Ralph Bates was born in 1899 in Swindon, where, at the age of sixteen, he was apprenticed in the repair yards of the Great Western Railway. At seventeen he enlisted in the Royal Flying Corps, serving later in the Queen's Royal Surrey Regiment until the end of the First World War. He then returned to the yards, but in 1923 went to Spain, where he worked first on the Barcelona docks and then as a travelling mechanic, fixing everything from village church organs to primitive electrical systems, and living mostly in the Pyrenees. (It was his skill as a climber that later enabled him to organise mountain scout troops against Franco.) In 1929 he returned to England, but was soon back on the Costa Brava, where he organised a fisherman's cooperative. He made his name as a writer of fiction with *Sierra* (1933), *Lean Men* (1935) and *The Olive Field* (1936), as well as his acclaimed biography, *Schubert* (1934). *The Olive Field* draws on his own experience of working as an *olivero*, his participation in the tremendous events leading up to the Spanish Civil War, and his sense of the remorseless onset of tragedy.

During the Civil War, Bates edited the publication of the International Brigades, *Volunteer for Liberty*, and served at the front and on the staff at the Defence of Madrid, until he was sent on a mission for the Spanish Government to the United States and Mexico. After the end of the war he lived first in Mexico – the setting of his novel *Fields of Paradise* (1940) – and then in America. He taught literature at New York University from 1948 until his retirement, as Emeritus Professor, in 1968. He married Eve Salzman in 1940; they have one son.

Ralph Bates now divides his time between Naxos, in the Aegean, and New York. He still writes, walks the highlands and, in the last ten years, builds telescopes. Since the death of Franco, he visits his beloved Spain frequently.

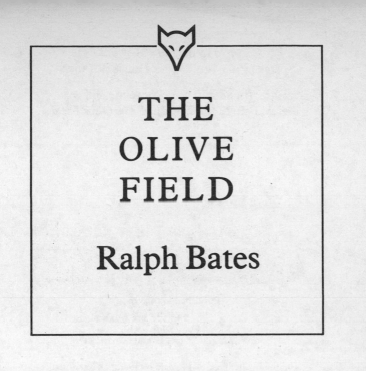

THE
OLIVE
FIELD

Ralph Bates

New Introduction by
Valentine Cunningham

THE HOGARTH PRESS

LONDON

In memory of
Esteve Pujals and Maria Canals de Pujals

Their friendship was dear to me and was
a great help in the writing of *The Olive Field*

Published in 1986 by
The Hogarth Press
Chatto & Windus Ltd
40 William IV Street, London WC2N 4DF

First published in Great Britain by Jonathan Cape 1936
Corrected edition first published in 1966
Copyright 1936 © 1964, 1966 by Ralph Bates
Introduction copyright © Valentine Cunningham 1986

British Library Cataloguing in Publication Data

Bates, Ralph
The olive field.
I. Title
823'.912 [F]   PR6003.A96

ISBN 0 7012 0674 8

Printed in Great Britain by
Cox & Wyman Ltd
Reading, Berkshire

INTRODUCTION

Thirties' writing is obsessed by utopia. Where, it keeps asking, is the Just City, the Great Good Place? Is it in Moscow, or Berlin, or Rome? Does it consist in socialist revolution, or fascist nationalism, or conversion to the Roman Catholic Church? Is the pastoral vision, in fact, ever possible – that wishful, dreamed-of existence, peaceful and creative, communally harmonious, organically in tune with nature, morally blessed and blessing? In the middle of 1936, when the Spanish Civil War brought Spain vividly to the notice of the world, it did seem to many writers that Republican Spain had become precisely that desired pastoral place where worker and peasant and intellectual together had made a social revolution that all moral persons should fight to preserve. When Orwell and others like him arrived in Barcelona in late 1936 and early 1937 they found romantic, lyrically welcomed, social renovation: 'startling and overwhelming' as Orwell's *Homage to Catalonia* puts it. 'It was the first time I had ever been in a town where the working-class had been in the saddle . . . queer and moving . . . a state of affairs worth fighting for.' It was what the writer and trades union organiser Ralph Bates had long striven for.

An ex-serviceman from the First World War, Bates had gone from his native England to Spain in the Twenties with the backing of the Communist International. He agitated for revolution among Catalan dockers and fishermen. When the Civil War broke out and the Comintern organised foreign volunteers into International Brigades of fighters for the Republic against the rightist forces of General Franco, Bates was a natural choice for jobs of high political importance. He edited the Brigades' paper, *Volunteer for Liberty*. His first wife, Winifred, helped organise the medical volunteers. Spanish history seemed to have caught up with his fiction and to be condoning its revolutionary thrust. For Bates had not only lived the revolution, but in his two great novels of the Thirties – *Lean Men* (1935) and *The Olive Field* (1936), which are about the struggles for revolutionary utopia in Spain that he himself had worked for, and which ask how the socialist pastoral ideal might connect with the real lives of the peasants who worked the Spanish fields – Bates had also written the revolution. No wonder they called him *El Fantástico*. Cannily, Bates had got inside the character of Spanishness, had taken the measure of the curiosities of Spanish political life and style. He knew Spanish life as only a few British writers – they include V. S. Pritchett and Laurie Lee – have done. One major result is the strangely prophetic power of *The Olive Field* in particular. Its narrative, culminating in the failure of the Asturian revolt of 1934, anticipates the pattern of demoralisation and failure on the Republican side in the Civil War, especially in the internecine struggles between Anarchists and Communists that so dismay Orwell's *Homage to Catalonia*.

Bates's fiction plunges its reader into the barbaric oddness, the exotic difference of Spain. Spain's extreme weather (no novel I know describes parching heat better than *The Olive Field*); its rebarbative religion (even English Catholic writers, such as Graham Greene, felt occasionally estranged by the dark forms of Spanish Catholic devotion); its messy and complex set of political parties: all these are what preoccupy Bates's Spanish novels. Had Orwell paid these writings attention, he wouldn't have suffered his initial (and continuing) confusions over the nature of Spanish political life – initial letter confusions, no less. 'As for the kaleidoscope of political parties and trade unions, with their tiresome names – P.S.U.C., P.O.U.M., F.A.I., C.N.T., U.G.T., J.C.I., J.S.U., A.I.T. – they merely exasperated me.' Learning the meaning and weight attached to those alphabetical tags almost cost Orwell his life, and did cost him the loss of the utopian socialist innocence he took with him to Spain. *Lean Men* and *The Olive Field* patiently illustrate just how much the great gulf dividing the Spanish Anarchists (the F.A.I.) and their allies in the syndicalist trade union (the C.N.T.)

from the Spanish Communist Party, interfered with simple revolutionary pastoralism, and generated unhealable rifts in Spanish agricultural (and urban) daily life. They are texts with none of Orwell's ignorance and illusions to shed. Unsentimentality about civil warring in Spain had come to Bates long before the Spanish Civil War broke out.

The hard-nosedness that inside information granted Bates did not, though, preclude sympathy and affection. Far from it. *The Olive Field* is an extraordinary celebration of peasant life as a tough existence eked out at the mercy of landlord, overseer, priests, policemen and weather. This novel must rank with D. H. Lawrence's presentation of the organically natural life of the Brangwen family on their English Midlands farm at the beginning of *The Rainbow*, or with Lewis Grassic Gibbon's eulogy of Scottish peasant existence in the first part of his *Scots Quair* trilogy, *Sunset Song*. *The Olive Field*'s reassertion of such warmly romanticised pastoralia in the Grassic Gibbon mode as a legitimate kind of proletarian, socialist realism was a timely response to William Empson's cheeky dismantling of that connexion. (In *Some Versions of Pastoral*, 1935, Empson had claimed that the obviously faked, literary sorts of pastoral, from Marvell's poetry through *The Beggar's Opera* to *Alice in Wonderland*, were, in fact, literature's best way of responding to calls for proletarian realism in writing.) And Bates's version of pastoral goes on having powerful effects on the reader. This presentation of the alliance between men and women and the trees they cultivate; the novel's sense of animated, communal participation in the diurnal work of grafting, watering, gathering; its apprehension of the relationship between people's selfhood and the tools they handle, whether agricultural implements or guitars, all offer a steeping in a way of life – not to say in a kind of seedsman's or grower's catalogue of technical terminology (*munzanillos*, *zorzalenos*, *verdials*, *dulzars*, *budiegos*, and so on) – that is as engrossing as it is informative.

Mere recognition of such realities would not by itself, of course, make *The Olive Field* all that special. Cyclical, rhythmic agricultural life commanded by the procession of the seasons is one of literature's most enduring subjects. What, however, makes Bates's account distinctive, particularly among left-wing novels of the Thirties, is his stress on the religious nature of these communal and natural rhythms. The medieval, ritualistic, liturgical connexion that had gradually leaked away from peasant life in the Protestant world survived vividly in Spain – to the surprise and consternation no doubt of Bates's Communist comrades. And Bates knew that the Spanish observer, and anybody anxious like himself to effect social change in Spain, must reckon above all with this essential aspect of Spanish character and politics.

In *The Olive Field*, the agricultural year is shown running hand-in-glove with the Church Year. Catholicism may be the landowner's religion. The devout Don Fadrique may be tight-fisted, selfish and arbitrary, and his mysticism charged with his fears of assault from revolutionary hordes of his own workers. The local priests may be hostile to reform and act freely as squires' and coppers' narks. The terrible and murderous Civil Guards may be deeply involved in what the novel calls the general Church-sponsored 'fatal liturgy'. But still an old man sings traditional songs of Christ's Passion as he ploughs. And the Communist Robledo rants drunkenly about Christ in the wilderness and the Church's appropriation of human rhythms, while the Anarchist Mudarra responds to the enchantment of holy pictures and images – both of them supersaturated, as Stephen Dedalus's friend Cranly puts it in Joyce's *A Portrait of the Artist as a Young Man*, with the religion they profess not to believe in. There is much spilt religion about in Bates's Spain, and above all, the novel suggests, among the members of the Anarchist F.A.I. 'Anarchism is nothing more than Christianity without God,' declares Robledo, and Bates agrees. But though they might feel superior in their opposition to Christianity, neither the Communist character nor his pro-Communist author can blunt the novel's major point, that the life of ordinary Spanish people, however left-wing and overtly irreligious, is ineradicably marked by Catholicism.

One particularly striking element of Catholicism's infiltration into the assumptions of Bates's people and the substance of his novel is violence. Spanish cruelty – the cruelty of the landscape, of people's behaviour on Left and Right, the dark imaginings of Spanish art and history – was something most visitors to Spain, not least in the Civil War, found hard to stomach. And Bates keenly spells out the wildest of Spanish paradoxes, that in this ancient Christian country, the land of the olive and the olive branch, those most enduring Judaeo-Christian emblems of peace, there should be so much opposition to peacefulness, especially opposition based in Christian practice and observance.

Reality in *The Olive Field* is intensely symbolic. Bates's novel comes packed with emblems, allegorised people, parable encounters. It's almost as if the ancient symbolic power of the olives that so dominate this story of Los Olivares had infected all of the place's realities. Trees, a weakling giant, a ludicrous elephant, numerous religious effigies, the amazing mayordomo Argote, the effetely scholarly Don Fadrique, singing, a brothel, and so on and on, are all granted meanings beyond their mere selfhood. This intensifying, even over-determination, of meaning, the persistent effort of the writing to perceive, arrest and squeeze out significance, register with great power Bates's sense of the historical importance of Spain's Thirties' crises. And it is notable that much of the emblematic activity the text goes in for is harsh, bitter, violent, the opposite of olive-like. The bed of aloes in the very first chapter – 'Their massive and fine-lined blades, cruel as an imperial lust . . . At their points, the unexhausted venom of the aloe leaves thrust forward sinister brown spines that had caused Mudarra to say that they forced one to think of blindness, of pierced and streaming eyeballs or the cheek cleft through to the root of the tongue' – strikes what will be the novel's characteristic and recurring note. This bitter, cruel plant is to be construed as being as much the typical product of Spanish soil as the more genial fruit of the olive. And in its preoccupation with this cruelty and violence and the meanings of violence, *The Olive Field* outdoes most twentieth-century fiction, even holocaust fiction.

Rural life is here a matter of knife and fist, of fights over water, fights between overseer and men, fights between rivals for a woman. Spanish politics, from Andalucia to the Asturias, is an affair of dynamite and bullet, of torture casual and systematic, of death-dealing Civil Guards and repressive soldiery.

Transgression runs as an enticement and a necessity through the whole story. Sexual and religious transgression, of course; but also more obscurely presented transgression, like the mating of donkey and horse to produce the mule, that sterile, barren offspring so characteristic of Spain. This is the mode of transgression that provides Father Martinez, the parish priest of Los Olivares, with a curiously magnetic clue to all Spanish ills, and is the occasion of one of the novel's most bizarre and mysterious emblematic scenes, the failed mating of a donkey with a mare, in Chapter 14. Grafting, too, the horticultural process at the very heart of olive-culture, is itself a kind of transgressing, the union of wild and cultivated stock – again as Father Martinez suggests. And, as the text repeatedly insists, grafting is a deed of violence, a matter of cutting, no matter how lovingly and surgically it is performed. Grafting is one reason why all the novel's olivars go about armed with knives. And it's no accident, either, that grafting is a central metaphor in the Christian theology of redemption: another instance of the idea that salvation necessitates pain, especially the pain of the crucified Christ. And here, of course, the violence endemic to the novel's Spain is returned to its perennial analogue and source in the Christian faith. If, in general, this novel's Anarchism can be said to be generated out of Christianity, how true that is, in particular, of the Anarchists' taste for violent action. Mudarra sticking his knife into the gums of the herbalist, or the *dinamitero* calmly walking towards his death, his body strapped about with sticks of dynamite, are offered as natural extensions of the ancient Spanish cult of the bleeding Christ. On the other side of the political coin, the Civil Guard take up their firing position with no sense of contradiction on the steps of San Andres church and the soldiers of repression fortify convents and cathedrals. Every party is presented as being kin to the effigy of Santo Cristo del Olivar ('broken . . . torn . . . blood . . . gaping . . . blood . . . crown of thorns . . . ghastly death') that incites Father Soriano to 'a rapture of devotion'.

The degree of Ralph Bates's imaginative sympathy with Spain's nightmarish intensities, as well as his evident joy in its easier-going peasant simplicities, are truly astonishing. To be sure, his sympathy is spurred more readily in some quarters than in others. The novel's liking and admiration for Anarchists as bold, if too reckless, men of Action has clearly something to do with this atheist and socialist author's own satisfaction in the destruction of churches and his shared sense that all revolutionary struggle involves facing pain with the courage of Mudarra and the Asturian *dinamiteros*. But it is a sign of Bates's stature as a novelist that he is also surprisingly liberal to characters like Argote, the cruel and socialist-killing overseer, to Father Martinez, agent of what is to Bates a dangerous and historically finished cause, and to the Anarchist Mudarra – that he is far more open than his own leftist politics would officially allow.

Nevertheless, that said, Bates does remain, throughout this novel, deeply hostile to his Catholics and his Anarchists. He is forever anxious to point up the repressiveness of Spain's Catholicism, and constantly arranges his plot to display the political and communal recklessness of what the Anarchists like doing. Anarchists' individualism, their impatience for premature action, their indiscipline in action, all cause trouble, whether it's local trouble like the sour olive oil produced by careless picking during the insubordination on the olive slopes, or a catastrophe of wider dimensions like the failure of a whole revolutionary uprising. When the awkward, somnolent, weakened giant of Spanish aspiration, emblematised in the novel's travelling freak-show giant, rises up for freedom, the revolt pithers away because, it's implied, the Anarchists, who may be admirably high on hatred of tyrants and on personal bravado and courage, turn out fatally to lack keenness for organisation and discipline.

The novel ends with a little demonstration that the better

way forward is the Communist way. Workers cooperating together can mend burst water-courses that individuals are powerless to repair on their own. Revolutionary pastorals are still possible, it's suggested, but only 'Tomorrow'. Alas, that Tomorrow did not speedily turn up. Indeed, in the Civil War which broke out just as *The Olive Field* was published, Ralph Bates's friends were to be found still laying the blame for the Republic's failure to defeat Franco on what they defined as the craving for premature revolution among the Anarchists and other non-Communist leftists. A year later, the most important piece of British literature produced in that war, W. H. Auden's great poem 'Spain' (1937) was left, at its own end, still sunk in the despairs of revolutionary hopes deferred, still looking forward to as yet unachieved revolutionary pastorals, 'Tomorrow'. What, though, Auden's 'Spain' captured with great power, was the necessity of the present pain, distress and sacrifice required if the Tomorrow was ever to arrive: 'But today the struggle.' And it is Ralph Bates's presentation of a part of that great and aweingly violent struggle for peace, liberty and justice as it affected the lives of ordinary, simple – and heroic – Spanish people, that makes *The Olive Field* one of the most compelling of mid-century English works.

Valentine Cunningham, Corpus Christi College, Oxford 1986

CONTENTS

FOR the convenience of readers who may wish to refer to it, there is printed on page 439 a brief note on Spanish politics, and also a list of the chief characters in this book on pages 435–438.

THE OLIVE FIELD

Mater Purissima

THE February sun slipped down behind the tiger-colored hills across the tawny Jabalón valley and they became solid and disturbing; the cliffs above the olive slopes ceased to glow, and of the three voices singing among the dark multitude of olive trees·two were suddenly quiet. The one singer, as if in response to the silence of the others, raised his voice and took more care to pronounce clearly the melancholy words of his song, and the echoes that fell from the cliffs now repeated intelligible sounds. But then he began to sing in broken phrases, between which the only sounds to be heard on the olive fields were of the sharp closing of steel cleaning scissors and the soft thud of metal against wood. Then the cracked bell of the white sanctuary on the green-gray middle slopes knocked sharply, the voice broke off in the high launching of a phrase, and the last echoes idly, like ravens, drifted up the darkening cliffs towards the scarlet-tinged domes above and were gone.

The workers of the olivars of Don Fadrique Guevara y Muñaroz laid down their ladders or shouldered their iron implements to go down to the sanctuary, but Diego Mudarra, who had been singing when the bell knocked, rapidly climbed through the upper region of narrow terraces and sat upon a heap of stones below the cluster of wild fig and albardín bushes at the base of the riven cliffs. A few shouts began to be heard below. Presently he called: "Hola! Joaquín."

Only Joaquín Caro's legs and lower trunk were visible below the lower branches of the little frost-defying arbequín olives, but Mudarra stood up and awaited him, though, when they

met, they exchanged no greeting but a casual "Hola." Mudarra
rolled a cigarette upon his knee, licked it, sealed it and gave
it to Caro, and for several minutes they sat silently upon
the stones.

They were a contrasted pair. Caro was of medium height,
square-set in the trunk, but with small limbs and hands. His
head was long-shaped and the fleshless, dark-skinned face with
closely shut lips suggested an ascetic reserve. Mudarra was tall
beyond the normal and already stout, although he was only
twenty-eight years of age; his head was large, the forehead high
and slightly receding, his eyes sunken and intense, the nose
aquiline, and his mouth wide and sensual. Fine black hair,
rather thin, was flung loosely back over his head, and one lock
continually falling over his right eye caused him to squint a
little. His hands were large but not fleshy, and across the ball
of the left ran a long white scar. Good humor pervaded his
face; though his carriage suggested sloth, his movements were
quick and extravagant.

"What about tomorrow afternoon?" Mudarra began. "Aguiló
has arrived; it'll be all right to bring him down to your place?"

Caro nodded. "The old man muttered a bit, and he won't
like it, of course, but that won't matter. Marcial wants to
speak."

"How is your brother?" Mudarra said, though there was no
question in his tone. A click of the tongue was all the reply
Caro gave.

"Speaking doesn't do him any good," Mudarra added after
a pause, and Caro at once said:

"Robledo is coming down to the meeting."

"Ah, Robledo," exclaimed Mudarra contemptuously. "Asking for trouble, isn't it, bringing Robledo and Aguiló together?"

"He's got a point of view that ought to be heard."

"Aguiló wants action; he told me he had to be got out of
Cazorla on the quiet when the Civil Guard heard about his
meeting there."

Caro stood up, and without more speech of the Anarchist
meeting they hurried down the slopes. From time to time they
spoke, commenting on the condition of the trees or on the work

that was being done. Here, where the arbequín olives gave way first to the verdiales still bearing late fruit and then to the more exigent trees long since stripped, the sap was already beginning to rise in a few trunks and one or two fresh shoots had been put out.

"Chance of there being a good crop this year!" Mudarra turned to examine a tree. "They've come through the winter well; last year's shoots were good; so they should bear well."

Caro replied: "Let's have a look at the late grafts in the Little Gully; we can go round to Mater Purissima by the fountain path."

The sanctuary of Mater Purissima, around which stood the tool houses, was the lunch-hour rendezvous and resting place most popular with the olivar workers. Larger than most, its plain baroque front stood high among the great dulzar olives which had been planted around it. Here and there the bullets of last year's troubles had flaked the limewash of two centuries from the then red bricks. In May of 1931, when churches and convents had been burned in Málaga and other places in southern Spain, there had been no such event in the town of Los Olivares de Don Fadrique. But one night the town had been mildly startled to hear shots ring out upon the slopes above, and in the morning the workers had discovered the sanctuary front to be pocked with bullet marks. Within, the reredos of gilded plaster had been smashed by two shots. Mater Purissima herself, lying upon her back upon the littered altar cloths, was undamaged. There had been little comment, though the assault was resented by the majority of the workers, for the place was regarded with affection for its beauty and the comfort it gave. Its deep arcaded porch, along the inner walls of which ran broad stone seats, gave cool shade in summer. Nearby in Broad Gully, sweet water, too cold for immediate drinking, abundantly poured out of the earth. The goodness of Doña Inés was often spoken of by the women who drew water there and who summed up the past or passing things of goodness with a long-drawn "Ay."

The sanctuary itself stood upon a flat-topped outcrop of brown rocks upon one side of which was a bed of aloes. Their massive and fine-lined blades, cruel as an imperial lust, of deep cuprous green, brown-dusted, reached out of yellow-green spider-haunted sockets. At their points, the unexhausted venom of the aloe leaves thrust forward sinister brown spines that had caused Mudarra to say that they forced one to think of blindness, of pierced and streaming eyeballs or the cheek cleft through to the root of the tongue. Paper and preserve tins littered the slope among the aloe clumps; their thick scarred masts stood high above the level of the shallow bluff, and from the sanctuary porch seemed to lean out over the green-patched floor of Jabalón.

At one end of the roof stood the belfry; its cankered bell, green as an unripe orange, swung from a beam of sun-whitened oak; at the other end was the weather vane, the eastern arm of which had lost its E. To this weather vane came the white doves from Don Fadrique's señorial house higher upon the slopes beyond the next ridge, and these, when some gust of laughter from the shelter disturbed them, circled out against the intense blue of the sky and the violet haze of the heat-masked hills like ivory motes, lazily circling after the first loud-winged flight.

Below the bluff of Mater Purissima the olive fields sank slowly down and the gaze traveled over the thin shadeless nets of foliage to the brown-turreted walls and the motley roofs of Los Olivares. Away to the southwest and northeast, around the bay of hills in which Los Olivares stood, swept the olives in level rows, like an army of cowled monks, dark and uniform. It was this regularity of row and uniformity of hue which gave its lugubriousness to the landscape and overcast all the mentality of that place with its slow nostalgic quietude, against which man contended only with short-lived violence.

When the two men approached the tool houses they were hailed with shouts by Argote, the olivero, as he was called, because, though he was really Don Fadrique's mayordomo, he spent all his time in the administration of the olive fields. The man himself they could not see, but presently he emerged from a shed, clasping a load of tools, which he dumped against a dulzar olive trunk.

"Help me shift these into that shed yonder," he grunted; "I'm having some manures put into the other." They smiled

and set about the task at once though it was long past knock-
ing-off time. Argote regarded chemical manures with more
veneration than the blessed sacrament itself, as Father Martínez,
priest of San Andrés, had once said. That was why the mayordomo had removed his coat and waistcoat and was working
himself; he was always impatient about his special enthusiasms.
They paused a moment before beginning to put the tools
away, and he came over and glared at them, his thick, bursting
fingers tugging at the neckband of his shirt, over which black
bushy hairs protruded. Though it was winter, the smell of his
sweat-drenched shirt came to them, and sweat was running
down his red taut-skinned face. Sudden anger showed itself,
and his thick lips, from which at all times the blood seemed to
be trying to burst, pressed together tightly. His bulging eyes
seemed to distend.

"Pretty lovebirds," he grunted, rubbing his chin with his
black tufted fingers. Mudarra grinned and pushed the falling
lock out of his eyes; his lips opened; the large yellow teeth
tightly closed.

"Well, put the bloody things away," Argote said, and still
staring at the olive worker, he grasped a bundle of tools and
held them out.

As they placed the last stack in the shed, Argote's huge body
suddenly blocked up the doorway; leaning upon his raised fore-
arms against the uprights, he thrust his head into the gloom,
near to Mudarra's face.

"Listen, you two lovebirds, I want you to work together for
the next few weeks; you'll be over at the top of Broad Skirt
tomorrow."

"All right," Caro said, struggling to get upon his feet among
the hafts of the tools where Mudarra, retreating from the doorway, had pitched him. The insult was meant to be ignored
and he ignored it.

"Course it's all right. . . . Let's see if you can make insertions
into the trees I've marked. Cut your trunks down one at a time
and get your grafts from the charge hand Calasparra. And
listen, disinfect your knives when you make the slits or I'll cut
your teeth off with a rusty sickle." Argote spoke ferociously,
boring vigorously into the growth of hair in his earhole with

his forefinger as he did so. The two men grinned at the threat.

"You don't say so," Mudarra replied. "What's the variety?"

"Abadejos into wild olive," Caro said, without waiting for Argote's answer.

"That's right," the mayordomo continued. "They're good strong roots. God rot yours." Mudarra clicked his tongue at the man's sudden truculence and made an obscene gesture towards his back as he departed. Then the two shook hands; they had never been coupled for work before; gratitude and an admiration which all the workers, even those whom he tyrannized, felt for Argote kept them staring after him for several minutes.

Men instinctively respected the mayordomo for his impressive presence; his massive head, broader at the jaws than at the forehead, seemed to disclose his thrusting truculence and undeviating will; the huge, hard-fleshed buttocks proclaimed his energy, so that the townsfolk still said of him, in his advancing years, that he was the terror and the delight of the women of Los Olivares, and they wondered that he had never married. But it was Argote's enthusiasm for olive trees which gained him abiding respect. He had never been trained as an olive worker and had taken to the trees several years after he had been appointed mayordomo, yet from the collection of the fruit and the pressing of the oil, the cleaning and pruning and grafting round to the collection again, he was to be seen riding along the paths of the Peral estate early and late.

Argote was not really a tyrant, though before the Republic he had been the Los Olivares political boss. Brutal, imperious and obscene of speech, he esteemed a good workman at more than his utility value. He did not evade responsibility in case of failure, and his knowledge was not to be questioned. While yet the former olive-field superintendent, Morcillo, had been in charge, Argote had harassed him into resignation, not only by intrigue and misrepresentation, but by the exhibition of superior knowledge, deliberately and brutally used to that end. Or rather, to the end that Indalecio Argote should have control of the olive fields he loved, and which at once prospered under him. It was Argote who, contrary to local tradition, had first tried watering the olives of the Little Gully. The year of that controversy was still spoken of, for, not content with informing the Marquis, who took no interest in his trees, he had sought to convince the workers. Mudarra sometimes drew a laugh, during lunch hours at Mater Purissima, with his impersonation of the mayordomo.

"Ha! Let me tell you! Every grass, herb, bush or tree that moves sap needs water. You need water, there wouldn't be any sap in your teeth if you didn't, and then what would your woman do for firewood! Hey, break up those clods into pieces as big as a pigeon's egg, and a bloody ordinary pigeon, too."

Finally the olivero had turned the water through the gully, and the trees had doubled their yield. A few had contracted tuberculosis, whereupon he had scored a resounding success by planting the sturdy damp-scorning, frost-resisting Catalan arbequín. It was Argote who had planted the famous groves of lechin olives upon the White Hill, locally called Golgotha, where no other variety had flourished.

And even in this year following the Revolution of 1931, when there was talk everywhere of Governmental expropriation, the mayordomo had not slackened his vigilance. Only his pushing of the little arbequíns higher and higher up the sierra had been relinquished. It was as if that extreme labor of building terraces and gathering basketfuls of nutritious earth from crevice and gully was just beyond the limiting effort now that the future was insecure. About the sun-corroded upper slopes of the Sierra del Jabalón this year there were to be seen abandoned terrace walls and level patches that bore no living timber.

That dereliction, the pockmarked front of Mater Purissima, and the felled Olive of the Infanta were the sole results upon the Peral estate of the bloodless Revolution of April, 1931. The Olive, of the variety called royal, had long been renowned in Andalucía. Then a daughter of the Royal House had visited it, whereupon it had been named "of the Infanta." The royal olive had become Royal, it was said. One morning, in the third week of that April, the Olive of the Infanta had been felled by unknown hands.

As Mudarra and Caro descended the track towards the town they met Argote, walking beside a small cart upon which were

sacks of manure. "Good night," he shouted with a long-drawn
"Buenas"; they replied cheerfully and hurried on. Then, hearing Argote repeat the greeting shortly, Caro turned round
and saw a girl coming towards them.

"Lucía," he said and they halted. As she drew level her pace
became slower, and when they saluted her she stood still. Her
timidity was obvious.

"Buenas," she replied at length to Caro's greeting.

"I'm thinking of coming down to Gordito's tonight, Lucía,"
Caro said.

"I hope you enjoy yourself," she replied; the traditional
scorn of Andalucian women was not matched by her tone.

"He means he'd like to step across the pavement and chew
iron," Mudarra added, meaning that Caro desired to court her
at her window.

"You are very kind to him, señor." She lifted her eyes to
Mudarra, and the air of abstracted and melancholy repose,
which they normally bore, for a moment faded from them.
The mockery in her words was intended for the bigger man, but
it was Caro who replied, quickly:

"Will you come to the window, Lucía?" he said, holding his
hand stiffly by his side. His intent gaze seemed to disclose that
he was pressing through his own extreme reserve. The girl
lifted her face and gazed over Mudarra's head. "Yes," she
replied, and hurried away towards the town.

Lucía Robledo, employed as an out-living maid at the
Palacio, was twenty years old and the second daughter of a
family of poor tenants, cultivators who had been forced to
take other employment. Juan Robledo, the father, now a
stableman at the Palacio, had fallen permanently into a sullen
temper at his ill fortune. His wife was called "the half-beata,"
because of her occasional fits of vehement piety. Soon after
their surrender of the farm, Gloria, the other daughter and a
renowned beauty, had taken service in the city of Sevilla, they
said, though the postman had more than once expressed
skepticism about the name of the city. Señora Robledo never
complained of Gloria's departure, but the father ceaselessly
muttered about it angrily. Lucía, the younger daughter, was
considered to have little of the beauty of her sister. Slender of

figure and not without a certain bodily beauty, only her face had distinction. Her lips were of beautiful and unusual wavering line, the upper much thinner than the lower; her chin, slightly thrust forward, was nevertheless small. Beneath her high cheekbones were faint and delicately shaped hollows which, with a high and sensitive forehead, made a curious and remote appeal. Over her brown eyes were brows widely set, black like her coarse hair which, dressed with olive oil, lay closely, disclosing the beautiful shape of her head. It was a face of disturbing sadness, and no one but Caro had paid court to her. Nothing definite had she replied, however, despite a year's persistence.

"Well?" said Mudarra, after a long silence, as they drew near to the town.

"What are you doing after the meeting tomorrow, Diego?" Caro answered.

"Nothing in particular."

"See you at Gordito's then," he continued, naming the café which faced Lucía Robledo's house. His companion did not reply at once.

"I was going up to the Republican Center to play a bit. Acorín will be there."

Tomás Acorín, "El Chino" as he was called, from the Oriental set of his face, the municipal clock-winder and repairer and formerly night watchman, was the other accepted guitarist of Los Olivares and Mudarra's rival. Between the musicians was no friendship.

"Christ, you don't want to concern yourself with Acorín; come down to Gordito's and play."

"All right, where are you going tonight? I'm playing at the Rincón."

"I may come up, but I'll be late. I'm helping the old man a bit tonight."

Mudarra nodded; with the father enfeebled by advancing years and Marcial, the elder son, consumptive, Caro was forced to assist with the father's land after his day's work upon the Peral estate, often working far into the night.

"Well, in any case, have supper at my place tomorrow as usual," he said.

At a bend in the track they took a shortcut across the last narrow lines of olives, and stood awhile on the Gallows Rock gazing at the town. The massive brown walls that encircled Los Olivares seemed larger and more impressive in the rapidly declining light. And the half-light cleared away the litter and refuse that lay before the walls; the old motor tires, the tangled and rusty wire, the burnt stones of gypsy camps, the rotting mattress which the children had dragged about the waste land as a chariot, the paper and the tins, all the melancholy detritus which everywhere confronts the beauty and grandeur of Spain. The darkening half-light hid from view the stinking squalor of the shacks of old timber and sacking that leaned against the foot of the walls, in which lived the debased and unfortunate of the town. Against the darkening valley, standing immense above the slowly moving black dots that passed in through the Gate of San Andrés, the walls seemed not to be the work of man, they were remote from him, and timeless. It seemed that the walls had been there before man had broken the mountain-side, as if the walls with their now blackening towers were immobile gods around whom man had gathered for protection. And as the night drew on they were gods of macabre and obscure power who had drawn bewitched men around them for the sustaining holocausts. In the darkness, the walls and the countless rows of black and silent trees halted upon the mysterious hill confronted one another and neither were the work of man.

Below the two men, the bellows in the Gallows Rock smithy began to respire, and the yellow light of the fire shot up the walls to their crenellations. Then, as the bell of San Andrés sounded its slow nang-nang, Joaquín Caro turned down the rubbled gully of the Huerta path towards his house outside the town.

As Mudarra left the Rock, away on the vast blackness of the sierra across the valley a solitary red bonfire was flaming.

2

The Song of the Plow

FROM the Gallows Rock, a hundred yards outside San Andrés Gate, a narrow rubbish-filled gully ran to the west, sinking rapidly into the yellow-brown earth. Having made an arc round a quarter of the town, the gully turned sharply southward, its right wall receded and fell away into a steep slope covered with a stunted growth of baladre and ricino bushes, among which threaded many goat paths. A little farther on, the rift became a valley whose bed ever widened until at last the watercourse from the Peral reservoir came in and the first small fields of the Upper Huerta began.

It was here that the Caros had their holding. The white-washed house itself, a simple rectangular building, with small and undecorated balconies of sawn and unpainted wood and red-tiled roof, stood with its back to the vertical cliff which bore up the promontory on which Los Olivares was built. Before it lay the patterned Huerta, or Gardens of Los Olivares, dotted with white tool houses and the cortijos of the larger tenants, and through which ran the meager yet vital waters of the yellow-bedded Jabalón. To the left, a buttress of the cliff cut off the view farther down the path, which curved again shortly beyond.

This Saturday afternoon of springlike warmth, Pascual had gone out with the mule and the donkey to plow the small field called "of the Well," which abutted on the house garden and ran down to the buttress which shut out the view to the left. Within the house the man Aguiló, brought there overnight by Marcial Caro, was conversing with the first workers

to arrive. From time to time Pascual Caro's feeble voice, singing the plowing song he had brought back from Castile, where
he had worked in his youth, mingled with the conversation and
the laughter of Ana, the mother, and her daughter Ursula. Ana
Caro, a slow-moving woman with a large, heavy face, dark-
ringed eyes and thin gray hair, was the real comfort of the
Caro house. Little time passed by without her laughter being
heard or her voice raised in some sally against the members of
her family. Ursula resembled her brother Joaquín, but she
also possessed something of her mother's disposition.

One by one, and observing caution, the workers came in,
until at last Joaquín Caro opened the meeting, calling upon
the Anarchist doctor, Aguiló, to speak.

Aguiló was a frail-looking man of small stature. His head,
somewhat oval-shaped, with very high cheekbones and thin lips
tinged with blue, was held back as if the effort of throwing
his voice over to the edges of a crowd had given it a permanent tilt. Thick glasses prevented his eyes, small and gray and
discolored, from being easily seen. His voice was clear but of
rasping quality. From his first sentence onwards there were
only occasional cessations of that confused hail of words.

His speech began with general references to the hardships
of the agricultural worker's life and that of the small tenant.
In all this he appeared to be thoroughly informed. As he
began his exposition of Anarchist doctrine, Justo Robledo
entered and sat down at the back of the room. His entry was
greeted with murmurs and turnings of the head. Many were
displeased, as Mudarra had foretold. He sat with his body held
stiffly; his pale face, with its expression of fatigue on the delicate features, was twitching with nervousness. During the
interruption of Aguiló's speech which his entrance caused, the
assembly could hear the old man's broken tenor outside; the
words "The mysteries of Christ's Passion" were distinguishable.

"It is necessary to destroy the State, for the achievement of
liberty, it is necessary to reorganize the whole of life from
below upwards with absolute liberty for all," shouted Aguiló,
banging the table with his open hand. "With liberty for every
man to enter or to leave the free associations which must take
the place of the State, when he pleases."

As Aguiló paused, Pascual's voice and the chink of the harness could be heard outside upon the field of the Well as he drew near the house. Instinctively the orator paused a moment to listen to the song, and then continued:

"We demand the destruction of all and every law, of all and every State, whether democratic or dictatorial. Every State is an oppressor within the country and an imperialist without. Why do we oppose the democratic State? Because with the pretence that it represents the general will it can be more despotic than a king, or a pope. What has the Republic done for the worker? Were we not promised a paradise? Has the peasant a square inch more land? What is the State, and its horde of officials?"

"Nothing but tax-gatherers," shouted another tenant from lower down the valley.

Once again the plower's voice was heard, exhorting the beasts at the far end of the field. Then Aguiló began a furious attack upon the Church. God was a fantasy created by the mind, a self-deception practiced upon oneself or a criminal deceit if inculcated in others. There were numerous cries of approval during this part of his speech; as before, he brought no arguments to bear upon the question, he advanced no data, but nevertheless the workers were excited by his denunciation.

"Why not get to the point?" called Robledo suddenly. There was an immediate hush, broken as many turned towards the interrupter.

"I thought we were going to discuss the land question," continued Robledo. His interjection was drowned in a storm of protest.

Aguiló skillfully changed the course of his speech and presently called upon those present to give statements of their own conditions. In the brief silence the words of Pascual's song could be heard clearly.

> The plow I shall sing
> and all its parts

his wavering voice declared.

> And I shall tell forth
> the mysteries of Christ's Passion.

Hearing the song, one or two glanced at Joaquín Caro's impassive face. Presently an olive worker, Ojeda, stood up and told them of his family life.

"I am thirty-four years of age, I get four pesetas a day and I've got to keep my mother and my sister; they earn one and a half pesetas a day between them. I want to marry. I asked at my novia's house four years ago and we are still waiting. Next week I am going to Asturias to work in the mines. . . ."

They nodded; Ojeda's story was common enough.

Then a harness-maker's young apprentice spoke passionately against the length of his working hours.

Florez, a small tenant, then rose, and though at first the workers listened with less sympathy, the man's story soon fired them. After Florez another tenant spoke, then another and another, some pouring out their hate for Peral, others for the land tenants for whom they worked. At last Marcial Caro rose to his feet and in a quiet voice began:

"We are poor farmers and we work no more than the lands you can see around the house. My father, when he was a young man, was forced to leave home because there were too many for one holding to support. Then, upon his return, he took over the land and married, hoping, as all fools hope, to live in peace with his wife and children, to gain their bread." He coughed once or twice, and paused to compose himself. Upon the field of the Well the father was heard glozing his song to the same beautiful melody:

> *And in the night before he was betrayed*
> *Jesus took bread and broke it in*
> *pieces . . .*

The father broke off his song to urge on the donkey.

"Burra, step out, step out, burra. Ay!"

"I was born to them," continued Marcial, putting his hand upon his chest, "and I was sick from the first, and my sickness turned later into this disease. Then came a child who was born dead, for my mother fell in working in the field down by the cliff yonder. Then came Victoriano, who was killed in the Moroccan war. Then Joaquín here, then the sister who died of my sickness, and last my sister Ursula. What has life been for my father, or for my mother? From morning to night a life of labor, working, hoping and praying; for my father is a pious man. And for what? We have nothing; last year we were forced to let half of our crops die on the field across the valley because we could not afford water at the price it was selling at. . . ."

Down the length of the field came Pascual's voice:

> *I shall sing the plow*
> *and all its parts,*

and again the urging cry, this time to the mule. And as the son went on they heard to the melody of the plowing song the words:

> *And an angel came to him, with the chalice*
> *of his passion, in Gethsemane, in that garden.*

"A little more plow and a lot less passion would suit me better," exclaimed Mudarra, and then he lifted his head sharply and caught his breath; it seemed almost that he blenched, and for a while he paid no attention to Marcial.

"Is it that my father is a bad worker? He takes pride in his lands, this field of the Well here is like a child to him, he talks of it and sits out there of an evening in summer. Yet when he is too old to work he will be compelled to live on charity, upon Joaquín's money, or perhaps if my sister marries . . ." He sat down suddenly and struggled for breath. Aguiló gazed at him sadly, and then began to speak again, launching upon a fiery appeal to the workers to prepare the Anarchist revolution.

At last Robledo stood up and motioned the speaker to sit down. Aguiló ignored the sign, however, and for a moment the two men faced one another; then a dozen workers sprang to their feet and uproar broke out. A bench fell to the floor and an old man, in trying to avoid it, fell heavily. There were threats mingled with the protests.

"Who invited you to come?" demanded Marcial Caro at last.

"Your brother," answered Robledo shortly. Joaquín Caro got to his feet.

"Compañeros, Robledo's views are not my views, but I invited him to come here and explain them."

The word "Whoremonger!" was heard as Joaquín finished, quietly spoken. Silence fell upon the room; outside there was silence also.

The harness-maker's apprentice said aloud in a high-pitched voice, "Drunkard!" and again there was silence.

"Well, that's that," began Robledo; "now that you've got that off your bloody chests we can go on." There was no interruption.

"I want to ask Señor Aguiló one or two questions." The "señor" was contemptuously spoken; Robledo had obviously been drinking.

"This isn't the place for debate," interjected Marcial Caro. "State your views shortly."

"Very well. We have heard and seen too much of this Anarchist revolution in the past. I say the workers will never win out until they form their political party, conquer the State by revolution, use the State to transform society, and then having made a new army and a new administration, turn upon the Church and destroy its power. . . ."

"Communist!" shouted Marcial Caro hoarsely, and for the next five minutes Robledo was engaged in a fierce dispute with nearly everyone present except Joaquín Caro.

Finally Aguiló secured silence, but it was Robledo who took advantage of it.

"If the workers had their own political party in April of last year they would not have been content to expel Alfonso. The land would have been given to the peasants and they would have protected the Workers' State. The peasants don't want nationalization, nor yet free associations; they want the land. Mark my words, the Republic will pay dearly for not giving it to them. . . . Spain has missed her opportunity. . . ."

"That's the kind of talk you give them at the Black House," screamed the harness-maker's apprentice. The Black House was one of the brothels of Los Olivares.

"I think it would have been better if that speech had been delivered by someone of greater moral repute," Aguiló said coldly.

"Moral repute!" Robledo exclaimed, his face white with anger. "Last week when Viñedo the gunman and bandit died in Paris, you wrote an article in *Land and Liberty* praising him as the true type of the free man. Viñedo, a common thief, a common murderer as the ideal revolutionary!"

"And you a married man, too," interrupted Aguiló.

"And you, Señor Aguiló, when you were in prison for inciting some little village flare-up, you wrote to the Civil Governor pleading for pardon. You were repentant, you had been misled, and so forth. You wrote three letters, one to the Bourbon himself, anything to crawl out of prison while there were three dead men in—"

A knife broke out the wall plaster to the left of Robledo's head. Those on the benches in front of him turned and two of them rammed the bench against his knees. Another brought the haft of an agricultural tool across his shoulders. Robledo, cursing and dragging at his belt, fell to the floor as Ana Caro flung open the door and screamed at the men. They took no notice of her, and presently she slammed the door and retired into the kitchen, where Ursula was weeping.

It was Aguiló himself who restored order. Robledo, his mouth bleeding, a bruise upon the side of his closely shaven skull, his left hand bloody from a knife wound, was silently escorted by Ursula and Joaquín Caro as far as the Old Well.

When two hours later the meeting broke up, the disk of the sun was already corroding away the summit crags of the western crests. The Huerta lay well below the reddening beams and was to be seen ghostly and gray by peering eyes. The newly plowed field of the Well, the goat pastures and the tawny cliffs behind the Caros' house glowed more deeply. The weeds in the chimneys and flutes of the cliff hung motionless and the few olives of the Caro patch seemed to possess the stillness of unreality. This stillness of the olives, their impassivity, was what had made them the symbol of peace.

When Mudarra had also gone, Joaquín Caro came out and went about the minor duties of the holding. Within the house Ana and the daughter were awaiting the return of the father, whom they could hear singing to himself in the stable, singing still the same song.

> *The plow I shall sing*
> *and all its parts . . .*

He wavered, and then after a pause:

> *I shall tell forth*
> *the mysteries of the Passion of Christ.*

Then they heard the father coaxing the mule to "move over, move over," and next he sang:

> *And Jesus was scourged*
> *and his blood ran down and watered the earth.*

Then, closing the stable door, he came to the front of the house, crossed himself, and entered as Ana was lighting the lamp wick in its bowl of olive oil. Looking into the shrunken kindly face and tender eyes of her husband, Ana smiled and came a pace towards him; he did not smile, but greeted her with the one word "Buenas."

Above in the town the angelus rang, and Pascual Caro, taking his rosary from a nail on the wall, sat down by the fire of dried broom just struggling into flame. Ana sat down also while Pascual recited the Paternoster and the first Ave María, and then, as her husband continued to pray quietly, she commenced to peel the potatoes for supper. Joaquín entered, and glancing at his father, walked quietly across the room and drank water from a pitcher.

"I'm eating with Diego tonight," he said softly and went out. Nothing broke the silence but the whispering of the father telling Ave Marías in honor of the Five Glorious Mysteries proper to Saturday: the triumphant Resurrection, the Ascension, the Coming of the Spirit, the Assumption of the Virgin, and her Coronation in splendor. Nothing broke the silence but the father's whispering, the mother's quiet labor in preparing supper, and the coughing of Marcial in his alcove above.

That evening Caro ate his supper at the house of a brother-in-law of the charge hand Calasparra, Oliverio Pérez by name, with whom Mudarra lodged. Pérez, a fervent admirer of Mudarra's guitar playing, rented a house in Villa Alta, or

High Town. When he entered, the guitarist was holding the seventeen-year-old daughter Concepción by the hair and pointing at his chair.

"Wine spilled upon it. What happens to women who spill wine?" he was saying with mock severity.

"Their men keep sober, you beast, animal, savage," the girl protested, screwing up her face.

"Do I ever get drunk then, that you must upset my wine?" he answered, releasing her.

"No, señor, you misbehave without. And thanks be to God you are not my man." She dodged the blow he aimed at her with his napkin and took the soup from her mother.

"Now Dieguito, now little brother," she scolded as he rose, "have respect for the soup if you can't for a woman."

It was a joyful meal for Caro, for the Pérez family treated Mudarra with open affection, and much of this also came his way as the guitarist's friend. Conchita, as the daughter was usually called, frankly accepted the part of adoring sister, and waited upon Mudarra even to the point of his annoyance, whitening his canvas shoes, repairing his clothing, making his bed and tidying his room jealously. This latter was a task which gave her much to do. Once at least during Caro's visits Señora Pérez would say:

"Diego has only to go into his room and all the things fly round like neighbors' cats." She said it during the dinner, and Pérez added in invariable antiphon:

"He's a marvel, I wonder the clothes stay on his body."

Since Mudarra's coming things had very much improved at the Pérez's house. A devotee of *cante hondo* and formerly a partisan of Acorín, the older guitarist, Pérez had welcomed the younger rival, promptly ceasing to champion Acorín. Mudarra was cheerfully cynical about this and never lost an opportunity to offer an explanation for this improvement.

"Good soup, eh, Joaquín?" he said, winking at the girl. "I find it best to praise the food here, it gets me into favor. You see, Oliverio's forever and amen drinking herb tea for his poor stomach; the herb tea puts him off his feed so he can't enjoy anything he eats, and the wretched woman pines

for praise and chastises her husband for not giving it. I give
her praise. Result, she gives me good food and looks after me
like an angel."

"Don't you believe him, Joaquín," Señora Pérez protested.

"Oh, I believe him," Caro replied.

"Believe what?" Conchita said maliciously. "About father's
stomach or mother's wickedness or Diego's artfulness?"

"It's a good place, anyway," Mudarra said. "If you can eat
good food."

After coffee, Mudarra rose and snapped his fingers towards
the ceiling, and Conchita ran upstairs for the guitar.

"We're going down to Gordito's. Care to come, Oliverio?"
Mudarra said, addressing Paca Pérez rather than her husband.

"Of course, go down and enjoy yourself, man," Señora Pérez
replied, and he at once reached for his hat.

"Conchita, if you were the last single woman in Los Olivares
I wouldn't marry you, for fear you'd get like your mother."
Mudarra shook his head at the laughing girl. This was the cere-
monial of departure whenever Pérez accompanied Mudarra,
but there was not a grain of truth in this reflection on Señora
Pérez.

Gordito's café was situated in the Callejón del Milagro,
Miracle Court, in which the Robledos also lived. The café
was popular with the olive workers and was used for political
meetings, it being easy to guard the approach to it. The Court
was a narrow and high-walled well off the steep Street of
Olive Oil and a place of intimacy and cheer. In summer, the
dweller's tables would often be brought out of the houses and
supper would be a public meal, during which sallies of wit
and good-humored jeering would pass from table to table. In
one corner, next to the steps which descended to the olive-
oil merchant's and the baker's shops, was a well and over it a
pulley, which the children delighted to operate during these
meals but disliked at other times. Its houses, whitewashed at
Easter, rose to irregular brown and chrome tiled roofs; iron
balconies overlooked the Court and gave a vantage point for
raillery.

The café differed from the other houses in having a broad
arch for a doorway, a vine hanging over a lattice framework

before the door, and in consisting of one large room only on the ground floor. Within, its only distinctive feature was the collection of bulls' heads, a great-uncle of Gordito having been a torero. That evening, Mudarra was at once asked to play, and he, readily complying, spent an hour upon the *flamenco* rhythms. Finally, his rival Acorín entered and gloomily sat down with his arms over the back of a chair, from time to time ejaculating a gentle "Ca!" or sighing abysmally. As a piece of virtuosity, Mudarra at last began to play a piece of "aristocrat's music," as his friends called it, music whose strange resurrection was the achievement of that stranger friendship between Mudarra and Don Fadrique Guevara y Muñaroz, Marquis of Peral. Then, Acorín having gone out in the desired dejection, Mudarra told several stories to the delight of the "parishioners," for he was considered the best storyteller in Los Olivares. Soon after midnight he rose to go, and the others with him.

"Look!" whispered Mudarra to Caro. Behind the grille of the lowest window in the Robledos' house something white was moving.

"Let's have that song about the bread and oil, Joaquín," Mudarra said aloud as the other drifted away. The song had been improvised by Mudarra and sung to Gordito in Miracle Court one evening when the early drawing of new bread at the bakery had filled the place with its sweet fragrance and a barrel of olive oil had been standing outside the neighboring shop. With especial care Mudarra began a prelude and then, while his fingers pulled the strings quietly well above the sound hole, he waited for Caro to begin the song.

> *Ay!*

At the long note the guitar swelled loudly and then was silent a moment.

> *Ay! When I saw sweet bread drawn out my thoughts*
> *to you this evening fled.*

And as Caro continued with falling notes the guitar began to play isolated chords.

> *And when they laid it on the white-wood boards*
> *I thought of you, O woman, sweet as bread.*

"Olé!" ejaculated Mudarra with quiet intensity.

"Ay!" began the singer again, and then he sang that she had the sweetness and the purity of the olives' press lying still in the wooden vats.

"Olé!" Mudarra ejaculated fiercely, beginning a glittering cadenza.

> *Ay! Man liveth aye by bread and oil*
> *Man dies, they say, with oil and bread,*

Caro began again, and with the last insistent but quiet phrases he told the woman that she was as bread and oil.

The guitar died away with the faintest touching of a high harmonic and the Court was silent.

"Buenas noches, amigo," said Mudarra, turning towards Olive Oil Street. "Good night, friend," The sereno was crying above in High Town: "Middle Night, señores, and the night is serene."

The woman at the grille watched the singer gaze after Mudarra until he had turned the corner, she heard the scuffing steps of the guitarist as he mounted to the Plaza change into a soft stride and die away. And then Caro was already approaching the window. By all the traditions of Andaluz courtship he should have begun by paying Lucía extravagant compliments; he did not do so but greeted her simply.

"There were many here tonight? I thought I heard Conchita Pérez."

"Yes, she came down and asked if she might watch us; she's friendly with my mother."

"But she's from the High Town; how's that, didn't the women of the Blue mind?"

"She doesn't belong to either of the Companies, so it doesn't matter. She came because . . ." The girl broke off sharply.

"I see. . . . They say the Company of the White are going to outdo you completely this year; they've got two new scenes to present."

"They said that three years ago when we made them look like beggars and traveling tinkers, Joaquín."

"Lucía, my dear . . ." Caro said, forgetting the Lenten Companies.

"Yes?"

"Lucía, you must answer me."

The girl opened her lips to make a quick retort; and then, glancing at the eager form beyond the grille, was silent.

"Tell me, girl, do you like me to come to your window?"

The girl did not reply.

"I've been coming for a year now; you know how I feel about you."

"Yes."

"Do you wish me not to come? Lucía, you must tell me. I must know, do you want me to stay away?"

"No . . ."

"Then tell me, Lucía my darling, do you love me?"

"I don't know," the girl replied at last. The man did not make immediate answer.

"Joaquín . . . I do love you."

"You do!" Eagerly he reached through the grille and took her hand and drew it to his lips, then as he released it she caressed his cheek with sudden impulse, releasing in him a flood of words he had never spoken before. The girl's laughter excited him the more.

"Be quiet, be quiet, man," Lucía said at last. "You talk like an orator."

"An orator. No, you make me more of a poet than Diego."

Her hand suddenly lay limp in his.

"The song I sang was his, you know, dear; don't you think it is beautiful?"

The girl was silent awhile.

"He is your friend," she said almost inaudibly and turned her head away.

"Ah yes, of course, but still it is beautiful."

From near the Lower Gate the sereno cried again, and when he had finished Lucía stood up and said:

"You must go now."

"But Lucía, so soon . . . why, it is only half-past twelve."

"Yes, please go now," she urged timidly, putting her hand through the bars.

When Caro had gone, she stood awhile listening to his steps as he mounted to the plaza, and then slowly went up the stairs to her room.

A long time Caro stood in the warmth that still radiated from the smithy, looking back upon the town, and then, as he stumbled down the groove of the Huerta path, his feet colliding with old refuse and tins that glittered sharply in the moonlight, the sereno cried again: "It is one o'clock, señores, and the night is serene." The cry disturbed Caro, and he hurried on down to the warmth of his home, beyond which a vague mist was rising from the newly plowed field of the Well.

3

In Contumely of Mules

JUST as La Cándida had discovered that there was no chocolate in the rectory cupboard and had commenced to suspect "that other" of stealing it, a boy's voice called from the porch, "Ave María." "I wonder whether 'the other' could have made himself a cup of chocolate while I was shopping yesterday," she mused. "The water was on the fire. . . ."

"Ave María," called the boy again. Ah yes, the serving boy, she must give him the piece of bread and sausage which was his wage.

"Gratia plena," she called out, and the boy answered "Bueno" and sat down on Father Martínez's bench. Carefully she measured off a thumb's length of sausage, cut off another thin slice from the piece because it was too long, took twenty-five centimes from the drawer, gave the breakfast to the serving boy and went round to her sister's little shop for chocolate.

" 'The other' is saying Doña Inés' requiem at Don Fadrique's today," she said to her sister.

"It's Father Soriano's turn this week?"

"Yes, 'the other's,' " she replied. "The Father will be back from San Andrés in a few minutes," and taking the piece of chocolate she hurried back to the rectory. Today she was pleased that she would not have to give breakfast to the curate to whom, even in her best temper, she never referred as Don Mamerto, nor yet as Father Soriano. Once or twice Father Martínez had rebuked her for the way she spoke to the curate, saying, "Father Soriano, though young, is a priest of God, Cándida," or "Don Mamerto has received Holy Orders."

Her reply was invariably a grim "Yes, I know," which succeeded in conveying a withering scorn of Soriano individually, contempt for the younger generation of priests in general, and a submerging pity for the misinformed bishops who had laid hands on Father Soriano's head.

La Cándida was in her late sixties; bent in frame, nearly bald and suffering from cataract as she was, she still moved with the determined gait she had possessed when she had refused a Huerta tenant's suit in order to enter the rectory as housekeeper. When a young and handsome woman, La Cándida had known of the classical accusation of her concubinage and once or twice had heard herself spoken of as "La Rectora." Well, what had they known, her accusers? They had known nothing. That imputation had been lived down many years now, but in some vague way it made La Cándida feel that Father Martínez had an extra claim to the rectorate, as against "that other." She feared and hated Soriano's courting of the more prosperous families of Villa Alta, for their gifts would possess far greater importance now that the Republic had declared that it would not make budgetary provision for the salaries of the clergy. The Marquis's quarterly grant would not keep body and soul together and La Cándida had no confidence in the charity of the Rector's flock.

When La Cándida returned to the rectory, she found the two priests already in the dining room. Father Martínez, his tall stooping frame nearly filling up the window alcove as he was reading the morning's paper, turned to her at once.

"Quick with my chocolate, Cándida, it is nearly time for Father Soriano to start for the Palace, and I am going with him."

"You are going with him?"

Father Soriano suppressed a smile. Why did that thin-nosed yellow-faced weasel smile, thought Cándida.

"I have to meet the Marquis today, woman," said the rector testily. Today he would receive his quarterly allowance. "The other" was sneering at her as if she had forgotten. Look at the poor creature. He was nothing beside the tall, massive-shouldered rector with his great iron-gray head.

"I should like you to provide me with an apple or some other fruit, please, señorita; his lordship's housekeeper frequently forgets to serve fruit with the breakfast," said the curate quietly.

Why did he speak like that? the oily, smooth-tongued rascal. Why didn't he say, "Give me an apple, woman," like the rector. Carefully weighing oranges in her hand to select the driest, she placed one on the table.

"There are no apples," she said, and went into the kitchen. When the priests left the rectory, La Cándida hastened to the window to see them cross the square to San Pedro's gate. "The yellow-faced, thin-nosed little creature, and in Holy Orders, Ca!"

"I wish Don Fadrique would come back to his house in Villa Alta," thought Father Martínez, as they walked up the track to the Palacio. He was finding it difficult to keep pace with the young priest, who, with the arrogance of youth, always appeared to be trying to outpace him.

"His lordship will never leave the Palacio," he said aloud to Father Soriano. "Ever since Doña Inés died he has not even opened his house in the Square."

"No, of course not," said the young priest, thinking "He has told me that at least four times. Always these local anecdotes and nothing of the Holy Ministry."

"A sad thing that was, brother, the death of Doña Inés. She died in childbirth, you know. She had had two miscarriages before and I well remember Dr. Torres coming to me—just for advice, of course and saying that another such thing would surely kill her. And it did, it did, brother. It killed her right enough. Ha! They've given the earth a plowing at last on this lot of terraces." The old priest stopped, out of breath, and pointed across the flank of the hills. "Too late, you know, brother; here we are near the end of February and that's the first working Señor Argote has given."

"Very late," Soriano murmured, gazing at the fields. He was thinking of Doña Inés and her fate with a horror that he could not keep from showing on his face. Why did Father Martínez always seek to remind him of that death? How frail was the flesh and how terrible concupiscence, which might take a woman and . . . tear her to pieces, tear her to pieces, his imagination insisted, and as a girl went by towards the Palacio he stared with fear and repugnance into her melancholy face with its womanly lines and its air of abstracted repose. His gaze followed the slender figure of the girl and in his imagination . . . it was terrible. Only last week a woman had groaned into his confessional, large with child, and shuddering he had been compelled to go in and listen to her.

"Well, the land and everything won't go to a son of Don Fadrique's for all his trying. Hola, Argote!" The rector suddenly raised his voice in a shout.

"He's one for a horse, brother," the rector chuckled; "no mules for Indalecio Argote." The mayordomo rode over to them and drew rein suddenly; the horse wheeled and spattered dust over their black cassocks. Argote did not apologize.

"Buenas," he said curtly.

"I was telling Father Soriano that it was high time you gave the land yonder a good working."

"Ca!" replied the olivero, staring hard into Soriano's face. "Middle of January to the end of February's my rule, but it wants understanding, señor," and he flung his thick hand down upon his enormous thigh. What a brutal head, thought Father Soriano and tried to avert his gaze, but the man on horseback stared so hard at him that he could not do so.

"What's the prospect this year? Looks to me as if there might be a good crop."

"Last year's shoots good and strong and all new wood sound, trust me for that, Father Martínez, and the trees have come through the winter much better than usual. Yes, a good crop, I think; they'll be flowering soon, anyway."

"A good crop, if God wills," the rector added.

"If God wills," grunted Argote, staring down into Soriano's face as if his gaze were a physical push. "Well, you're anxious for your breakfast, Father, I suppose," he said to the curate; "you'll be wanting to get that little job over at the Palace, eh?" And with a fresh cloud of dust he rode off along a side path, shouting: "Adios, señores."

After the requiem the Marquis led the way to his library and sat at a table with his hands crossed at the first joints of the fingers. Father Martínez walked to the other side of the room and sat down also, laying his hand upon the back of a chair as a sign to the curate to be seated.

"Please be seated, Father," said Don Fadrique, "or perhaps it would be better for you to break your fast." Father Martínez rose and pulled the bell rope. Presently the housekeeper came and beckoned to the young priest to follow her, and, as he did so, the rector sighed.

"I should like you to return here afterwards, if you please, Father Soriano," said Don Fadrique without looking up.

"Your lordship looks a little unwell," ventured the rector, looking into the long, grave face of the lord of Los Olivares. It seemed to him that the skin, stretched tightly upon the aggressive skull, was paler than ever, that the dark expressionless eyes were even more cold. Don Fadrique bowed his head slowly.

"How are things in the town, Father?" he said quietly.

"Ah, not so well as I should like them." He paused awhile as if searching for permission to continue speaking. "In some ways I am hopeful, your lordship. The preparations for the Holy Week processions have really begun in earnest now, though there is little chance of them being performed . . . your lordship will understand."

The Marquis of Peral watched the old priest steadily without speaking, motionless.

"And with the permission of your lordship I should like to say that both Companies very much hope that you will be able to make your usual grant to assist with the purchase . . ." Father Martínez faltered.

"I am very sorry," Don Fadrique said at length, "but I shall be unable to make the grant this year." Slowly he parted his hands.

"Yes . . . ? But if I may venture, even supposing there are no processions," began the rector. The Marquis joined his hands and the priest was silent. After a while he said:

"There have been several meetings in the town recently. The Anarchist, Dr. Aguiló . . ."

"Aguiló?" There was a sharp inflection in Don Fadrique's voice.

"Yes, he is in these parts, and two others, I am told. There was a meeting a little while ago at the house of the man Caro. There was another this week at Ojeda's, the man who is leaving, and two more elsewhere. There is much excitement. I need hardly say I am well informed, your lordship."

"What is the cause of it, the immediate cause, I mean? The excitement of last year, perhaps a certain measure of disappointment with the results?"

"The disappointment perhaps and excitation of spirits, yes . . ."

"The immediate causes? Wages have not been lowered, surely the men have no reason for complaint?"

"They complain, of course, your lordship. The shutting of the shoe factory in Puente Nuevo has brought a lot of young people back home again. Puente Nuevo is a bad place, of course. . . . Sometimes I think the country is tired, the earth and the people; perhaps the earth itself is tired, even the Huerta people complain they can't live upon it. Of course, your lordship, I tell them they ought to work it better as their forefathers did. Ah, señor, Spain has never been the same since the farmers gave up using the horse and the ox. You cannot plow with the mule; first it doesn't draw the share deep enough, and secondly it is an unprofitable beast, a monster, señor; whereas the horse has offspring . . ." Father Martínez edged himself forward in his chair and waved his hand vigorously. "I mean, señor, Our Blessed Lord Himself rode upon an ass with palms before him. . . ."

Don Fadrique laid his hands upon the table, and the rector's enthusiasm collapsed; a moment later there was a knock on the door. The Marquis of Peral looked up with interest in his face, and then glanced at his watch. Warmly he said, "Come in." Father Martínez stared at the door. Father Soriano and Mudarra entered, and behind them a stranger who advanced at once to the table, near which Diego had taken his customary seat.

"His Lordship the Marquis of Peral?"

"Yes."

"I am instructed by Señor Carlos Bustamente, my employer, to give this to you, with this letter, your lordship." Don

Fadrique's face became suddenly animated, and he opened the letter with haste. It read:

Acting upon your greatly respected instructions of February last year we have secured for you the volume which our fully authorized messenger will deliver to you. This copy of The Six Books of the Dolphin of Music *was formerly, we understand, in the Medinacoeli Library at Madrid, in which it was deposited by a member of the House of Alba upon his retiring from the Grand Priorship of Malta. The edition is that of Vallodolid of the year 1538, which, as your lordship will know, is the first and most prized. We regret to state that the foot of one page in Book III, containing a vihuela arrangement of a song of Joaquin des Prés, is missing, and that the colophon is badly stained. The binding, we have reason to believe, is Italian work of the last quarter of the sixteenth century. In view of the rarity of this book, which your lordship so urgently desired us to obtain, we feel sure that the enclosed account will be acceptable to your lordship.*

The account was for twenty thousand pesetas.

"Permit me," the messenger said, producing a pocket knife, as Don Fadrique began to fumble with the parcel.

"Oh, please be seated, Father Soriano, be seated." The Marquis waved towards a chair.

"Sit down, man," growled the rector.

Don Fadrique turned the book over in his hands before opening it. Within was the familiar title page, a badly drawn sketch of which, copied from the National Library copy at Madrid by his own hand, lay in a drawer of the music-room desk. He gazed long at the steep-pooped three-masted ship with its flying pennons, and at the dolphin as big as the ship going before it, with a musician perched on its back playing a vihuela. The title page fascinated him, and again and again his gaze moved from the castle-like ship stately progressing over the formal sea to the sporting but formal beast. Sometimes his attention lingered over the musician not rapt in his music yet ignoring the hazards of his position, gazing out of the title page at Don Fadrique. As he contemplated the engraving,

the things around him, the table, the messenger standing
motionless before him, the room and the sounds of the wagon
being drawn over the small stones of the yard outside, all
faded away, the title page itself faded away and Don Fadrique
was gazing at a musician who regarded him from the back of
a dolphin, a musician secure. A subtle nostalgia was mixed
with the serenity which the Marquis experienced as he contemplated the ideal life of the imagination which the long-
dead artist had surely known, and the pain was pleasure to him.
A melancholy of the utmost refinement took possession of him,
so keen that he could not have spoken of it even though, as in
fancy he had done, he had addressed the musician upon the
dolphin's back. What was the secret, the symbolic significance
of that simple engraving? Its peace . . .

"Your lordship will have even greater reason to be proud of
your library," the messenger said, and Don Fadrique looked up
to see the world about him, the two priests, the guitarist, and
the man from Madrid. Father Martínez, watching the Marquis
buy a book, was mildly surprised at Don Fadrique's appearance.

"If your lordship cares, I am fully authorized by Señor
Bustamente."

"Ah, yes." Don Fadrique's sigh as he laid a check book
before him was wrongly interpreted by the messenger. His
regret that he had been forced to reduce the amount of Father
Martínez's quarterly check was revived by the transaction he
was about to conclude. But the Dolphin was cheap at the price;
no doubt some collector troubled by the advent of the Republic
had been compelled to sell this treasure. Well, it was a good
investment, small and easy to carry away. But the pleasure of
it! He caressed the book again.

"Señor Bustamente will send me the usual document of
rightful tenure with the receipt, I suppose," he said, as he
handed over the check.

"I am empowered to give both, señor." The messenger's
relief was audible.

"Very good. No, don't get up, Mudarra; kindly bring a
chair for this gentleman, Father Soriano." The priest started
violently, and brought over his own chair, looking down for a

moment at the book, the papers and the check upon the table. With nervous movement the messenger signed the receipt.

Sadly the old priest made his way back to the town, relieved that Soriano had been asked by the Marquis to remain behind awhile, for the young priest had not yet learned to be companionable, and his nervous earnestness often displeased the rector. The reduction in his allowance was not a serious one, but it disturbed him greatly. First the cessation of the Holy Week grants and then this reduction! What was to happen to Los Olivares, he thought, as he looked around at the wide acres of Don Fadrique's lands. Ridge after ridge ran down from the iron hills and spread out first into buckled and broken planes and then into suaver but still sharply edged folds. Saddle after saddle of earth swept away round the great bay in the hills and all of them were covered with the olivars of Don Fadrique, olivars that had been first laid out when the knights of Castile had driven out the African invaders, olivars which had given their very name to the town below. Such lands must surely arouse the covetousness of the men now in power at Madrid. There was talk of land nationalization, of expropriation, of giving the land to the workers. But supposing the law of property were violated, how could this land be used for ought else but olives? Father Martínez stood still in the dust and stared across at the vast waterless slopes. Perhaps he would himself be driven out of Los Olivares; indeed he would not wish to stay if all this were to be broken up and destroyed. He had saved enough for his own and Cándida's declining years, but with all the strength of his heart the rector desired not to leave the town of his forty years' ministration, nor the lofty darkness of San Andrés with its stale-sweet smell of incense and its warm smell of the wax he himself had burned. These thoughts wearied him with their sharp insistence, and it seemed again that the whole country was tired and despairing, that repose and strength and peace had gone forever. "Just as the horse is disappearing," he murmured. It was as if something brooding over the country for years and years had absorbed the energy of Spain, its intelligence and its strength alike. Slowly and sadly he made his way towards the enormous brown walls over which the roof of San Andrés was visible, watching over the town with its imperious tower and gaunt iron cross.

Father Soriano was filled with pleasurable excitement when he left the Palacio. The labors the marquis had asked him to undertake, of reporting upon the state of affairs in the town and in the Cortes and particularly upon the progress of land legislation, would be easy and agreeable. It was not the silver in his pocket that pleased Father Soriano, nor yet that it was the Church's duty both to warn and to defend her sons against mortal transgressions, but—somehow it linked him with the place, something he had found impossible to do. When the families of Villa Alta heard of Don Fadrique's confidence in him surely they would unbend and his loneliness would be at an end. Two years of loneliness, two years of isolation from mankind save through the contacts of his ministry—Father Soriano rebutted the thought. Surely the exercise of his ministry should give him peace, and yet . . .

A scream of shocked laughter startled him. Argote was shouting to a group of girls, from the vantage point of horseback.

"Eh?" he was shouting. "Too old, am I? God's teeth, I could . . ." His words were lost in a fresh scream, and the laughing girls ran down the track.

"Hola, padre," called Argote roughly as he rode up.

"A very good afternoon to you."

"So you didn't go down with the rector?" Argote began, throwing Soriano into fresh confusion. "I saw him looking at the men at work down by Mater Purissima. Ha! He's a fine fellow! Thinks he knows all about olive trees, señor, he thinks he does, but he knows less of olives than a young priest knows of . . . God bless my soul, it's nearly time for me to be indoors."

"There must be much to know, Señor Argote. There are fine trees here, I see."

"Fine trees! God's wounds, man, you've never been out to the Great Skirt, have you? You must come with me someday and I'll show you something."

Father Soriano's heart beat faster, and he hastened to reply: "I should be delighted, delighted, Señor Argote. I know nothing of olives."

The mayordomo's face seemed to be less brutal now.

"Wounds, man, I know you don't, but it'll do you no harm to learn. Say, there's time to have a look at the Chapel Olive." Argote swung from the saddle and, giving the beast a resounding smack on the haunches, at which it set off towards the Palacio, pointed along a path and with a single "Follow me," strode away. It would be as well to begin, thought Argote, by showing the priest a few curiosities and telling him a few anecdotes; the serious talk about the care of olives could come later. The path was a steep short cut to the Palacio, and soon Soriano was wishing Argote would not walk so fast, it was as hard to keep up with him as with Father Martínez, who always seemed to be challenging him to walk faster, as if proud of his prowess in old age. Eventually the path led round to the rear of the Palace.

"There," said Argote, pointing to the summit of a wall in Moorish style. "That's the Chapel Olive and I reckon it's the most remarkable tree in Andalucía. Let's go inside and see it better," and with a leap he slid down a steep ten-foot bank, leaving the curate to find his way down alone.

"It's been there for well-nigh three hundred years," Argote continued, "and there's less soil on the top of that wall than muck in that pigeon house yonder."

Soriano contemplated the little tree which stood bravely atop the high wall. "But surely the roots must go down to this well," he ventured, pointing to the Moorish well below the tree.

"That's what I say," bellowed Argote, "but some of the fools think otherwise. I reckon some thin feeler or other must get down to the water or it wouldn't live."

"Does it grow good olives?"

"Not a goddamned one, nowadays. But they say it used to provide enough oil to keep the lamp burning before the Santo Cristo in the chapel. Wants pruning and cleaning, I expect, and a few new limbs grafted on, too, but there's no time for that kind of thing nowadays. Still, it's curious."

"The Santo Cristo, you say, Señor Argote?"

"Yes, that building's a chapel. You'll see the inscription in a hole in the wall. By the way, there's another interesting tree just over in that gully . . ."

"Just a moment, please, señor, I should like to read the inscription." He peered into the little oven-like recess. It read:

Upon St. Michael's day of the year MDC, *the head of the apostle Saint Peter and the Image of Santo Cristo del Olivar were discovered at the spot indicated by this inscription, after having remained hidden for over a thousand years. This discovery was due to a fowl which, pecking at the wall, succeeded in opening the hole in which the miraculous image was resting.*

"Doesn't say anything more about the head," Argote gruffly commented.

"But the · image! Sincerely, I should like to know what happened to the miraculous image." Soriano's eyes glittered.

"Oh, that," Argote said, "that's in the chapel; the door's open."

Soriano stood before the image. It was a wooden crucifix of veined olive wood of expressive workmanship. The body twisted in pain seemed to writhe · away from the cross, the arms, unlike many such images, were supporting the body's weight, by which the hands were visibly torn. Father Soriano had never seen such realism. The crucifixion print by Guido Reni which hung in his room, with its open horizontal hands unlacerated, unbroken by the blows of the nails, was henceforth uninspiring. Even the Velásquez crucifixion print in the confessional box, with its closed hands dripping with blood, had not the devotional power of this terrible work. The weight on the arms made more visible the gaunt ribs of the emaciated body, and the feet, broken by the journey to Golgotha, were torn hideously by the nails, around which blood had been painted. All this was fine and spiritual, Father Soriano could see, but the glory of the crucifix was the agonized face with its open gaping mouth and the eyes turned upward, and in the sunken cheeks covered with blood that poured from beneath the crown of thorns upon the head. All the horror of that ghastly death was depicted in the Santo Cristo del Olivar, and gazing at it Soriano fell to his knees in a rapture of devotion. Tears came into his eyes, tears of exquisite joy, and when at last he wished to pray he was forced to swallow before beginning, "O Jesu, Jesu . . ."

When he came out of the chapel Argote had gone.

Striving to recollect where the head of St. Peter had been taken for veneration, Soriano descended to the town. He stood a moment before San Andrés, undecided whether or not to enter. If ever he were rector of San Andrés, he reflected, he would certainly try to get the Cristo del Olivar translated to the church. Rector of San Andrés! Perhaps now that the Marquis— he rebuked himself for the thought.

"The soup is ready and the rector is waiting," said La Cándida with her inevitable hostility as Soriano entered the rectory. He blushed and went at once into the dining room.

4

The Wood and the Steel

WHEN the Mater Purissima bell knocked at midday upon the second Saturday in March, Mudarra called to Caro, who was working lower down on Broad Skirt. Turning towards the answering yell, Mudarra saw the foliage being shaken and, gathering up Caro's jacket and the tools, he descended to the foot of the tree in whose branches his friend was working.

"Here, catch," Caro said, dropping a few slender branches. "What do you think of them?"

"Ought to do well, budiego olives; what are you going to graft 'em into?"

"Budiegos, about two dozen of them, and a few manzanillos and zorzaleños is all the Ojedas have got."

"Quite enough for that patch, too. That's six branches, Joaquín, you won't want any more."

Caro stepped down from the mother branch to the trunk and leaped to the ground. "Now to trim them a bit and stick 'em under our coats."

"Argote wouldn't mind."

"Well, I've not asked him, so we won't take any chances. You take the tools down to the chapel and come back to me and we'll cut across the gullies to their field. Sure you won't stay this afternoon, Diego?"

Mudarra shook his head. "I've told you twice that I'm going to Aguiló's meeting at Puente Nuevo. It's going to be a pretty hot one, I gather. The shutting down of the shoe factory has wakened things up. By the way, have you heard about Peral refusing the Companies a few duros?"

"You're not protesting about him not giving to the Companies, are you? They say he bought a music book for thirty thousand pesetas though!"

"Am I hell." Mudarra shrugged his shoulders and then regarded his companion inquisitively. "Do they?" he added, remembering the scene he had witnessed. "Why not forty thousand?" Of those present at the transaction who could have spread that story? Surely not that old hater of mules, Martínez. Soriano, then. But to whom?

"I wish I could come this afternoon, but I've promised Señora Robledo to help them," Caro said.

"Oh, what's she to do with the Ojedas then? You didn't tell me that."

"Nothing, only when Ojeda went away it seems he told his mother that I would look after their trees, for a while at least. She didn't know me, but she's friendly with Señora Robledo."

"Oh ah."

"And Señora Robledo came down to our place and asked me if I'd do a spot of grafting for them, and suggested that if the weather kept good we'd all have lunch out on the field. I didn't want to lose the chance."

"Well, the weather's kept good all right." Mudarra grinned. "There's chance in that."

"What about tonight?" the guitarist asked as he was about to leave the Ojeda field. "I'm going along to the Rincón café; coming?"

"Why not go down to Gordito's?"

"No, if I go anywhere else it'll be to Manuel's bar. Acorín will be there and I've got one or two to get back. Last time I was at the Rincón he came and sighed all over me like a mare in heat. What the hell's he want to follow me round for?"

"You dog him round, too."

"He's such a melancholy devil. Well, you know where to find me."

The Ojeda olivar was no more than a small plot upon a saddle of one of the ridges that ran down to the Jabalón valley, about a mile distant from the town. Nearby were a few ruined walls, blackened by the fires that had been built against them, and a circular threshing floor paved with red bricks. To the field led a narrow path which, starting from near the Caro's house, obliquely traversed the whole of the Peral olivars upon that side of the town. Often it curved into gullies filled with broken and sharp-angled blocks and thin slates of stone that rang lightly as passing feet sent them down the gully, often it crossed cones of yellow scree held together by the wiry ace-buche, from the wild olive, or passed under strange cones of rain-denuded earth, like penitents in a Lenten procession. Finally the path divided, one branch disappearing into the superb grove of holm oaks in which stood the Sanctuary of Our Lady of All Unprotected Ones, while the other climbed to the shoulder on which lay the Ojeda field and where a quite un-founded tradition asserted a Moorish village had once stood. In the field were some forty olives and of these a good half were young trees, the former having been renderd unproduc-tive by disease. Almost the last act of old Ojeda had been to replace them by others.

Soon after Mudarra had gone the party arrived; with Señora Robledo were Lucía, Señora Catalina Ojeda and her daughter Escolástica, the latter a pretty girl with an ugly name, her neighbors said. Señora Ojeda at once apologized for their late-ness, the journey had been too much for her. Joaquín Caro made seats from the stones of the ruins, arranging them against an angle of the walls facing the sun and then, after the lunch of bread, wine, omelet, and meat cooked over the ash of a fire of holm oak and olive twigs, conversation became lively.

Escolástica had formerly been a nun in the Carmelite Order and had reached her seventh and last year of membership of that Order before finally taking the veil. In 1931 she had been living in the Convent of Nuestra Señora del Carmen in the city of Murcia. When the convent had been burned to the ground by revolutionaries, the girl escaped in a motor beneath a pile of empty sacks. Finally, life outside the convent, which she had entered at the age of seventeen, proved more to her liking, and she had left the Order after an all-night argument with one of the superiors who had arrived posthaste at Los Olivares. She was now engaged to be married to the brother of the harness-maker's apprentice, who had promised to come to the Ojeda olivar later. Escolástica's story was invariably the principal subject of conversation whenever she was present.

"Life is very strange," concluded Escolástica. "Sometimes when I'm working or lying in bed it all seems like a dream. I can't believe I've spent seven years in a convent."

"You're better off now," her mother remarked abruptly. "I can tell you it was a great displeasure for us when she went into the convent." She did not add that at first she had been more than a little uncomfortable in the presence of her returned daughter, whom, despite her love for Escolástica, she had regarded as a disloyal nun.

"Yes, yes, I am happy, but I was very happy then, too, everyone was kind to me. The worst is that everyone's an invalid in a convent."

"You were happy?" Caro inquired.

"Yes, everyone loved me. There are many who suppose nuns don't laugh, but I could tell you things. Holy Innocents' Day was the best, that's when the Mother Superior doesn't count for anything and the youngest commands. Mater Santissima, you should have seen the things we used to do. I remember how Sister Chastity and two of us tried the chapel door key in all the cell locks until at last we found one it would open. Then we dressed up some pillows in a habit and put a broom through both sleeves and drew a face on the pillow with charcoal, so that it looked just like a dead nun with her arms stretched out. When the sister came back, of course she didn't expect anything in her room, because the key was still with the Mother Superior. My, you should have heard her scream! She had hysterics and we had to send out for the doctor! Another time one of the nuns painted her face with some stuff that shone in the dark and put a sheet over herself. I ran down the stairs by fours when I saw her, I thought it was a wandering soul. And then . . ." Escolástica looked at her mother inquiringly. Señora Ojeda nodded a little doubtfully. "I don't think they will mind."

"Once, one of the nuns emptied a lot of packets for making effervescent water into the sisters' night chambers, so that . . ."

"That will do, Escolástica," her mother cried. "No more."

Then, as Lucía was working upon the embroidery of the

dress which Escolástica's *novio* would wear in one of the pasos of the Holy Week procession, which it was hoped that the mayor would authorize, Escolástica began to tell them about the Murcian celebrations.

"You should have seen La Dolorosa. They say that when the image-maker tried to find a woman with a face beautiful enough they brought him a married woman who looked something like the Virgin. But this woman had a happy face and the image-maker was in despair. So at last they found a way out of the difficulty. They brought the woman to the image-maker and then accused her of adultery against her husband, and as she began to weep and her face became agonized they took a photograph of her. And that's why the La Dolorosa of Murcia doesn't look like a virgin, they say, because this woman was a married woman. They say she died of the sorrow and the scandal. That's the story they tell, but I don't know whether it is true or not."

"I don't believe it," said Caro. "Nor I," added Señora Robledo.

"It's what they say in Murcia," Escolástica repeated with heat.

"They say," Lucía remarked.

"Well now, I suppose it's time you began the grafting, isn't it?" Señora Robledo asked. "Will you want any help?"

"It would be better, though I can manage."

"Lucía, you go and help Joaquín."

"But, Mother, I've so much to get done."

"Oh, but you're nearly at the end of those red flowers."

"But there's the leaves to do yet."

"Now run along, child, and help Joaquín. When Escolástica's *novio* comes he'll want her to himself or she could help."

The couple went over to the field, Lucía carrying a basket with the little shield-shaped pieces of living wood, each containing an "eye" which, during the conversation, Caro had cut from the boughs he had provided, and he carried the wool binding and the thin-bladed knife.

The couple approached the tree which Caro pointed out, and Lucía stood still while he walked round it slowly several times. Then he came to her side, and laying his hand upon the smooth young bark he said: "We'll make a branch grow out of here. That will balance the tree and make it like a tripod upside down."

"It will be like a candelabra," Lucía added quietly.

"That's right; when it is grown they can cut off one or two of the son and grandson branches on the other mothers so that light and air will enter and keep the tree healthy."

"Yes," replied Lucía.

"Well then, that's settled." Caro did not at once begin work, but remained by Lucía's side regarding the tree gravely. It was a healthy young tree, slender of trunk and delicate of limb, and its bark was smooth and light in hue, having that tender appearance which told him of the sap moving up from the roots to the topmost clusters of leaf. Something in the tree pleased him, and it was a pleasure he could not have described. Caro looked around at the enormous and barren hills standing behind them and across the already brazen bowl of the valley, a land bare of trees save for the glistening but lugubrious grove near which they stood, a few pines and the olives of the lower fields. It was a motionless land, a still land of bitter earth and vast forces in rest, and about it there was no trivial grace. The olive trees themselves, though young, seemed already to have the immobility of the older olive trees of those hills, that gravity which makes them at one with the hills. The breeze which from time to time ran down the immense slopes behind them seemed not to cause the least tremor in the branches. And spring, which had already tinged the broom clumps with gold, had awakened no colored display in the olives but a sober putting out of waxen green leaves that mingled with the old without contrast. It seemed that the olives were the very spirit of that land and, at peace with it and its iron law, stood patiently regarding the dry unnurturing soil from which the sun's fierce round mouth had long ago sucked all the juices, content laboriously to move the little sap it afforded and content also at length to produce their little green and red and purple-black fruit.

Caro at last stepped forward and laid his hand upon the tree. Neither Lucía nor he had spoken for several minutes.

"See, Lucía," he began, "first we draw a letter T like this, on the bark," and with his nail he made the letter. "Then we have to cut into the bark as far as the wood, so, along the lines." He was silent awhile, working the knife into the bark with firm and deliberate pressure. The girl did not move or speak, watching him with absorbed interest, though she had seen this shield-grafting done many, many times.

Now Caro had incised the letter T in the mark and was working the thin blade under it, loosening it and tenderly pulling it away from the wood till the flesh of the tree shone through the parted bark.

"It seems cruel," Caro said.

"Yes," she replied.

"But the tree must be hurt if it is to be fruitful and profitable, and soon the sap will flow into the wound and it will heal and the new wood which we shall graft in will take life in it and grow. See, it's done like this," and he held out his hand for an "eye." "Budiego grafts," he said, gently taking the shield from the girl. "Like unto like makes the surest and best of grafts, but there's a golden rule, Lucía. Hard wood over hard wood and tender over tender, that way the two natures are at peace and the tree is in comfort." Caro placed the graft between his lips, holding it by the little shoot that would soon grow into a new branch. Then carefully parting the loosened bark with his fingers, he leaned forward and with a downward movement of his head slid the graft into place. Firmly he closed the bark over it so that only its shoot protruded.

"Now we bind it with the wool," he said softly, "not too tightly, for the sap must flow into the new wood or it will die . . . and that's that," he concluded, stepping back from the tree to the girl's side. For more than a minute they gazed at the tree and then Lucía sighed.

"Why do you sigh?" he asked.

"I don't know," she answered, smiling. Caro put out his hand and she took it and held it a moment; he made no movement to approach her more closely but stood so, gravely regarding her, and was content.

When at last the grafting was finished, voices were suddenly raised upon the threshing floor. "Mother of God, you're late," Señora Ojeda called shrilly. "We shall have to be going back in half an hour." Justo Robledo and his wife and Escolástica's *novio* were coming up the path. Presently the party came over and examined the work, approving with loud outbursts of praise followed by solemn noddings and a few discreet questions. They did not invite Caro to return to the ruins with them, and although Señora Ojeda offered her a shawl against the rapidly cooling air, Lucía did not go back with her.

"Let us see how the other trees are getting on," Caro said, and they went over to the older olives.

"Zorzaleños," remarked Caro. "It gives good oil, though it's not really the best tree for this high ground. It doesn't resist the cold very well, but it is very fruitful. See!" He reached up into the lowest foliage. "The flowers are coming, it will be a good year if the weather is kind." In his hand lay a fragile cluster of waxen yellow buds, their little globes marked with the cross of the still folded petals.

Behind them a gramophone began to play American dance music and they heard shouts of "Come over here," "Come and dance," so they returned to the threshing floor, where Justo Robledo and his wife and Escolástica and her lover were dancing.

"Would you two like to dance?" Lucía's mother questioned.

"I, no," replied Caro. "Do you want to dance, Lucía?"

"No."

"Then put this shawl round you, daughter."

They sat awhile side by side on the stones and then, as the party returned to the town, separated, Lucía going ahead with Escolástica, while her *novio* and Caro walked by Señora Ojeda. Before they had reached Los Olivares night had fallen.

5

To Dust

AFTER a breakfast of bread and water Don Fadrique entered the chapel in which the requiem was to be sung, though there was still an hour to wait. Of the nine choristers who had arrived late the previous evening from the cathedral city, six had already sung at the Palacio upon many anniversaries of the death of Doña Inés and they would therefore know the custom of the house. Today he did not wish to be disturbed by the business of the estate, and Argote rarely took any notice of his desire to be undisturbed if he was accessible.

Five minutes later the door opened and Father Martínez and Soriano entered.

"You wished to speak to me, my lord," said the curate, who was to celebrate the requiem Mass.

"I wished to ask a dispensation from you."

"Your lordship may command."

"Not in this. Father Martínez will tell you that it is my custom to have the motet 'Emendemus in melius' sung at the end of the mass."

"A motet, 'Emendemus in melius'!" Father Soriano's surprise was such that he stumbled in pronouncing his Latin. "But, your lordship, that is the motet for the Sundays in Lent, and this is Thursday."

"That is so."

"At the end of the Mass, brother," interposed the rector with a frown, "his lordship would like you to go to your seat before leaving the chapel and pray for the soul of her ladyship, while the motet is being sung."

"But, señor, that is very contrary to the rubrics; I understand that I am still to be vested?"

"Of course, of course." Father Martínez's frown deepened.

"May I propose a solution of Father Soriano's difficulty?" Don Fadrique remarked coldly. "When the Mass is finished perhaps you could take off the chasuble and the maniple and be seated, or perhaps you would still care to leave the chapel. It has merely been my custom."

"Very good, your lordship," replied the curate, in confusion. "I will take off the chasuble. My prayers shall be exclusively for the intention of the Mass." He looked at the ground, blushing.

"Thank you."

When the parish priests had gone, Don Fadrique gave himself once more to his mood. The austere chapel with its high windowless walls and miniature clerestory was bare of ornament, save for those things ritually necessary. Upon the altar stood two three-tiered candelabras of the Catalan lily pattern, splendid examples of early-fourteenth-century work.

But it was towards the reredos that Don Fadrique's eyes most often wandered. He felt indeed that it was almost a part of his own being. The reredos consisted of a large unsigned painting depicting choristers singing with their faces towards the observer. In the background was the Virgin, holding the naked child upon her lap with one of his feet in her right hand and the left lightly clasping his stomach. The Virgin, with no crown, but loose flowing hair, wearing a magnificent copelike dress of scrolled fabric over a blue robe trimmed with narrow, exquisitely painted lace, was gazing shyly at the ground to the right of her feet.

It was neither the devotional nor the artistic quality of this retable which for so long had fascinated Don Fadrique. It was his discovery concerning the choristers that endeared the picture to him. Ostensibly they were singing a Mass, for on the altar steps lay an open manuscript, showing the tenor part of Morales' Gloria in the Mass "Benedicta est coelorum Regina," the identifying of which had been the first step in the erection of Don Fadrique's private historical theory concerning the life of the great Spanish composer. Then, curiosity one day prompting him to find out the composition of the choir, he had examined the scores each of them presented. Six of them could be read and, to his surprise, the Marquis had found that they all bore the first notes of the tenor part of the Gloria of six different Masses by Morales. There was in the Palacio library a copy of the magnificent Missarum Liber II dedicated to Pope Paul III and it had been possible for Don Fadrique to determine that the tenor on the extreme left was singing from the Mass built on that peregrine ubiquity, "L'Homme armé," while his neighbor was singing from the score of the five-part "Quem dicunt homines."

From this point, step after step had led Don Fadrique to the conclusion that the great Spaniard had once been chapelmaster to the house of Guevara, and this conclusion he had sustained by methods of scholarship that had much of distinction about them. At one time he had been perplexed by the fact that there was in the painting one less chorister than there were Morales' Masses. Then with a flush of triumph he had remembered that in the "Pro defunctis" there would of course be no "Gloria." Then, clearly, the altar and retable in the picture were the same as he now beheld before him, and Don Fadrique found in this a special commemorative intention. Ribas, the master of the cathedral music, had scouted all this by saying that early artists often played jokes of the most farfetched kind. His own stall, he added, had upon the reverse of the seat an obscene carving of a woman and a dog. But then, that gentleman had not known the least fact about the life of Morales, and had supposed that his protector Alexander Farnese had become Pope Paul the Fourth in 1533, by a whole year misdated and incorrect in the title; clearly Morales had been master of the chapel.

These meditations were suddenly broken by a vigorous rap on the chapel door, and with a sigh the Marquis opened it.

"If you please, your lordship, there is some business that must be attended to." Argote's tone was deferential but firm.

"I cannot come."

"If your lordship will have the goodness."

With no more protest he followed the mayordomo.

In the salon a thin-faced peasant was standing bareheaded,

and when the Marquis had taken his seat Argote motioned the man to speak. With nervous glances to right and left the peasant opened his mouth.

"Your lordship . . ." No other words issued.

"Speak up, man," commanded Argote.

"If your lordship . . ." Again the peasant broke down.

"God's . . ." Argote suppressed an oath. "Your lordship, he wishes to know if you will buy the three fields adjoining the property he rents from your lordship."

"I have already announced that I shall buy no more land," said the Marquis, crossing his hands at the first joints of the fingers.

"Then he wishes to know if you could find it possible to reduce the rent of the other land."

A frown appeared and disappeared upon the Marquis's face.

"That, I fear, will be impossible this year, and in any case Señor Argote manages all such business."

"But, Lord God have mercy, it was but three years ago you put up my rent," the peasant burst out.

"That may be so, I do not know. Is that so, Señor Argote?"

"Yes, your lordship. He says that unless he can sell his own land or secure a reduction of rent he will be unable to purchase water this year."

"God have mercy!" the peasant exclaimed, fiercely addressing himself to the mayordomo. "I cannot bid for the reservoir water against the bigger farmers and against . . ."

"That will do," ordered Argote.

"You must fetch water from the Jabalón as others do," began the Marquis and was silent. The peasant was staring blankly at him, his lips moving silently, his body trembling.

"Sufficient," the mayordomo began, but suddenly words burst out of the man's mouth.

"Don Fadrique, I tell you this means begging for me. We *cannot* pay, sir, we *cannot*." The Marquis parted his hands and laid them upon the table. "God punish you, sir, before you built the water reservoir . . ."

"His lordship did not build the water reservoir," shouted Argote.

"His father."

"Nor his father." The great figure of the mayordomo bore down upon the man.

"His grandfather."

"At the request of the Huerta tenants his lordship's grand-father built the water reservoir to store the winter rains. You know the truth as well as I do." Argote took the man's coat in his huge fist.

"But we hadn't to pay for water then, sir," the peasant whined.

"It was agreed by the tenants that they should bid for the water to repay the cost of the reservoir and to maintain the watercourses. If they bid high it is not his lordship's fault."

"But, sir . . ."

"Well?"

"If you could only lower the rent we might live, sir; we have *nothing*."

"I may have . . ." The Marquis checked himself. "Once my father was blamed for buying land; I am to be blamed for not buying it," he concluded.

"May God punish you for ever and ever," the peasant whispered at last.

Don Fadrique crossed himself. "May God Almighty forgive you," he said quietly, and walked towards the chapel.

Kneeling before the seat of the Guevaras the Marquis tried to forget the incident. The peasant had confused him with his grandfather. "His father," he had said. "Nor yet his father." "His grandfather." "His lordship's grandfather . . ." The words echoed still in his memory. The ignorance of the tenant was a measure of the trust that could be placed in him, he thought confusedly, for some proposition that did not make itself clear was disturbing him. That the man should have been confused with his ancestors must show how irrational the peasant's censure had been. The reservoir—up there on the hill—for a moment an image of the light-hued dam glimmered among the shapeless crags of the Barranco . . . and then he saw the blue surface of the water from the observation platform and the long tree-shaded path leading back to the white Palacio. Were the Guevaras, then, nothing but the reservoir to those men below, nothing but the white palace among the olivars? So that

the whole line of Guevaras stood as one man to bear the hate
. . . and the respect and the fear as well? Yes, he saw that now,
the peasant had merely been thinking as he himself would have
desired had he wished them to think of him. And yet, Don
Fadrique shrank from the thought, all of these around him
and below him—around him and below. He lowered his head
upon his arm and prayed for spiritual comfort. Through his
prayer the same images persisted, of himself standing upon an
eminence of the mountainside and of all these people, red-
faced red-handed, moving slowly among the trees a long way
off, around him and below. He imagined the house in the
Plaza Mayor—and the word República for a moment pained
him like a knife turning in his mind. The spiral pillars carved
with leaves, the fluted columns supporting the tabernacle like a
canopy beneath which the arms of Los Guevaras now crumbled
slowly to powder. The hanging fruit of stone, the masses of
stone leaves across the lintel and the obese children with lyres
upon each side of the arms. The people passed by it now indifferently, children played upon its steps, dogs mounted them,
dust collected upon them and against the paintless door behind
which no one lived—once he had lived among men, yet had
he—he had left the Solar— A voice interrupted his reverie.

"Confiteor Deo omni . . ." The voice was his own, he looked
up and his lips continued to follow the words of the confession.
Again the strange uneasiness for a moment took possession of
him, and then he was gazing at the Virgin in her scrolled
cope and dress of exquisite blue with its narrow edging of lace.

And as he regarded the Virgin's dress he heard in his
imagination, as if far off, the ripple of a woman's laughter and
it disturbed him in yet another way. Now the "Kyrie eleison"
was rising higher and higher and he lowered his head again
to listen to its loveliness, yet could not lose himself in it. The
thoughts that had persisted since the incident with the peasant
still lingered in his mind.

Again he was contemplating the Virgin in her blue dress
with its narrow lace, and then suddenly his eyes turned to the
trimming of the altar cloths and thence to the white linen.
"Inés, Inés," he murmured, seeing there her own clothing, her
own lace, the linen and laces of her nightdress and bridal

sheets, now lying upon the altar of God that the Holy Sacrifice might be performed upon them. Then as the "Sanctus" began, hushed and trembling yet confident, the memory of Inés faded and he was listening to music, with the same cold discomfort in him.

Slowly the Mass moved towards its end. Don Fadrique barely heard the consecration bell, though as the opening phrases of the "Agnus Dei" were murmured he prayed for the soul of Doña Inés; not the shy, laughing girl he had married, but the frozen woman of the house of Guevara lying in her fruitless bed. Innumerable plenary indulgences had already been gained for her soul. Now the Mass was ending and the voices were singing, "Libera me, Domine, de morte" and were suddenly hushed to a whisper at the word "æterna." "Deliver me, O Lord, from death eternal," the voice far-off within him said, "in that tremendous day when earth and heaven shall be moved and Jabalón and olivars and palace, all, all of it, shall burst into flame and the encircling hordes shall rush in to judge . . ." Don Fadrique trembled. "Libera me, Domine, libera me," the music pleaded. And was silent.

The celebrant had gone to his seat upon the epistle side and sat down without removing his chasuble, and Father Martínez was making signs to the choir to begin the motet. The canto fermo tenor moved a little away from the other tenors.

Now the timid contribution of the word "Emendemus" was rising through the web of music. "Emendemus, emendemus"— the phrase echoed in his mind and made a fifth counterpoint to the incomparable art of the former chapelmaster of the Guevaras. The voices were pleading, not for worldly gain, nor yet only for emendment of life, and then through a sudden hush, the grim solemnity of the canto fermo obtruded: "Remember, O man, that dust thou art and to dust thou shalt return." The phrase, stirring Don Fadrique more deeply than any other music or thought he had experienced, rose again and again through the inter-twining sounds, each time more grim, more ominous, more coldly implacable. "Remember, O man, that dust thou art *and to dust thou shalt return*." Then the four voices once more affirmed their contrition, with the fear of death in them, and the listener was contrite also and afraid. Don Fadrique did not know for what he was contrite and of what he had fear. And then another hush let through for a moment the stark solemnity of that "et in pulverem reverteris," and this was followed by an anguished vehemence that rose wailing against the persistent specter of death, rose wailing and desperate to fall back in a cry of mortal sorrow that suddenly obsessed all the parts. Grief hung over the chapel, wringing its hands, wringing its hands over the grim hills and the solemn olivars, sobbing, lamenting, and suddenly the slow steady tread of that fatal prophecy was again heard, *"Remember, O man, that dust thou art and to dust thou shalt return."* Don Fadrique lifted his head nervously and looked around him. He was in the chapel of the Guevaras, the aged priest of San Andrés was kneeling near him, his head bowed, the stupid old priest with his queer hatred of mules and his strange obsession by them, and as the music swelled suddenly, and the words *"Remember, O man"* inexorably forced their way through the counterpoint, he wanted to go over to the priest and lay his arm around the old man's shoulders. The impulse faded instantaneously; *"to dust thou shalt return"* announced the canto fermo, and then suddenly an uprushing paroxysm of fear flooded out over the music and took possession of Don Fadrique and for the moment all the cold pride of line and person, all the aloofness and reserve and dignity were futility. *"Dust, O Man . . ."* tolled the prophecy and it seemed that the white town, the great brown towers and the tawny hills were shaken, that the hills were darkened with the smoke of conflagrations, the Palacio itself—that through the swirling crackling olivars ran thin-faced men, towards the Palacio—*"Remember, O Man, that dust thou art and to dust thou shalt return"* and darkness settled down over the landscape of Don Fadrique's imagination.

Somewhere beyond the darkness a music of fear was hovering —and then feet were shuffling, the chapel door closed at last and the Marquis of Peral was alone, empty of feeling, cold. The grave face regarding the Virgin with her scrolled cope and the blue dress was the face men knew in Los Olivares. But still faintly he heard the cry "Remember, O Man," and by it his emptiness was made more cold.

Many minutes passed. Again there was a knock upon the door; he opened it and waited for the people standing there to speak.

"Upon the part of your tenants, we have brought these for the soul of the departed. May she rest in peace." The first couple, an old landworker and his wife with lined and weary faces, placed two long candles in Don Fadrique's hands. And he inclined his head and said, "May her soul and the souls of your departed be in peace. I thank you for this charity, and God be with you."

A young couple now stepped forward, an olivar worker and a girl of the outliving staff with a sad resigned face already lined, and, placing two more candles in Don Fadrique's hands, they said:

"Upon the part of your workers we bring these for the soul of the departed. May she rest in peace." The Marquis did not incline his head but looked searchingly into their faces. The melancholy eyes of the girl slowly lowered their regard and the youth shifted his feet nervously; only the weary faces of the old people returned his gaze, without changing. Nothing could be read there. He sighed almost inaudibly and said:

"I thank you for this charity. May her soul and the souls of your departed be relieved. Requiescat in pace," and all crossed themselves. Slowly and in disorderly manner the people went away.

The candles had burned two inches before the Marquis left the chapel and then, having lunched, he spent an hour sitting in his library, wearily transcribing from the Dolphin of Music. The task had lost its interest and from time to time he wandered about the room, idly searching for something more absorbing to do. Nothing suggested itself, and will-lessly he decided to ride through the olivars. As he left the stables, he heard the harsh passionate voice of Argote shouting at a worker and the fierce reply, and the two voices increased his loneliness. Suddenly he called to the stableman and dismounting, said, "Send a boy to the man Mudarra and tell him to come to my library."

When Mudarra was announced Don Fadrique rose to meet

him and extended his hand; with a momentary hesitation Mudarra took it and shook it vigorously.

"What have you got this time?" he inquired with a grin.

"Nothing, I am afraid; I have not been able to make much of this," and he pointed to the Dolphin.

"Narvaez—who was he?"

"A sixteenth-century lute player, who could add four more parts to his lute above a four-part organ piece."

"Jesus!"

"He was also player to Philip II."

"Ah! You say you've not made much of it; let's have a look, man." Mudarra studied the sheet attentively. It was headed "Second Fantasy for Vihuela." "Well, I don't know what's in the book, but by God you're right! You haven't made much of it. See here, that's a good idea right enough, but it wants filling out. Give me a guitar." Don Fadrique walked quickly to the wall and took down an instrument. Soon the skeleton sounds of his transcription, lovely, calm in their nakedness, were vibrating throughout the library.

"No, no, no!" burst out Mudarra at last. "God alive, can't you see that passage is phrased wrongly? It'll be too damned difficult without a lot of practice, but it goes like this." Don Fadrique nodded. "That's the result of not being a player myself, man."

"Your bars are all wrong, too, by the feel of it. You can't make sense of the rhythm if you put them there and there and there like palings. But it's good stuff. I'll take it away and work at it. Anything else?"

"No, but I've turned up these old song transcriptions. Caramba!" exclaimed Don Fadrique suddenly. "There was a girl singing these very words in the patio yesterday. 'The Moorish king was walking in the city of Granada'." He hurried over to the bell and waited for the housekeeper to come.

"Fetch the girl who was working in the patio yesterday. I think she was one of the candle party this morning." Presently Lucía Robledo came to the door.

"Please come in." Lucía nervously took the chair Don Fadrique offered her.

"Listen, Señorita. Yesterday you were singing a song in the patio, about a Moorish king. What is it called?"

"Ay de mi aljama," replied Lucía.

"Ay de Mi, Alhama," Don Fadrique read. "The same! Sing it, please."

"Ah no, your lordship . . . I cannot sing."

"Sing it, please, it doesn't matter *how* you sing."

"The melody is a bit different, señor," the guitarist said.

Timidly the girl commenced but as Mudarra pulled the strings more vigorously she sang with more confidence; she seemed to have forgotten the Marquis until he spoke.

"It is a little different. You must sing this version some other time. Do you know any others?"

"No, your lordship."

"Only the popular songs," Mudarra added. "Señorita Robledo is not a singer."

"Let us hear one of the popular songs then."

Again Mudarra began, tapping the splendid rhythm with his fingers behind the bridge. "Olé, Olé," he said quietly at the end of the first verse of the seguidilla.

"Now then, *guapa!*" and he stood up and played with more brio and with sudden pianissimos and when at last Lucía entered she also stood up and faced Mudarra. Over his face there passed the hint of a taunt and he drew his body up and stamped a level beat with his heel while this thumb and fingers drummed the hollow instrument between the chords. "Olé, Olé," he cried, and with a fierce nod brought the girl into the music at once, her eyes shining, her head flung back and her hands upon her hips, her breast thrust up towards him. Mudarra advanced upon her and as she sang her lips seemed to curl in a challenge of disdain. "Olé," he concluded, with a downward run and a rapid softening of tone.

The girl glanced nervously at Don Fadrique, shaking his head from side to side. "You seemed to enjoy your music. Well, tell the housekeeper you may go home now," he said, with a nod to Mudarra also.

Outside in the corridor the girl did not glance at the guitarist, until he patted her on the shoulder and said; "Bravo, Lucía; if only you had a voice, you'd be a good singer." Suddenly he put his arm round her shoulders and drawing her to him kissed her upon the face. "No!" she exclaimed, but when he released her she was trembling violently and her face had turned pale. Without word of leave-taking she hurried away along the corridor while he watched her, in indecision.

In the library, Don Fadrique sat down with contentment to the transcription of music, hearing still the tones of the guitar in every note he wrote. An hour later at the sight of the black-bound score upon a chair he sighed. In his memory he heard faintly, but clearly, the steady beat of that canto fermo of his life, "Remember, O Man, that dust thou art and to dust thou shalt return."

6

Iscariot Steadfast

THERE was much to excite the people of Los Olivares during Holy Week. The first olives were now in flower and rarely had there been such an early flowering. Then, while the processions representing the Passion of Christ had not been held in most of the cities of Spain, they had emerged in Los Olivares. Fierce anguished hate of the Church flared up on one side and stubborn but nervous assertiveness on the other. Rumors began to flash through the town, especially on Maundy Thursday when the electric light failed in San Salvador church at the moment when the Host was being carried up the steep flight of steps through a blaze of light to the monstrance at the top of the "Monument."

It was rumored also that some drastic protest was to be made, and that Don Fadrique had declined to take his traditional place among the barefooted bearers of the symbol of the Redeeming Faith, on Good Friday. A disciple of Mudarra named Baeza claimed that Argote, who spent these days peering delightedly with goggling eyes into the minute crosses of the olive blossom, had been ordered by Don Fadrique to take his place. This report excited much laughter throughout the town. Finally, late on Maundy Thursday night it rained heavily, and this made yet another theme for conversation. Never had Los Olivares been so animated.

Good Friday morning broke fine, and by eight o'clock the streets around the church of San Salvador were filled with people. This was the great day of the Holy Week celebrations, the only day upon which the Company of the Blue, of Our

Lady of Sorrows, and the Company of the White, of Our Lady of Bitter Grief, united in one procession.

Señora Pérez and Conchita rose early, and with much urging of one another arrived at the square in time to see the first guildsmen arrive. Before long Attila and his men, Cambyses the Great with a company of Assyrians, Nebuchadnezzar, Nero and his infantry, Saul and David and a score of classical and biblical characters were clustered vividly in the center of the crowd of black-dressed peasants from the hills, their embroidered cloaks blazing with gold and scarlet and green emblems and glittering paste. The band of the Blue suddenly struck up and was answered by the band of the White, playing a different tune. Neither band would cease and partisan cries increased the din.

Suddenly a shout drew all eyes to the step where the sacristan stood dressed in a ragged cassock, waving his arms to a group of Hittites. Hittites and peasants raced up the steps and dragged back the great wooden doors. A tremendous roar went up; within the gloom of the nave the first paso was seen moving towards the doors. In the darkness, it might have been the movement of a living God, so slowly and steadily it advanced, towering above its bending worshipers, who appeared even in that short distance to be bent beneath its weight. And then as the light struck it and the wooden figures were revealed, the crowd in the plaza saluted Judas kissing the Master. The paso tilted at the head of the steps, the figures leaned forward over their escort of Ammonites, swayed and were erect again. A patrol of the Civil Guard with their green uniforms and with the sunlight arrowing from their glistening hats moved to the head of the procession. To show that Christ was dead they carried their rifles at the reverse. The rifles were loaded.

Again there was a shout; another paso emerged, and now the "Miserere" rose from the choir already gathered at the steps, its bare monotonous melody full of a sorrow that was too vehement for singing and must be shouted with the full voice. "Miserere mei Deus." The fore part of the choir sang not slowly but swiftly, as if this were an incantation before urgent battle; the disturbing intensity of the singing was immeasurably increased by its rapidity. "Secundum magnam misericordiam tuam"; there was no pause between the two sections of the verse; as the sibilance of "Deus" was heard it mingled with the urgent shout of "secundum." There was in the singing of the rear part of the choir a note of taunt, of challenge against the leading band of singers, and at once they answered, "Et secundum multitudinem miserationum tuarum." There was no supplication in the "Miserere" of Los Olivares, no contrition, nor yet attrition. It was a direct and imperious conjuration of God.

Paso after paso emerged from the church. Shrill voices of girls and women were heard in the crowd screaming the "Miserere." At last the Redeeming Faith was seen in the darkness and with the acclamations were mingled cries of "Olé," "No, he's not there." In tunicles of purest white satin and silk twelve of the most prosperous of the gentlefolk of Villa Alta were bending beneath the crushing weight of the Redeeming Faith, their feet bare. Behind them marched a relief of twelve, their feet unshod also. "Don Bartolomé, the banker"; "Don Francisco, the one who owns the new olive oil factory"; "Señor Marcial Barrera and Pedro Barrera!" "Yes, *by God,* he's here!" The news that Argote was among the bearers of the paso of the Redeeming Faith ran like fire among the crowd and away up the steep street to the plaza before San Andrés. "He's there." "The olivero is under the Faith!"

Indalecio Argote wore a white tunicle too short for him so that it disclosed almost to the knees his great calves, over which ran swelling blue veins. His massive shins were covered with dense black hair. His face, redder than ever, was filled with humiliated fury, the blood was pressed from his thick lips with the clenching of his jaws. Of the bearers of the Redeeming Faith Argote alone seemed oblivious of his burden; with his left hand he was thrusting forward the bearer in front of him. "Room, God's . . . wounds, give me room, *hombre.*" The olive oil factor, sweat pouring down his quivering cheeks, stumbled and tried to turn an agonized face to the mayordomo.

High above the twelve rich men of tradition rose the platform of the Faith, its sides carved with rococo ornament of lily and rose and grapes, fluted and whorled and embossed, and painted in white and blue and gold. Above this rose another tier covered with imitation flowers, among which knelt an angel with enormous spread wings pointing down at a prostrate devil in chains. Higher still among tapestries embroidered with white clouds and pink cherubim, supported by silver-painted scrolls of metal, stood the brazen cross, draped with the richest lace which Doña Inés had been able to buy in the capitals of Europe. Around the Faith thronged the Roman soldiers of the Company of the White. Then, as the final paso of Our Lady of Bitter Grief, surrounded by white Nazarenes, emerged, the choir closed in behind and after them the clergy: Father Martínez, his face vacant of excitement, and the trembling Father Soriano, his eyes filled with tense anxiety and his fingers nervously playing with the leaves of his book, walking between the two clergy of San Salvador. "Miserere mei Deus" . . . "Secundum magnam misericordiam tuam" came the answering shout. Slowly the Civil Guard followed with reversed rifles.

The head of the procession had long disappeared round the corner of the white Calle de la Huerta and was mounting the Street of Olive Oil. Now the salutations and the cheering became partisan. As the first paso of the Company of the Blue began to climb the hill there were cries of "Espléndido," "Magnífico," from the wearers of the blue badge among the spectators. The wearers of the white were silent. A minute later they cheered wildly, trying to make up for the few of their numbers in this lower town by the extravagance of their praise. "Looks like living flesh" . . . "Ah Lord, what pains, what agony, see what agony!" An answering challenge came from the Blue as another paso rounded the corner. "Espléndido," screamed Baeza from a balcony, the veins in his neck swollen and his face inflamed.

As the Redeeming Faith, eleven of its bearers already gray with exhaustion, turned into the Street of Olive Oil, the spectators fell to their knees, some of them bowing till their foreheads touched the ground.

"Change . . . change . . . bearers," gasped the foremost bearer on the left.

"Change bearers," the onlookers shouted from the balconies, and the gentlemen of the relief hurried forward and sidled into place beneath the swaying platform. A cornet call sounded

and up the length of the street the procession halted. The
first bearers of the Redeeming Faith stepped away from the
paso, some of them staggering; Don Francisco, the olive oil
merchant, collapsed at the curb.

"A chair, a chair for this señor," the onlookers shouted. A
father, his daughter and two children turned to obey, and
jammed in the doorway of their house.

"God strike me," shouted the man, aiming a flat-handed
blow at the child. He ran in and brought out a chair.

"Wounds, man, no! I am all right," Argote was protesting
to the relief bearer.

"But, Señor Argote, it is my privilege."

"Privilege be ———. I don't want any relief. That one won't
carry any more," he added with contempt. "You can take his
place at the top of the hill."

Once more the cornet sounded and the procession moved
up the hill pace by pace, the fierce yet wavering music of the
"Miserere" seeming even yet more intense because of the flooding sunlight. Upon either side the people fell upon their knees
as the Redeeming Faith crawled by, some groaning, others
beating the ground, others crying out, "May the Holy Cross be
forever adored," and a few stood without gesture of veneration.

Father Soriano watched the spectators anxiously. They
were cheering and agape, but it seemed to him that there was
less excitement than in the first year of his ministry in Los
Olivares. There were some who gazed intently but with
insolence, and more than this, there were many who regarded
them with an air of envy. And many went slowly to their
knees. His thoughts were interrupted as a little child ran out
of the crowd towards Father Martínez; the old priest put out
his hand for the child to kiss and then patted her upon the
head. For a few paces she walked side by side with the rector
of San Andrés, and then her mother fiercely recalled her.
Father Martínez waved his hand to her as she returned to the
pavement. Soriano stared back at the child, whose gaze still
followed the rector.

Near the top of the Street of Olive Oil and upon the right-
hand side was the little Square of Our Lady of Carmen,

from which the people of the poor quarter behind the chapel were accustomed to watch the Holy Week processions. Now the Square was only half full; women occupied the front places, while a few men were seated on a motor lorry drawn up before the Chapel of Our Lady of Carmen. A little below the corner of Olive Oil Street and the Square the Robledo family stood, Caro by the side of Lucía. Justo and his wife were a few paces removed from the others. They were watching for the appearance of the first *paso*, in whose escort Escolástica's fiancé would be walking, wearing the robe which Lucía had helped to embroider. Presently the Agony in the Garden came in sight, greeted by frenzied shouts and a rapid fluttering of hands making the sign of the cross. Escolástica's *novio* was upon the side nearest them, his yellow robe with its red tiger lilies and emerald-green leaves blazing in the sunlight.

"Very good, child," said Señora Robledo to Lucía; the mother nodded excitedly and kissed her daughter. Justo smiled in recognition of her work.

Suddenly, just as the Civil Guard had passed the Square, the leading bearer of the second *paso* slipped upon the cobbles, still greasy from the night's rain. The figures of Iscariot kissing Jesus leaned drunkenly. From the street there were cries of "Ah!"; from the Square, laughter. Hisses challenged the laughter, derisive shouts threw back the challenge. Then shouts and countershouts ran out amid women's screams and cries of "Beasts," "Animals," "Infidels." A part of the Civil Guard returned swiftly to the Square, hands upon Mauser holsters, and the senior of them shouted something which brought a yell from the men pouring out of the narrow streets into the Square. Immediately massive pistols were drawn from their holsters and held aloft for the jeering workers to see. In Olive Oil Street the procession faltered, moved on again, and then the foremost pasos doubled their pace.

At once a volley of stones rattled among the images of Christ before Caiaphas, leaving scars upon the bright paint. The Roman lictors fell back and parted, and another volley of stones flew out of the Square; the Civil Guard turned down to join their colleagues at the head of Olive Oil Street. Those who could fled indoors, but the majority could not escape from the

choked pavements. The "Miserere" was being sung more
loudly now. In a momentary lull there was a crash and a tinkle
of glass as a stone broke the pane before the shrine in a recess
of a house wall. Then with a rush and fierce commands the
side streets discharged another reinforcement of procession
breakers. The tarpaulin was pulled off the lorry, disclosing
petrol cans and bundles of wood, buckets were flung from a
window, and in a few seconds black smoke was belching into
the air from a whitely blazing fire. Little streams of burning
petrol ran to the gutters.

Screams and wails mingled with the shouts. At the top of the
street the Civil Guard, rifles at waist level, stood motionless.
To open fire would mean killing men, women and children,
sightseers as well as procession-breakers.

"Into the air!" commanded the guard sergeant suddenly, and
round after ear-splitting round crashed out in the narrow street.
Bullets whizzed away to the blue sky above the rooftops. Those
in the Square were aware of their vantage. Above them in
Olive Oil Street were two pasos abandoned by their bearers,
now crowded upon the pavement. Below them the bearers,
escorts, spectators and breakers were thronging, and jamming
about the statues.

With a fresh outburst of defiance and before the upper
spectators could leave the street clear for the guards to draw
sabers, a group flung themselves upon the paso of Judas betraying Christ and with a balk of timber broke the Christ from
its stand.

"To the fire," they yelled. "To the fire with this Santo
Cristo!" Cries of horror rose louder than ever as the image was
flung into the flames and its white paint curled and blackened,
women fell upon their knees, white-faced, praying distractedly.
"Barbarians! You condemn yourselves to hell," shouted Señora
Robledo, "to hell, to hell." From a rooftop Don Bartolomé,
one of the first bearers of the Redeeming Faith, shook his fist
at the iconoclasts and shrieked, "Infidels, infidels," with cracking voice. Again the Civil Guard lifted their rifles; at the first
shot Don Bartolomé ducked and fled across the rooftops, leaving a borrowed shoe behind him. This time the Civil Guard

was answered with a pistol shot, which struck the wall to the left of the shrine, tearing out a broad patch of plaster. Fighting a way up through the throngs now pressing down the street, a new contingent of image-breakers arrived, carrying with them a crucifix and another Christ. In the Square, the iron grille of Our Lady of Carmen was resisting the blows hailed upon it by the infuriated men. The iron bent before the swinging balk, but the nearness of the motor lorry prevented the incendiaries from exerting their full strength.

Suddenly Lucía, who had been clutching Caro's arm, darted forward onto the cobbles and shrieked and lifted her hands in the air. "Diego, Diego," she screamed. In the middle of the road, Mudarra, his pale face burning with intense purpose, was swinging a bar of iron at the feet of Judas Iscariot. He did not hear her and she screamed again, "Diego . . ." rushed forward, and received upon her legs the backward blow from the iron bar. Mudarra turned and, dashing the hair from his eyes, panted, "Lucía . . . ah, my dear . . ." The girl staggered and, flinging herself to her knees, frantically clutched him round the legs. "Diego, Diego . . ." Words would not issue from her dry mouth, but in her eyes was the terror of hell.

The guitarist tried to break open her arms, his gaze fixed upon her bloodless face and closed eyes, then swinging the bar over his head he brought it down against the back of Iscariot, and lunging forward violently broke open her arms. The wood resounded dully and chips of paint flew from it, but it resisted the blow, and the second and third blows also.

"Stronger than Christ," shouted Mudarra, and the panic-stricken girl called faintly, "Diego."

"Ah, woman, woman!" he cried, flinging the bar along the cobbles as she clutched blindly at his ankle.

"Diego . . . don't, for the love . . . of God."

Mudarra wiped the sweat from his face and, catching sight of the girl's father, waved his arm at him to fetch the girl. The father nervously stepped forward. A racing man cannoned him aside and he fell.

"Here, this is no good, Caro," yelled Justo Robledo, dragging with him his wife, who had fainted.

"No . . ."

"Up there," Robledo shouted, pointing to the balcony, "with me."

"Yes!" Robledo laid his wife against the wall and called to his mother, then forcing his way across the road, put his face through the bars of the grille and shouted to the people within. A moment later the door opened and they slipped into the house. As they appeared on the balcony a bucket of petrol caught fire among the women and youths in the side street, and screams of panic rang out.

"Compañeros!" Robledo bawled, "this is not the way to make revolution." No one heard him.

"They'll recognize you, Caro," he gasped.

"Compañeros!" Caro waved his arms, a few looked up at the balcony, but his voice was too weak for them to hear. "Try again, Robledo."

"Compañeros . . ." Robledo called above the din.

"Infidel . . . corrupt and evil son." The father's whimpering cry could be heard by those around him only.

The Civil Guard lifted their rifles. "Independent fire," called the sergeant. In the declining uproar the first rifle shot crashed more loudly. Above Robledo the roof tiles flew into the air. "Idiots," he yelled, waving his arms at the guard. *Crack, crack —crack,* three rifles spoke. Robledo lurched, spun round and tottered backwards. His waist catching upon the balcony rail caused his feet to lift from the floor. As he swayed Caro clutched him desperately and pinned him to the balcony rail, waving to those below. Another and another bullet thwacked into the wall behind him and with a crash the window flew into splinters. Below he saw Lucía in Mudarra's arms, motionless. Her mother was shrieking and hammering at the door below.

The sight of Robledo hanging over the balcony rail, blood already dripping from his shoulder, stayed the iconoclasts. Many of them stood motionless for one moment and then came racing up the street through the deserted images; down the side streets the people were madly streaming back to their homes. The banging of doors resounded. Seizing the opportunity, the Civil Guard charged down Olive Oil Street and into the Square, Mausers drawn, rifles slung.

From beneath the lorry two spurts of flame shot out and the foremost guards, flinging themselves aside, returned the fire. Dust and stones flew up and the man beneath the lorry scrambled out and made his escape before a pressing hail of shots. At the bottom of the hill another patrol of the Civil Guard arrived and fired their warning into the air.

In the Square of Our Lady of Carmen the fire smoldered; a wooden head, charred beyond recognition and glowing red at the neck, had rolled towards the street now empty and silent save for a crouching group upon the pavement and a girl sobbing at the feet of Judas Iscariot proffering a kiss to the empty air. At the bottom of the hill the weeping Soriano knelt handle of which sat Argote in his white tunicle, surveying his against the platform of the Redeeming Faith, upon the fore-bare feet with melancholy disgust. One of the guards slowly reversed his rifle.

Up the length of the steep hill, littered with the helmets and spears and trampled embroideries of Cambyses' and Nero's and Caesar's men, stood the abandoned images, glittering and gaudy in the sunlight. Nothing broke the silence save from the back streets the long declining cry of a blind woman hawking fish.

7

A Symbol

JOAQUÍN CARO was working in the tiny vine plot at the end of the field of the Well, when the captain of the Civil Guard, Montaña, and a man in black, came down the path from the Gallows Rock. He watched them enter the house without formalities and then laying aside the tool, walked quickly to join them. Within, Ana and Ursula were inviting the two men to be seated. The man in black at once accepted; his large white pulpy face was dotted with perspiration and his breathing was quick and short. Montaña was at his ease; his deeply grooved dirty-looking face, fleshless and dry, showed no emotion.

"This gentleman is Señor Rosich, the Fiscal of this province. This is the man Caro."

"Ah yes. I am pleased to meet you, Señor Caro," began the Provincial Prosecutor, with a wheezing voice and a pronounced northern accent. "First of all I should like to thank you for your attempt to frustrate the public indecency—I refer to the sacrilegious and insensate disturbances of some three weeks ago." Señor Rosich paused a moment to breath very deeply, and with no more than a glance at Caro began again. "I refer, of course, to the barbarous interference with the processions of Holy Week. I need hardly say that I—and you must understand me, Señor Caro, to be speaking not for myself alone, nor merely for cultivated and civilized opinion, but for the Spanish State, which, of course, while it recognizes that there must be an amendment in the relation of Church to State, cannot permit these intransigent and criminal overflows of passion—

that I am especially pleased to be able to congratulate you in that your action, h'm, your action must have in some sense—I mean that you yourself, I understand, have, in some measure, affiliations which might, in a man less reasonable, less sensible, less cultured than yourself, have reasonably led one to expect, h'm—shall we say participation, or if not participation, an approbatory neutrality towards the events to which I refer."

Montaña slowly rubbed the corner of his mouth with his forefinger. "Precisely," he murmured, staring at Caro with narrowed eyes. Ana had been following Rosich's speech with moving lips and she was out of breath.

"Moreover, I should like to express to you, Señor Caro, the sorrow which I, and Captain Montaña, feel that you should have been exposed to the risk of injury while you were attempting to restrain this . . . this . . . ."

"Exactly." Montaña crossed his hands behind his back. "I regret that we fired upon you, Señor Caro."

"And now, Señor Caro," Rosich said, with another glance at Caro, "I should like first of all to say that the authorities have decided that there shall be no repercussions in this matter. The Civil Governor has no desire to investigate this affair with any thought of prosecution. You understand that, of course, Señor Caro; nevertheless I should for myself, and purely as a layman, be exceedingly interested to hear your description of the events. As for example, what you saw which moved you to protest and what you observed from the balcony, etc." Rosich pressed the tabletop with soft flexible fingers.

"Well, señor, I saw the pasos being broken and the statues flung into the fire and I thought there might be bloodshed."

"Yes, but . . . please be a little more precise, Señor Caro."

"I am afraid that . . . that I was rather too interested in defending myself and someone with me to notice much, señor."

"H'm, ah, I see; that someone with you was whom, may I ask?"

"The daughter of the woman you examined this morning, señor," Montaña interjected. Caro was alarmed. Had Lucía's mother given Mudarra's name to the authorities as she had declared she would? He thought a moment. "Most of the de-

tails which I can offer you, sir, I have been told by Señora
Robledo and her husband. I am afraid I was very distracted."

"Well, Señora Robledo had many interesting things to say,
of course." Rosich glanced at his document case.

"The first paso to be broken was Christ before Caiaphas."
Rosich tapped the table quickly. "And I think it was the
bearers' slipping which started the trouble; after that it all
happened so quickly . . ."

"Quite, I understand all that," Rosich said, with a hint of
petulance. After half a minute's silence Caro added:

"You must forgive me, señor, I was thinking what to do, trying to make up my mind how to prevent the affair becoming
serious."

"Precisely," Montaña said quietly.

Rosich stood up. "You must allow me to thank you again
for your intervention, Señor Caro. I think, Señor Capitán,
that we had better visit the next person upon the list."

"The man Pérez, Señor Fiscal, but I am afraid . . ."

"Pérez? Ah yes." The prosecutor spoke testily.

Joaquín Caro and Ursula accompanied the two officials to
the main path beyond the threshing floor and stood watching
them slowly climb back to the town.

"Will Señor Pérez tell anything?" Ursula began.

"No, no, of course not. Montaña will have told the prosecutor where Diego lodges, that is all. They've been visiting
everybody."

"Why are you worried then?"

"Worried? You go on indoors; I shall go to the hospital to
see Robledo."

The Fiscal's behavior was very strange, Caro thought. He
had said there would be no prosecutions, yet he had tried to
obtain names of incendiaries, and why did the Fiscal visit them
instead of ordering them to appear before him? Surely, even
if Señora Robledo had not informed, there must be many willing to do so, besides the private agents of the Government.
Well, if they went to Pérez they would find the faked and predated bill announcing Mudarra as playing in a Sevillian café,
which they had prepared. And they would have been told by
now that Mudarra had left Los Olivares upon the Saturday,

which he had been on the point of repeating. All would be well so long as the Sevillian authorities did not make too close an inquiry and discover that the café had never before provided entertainment. If they did, Mudarra would be able to make a good getaway, he had no doubt, for he would be well warned and aided by the F.A.I., whose secret press had printed the bill. Perhaps Robledo would know what was happening, though as he had not replied to Caro's message, he might not desire him to call.

The Hospital of the Order of Nuestra Señora del Carmen was situated in a side street behind the Town Hall. In front of it stood a little garden, crowded with stumpy palms and rhododendron bushes and an orange tree, shut off from the street by a high whitewashed wall stopped with blue tiles. Over the blue door was a stone plaque engraved with a cross and a skull, in the eye sockets of which someone had put pitch. Now in the declining light of the sultry evening the hospital garden seemed dark and oppressive and the palms malignant. The door was opened to Caro by a little emaciated nun, who demurred long before admitting him.

"The patient has had so many visitors today. He hasn't slept for two days."

"I'm sorry, sister, but I must see him."

"His wife is with him."

"My name is Caro."

"Caro. So you are Joaquín Caro?" The nun looked up searchingly into his face. "So *you* are Caro," she said at length to herself. "Follow me."

At one side of Robledo's bed sat Celestina, his wife, a smile upon her pale and usually brooding face. At the other Baeza sat with a bandaged hand resting upon his knee. As Joaquín approached, he quickly put his hand in his pocket and then, recognizing him, withdrew it.

"So you've come at last." Robledo looked much better than report had described him. "Well, I suppose you've been having trouble of your own?"

"Trouble? Well . . . But how are you, how's the shoulder?"

"Going well; the nuns say their prayers have been answered." The truculence of his voice did not suit the remark.

"I'm pleased to hear it."

"So you've had no trouble?"

"The usual questions, of course."

"Christ, who hasn't? No trouble with the F.A.I.? Is that why you didn't come to see me? Didn't they like you breaking up their bonfire party?"

Caro flushed. "I am sorry not to have come. I sent a message by . . ." Celestina looked pleadingly at him. "Perhaps it was undelivered, or you were not well enough to receive it." Robledo's wife was afraid the result of that Friday's collaboration might mean friendship, no doubt; his own activity would awaken other fears. Or perhaps she was jealous of anyone being friendly with her husband, as everyone said. Well, that was understandable. Celestina's devotion to her profligate husband was the subject of much comment in Los Olivares. It earned her pity, or scorn, principally contemptuous scorn.

"To tell the truth, I came to find out something you might know."

"Ah! Well . . . Mother of God, speak out, man!"

Caro told him what had happened that evening and then said, "Do you know whether Señora . . . your mother has given information about Mudarra?"

"No idea, nor do I care. But don't worry about Rosich; what he says is true enough, there won't be any prosecutions. There can't be."

"No?"

"Hombre, the Civil Governor himself is to blame. I sent him a letter about the processions on Tuesday morning warning him of what might happen, and the news was in all the Seville papers, plus comments. He doesn't want this affair too much advertised."

"I see."

"Nor does the Civil Guard here; they feel a bit sorry about my shoulder."

"Well, that's good news, Robledo. I am grateful for it. An affair like that wasn't enough to lose a lot of good men."

"Wasn't it!" Celestina exclaimed. "I call it criminal to burn the figure of Christ."

"Several Christs—Christ on one foot, Christ on the other,

Christ sitting down, Christ standing up, all the Christs that ever were and a few . . ."

"Justo, Justo!"

"Ah well, woman." Truculent a moment before, Robledo now sounded aggrieved.

"Respect for art . . ." began Baeza.

"Quite! And how did you come to burn your hand?" Baeza was silent. "They say you nearly burst yourself with shouting when the Bitter Grief went by. You must have done a quick back-street dive, Baeza. Nothing like being in things, is there? I had to be in it, too, blast it. Besides, nowadays this art business is no good. What value do you think those statues have? Or nine-tenths of the stuff called ecclesiastical art? The Martyrdom of St. Paul in the chapel of San Andrés, for instance?"

"Ah well, that's different."

"No it isn't. A few glimmering patches of gray upon a black canvas in a chapel too dark to see your fingers. That's the greater part of ecclesiastical art . . . and when they get hold of a man like El Greco, how do they keep his pictures? They don't, until it's discovered he has money or publicity value."

"But, Justo," interjected Celestina, "that may be so, but surely it's nonetheless a crime and a sin to break up processions like . . ."

"Nonsense, woman, it's no crime, it's just damn silly. At the level at which the Church appeals to believers its enemies will attack it, that's all. Howling 'Misereres' through the streets is Catholicism. Burning images is Catholicism, too. The only thing that wasn't Catholic was the petrol and that was American capitalism. You'd have the Civil Guard shoot a crowd of living bodies for the sake of a dozen wooden copies?" Robledo burst into laughter at his wife's puzzled expression. "Woman, woman, these Anarchists are right bang in the good old tradition if only you could see it; they might be Jesuits working up a 'Back to the Church' campaign."

"They are not copies, they are symbols of the Faith," said the nun with a steely voice, from the other side of the ward.

"Ha! That's your Faith, never able to rise above its symbols. Never able to get behind them until you are forced. That's why you must hang this over *my* bed." Justo jerked his hand towards the black crucifix on the wall. "If I valued symbols as you do I would burn churches with joy."

"You talk like an Anarchist, Señor Robledo," the nun replied.

"Do I? That's a good answer, sister, but it won't do. . . . I've just thought that philosophically Anarchism is nothing more than Christianity without God . . ." Robledo was really talking to himself.

"But what do you want to do, Justo?" asked Baeza.

"The same old doctrine of every day," sighed Robledo. "First give the land to the field workers. That will mean they will be able to eat at last, also that they will be able to buy. Then you'll have a market for your factory goods for the first time in the history of Spain, and that will give your socialized factories a chance. Right, got that? Well, you abolish lock, stock and barrel the old Civil Service—that's me, by the way—and administrative machines and make a new one, then you scrap the old army and make a new one."

"And what then?"

"Hombre, what then! Leave it to the peasants to decide what shall happen to anybody who wants to be the little counter-revolutionary. And leave it to the political army to deal with the big ones."

"Yes, but the Church, Justo. The Church will never consent to Socialism."

"The Church? Well, when you've started the way I've described, all you do is wait a few months and then kick it hard where it sits down."

"Yes, I see," began Caro. "Well, that looks like making a new State."

"Of course it does; that's just the point where you Anarchists step on your beards," Robledo said with sudden weariness. "This bloody talk's no good for me, Caro, after all . . . it's all a bloody dream, isn't it, sister?" Robledo addressed the nun who had brought a bedpan. There was more of anger than coarseness in his remark. The nun did not smile or frown but without a glance walked quickly away.

"She's not a bad sort, in fact, she's a good sort. But it's all a dream, this plan of mine, for it's already too late. They're planning in Madrid to nationalize the land by buying it from the owners. How long will that take? And with the present Civil Service to do the job? And what will the land worker get out of it? Why, nothing, nothing, nothing."

Caro looked up in surprise; there was sadness in Robledo's voice and in his eyes there were tears.

"And listen," continued the injured man, struggling to raise himself, "by and by the town workers will rise against capitalism, in a few years they will have to revolt if they are to defend themselves against what will happen here. And they will rise and fight like hell and be smashed to pieces, for the land-workers will sit still and do nothing, they'll have been cheated. I tell you that in a few years' time property . . ."

"There, there, be quiet, Justo," Celestina said, laying her hand upon his head and trying to kiss his face.

"Be quiet, woman, and leave me alone. Property and the Church and all the old band of thieves will be back in power. They've never really been out of it, and with your precious Republic, too."

As the nun came hurrying to the bedside he sank back into the pillow, his face twitching with pain.

"My God . . . it's too late, too late," he whispered. "There's going to be hell on earth in this country soon."

The nun crossed herself and then spoke sharply to them:

"You two men must go at once. And you, Señor Caro, you are not to visit this patient again; you excite him without thought for his condition."

"Mother of God, sister . . . what the devil am I to do then? Learn little catechisms and sweet litanies from the novices?" Robledo's weary bantering suddenly flared up, "God," he shouted, "I hate this place." The nun, unperturbed, placed herself between Caro and the bed. "You must go at once. Celestina, watch your husband while I show them to the door."

When the two men had gone, Celestina began to arrange the pillows and the bedclothes, murmuring to her husband, alternately scolding and comforting him. "Ah, cowherd!" she said, caressing his head. "Be quiet, little one, my son." Soon he lay quiet and closed his eyes. Celestina began to rock to and fro, humming under her breath, "Ah ah, Ah ah," upon two notes a tone removed. After a while Justo's right hand lying upon the bed turned over and she put her hand in his and his eyes slowly opened. "Ah, little one, my son," she whispered, "worse than a cowherd." Presently his eyes closed and Celestina, still humming, leaned over the bed and laid her head upon the pillow. When the nun returned Robledo was already asleep.

The nun gazed into the face of the wife, whose wide-open, glowing eyes looked back at her steadily from the pillows. Pursing her lips, the sister was about to speak, yet the eyes of the wife stayed her. There was grief in the wife's disvirgined dark-ringed eyes, yet more than grief, and they were suddenly discomforting to the nun; she tiptoed away.

A week passed with many events that stirred tongues in Los Olivares. Three days after the Prosecutor had departed the mayor of the town was deposed by the Civil Governor. A day later there was a two-column attack on Father Martínez in the Puente Nuevo newspaper, suggesting that he should be tried for deliberately jeopardizing the public peace by encouraging the Processional Companies. Caro took little part in these debates, however, being distressed by wavering belief in his political doctrines and the absence of Diego Mudarra, from whom he had received no word.

At last, upon April 25th, exactly a month from Good Friday, Caro was working in the olive grove belonging to his home, breaking the ground beneath the spread of the trees which could not be reached with the plow. He had just straightened up to gaze once again at the rich and unusually prolific blossom when he heard a girl's shout.

Conchita Pérez was waving her arm excitedly. He flung down the heavy iron, grabbed his coat from a branch and raced to meet her. Without delay, the couple hurried up the path towards the town as far as the Gallows Rock, where Conchita hung behind lest the townspeople should think that she had been alone with a man. When he had gone a hundred yards ahead, she hastened after him to her home.

8

Our Lady of Unprotected Ones

IN this first week of May the conversation at Mater Purissima had moved back towards the work in the olivars and especially the likelihood of a bumper crop. About this possibility there was much mingled feeling. All the natural joy of man in the fruitfulness of his trees was aroused by this season of unusual florescence. From the crowded shelter—for the increasing heat now drove many more workers to its shade—the top of the dulzar grove in the Little Gully could be seen. The sweet olives had especial interest for the workers, for by the tradition of Andalucia they might take fruit for their meals during the harvest. Now the dulzars were covered with blossom, so rich that despite the minuteness of the flowers, even the inexperienced eye could perceive that yellow powdering of the hazy green domes in the gully. Worker after worker of the skilled grade would begin an excited description of the blossoming of the trees in his care.

"This year the bellotudos are *fine!*"

"Ca! You haven't seen the Cordova Whiteleafs on the Broad Skirt!"

"*Fine* olive, the Whiteleaf." With a screwing of the head, "Plenty of flesh and tasty."

"Yes, better than the gordal." An uproar of protest did not dismay the worker. "And *oil*, good white oil, what kind of oil do your blasted gordals give?"

"Ah well, oil, of course . . ."

"The manzanillos . . ." another would begin. "Yes, the Little

Apple olives are already showing fruit. Dios, we shall have to prop the branches this year!"

The excitement of the blossoming season was reflected in the temper of the workers. Horseplay and jest were more common despite increased fatigue; unskilled workers, the earth-breakers and the wall-builders and path-makers, disputed with the most skilled pruners and grafters about the care of trees, and were heard with deference. And when Argote rode by there was a note of affection in the shouted greetings and a sudden throb of the heart in recounting some derisively worded tale about the mayordomo. The trees were loaded with blossom, yellow-green blossom, little yellow chains and bunches of chased gold. God's teeth, Gloria in Excelsis Deo!

And yet, beneath this joy was fear, not because a few hands had already been put off, but because it had more than once happened that a heavy crop had brought a poverty beyond even the patient bearing of these men. The older workers especially remembered when the price of olives had fallen so low because of plenty that they had had themselves to offer a reduction of their daily wages of three and a half pesetas. The following spring they had worked for two and a half pesetas a day.

"Caramba! Nearly as bad as the poor devils down below on the Huerta or those God-forgotten souls out in Castilla!"

And one day the charge hand, Calasparra, summed up the general opinion. "What Los Olivares needs is a bumper crop here and a failure everywhere else."

The first week passed by, the weather set firm and golden, and soon the tawny earth was dusted with the tiny shriveled petals. Then upon Monday, May 9th, the Mater Purissima talk took up a new theme, the town pilgrimage upon the following day to the sanctuary of Our Lady of All Unprotected Ones.

"What about it, Joaquín?" Mudarra questioned. Caro shook his head and the guitarist pressed. "Christ, it won't hurt you to come up to the dancing after the Office, will it?"

"Go if you like, Diego. I'm not going."

"Oh well."

"That's what's wrong with these people. They say they want

to get the Church off their backs and then they go and pander to it like that."

"Ca! It's just a holiday. What kind of a Catholic am I? Besides, Lucía will be there."

"You go if you like . . . I haven't seen her for over a week."

"No? Hombre, I thought you were chewing iron down at Miracle Court."

"She won't let me stand at the grille nowadays; I've seen her once or twice on the path. Sometimes she talks . . ."

"Here, perhaps I can put this right."

Caro shrugged his shoulders. "Well, you might have a look at those grafts I did on the Ojeda trees when you come out of Mass."

"Oh, teeth!"

At nine o'clock upon the Tuesday morning the smaller bells of St. Andrés and San Salvador began a steady hammering, with occasionally an interrupting boom from the great bells. Soon the first groups began to pass out through the gates, each bearing the white-clothed basket of food that was also a challenge to the rest of the town. In the whiteness of the towel and its creaseless arrangement lay the pride of both men and womenfolk. A wife who failed to produce a cloth of dazzling whiteness, at the expense of chloride of lime, long beating, long rinsing and much sprinkling of clean water while it bleached in the sun, would accompany a frowning husband all that day. No family passed another without a careful glance at the basket cloth, or it might be a stare. Along the three principal paths a white-dotted chain of figures was soon moving; short snatches of song, shouted greetings and derisive yells resounded; practical jokes were played, though never with the baskets. Then, as the paths grew narrower away from the town, a few broke the chain and with an imperative "follow me" to submissive families set off across the olive fields, anxious to show off their knowledge of the slopes and terraces. The sanctuary bell began a frantic beating as the groups began to enter the holm-oak grove.

Mudarra, with an old guitar slung over one shoulder upon a blue ribbon and an enormous wine sack upon the other, led in the Pérez family, Conchita at his side but a yard in the rear,

Oliverio and Paca behind with the basket, broadly grinning at the welcome given to their group. "Olé, Olé!" Soon the crowded grove was ringing with shouts.

Suddenly the bell stopped. Father Martínez stood upon the low wall that enclosed the treeless space before the chapel and shouted:

"Listen, listen. All those who do not wish to hear the Holy Office be pleased to keep silence when it begins." Before he had finished speaking the hubbub had broken out again. A few entered the chapel, and the squeaking and grating of chairs and a din of conversation broke out within. Father Martínez, shouting orders to the persons rearranging the chairs, at last gave a prodigious spit, and strode in. A band of scuffling children ran out, laughing and screaming with delight, one of them rubbing his seat with evident pride. At one side Soriano and one of the clergy of San Salvador were talking in low tones. That year the Mass would be sung by a priest of the lower church, while Soriano was to preach.

The curate of San Andrés was already very nervous. He frowned at the children as they ran in and out of the chapel, and his face twitched when a boy grabbed a chair and pulled it out into the open.

At half-past ten, the celebrant nodded and went within, Jesus "Gordito" Caravaca once more began to hammer upon the bell, and the people gathered around the chapel rushed in and knocked over the chairs. The rector of San Andrés again stood upon the wall and shouted: "All those who don't want to hear the Mass be kind enough to be silent." A few looked up and some moved to the other side of the grove. "Mother of God!" ejaculated the priest, and, throwing his cigarette away, gave another vehement and exhaustive spit and entered the chapel. A band of youths and young men collected before the open door. At once the nasal voice of the priest was heard intoning the introit, and afterwards Gordito leading the women and old people in the responses. The shrilly-sweet voices of children trailed behind Caravaca's by several words. Outside the conversation began to buzz.

"Just as we'd passed the old well, the one with the sulphate splashed over it—you know, by Argote's own vineyard—the

mule that was carrying the double bass shied up." Mudarra
was speaking of the preparations for the dance.

"Caramba!"

"And that big fiddle jumped up and down on his back like
a priest on horseback. You should have seen the pantomime!
The mule lashing out and old Acorín with a face like Ash
Wednesday running round wringing his hands and moaning,
"Ah, mule, mule, you'll be the ruin of that double bass as sure
as you've been the ruin of Spain!"

The shout of laughter at the stroke against Father Martínez
drowned the singing within and Gordito came out and scowled
at the men.

"Then a string broke on the bass, poom! And the mule
dashed off up the slope like the devil with his tail on fire."
Again the laughter drowned the voice within; the Gospel had
just been begun.

"And poor old Chino came up to us and said: 'Now look,
señores, what can you do with a beast like that? God, how
much I have suffered with that mule today.' Poor old bastard."

A boy ran out of the chapel and made water against the wall
and then called shrilly to a child tethering a donkey; a chair
fell over within and there was a ring of money on the floor.
The men without laughed shortly, one of them began idly to
thrum all six strings of his guitar, and the conversation grew
louder still. A sudden silence within hushed the voices and
Soriano was heard beginning his sermon; a few hissed for
attention.

For a while the listeners outside could not catch Soriano's
words; then as the priest's nervousness disappeared he burst
into that eloquence which had already earned him local fame.
"And today our Holy Mother the Church bids us honor our
Heavenly Mother with this most comfortable of her titles, Our
Lady of All Unprotected Ones. And the Heavenly Mother
herself has especial joy in being saluted with this title. All
power in heaven and earth has been given unto thee, said San
Pedro Damiano, and She who presents Herself before the
Almighty has given to Her children this promise that no un-
protected one shall ever turn to her without succor." Father
Soriano's eloquence shortly took a fresh turn and he began to

condemn the folly of wordly men in supposing that they could work out their salvation by means not only not sanctified but condemned by Holy Church, instead of appealing to the Mother of All Unprotected Ones.

"Now he's getting angry."

"Listen; what valor, what fire, what spirit!"

"Wars and revolutions and poverty and sin, all, all this chalice of grief and woe can be removed from the lips of the sorrowing world by Our Lady of Unprotected Ones." For a long time Father Soriano's sermon was listened to in silence by those inside the chapel, and then the congregation began to grow restless. Long before he had ceased the noise within almost equaled that without.

When the Mass was continued, Father Martínez at last was compelled to come out and stand among the men in order to preserve some order. For a while he succeeded and then, after the Elevation, the jesting and horseplay began again. Amongst the laughing and conversing men, trying to ignore the ribaldry and the open jeers proffered by subdued voices, the old priest stood, his lips trembling but his head flung back as if proudly; in his eyes there was anguish. Presently the men heard the tinkle of the bell that marked the priest's communion. There was a momentary hush and then the hum of talk and the jests recommenced. Father Martínez's head was now lowered and he followed the Mass without his book, his hands holding his cassock girdle tightly. At the "Deo Gratias" his voice quavered and broke and he stood silent among the men, one of whom thrust another forward so that he charged into the old man. There was an immediate and vociferous protest from the others, shouts of "No, No!" "Eh!" rang through the grove, and many faces were turned towards the sanctuary. Father Martínez looked round in frightened confusion and slowly walked away, followed by the gaze of the men.

The priests emerged from the chapel and stood aside, the thin procession passed between the ranks of silent workers, the little statue of Our Lady of Unsheltered Ones borne by Jesus Caravaca. Lucía walked by the side of Ana Caro, Juan Robledo by the side of Pascual Caro. At the edge of the gully beyond the grove the crucifer halted and the followers lined up behind him. Father Soriano, now vested in a cope, took the thurible from the boy and swung it three times with short, jerky movements towards the tiger-colored hills across the Jabalón valley, three times to the burnt, mist-veiled hills at the head of the valley, three times to the steep desert of baked mud and calcined stone behind the grove, and finally he swung the rattling censer towards the dark and solemn grove three times. Prayers were read and then Soriano took from Father Martínez a small bottle of cut glass and with murmured benediction threw a few drops of holy water to the silent trees, a few shining drops towards the burnt wastes that bore up the grove, a few drops to the shimmering valley head, and finally waved the empty bottle towards the striped and tawny western hills. Father Soriano was perturbed that he had emptied the bottle prematurely.

Now the white cloths were taken off the baskets and the smoke of fires drifted in from the ruins nearby, a few peasants asked a blessing upon their meal from the priests and Soriano gave it.

Upon the edge of the grave near the Ojeda olive field seats of stones had been built and a cloth laid for the clergy; Argote, standing by, shouted to them.

"His lordship's wish is that you should honor him by accepting this lunch," said the mayordomo, pointing with his foot to a large hamper.

"Thanks, man," replied the rector of San Andrés, the senior priest, rubbing his hands.

"Right. Sit down then, señores, and we'll set to work; by God, I could do with a bite, my belly's rattling. You there, hey!"

Argote whistled to the worker González, who doubled over. "Unpack that hamper and pass the stuff round."

González took out five bottles of Valdepeñas and a bottle of muscatel, two bottles of Spanish champagne and a small bottle of cognac.

"Wounds, man, let's have the sherry first," Argote grunted. "That's vino rancio; the sherry, I said. Right."

"Good stuff his lordship has provided," said Father Martínez, looking into his glass.

"Eh! Trust me," the olivero ejaculated. "We'll take the soup as eaten because there isn't any, but here's pickled anchovies and a bottle of olives and a few little things. If one of you gentlemen will throw a blessing . . . Amen, right, now to it."

After an omelet and tinned tunny, the roast chickens were brought out, and after that came the grilled ribs of lamb and the braised tongue.

"Here, man alive," Argote exclaimed suddenly. "You're not eating anything." Father Soriano smiled nervously. "Isn't the stuff to your liking? . . ."

"Of course it is," the rector replied. "Another little rib, Señor Argote?"

"Sure, two if they'll go round. Hey, González, there's some sausage wrapped in a cloth in that hamper; fetch it out. That's right, pass it to this gentleman here." The priest of San Salvador looked at the label and nodded approvingly.

"Here, this tongue's going begging, Father Soriano," said the mayordomo. "You'll eat it, or I'll know the reason why."

"I'm very sorry, but I cannot . . . I mean, I prefer not to eat any more."

"Wounds, man, it won't hurt you. It's good stuff, or the butcher and the cook will hear something."

"Yes, it looks very nice, very nice indeed. But . . . tomorrow is my saint's day feast and . . ."

"Ah, of course, San Mamerto bishop, you're fasting," the priest of San Salvador remarked.

"God's wounds! A little sin like that won't choke you. Eat up and enjoy yourself, man, while you're alive."

Soriano smiled painfully.

"Let him alone," the rector muttered. "Vino rancio, did you say you had brought?"

"Hey, González, bring the vino rancio. Where is it? Hey, where's the vino rancio!" The mayordomo's voice rang out through the laughter and the conversation that filled the grove. A man ran over from another group with a bottle and a plate of biscuits.

"Vino rancio, did you say, Don Indalecio?"

"Right, man, Father Martínez here wants vino rancio. Give it him."

Other families sent over biscuits, fruit and bottles of anis; the rector shouted thanks and greetings, but waved the offerings away. "Thanks, thanks, many thanks, but we're well provided. Try some of this."

"That's right," shouted Argote, "try some of this, you dry-gutted tripeless unfortunate." A peal of laughter greeted the description and the man grinned, patted his flat stomach and took the leg of chicken, waved it aloft and bit into it.

"Well, that seems to be all," the mayordomo said at last, looking around him. "A little stroll to shake this down and then a nap for me. What do you say, gentlemen?" Argote strode off towards the Ojeda olive field and the clergy watched him sauntering round the trees one by one.

"That's a man for you! What would Don Fadrique do without him, eh?"

"Nothing, man, nothing at all. He might as well sell up without Don Indalecio Argote."

The voices sank to a steady hum. Argote returned and soon his long rasping snore was heard from beneath the jacket over his head. Half an hour passed and then an intermittent thrumming of guitars began; at times the thrumming would become a *flamenco* prelude, often left unfinished. At last a voice was lifted. "Yesterday I improvised a *seguidilla*," it announced and broke off at once.

The mayordomo awoke and flung the coat from his head, stared hard at the two clergy of San Salvador, shook his head violently and rubbed his face and said:

"God's teeth! There's nothing so ugly as a sleeping priest in all Christendom, unless it's a farrowing sow. Ugh!"

Half an hour later the orchestra began to tune up, and those who had wandered off returned to the dancing space, which was at the Jabalón side of the grove where the trees grew less closely and the drooping branches had been lopped off for the purpose. Seats of planks laid across stones served for the orchestra of one cornet, two violins, a clarinet, a trombone, a euphonium, double bass and percussion. Mudarra and Argote were the first to begin.

"Señorita Concepción Pérez y Calasparra, kindly honor me by giving me this dance," said Mudarra, bowing deeply.

"Yes," replied the girl, springing up and running into the crook of his extended arm. She answered laughter with laughter. There were one or two cries of "What a fine couple."

Argote approached Asunción Chapaprieta, the recognized beauty of Los Olivares, and carried her off, and soon the clearing was full of couples, mostly of those engaged to be married. At the third dance the space was already too small and the dancers were moving among the tree trunks.

During an interval Mudarra took his guitar from Pérez and at once began a prelude in the fandango rhythm; there were immediate cries of "Olé" and he accentuated the rhythm and brought a more metallic tone from the instrument, pulling the strings near the bridge. Asunción Chapaprieta and a few young folk stepped into the space and soon the rhythmic snapping of fingers and the castanets which many had brought with them were providing a magnificent stimulus to the dancers. At the finish of the dance Asunción was greeted with one or two cries of "Blessed be the mother who gave you birth," which praise of her beauty she acknowledged with a toss of the head and a gesture of scorn. At the third of the flamenco dances Acorín stumbled over the plank seat, gave his violin to Father Martínez and, seizing his guitar, began a *zapateado*.

"Viva El Chino," Pérez called loudly, and there were loud hisses from the Acorín partisans. At his last chord Mudarra began with an upward scale and a sustained trill that brought shouts of admiration from the guitar enthusiasts and then launched into a violent and extravagant improvisation. The rhythm which followed caused many to hiss at interruptions, as the brilliance of the tone, its immense vitality and the drumming counterpoint of Diego's fingers before and behind the bridge, the resonant whisper of pianissimo before and the harsher whisper behind, made an elaborate yet unfailingly rhythmic pattern. This was Mudarra's speciality as decoration was Acorín's, and the display excited the people. A couple preparing to dance were stopped by waving hands, and then a pianissimo upward scale in thirds to the eighteenth fret and a sudden fortissimo. statement in six-note chords of the principal figure brought the whole rhythm to its beginning again. The involuntary shouts of "Olé" obscured the following pianissimo, but a nod from Mudarra set the dancers in motion. The modern dances which followed had more life as a result of the flamenco stirring of the blood. At the second, Father Martínez strode over to the orchestra and amid cheers and shouts grasped Acorín's violin and put it to his shoulder. Shaking with laugher at his mistakes, more numerous than his correct notes, the rector took up the melody from the first violin. When the dance finished there were shouts and groans and a unanimous "Viva!" The priest waved his arm in acknowledgment and, wiping his forehead, picked up a pitcher and poured water down his throat. Father Soriano came over to him and said:

"If you will excuse me, I should like to go away and say my office."

"Ca! brother, stay here with me," the old man replied, taking up his book and going towards the Caro family. Pascual offered his stone seat to the priest, who at once began to read in his breviary. The curate walked through the gap in the piorno bushes at one side of the orchestra.

It was after Argote had danced with Lucía that Mudarra approached her.

"I am sorry Joaquín is not here; I asked him to come but he was as stubborn as a mule."

"He told me why," she challenged.

"Yes? Well, here I am and I want this dance. Will you dance with me?"

The girl hesitated a moment and replied, "Yes."

When the music stopped Mudarra did not escort her back to her parents but, meeting Justo and his wife, the couple joined their group.

"Give my wife a dance, Mudarra," Robledo said curtly. "This shoulder of mine is none too comfortable yet."

Lucía had few opportunities for talking to her brother alone and by the time she was taking her leave of him the dance had finished.

"I want this one, too, girl," Mudarra said, and before she could refuse Robledo exclaimed:

"Yes, you dance with Mudarra better than with anyone else. Give him another dance."

Silently she accepted the guitarist's arm and he commenced to mock at her diffidence as they moved among the trees.

"Why do you wish to dance with me then?" she flared after a jest that bordered on brutality.

"Why? Because I like you, what better reason?" As he spoke his arm involuntarily tightened and her breasts were pressed against him, and at once, feeling the movement of his body against her, she paled and her lips parted. As they passed a gap in the piorno bushes he reversed the movement and drew her along the path. "No, Diego," she murmured, and weakly resisted. For a moment the impulse wavered and then with a quickened step he guided her through another clearing, still dancing. Beyond, the path narrowed, and Mudarra stopped.

"I want to talk to you, Lucía," he said with difficulty; there was fear but consent in her face as he took her arm and led her along the gully path and over the line of the arete. Upon a little ill-defined flat that had once been a field they halted and silently faced one another for several moments. When he spoke it was about the feast, the dancing and the band, now muffled by the intervening arete.

"We must go back," the girl exclaimed urgently as the music ceased.

"No . . . not yet, please, Lucía," Mudarra said and reached out and took her arm again. "I wanted to . . . I wanted to ask your pardon for kissing you at the Palacio." The girl turned her gaze away from his inflamed face and he moved nearer to her. Suddenly he grasped her by the shoulder and roughly jerked her into his arms and stared down into her face, his fingertips boring into the vertebrae of her spine. She did not struggle until he kissed her fiercely upon her open mouth; as his hand cupped hungrily over her breast her resistance ceased. Half leading her, half dragging her to a depression among the piornos, Mudarra flung himself upon his knees and forced her to the ground. "No," she whispered faintly once only, as his hands fumbled at her dress. Kneeling, he laid his hands upon her shoulders and shook her. "Lucía, Lucía, don't yield, give, ah, woman, woman, if you are going to do it." She closed her eyes as his hot breath upon the corner of her mouth sent intolerable sensation coursing through her skin; gasping, she clutched him around the neck and lifted her breast towards him, her body shaking with terror and desire. Firmly he laid his hand over her mouth and stifled her scream.

Afterwards Lucía neither wept nor spoke. At times she turned to him frantically and pressed her head against him, trying to hide her face from the light, once her fingers groped among the hairs of his chest and one of her hands clumsily felt its way to his armpit. Then she would fling herself away without a word and stare into the ground and tremble, her lips moving. At one of these moments when she recoiled from him Mudarra knelt up and bent her head back towards him and kissed her upon the cheek, forehead and eyes. "Lucía," he whispered, "don't be afraid; let us marry."

With a moan she tore herself from his grasp and beat the ground with her hands.

"I will marry you."

She made no answer but stared blankly into his face.

"I want to marry you, Lucía."

"Ah no, Diego, Diego," she cried and burst into tears.

Twice the band had played when Mudarra said, "We must go back, there are only a few more dances." But the girl shook her head.

"I can't meet people, I can't, I can't."

"Be calm, my dear, let us go back at once. Listen, I'll protect you and there's no one will dare say anything if you are on my arm."

"No," she said wearily. "Go back alone, Diego."

Nothing would persuade her to accompany him; at last he rose and moved away and then returned and kissed her upon the lips and caressed her head.

Near the upper piorno bushes a group had emerged from the grove and were building a fire; he retraced his steps a little way and slowly picked his way across the broken slopes. At the promontory of the Ojeda olive field he leaned against a tree for a moment and gazed back at the girl crouching with her head upon her knees. He looked around at the trees a moment and then rushed from the field. Within the grove he stayed awhile with the families dancing apart, until the angelus rang from the Sanctuary of Our Lady of Unprotected Ones. Then, as he approached the band, the rector hailed him, but he went on and sat down with the Pérez.

"Shall we dance?" asked Conchita, still happy and excited. He put out his arm and began to guide her among the couples.

"What is the matter, Diego?" the girl said before a minute had passed.

"I am not well," he replied.

"We must go home. Come along." The girl took his arm and impelled him to the side. "Come along, little son, we'll go home and I'll make you some herb water."

9

An Antique Guitar

AT the threshing floor Father Soriano protested that he could not allow Pascual Caro to accompany him further; the old man took off his hat and held it before him in both hands.

"We are very grateful, Father, and we hope you will visit us again."

"Yes!" exclaimed Soriano. "Of course, of course, I shall be glad to visit you."

"Father Martínez is too old to come now, you see, he used to come." The old man's quiet voice seemed to stir the priest.

"Then I will come, but you must . . ." He was about to say that he did not wish to interrupt Pascual's labors. "I will come," he said simply. "And I shall mention your departed ones in my Mass tomorrow morning, and your family." And then seeing the leather purse which the old man had brought from behind his hat, he said urgently, "Ah, no, Señor Caro, no, I beg you, nothing of that."

The eager sincerity in the priest's voice surprised Pascual and after a moment he bowed his head and crooked one knee; there was a strange happiness in Soriano's heart as he gave his blessing. The old man crossed himself and let his hands drop to his sides. The priest had already begun to recoil, when Pascual took Soriano's white and trembling hand in his dry and blackened claw.

Ana Caro was pouring into a bottle the water which the curate had blessed, when her husband returned.

"Father Soriano seemed very ill," she said.

"Yes." Her husband nodded and thought for a moment. "I

watched him go up the path; sometimes he just walked like a very old man, sometimes he ran. He stumbled and waved his arms, also."

"They say he was in bed three days after his fall up at the grove; perhaps the shock to his head . . ."

"Ah, that was nothing, woman, no; perhaps he studies too much; they say he reads all night and prays."

"He is very kind," Ana said as she poured holy water into a china stoup hanging on the wall in the window niche.

"Pascual, look." The bottle clinked on the sill. "Marcial!"

Outside Joaquín was propping his brother against the stable door; the elder son's eyes were shut. Ana called to her daughter and ran out.

"Marcial, little son, what is it?" she cried. "Come, little son, put your arm over my shoulder. Joaquín, take his other arm."

"It's nothing at all," Marcial replied, pushing her away. "Just like yesterday, nothing more."

"But, Mother of God, why didn't you come in, when you felt it coming on, then?"

Marcial did not reply; then his eyes met Joaquín's, and the younger man's gaze wandered up the path towards the town and he sighed. Without warning Marcial collapsed.

That night when Joaquín Caro visited Mudarra's lodging, Conchita Pérez called from the balcony.

"Hola, Joaquinito, he's come back."

"He's back?"

"He came back this morning, but he's out now. I don't know where he's gone."

"But I thought he was playing in Córdova for a fortnight. It's only a week since the feast of the Unprotected. Did you know he was coming back?"

"Of course not!" the girl exclaimed indignantly.

"But didn't he write to you, woman?"

"Hombre! Why should he write to me? He wrote to my father, but he never told me what was in the letter except that Diego was all right and playing well and that they were pleased with him at the cabaret."

The following morning, a Wednesday, Mudarra was already at the tool sheds when Caro arrived, and was carrying on a violent dispute with the mayordomo, about nothing, as usual. Caro greeted him warmly, and after a moment's hesitation the guitarist linked his arm in his and they walked towards the Broad Skirt.

"Why didn't you write and say you were coming back?" Caro opened.

"I didn't know I was . . . the night before last I got fed up halfway through the show . . . couldn't stick it any longer."

"But the pay was good, you said."

"The pay? That was all right, though they wanted me to sing. But it was . . . Joaquín . . ." Caro looked up in surprise. "You know what a cabaret is—there was a taxi dance in the front of the house, noise, chatter, and . . . all that, it sickened me." Caro, perplexed, gazed round at the trees, many of which had been whitewashed; below, a clanking of buckets could be heard and the voice of children singing.

"Well, I'm glad you're back, anyway."

"What's the job for this morning?"

"I've just been cleaning off unnecessary shoots. Things are not going too well with the trees. Almost a third of the blossom hasn't fertilized after all, though everything was favorable. Look here, not a sign of fruit coming on this branch, and they're all the same up here."

"Too much blossom."

"Too much? Well, perhaps so. I don't trust those freak flowerings myself. It happened like this in '23, they say, and our verdial flowered like it two years ago. But the trees are much better down below."

Mudarra went from tree to tree, examining the stems upon which the little green nodules should be hanging. Presently he climbed first into a budiego and then into another and another, finally going over to a bulky one upon the next terrace. He climbed as high as the strength of the limbs would permit and then quickly descended, leaping down from the fork.

"That's remarkable," he said. "They seem to be doing better at the top of the tree, though even the highest are bad. There's no sense in it, trees go their own way like . . . Well, it won't do any great harm."

When they had been working for half an hour Calasparra

approached them and announced that he would have to separate them for a week or two as the trees were to be whitewashed and he would need one of them to superintend the women and children who would do the work. Caro at once protested, there were many more men below who could be better chosen; there were older men to whom a rest would be welcome.

There would be no rest, Calasparra declared; the man in charge would have to mix the whitewash and deal it out besides seeing that the work was done well. At a piece-work wage of one to one and a half pesetas a hundred trees, supervision was necessary; despite the fact that the children delighted in the unusual task, their mothers often urged them on to the detriment of the work.

Caro was not content with this and argued that a skilled worker should not be put upon his job, and at last Calasparra surrendered. Mudarra had not spoken throughout the conversation.

"What's the matter with you today, Diego?"

"Nothing."

"Listen, is it what they're saying in the town?"

"What are they saying?"

"About you and Lucía; they say you danced with her three times."

"Twice, I danced with her twice."

"Well, what's the matter with that, *chico?* I don't mind that; I shouldn't if we were promised, and we're a hell of a way from that."

Mudarra flung his cleaning hook upon the ground and hurried over to Caro and grasped his arm.

"Joaquín, boy . . ." he burst out.

"Yes? What's the matter with you?" The glitter went out of the guitarist's eyes and he flung off Caro's hand contemptuously and walked away. A few minutes later Baeza climbed up to them, leading a group of women and children. Two laborers followed carrying a tub of thick limewash slung across a pole. Soon Mudarra was wrangling with a laughing circle of women, and Caro drifted away and recommenced work.

At midday, when Caro shouted to the guitarist, he replied

that he would not be going down to Mater Purissima but that he would try to sleep in one of the storm caves dug in the hillside; he was tired with the unnatural hours of the cabaret and the journey. Caro did not try to dissuade him, yet despite the jests and the horseplay at Mater Purissima he felt lonely and uneasy. Father Martínez hurried by towards the Palacio during the lunch hour and halted a moment to acknowledge the boisterous salutes; not even a neat allusion to the incident of the mule's escape with the double bass amused Caro and before the two hours' rest had expired he set out for Broad Skirt. Then he suddenly remembered that Mudarra spent Wednesday afternoons with the Marquis of Peral.

That afternoon Don Fadrique himself remarked upon Mudarra's apathy, his playing was far from possessing its usual precision. Was the music uninteresting?

"Perhaps it's the state of the trees affecting me," Mudarra exclaimed irritably.

Don Fadrique smiled and said, "The state of the trees? Now what about that Narvaez Fantasia you were going to practice for me?" and there was a hint of melancholy in his voice that awakened an unusual sympathy in Diego. "Give me the guitar with the capatastro fixed, it's too difficult for straight playing . . . I'm sorry, man, I am unhappy and I never play well then." There was a faint accent upon the pronoun.

"You are unhappy?"

The Marquis of Peral looked steadily at the guitarist for a few moments, and then his face was suddenly illuminated and Mudarra thought he had never seen the man look so well; his whole bearing had changed, his thin bloodless lips had parted and he was breathing quickly. Without a word he strode over to a cupboard and, opening the doors with a violent movement, took out a guitar. It was of a kind Mudarra had not seen before.

"Take it." The guitarist took the instrument in his hands and slowly turned it over and over, his face disclosing his delight. The table was of a beautiful and rare ivory-white wood with a fine narrow grain and an exquisite varnish and the pinheads in the Italian-shaped curled bridge were of opal. The silver-fretted finger board was of the densest ebony and very narrow, the sides of the body a lovely chestnut brown. It was not only the materials which delighted Mudarra, but the balance, the feeling of soundness and unity, and the indescribable thing which he himself called the *fraternidad,* the "brotherliness" of the instrument. It was a long time before he pulled the lowest string.

"Ay!" he exclaimed, "listen, man," and he pulled the string again.

"I bought it during Easter week, for little money. It is of the early seventeenth century. If the maker were known it would be worth four times the price I paid."

"It's a grand thing," murmured the guitarist.

"You think so? Well . . . well, it's yours, Mudarra."

"For me? No, by God, no!"

"I want you to have it; it'll be hard to play, perhaps, because the six strings hardly lie on that narrow board. It must have been intended for five strings, though the head looks as if it had never been reformed. But it's yours . . ."

"Don Fadrique, I can't take that instrument." Mudarra held it out to the Marquis.

"It is yours. Now play the Narvaez again."

Diego did his best to play the Fantasia, but he failed and he was forced to lay the instrument down. It was not the excitement and the embarrassment of the gift, it was the guitar itself which prevented him playing, he said. It was too lovely to be played upon straightaway, you had to live awhile with a thing like that, to look upon it, to touch it, to consider its nature and discover its capacities; only after such acquaintance could one handle it with the strength necessary for good playing.

"Very well, play something easier. Ah! now that you have an old instrument we'll have those songs we tried last time you were here. I'll send for the girl who sang with you."

"Don Fadrique, I . . ." began the guitarist, but could not finish the phrase; the sweat burst from his hands and he put the instrument down hurriedly.

Lucía came slowly across the room, and stood before the table.

"I want you to sing that song of the Moorish king," said the Marquis. "Don't be afraid, here are the words." The girl lifted her head, her eyes were closed and her closed lips were twitching.

"Don't be afraid." The voice was harder. "It doesn't matter how you sing. Begin the prelude, Mudarra."

As Mudarra picked up the instrument it slipped from his fingers, and though there was no danger of it falling to the floor he snatched at it desperately. The girl started and screamed.

"Very well, go on back to your work, Robledo," Don Fadrique said coldly. The barely audible contempt in his words snapped like a thong across Mudarra's body and his hands jerked involuntarily. Swaying, Lucía moved to the door and struggled to open it; the Marquis suppressed an ejaculation of impatience.

"The woman is stupid," he said when she had gone. "Well, play that lovely little festal piece of Luis de Milán."

"I . . . I don't feel like playing." Mudarra's body was shaking, yet he succeeded in preserving the appearance of calm.

"Oh, please!"

He sullenly struck the descending minims of the chord of A flat with which the piece began, then at their repetition the anger and the hatred which he could not express burst into the music and the snarling guitar flung out the music as if it were an imprecation. Don Fadrique lifted his hands in astonishment, but the musician paid no heed until the other stood up, and then he sprang to his feet.

"Too passionate, Mudarra, but there, you play all this old lute music too passionately, it should be played with calm, with reticence . . ." The guitarist wheeled towards the table. "No," he burst out. Don Fadrique smiled and shook his head. "Contain yourself, man. The old music should . . ."

"I play it as I play it," shouted Mudarra. "Those people were flesh and blood, their music . . ." He stumbled in his speech and then continued, ignoring the fact that this was courtly music, a music of aristocrats. "Their music is the music of passions like ours, their feasts, their dances, their joys, their sorrows, their loves, for women, for men, their hates for men

. . . the same miseries, poverties . . . the same goddamned aristocrats to wipe out . . ." He stopped, gasping, and put his hands
upon the table.

There was silence in the room.

"So," murmured Don Fadrique. "Very well. You may go
now. When you are calm you may care to apologize." He sat
motionless, his fingers crossed at the first joints, his face empty
of expression. "But your apology will not be accepted."

"No, by God! When I say such things it is because I have
done with a man."

Mudarra slammed the door behind him and hastened along
the corridor. In the room which served as antechamber the
rector of San Andrés was sitting and as he entered the priest
addressed him. Mudarra was about to pass on.

"I wish to know if his lordship could be seen now, señor?"
the old man said with comical timidity.

"No, useless to speak to him now." Father Martínez sat down
and, fumblingly putting away a well-thumbed letter into his
cassock pocket, said dejectedly, "I have been here since midday."

"Here, come on down to the town," Mudarra exclaimed,
grinning.

The two men walked silently side by side as far as Mater
Purissima, and then the guitarist began to speak of the infructa-
tion of the olive trees. The old priest put out his hand and,
staying their march, asked repeated questions. He was distressed at the news and wished to see for himself; perhaps
Mudarra could show him a few cases. They picked their way
along the top of the terrace walls, for the fortnightly harrowing
which would now be kept up throughout the summer had
been begun. At a budiego field Mudarra halted and gently
pulled down a branch. They stood long discussing the plight
of the trees, going from terrace to terrace, the priest, tucking
up his cassock to clamber down the walls by the projecting
steppingstones, disclosing a patched pair of trousers.

"I remember it was like this in '23 and in '07 and '89 or '88,"
he said. "You know, Señor Mudarra, I often wonder whether
there is not something *wrong* with the olive tree as a species.
Think of the way we cultivate the tree; it's forced to give fruit

so much bigger than the wild olive. We cut its branches and twigs to make the fruit bigger, we graft like over like to make the fruit bigger; its natural state is far behind." The priest waved his arm towards the town. "Sometimes I think old trees like that one are twisted and crippled not with age but with the cruelties we practice upon them. I love olive trees and nothing pleases me better than to come up here and walk along these paths. I often say my prayers up here, you know, but it does seem cruel they must be cut about like that in order to be fruitful. Perhaps they like it. The species is old, very old, like the soil and like man, and perhaps it is tired like them. I have an old book by a monk of Sevilla named Baeza, in which he says that the golden era of the olive was during the time of the Moors. Why, even the seed within the fruit is mostly infertile and you have to propagate the tree by planting slips. And you know, man, when the seed of a tree or a beast becomes infertile . . . Thanks," said the rector, taking the letter Mudarra had picked up and stuffing it back in his pocket. "God doesn't like infertility, or that which produces it; in Leviticus, chapter 19:5, he forbids us to cross one animal with another: 'Jumentum tuum non facies coire cum alterius animantibus.' "

"That's right, Father," laughed Mudarra, "but this is a simple matter: with so much blossom the tree cannot move the sap quickly enough, or there isn't enough of it, and the fruit stems, being so fine, shrivel up and pollen isn't formed; or perhaps it is formed and the stem dies. Look what a long way it has to go, Father," and Mudarra pointed first to the powdery, stone-choked soil and then to the top of a great verdial, famed throughout the Jabalón valley for its enormous stature.

The rector resisted Mudarra's arguments for a while and then commenced to ask questions about the work. They stood at San Andrés gate engrossed in the theme for a long time before they entered Los Olivares. As the guitarist drew near to his lodging Conchita waved to him from the balcony and he jeered at her from the pavement. She replied excitedly and then suddenly he was sad again.

Searching for his key, Father Martínez again encountered the letter in his pocket, and because of the conversation with the olive worker, who, for all that he was a sacrilegious iconoclast, was a likable man, a deeper melancholy than ever took hold of him. Within the rectory he opened the letter again and read the command to appear before the provincial prosecutor, who had been instructed to report to Madrid upon the celebration of the Holy Week ceremonies. How foolish he had been to yield against his own better judgment and how unjust men were to forbid Holy Church her rights; it proved that these doctrines were mortal heresies to be stamped out. Perhaps Don Fadrique would be able to help him, yet, as he thought of the palace, he saw also the olive trees and the great hills of the land he loved and he was shaken by a fear that he might have to leave Los Olivares. He was lonely and there was nothing to combat his loneliness save his books, and they often increased it, and the priest his helper. He shuffled along the landing and tapped upon Soriano's door. At the curate's invitation he entered.

Soriano looked up from the volume of Albertus Magnus and thrust forward a chair; it was not often that Father Martínez came to his room nowadays. Hastily he took out of his cupboard a box of cigars. To Soriano's pleasure the older priest took a cigar and then, pressing it between his fingers, replaced it and carefully selected another.

"How are you today, brother?" the rector asked.

"I am better, thanks be to God."

"Did you try the water I told Cándida to make for you?"

"Yes . . . perhaps it has benefited me."

"She knows much; but tell me how you came to fall; they found your breviary a long way up the slope; I can't understand how you came to be down there unless you ran down the slope. Did something frighten you, brother? Did you see something? Sometimes the people misbehave. They go off into the bushes—vamos—a man and a girl . . ."

Soriano's face disclosed anguish and he replied faintly:

"I do not know," and after he had spoken the words his fingers made a minute sign of the cross upon his breast. Tears appeared in his eyes and the rector sighed and laid his hand upon his shoulder.

"Come out with me for a walk, brother. Too much reading

is harming your health. Ah, Albertus Magnus, *The Paradise of the Soul*. He was a great bishop; I used to use his book when I was first ordained also. 'Of chastity,' " the rector read aloud. " 'Chastity is preserved with temperance in eating, with base clothing, with affliction of the body . . . And not less should one be on one's guard against all suspicious persons, and such for a woman is whatsoever man and for a man whatsoever woman.' Brother, tell me, are you suffering temptation?"

"No, no," cried Soriano in horror, and covered his face with his hands.

Father Martínez pressed the shoulder beneath his hand. "I am going to take a stroll through the town; come with me if you will." Soriano did not answer. "You must pray, brother," the rector said abstractedly and left the room.

Perplexed by Soriano's sickness, yet himself feeling a little comforted, Father Martínez walked across the square and by an alley came to the top of the Street of Olive Oil. In the Square of Our Lady of Carmen children were playing and he halted and watched them.

The child in the center of the ring was singing that she had journeyed to France to see the three beautiful daughters of a Moorish king. Then the ring began to chant that the king knew how to keep his own children "with one loaf which God has given me and another which I .shall earn."

The girl in the center gabbled, "Then I shall go back to France to the palaces of the king because you will not let me see your three fair daughters." Now the chorus, shaking their linked hands, gravely sang. "Turn again, turn again, knight, and do not be discourteous. Of my three beautiful daughters you may choose the one who pleases you." The excitement became now intense, the children glanced at one another with jealous and knowing eyes, some of them skipping with suspense, others thrusting themselves forward. The girl-knight walked slowly round the ring. "Take me, take me," whispered a girl, thrusting out her stomach. The chooser passed by and the girl was downcast. At last the knight seized a little child of four or five, who wriggled with delight. "I take this one for my wife because she has seemed to me a rose, because she is a red carnation." The girl-knight covered the child's face with kisses, and she gave them back eagerly and laughed and danced clumsily round her husband.

"Shameless little creature," said Father Martínez, laughing. "That's the girl who minds the three sheep out by the Gallows Rock and the little one is the carbon-seller's daughter in Jaen Street."

The chorus began to dance round the husband and wife and sing with shrill excitement that the bride would be given a chair of silver in which she would embroider queenly robes, that she would receive little whippings when necessary and at the hour for eating she should have a little pear in her mouth.

The girl-husband, seeing Father Martínez smiling at her, ran forward and he put out his hand for her to kiss; she curtsied and he waved an unspoken blessing over her; the former bride was hopping and skipping in the center of the ring, pulling up her dress with excitement and disclosing a dusty bottom. Smilingly, the rector walked on. The curate would have done well to have shared the cheer of the street, he thought. And when he ceased to smile it was not the memory of the events of Good Friday which saddened him but the sight within a dark store of the tall glass jars containing samples of olive oil, yellow-green, yellow, tinged-with-yellow oil and sweet white oil with the faintest glow of early evening in it. If only the world were as tranquil as a pool of olive oil, he murmured. The popular simile had always been on his lips when he preached.

10

Circus

TOWARDS the end of May the theme of water made its annual entry into the conversation of café and casino. Since Maundy Thursday it had not rained over the Sierra del Jabalón. Once only had clouds been seen and these had let down but one faint blue-gray net of rain upon the barren uncultivated sierras across the valley. Every worker in the Huerta and upon the olivars above had watched that waste of water anxiously, yet, as if the clouds, like huge indigo balloons, had been tethered to the opposing hills by that single almost vertical column of rain, the water had never reached Los Olivares. A day later a hot wind from the direction of Africa had blown the clouds towards the far-off deserts of Estremadura and Castile. Everywhere men spoke of water, yet between the talk of the casino of the upper town and that of the cafés and taverns of the lower town there was much difference. In Villa Alta men remembered when the bidding for the "thread" of water had forced it to the price of fifty pesetas. At Gordito's, at the Rincón, and at Lower Gate, men talked of the crops upon their patches of garden or their small holdings. At the casino the quantity of water available and the price of it was the principal theme; in the taverns men spoke of onion beds, or of a row of tomatoes; and in the siesta hour they sometimes went down to their patches and stood picking their teeth, brooding over the wilting produce. The history of former years was revived, of dry years and burnt years and of the making of the dam, the builder of which had been found one day lying injured upon the Gallows Rock. Stories of disaster were told,

even of distant places such as Lorca, where long ago the dam
had burst and drowned six hundred people of the thickly
populated Huerta. That builder had flung himself into the
raging torrent to escape the fury of the survivors. There were
not lacking those who said that dynamite would be well taken
to Don Fadrique's dam.

In the first week of June the heat suddenly increased, men
worked in the olivars with the hot stink of their sweating
bodies rising to their nostrils, the incessant, ear-piercing, head-
throbbing noise of the cigarras in the olive trees hung over the
land like something tangible, like a roof of sleep-bringing or
maddening sound, the monotone of the earth's obsession with
heat and thirst. At early morning the shrill grinding rods of
sound suddenly began, at noon the swimming heat seemed to
double the sound, and at night to go out of the town gates was
to walk into a sea of sound like the grinding of the axles of
ox wagons.

Two things had provided conversational relief. Upon May
29th, the Sunday after Corpus Christi, after Mass, when the
first communicants in their white dresses were being jealously
shown off through the streets by their parents, the handbills
announcing Guido Chapman's Great American Circus were
posted up. For two nights only Los Olivares would enjoy a
visit of this world-famous company. On the Tuesday the
caravans had arrived at the Arenal, the sandy waste outside
the lower gate, and a dingy and patched canvas tent had been
put up, watched by half the population. But the excitement
reached its peak when on the Wednesday morning the elephant plodded through the dust from Puente Nuevo, carrying
its keeper upon its head and upon its back a tarpaulin bearing
the words "Circo Chapman." That afternoon the elephant had
paraded through the streets, once only.

The more timid shut and bolted the doors at once, though
the uniformed herald declared the beast was as docile as a
little lamb. Presently confidence was regained and the Street
of Olive Oil was packed with gesticulating, shouting and
laughing people watching the procession of two white ponies,
three white horses, a couple of clowns and an elephant mount
the hill. Several boys earned fame by running under the beast

when the procession halted at the Square of Our Lady of Carmen.

It was in the Square that afternoon that Father Soriano first became Don Mamerto. The two priests of San Andrés visited the chapel that afternoon to prepare for the evening rosary said there throughout the month of Our Lady. As they stood before the chapel the herald arrived, dressed in a cherry-red silk jacket that nowhere fitted him, green breeches and white stockings. He bowed to the priests, blew a piercing blast on a dented trumpet and reeled off a nearly unintelligible announcement. The procession filed into the Square and the elephant at once tried to take the umbrella which Father Martínez carried against the sun.

"She won't do any harm, your reverence," said the herald with a lisping German accent.

"I have no confidence in you or the beast," declared the rector, "and I want my umbrella," and as he stooped to retrieve it the animal's trunk uncurled before his face and he withdrew hastily; the herald smacked the trunk smartly and returned the umbrella.

"That elephant will be the ruin of your umbrella, Don Bautista, as sure as mules have ruined Spain," someone shouted clearly. During the laughter the mayor's beadle arrived and ordered the procession out of the town. The new mayor was taking no chances of disturbance.

"There's nothing in the laws of Spain against an elephant walking in the streets," declared the herald heatedly.

"I don't know about that," replied the beadle, "but animals can only be brought into this street on market day, and an elephant is a beast. Tell me if I'm right or wrong."

"Arrest him, Señor Zapato." . . . "Arrest the elephant, Señor Zapato." . . . "Turn the beast out." Jeers and advice came from all sides and the beadle indignantly marched off to the Town Hall for further orders.

During the dispute the animal had been gently nuzzling Soriano, who noticeably showed less timidity than his colleague; a boy carrying a bunch of bananas went by and the trunk reached out towards the priest. "Ha!" exclaimed the curate. "Sell me those bananas, son," and, having given a peseta to the boy, fed them one by one to the elephant. It was the first time Father Soriano had been seen to laugh; first he laughed shortly and nervously, then confidently, and then he burst into a high-pitched peal of laughter as the trunk swung backwards and forwards between his hands and the beast's mouth. Wits swore the elephant was laughing at Don Mamerto also, but it is certain that few priests had ever been seen to laugh like Father Soriano. "Take," he gasped, holding out the last banana and searching for a handkerchief in his cassock pocket. A moment later Captain Montaña and Sergeant Alvarez of the Civil Guard peremptorily ordered the procession out of the town. The circus performance itself was not so much discussed as the procession.

Upon the first Thursday in June the second event occurred. At seven of the evening, as people were hurrying into the town in fear of the bulging thunderclouds of greenish umber that were moving up from the south, the small clock tower that stood upon San Andrés Gate collapsed into the roadway beneath. No one was hurt; Mudarra, Aguiló and the harnessmaker's apprentice had seen the tower lurch when they were about thirty yards off, and, shouting a warning to a man driving a brace of donkeys, they dashed into the alley beside the inn of Rodríguez the Castilian. Thus ended not only a piece of masonry and a contrivance of metal but a comedy of many years diversion.

In Puento Nuevo, when it was desired to say of a married couple that they did not live in harmony, it was usual to declare they were "like the two serenos of Los Olivares." The long feud between the former sereno of Villa Alta and his colleague of Cuestas Abajo had provided Mudarra with one of his most popular tales, not the less willingly recounted because the High Town official had been Acorín.

To Acorín the collapse of the little baroque tower was a disaster, for his devotion to the ancient clock was great and had long endured. Within a few minutes of the fall he was searching among the crumbled stone and plaster for the remains of the clock, the pieces of which he brought to the fire station for protection. Through more than four hundred years the timepiece had functioned. It did not lessen the upper sereno's regard for it that it had once been housed in the former church of San Salvador, destroyed in a nineteenth-century political war. Nor was El Chino's devotion to Holy Clock measured by the small fees he received from the town council for its regulation and repair.

But if Acorín lavished devotion upon the "venerable machine," as the local press had once called it, it was chiefly a fruitless wooing. All one knew, it was said, was that if the wind was blowing the clock was certain to be fast, while when it rained it was sure to be slow. The heat and the cold likewise had effect upon the clock, and according to the Lower Town so had the state of the moon; and there were subtler influences than this, tradition declared, such as the condition of politics, or fashions in dress. At times it would mark the hours but fail to strike, at others it would strike but fail to mark, and sometimes it failed to do both. At the Rincón that night Mudarra at last threw off the melancholy which everyone had remarked in him and again told the story of the two serenos of Los Olivares. The presence in a far corner of one of the actors in the story only lent more malice of his tongue.

"Listen then; as everyone knows, when old Acorín, God bless his long face, was sereno for Villa Alta, Cariño, 'the gypsy,' was sereno for Cuestas Abajo. They never were friends, chiefly because Cariño couldn't stand mustaches that turned down and being a gypsy had some small notion of guitar playing. Look!" whispered Mudarra. Acorín had changed his seat for one a little nearer their corner. "It all began when a gentleman in the Lower Town got up too late for the carrier who was to take him to Puente Nuevo. Cariño had called the hours wrongly, he swore, and the gypsy swore he had not. Of course it was obvious that El Chino was going by the clock and Cariño by his watch. Ever after that there was war between them. 'It is midnight, señores, and the night is cold and clear,' Acorín would sing, and within ten seconds you'd hear Cariño yelling out: 'Half-past twelve, señores, and the night is cold and clear.' That infuriated poor old Chino, of course, and he took to singing out in reply. 'He's a liar, señores, and the night is clear and cold,' Chino would bawl out, or 'God have mercy upon his soul, señores, and the night is cold and clear,' till at last people got no sleep for their arguments and the mayor had to put a stop to it.

"Well, for a while all went well. Look!" Everyone stole a glance at the other guitarist, who was now reading a paper four tables away. "And then it all started again. This time the clock stopped altogether and the mayor, the secretary, and all the clerical staff of the town council stayed in bed all day and dreamed they were in heaven. They found Acorín prowling about with his eyes shut at midday. Then he became wily; he'd wait till Cariño down below had sung out, 'Two of the clock and a wind from the west,' and then he'd call out the same from Villa Alta. Cariño got so wild that he'd wait until one minute to the hour by the clock and then call out, 'A half-past three, señores, and a full moon,' and then the clock would strike three or four or five and Cariño'd let up a laugh that made the Buck Mule cross himself in bed for fear of the wandering devil. Of course it was Acorín got the blame for it and he was hauled before the Town Council more than once for causing a nocturnal brawl. Watch him now!" Acorín ordered a coffee and moved to a nearer table to watch a game of cards.

"Well, finally he began to call the right hours and that infuriated Cariño more than the wrong ones. So one night he crept up the steps yonder and waited till El Chino sang out, 'Half-past three, señores, and the night is serene,' and then Cariño let up a yell that made half the town shoot out of bed in fright. 'Four o'clock, he's bought a watch, and that blasted clock has stopped again, señores.'

"A minute later they were in the gutter yelling and cursing and scratching and biting and generally raising hell, till the mayor and his beadle came down in their nightshirts and separated them."

"It's a lie," shouted Acorín, charging across the room and pointing a long bony finger at Mudarra; there was an uproar of laughter in the midst of which Acorín could be heard shouting something about a clock. When quiet was restored he sat astride a chair and watched Mudarra; gloomily, till he was invited to have a drink, and then he returned to his table and drank his coffee at a gulp.

Everyone knew there was little truth in Mudarra's story,

though Cariño and Acorín had once quarreled noisily in the streets about the Town Clock.

"Give us another, *maestro*," the harness-maker's apprentice called. "Here, another anis for Señor Mudarra."

"Best keep your money in your pocket, boy," Mudarra replied, but a dozen voices asked for another story.

"All right, though, Christ, it's hot. . . . A new one about a circus elephant," he began. "Listen."

"About Martínez?" Baeza interrupted.

"No, the poor old devil will be back from the capital on tonight's bus, I suppose. But listen, I said . . ."

And then, as he was about to begin, he glanced at Caro's face. At other times when he told stories his friend's face would glow with pleasure and the ascetic calm of his expression would be transmuted to warm though undemonstrated enthusiasm. But now Caro's face disclosed nothing, if it were not that his reserve had become weariness and pain. Mudarra's heart beat heavily and he was sickened by the atmosphere around him; he could not tell the story, the ridiculous idiotic story.

"I'm sorry, it's too damned hot for yarning," he said, rising.

"But, Christ alive, man, you can't set us up like that and then suck us in."

"I can't tell it, too hot, I tell you." They heard the savage temper in his voice and desisted.

Beneath a black and suffocating sky, Caro accompanied him to his room at the top of the Pérez house. Conchita brought in a small lantern, the sides of which were smeared with honey and sweet wine.

"Now, you won't be bothered with mosquitoes, *chicos*," she said. "Ay, it's hot up here." The girl stared at the two men, alarmed at their strained and brooding faces.

"There are no mosquitoes," Mudarra said with suppressed voice; Conchita held her breath with anxiety, wondering what evil thing was happening, and then Caro said:

"It's too hot for mosquitoes."

Her mouth dry, with uncontrolled voice she replied:

"Yes, there are some, look!" and hurried out as if escaping from a menace.

They both gazed at the insect hovering before the lantern,

watching it with gloomy intensity as it approached and
withdrew from the light. The tiny whir of its wings suddenly
ceased to reach Caro, and a sharp movement on the bed made
him turn his head in Mudarra's direction.

The guitarist was lurching towards him with his eyes blazing
and his great hands stretched out as if he were blind. Caro
shrank back as Mudarra seized him by the shoulders and the
next moment his chair was resting upon two legs and his head
was bent forward by the pressure of the wall behind. Mudarra
thrust his face, streaming with sweat, into Caro's. Words did
not come to him, yet with the effort of speech his cramped
jaw trembled.

"Hombre!" gasped Caro.

"Hombre!" Mudarra murmured and then shouted, "I've
been a .traitor to you, God in heaven, Caro, I've got to marry
Lucía!"

He released Caro, who fell from the chair awkwardly, and
flinging himself back on the edge of the bed, stared at him.

"Speak for God's sake, man," he panted. *"Ah, Virgen Santa,
it was more than dancing we did that day."*

The two men faced one another. The man upon the bed
wanted to fling himself at the other's knees and plead forgive-
ness, the other, wild and bewildered, had no thought that
could have found words. The heat and the acrid vapors of the
sweat running down his belly to his clammy loins, the mosquitoes sticking one by one to the lantern, the bluewashed beams,
the rumpled bed, were unrealities that had suddenly become
real. He could not speak, yet as he grasped the meaning of the
words last spoken, an enormous Justice—not a sense, but a
thing with a will—filled him and demanded speech, yet no
words came. He did not feel hate, but Justice within him,
Justice that does the work of hate. He had loved this man, yet
he was now far off upon the bed, as if a pane of thick glass
cut him off from touch or sound of speech, and then he sat
without awareness of body at all save the creeping trickles of
sweat upon his face and the thudding within his skull. The
light seemed to go out.

The man upon the bed sat gazing at the other, his body too
weak to move him, the sickness in his belly sending cold waves

over him. "Joaquín, understand, let me tell you," his brain
shouted, but as the words reached his thick tongue they
stopped and fled back into the brain and tormented him. Ah,
Caro, you must know the truth, he tried to say and opened
his mouth, but failed to speak. And suddenly the room became
somehow like a furnace and the heat scorched his eyeballs as if
sweat were running into them. Thoughts, all of them clothed in
words, were clamoring for utterance and yet he could not
speak, for speech was futile. There was so much to say, the
other man would never be convinced, the man he had loved
but who was remote and strange yet with a hold over him and
a monstrous Right against him. Ah, God, it would be good to
have this bond broken, to go forth as enemies or as two men
passing in the street, to be as men in different cities never
having known one another. And as he was aware of this he
drew his knife and tossed it on to the other's lap. Still the
other sat silently staring at him.

The other stood up and the knife slipped to the floor, the
man's hand reached for his cap and he went out of the door,
stood a moment and then shut it with a slow care that caught
and held the bleared eyes of the man upon the bed.

Upon the landing a movement among the lumber made him
peer mechanically into the darkness. The girl in her pleated
nightdress came forward and, wide-eyed with fear, asked him:

"What has he done, Joaquín?" Caro suddenly wanted to
rush into the room and grapple with Mudarra, to fight, to
burst into passionate speech, to reason or to forgive.

"I don't know," he murmured, and went down the stairs.

The Flesh and the Steel

SINCE March it had not rained and the Huerta was rapidly assuming the color of the bordering earth, towards which numerous groups of men were now moving. The meeting place was to be a quarry-like hollow in the ghastly lands that rose out of the Huerta upon the down-valley side. Here were neither olive trees nor any trees, and no paths. The eye searching for relief encountered neither bush nor grass nor herb, no cigarras whirred and no bird ever crossed this macabre waste. The ashen-gray detritus of moonlike cordilleras, streaked with blinding white earths, was worn into gullies whose sides were flanked with bitch-ribbed aretes and tall crumbling cones of baked and eroded muds. Above the lower regions of this land the Sierra Seca, the Dry Range, rose, repeating the lower forms. Long ridges ran down from the striped canvas-hued upper planes, their sides grooved with black-lined gullies; all of them sprang off the ridge line at the same angle and the aretes between these gullies were divided again by smaller gullies running down at still the same angle; immense cones and fans of cindering earth guarded the base of the hills. These lands were the skeleton of death.

The members of the F.A.I. and the sympathizers who were going to the meeting entered this lower region from the Huerta or from the Puente Nuevo road. They crept on by ones and twos from the heat of the open and vestured lands to terrible furnaces of quivering air, where the heat dried the mouth to the root of the tongue at the first few breaths, where the skin dried and became stiff, where the eyeballs were knifed with pain till the pupils closed and from excess of brilliance the landscape darkened. These were the men who labored ten hours a day upon the Huerta and the olivars, in heat that rotted the clothes upon their sweating backs, so that over them hung the odor of burning cloth. These were the blackened men who hour after hour thrust spade into earth or guided the harrow whose metal was too hot to be touched, whose eyes were permanently bloodshot with stooping in that suffocating heat. Yet these men entering the canyon paused and gasped for breath, leaning against the crumbling rocks that were too hot to be sat upon. The exhausted air hung still and the scorching lungs dragged at it for breath, the heart hammered frantically at the ribs till it missed its beat, once, twice, thrice, and the men faltered and choked; the blood distended their veins and seemed to burst into their ears and they were momentarily deaf. Some who for reasons of precaution had entered this region higher up were thereby compelled to climb over ridges into the trench of the meeting place. In an agony of labor they scooped at the blistering earth with their hands, kicking at the breaking soil of the easiest slope; the sweat appeared and dried instantaneously, they knelt and gasped and fought on and rested face to the ground and at last crossed the line of the ridge and staggered down to the hollow. In this way thirty men came to the meeting.

As the sun had burned off the soil's cape of vegetation, so the heat burned away from these men all finesse of speech, oratory, caution and prevarication. They spoke in gasping jerks.

"At once," said the small tenant Florez, "the dynamite we got from the road workers at Cazorla will be enough to blow it in."

"Yes, yes." There was no excitement, but a dull murmur of breathless assents, save from Aguiló.

"But the water, where will it go? We do not wish to destroy life, it will not be the masters to die."

"No, the water will go down the old barranco to the river."

"All the fields are derelict within four hundred meters of the barranco."

"There are no houses." This was true; before the reservoir

had been constructed the water had not descended to the Jabalón by the present Huerta lands but by the old, less fertile and less extensive ones now worked only by the poorest tenants. To these diminishing fields the water was led by courses.

The speeches that followed were not in dissent even when they spoke of danger.

"The crops upon the Huerta . . . will die."

"They're half dead already . . . even with irrigation."

"Our crops are burnt . . . they could not be saved even . . . if we could afford water," screamed Florez suddenly.

"If we cannot have water . . . what does it matter? Ours will die . . . let theirs die."

"The Huerta workers will . . . lose their jobs."

"We shall . . . it does not matter . . . who cares . . . at two and a half pesetas a day."

"There will be danger . . . in blowing in the dam."

"Yes. It does not matter."

"Who will do the work?"

"I will."

"Mudarra said . . ."

"Mudarra wants to do it himself."

"Where is he? . . . and Caro?"

"Caro's working."

"And Mudarra?" Heads were shaken in answer. "He's not been working," one said.

"It does not matter . . . he's willing."

"Fuses?"

"Yes, fuses."

"I know where fuses can be bought," Aguiló gasped.

Stones suddenly trickled down the slope opposite the meeting; every nerve jerked taut, every gaze struggled to penetrate the light and then as eyeballs adapted themselves, searched every stone along the crest.

"Nothing."

"The earth broke."

Everyone continued to gaze, half a dozen hands moved slowly to jacket pockets.

"The earth broke."

"A stone . . . shifted."

"Yes."

Then for one second the foresights of a rifle described an arc atop the ridge. Arms shot up, a dozen pistols cracked and banged in the trench bottom and the earth along the ridge flew into the sky. The meeting divided like the bursting of the boughs of a lightning-struck tree. Aguiló put his pistol in his pocket and slowly crept up the steep slope towards the notch where the rifle sights had been seen. The men below, covering his ascent with their pistols, could hear his breathing as he paused to fight for breath. The stones began to rustle behind him. At mid-height he slipped and grasped desperately at a leaf of slatelike rock. It held and he moved upwards again. Higher and higher Aguiló crept until he was right beneath the notch. They watched him as he measured the distance with his eyes, tested a hold, searched around for thrust points. Then he waved their cover aside. The pistols slowly sank.

"Man!" Florez whispered hoarsely. *"Por Dios!"*

The men saw Aguiló's body grow tense as he put both hands into his pockets. He crouched and they held their breath.

"Now!" Florez shrieked as, madly thrusting at the earth, Aguiló dashed out upon the crest, both hands holding weapons. For a moment he crouched . . . and then relaxed.

"They're near the road . . . come up." Several men scrambled cursing to the summit. "Over there . . . don't fire."

A pair of Civil Guards were hastening over the ashen slopes above the gully heads towards the road.

"They heard nothing," Aguiló said, watching their faces.

"Who knows," someone muttered.

"Every man get away by himself. At once!" Aguiló shouted into the deep trench.

The workers hurried along the canyon floor and broke up as the Huerta came into view. Before they had reached the town, guards were galloping along the Puente Nuevo road.

As Joaquín Caro was cutting the varetas, the unnecessary

shoots, from the trunks of the mother branches in a group of verdiales, he saw the mayordomo riding up the path towards him.

"Where's your bedmate?" began Argote.

"I haven't seen Mudarra, if that's what you mean."

"Not seen him? You're always crawling round one another, aren't you?"

Caro did not reply, but went on cleanly removing the varetas with a single sweeping blow of the heavy steel. The olivero sat with his hands upon his thighs, elbows out.

"Ca!" he said at last. "Well, here's news for you; you needn't trouble to turn up from next Monday onwards."

"What the hell!"

"Got it? That's news, eh? You're not the only one either."

"What's the idea then—these bloody trees going to look after themselves?"

"Think you're the only skilled worker up around these parts?"

"I am as good as most."

"Ha, no doubt, Señor bloody Caro." Argote's voice lost its aggressiveness.

"Well, then, what's the sense of it?"

"Christ knows, but you're bloody well sacked," shouted Argote, and giving his horse a furious kick, drummed down the path.

The olivero's temper had been growing insupportable lately; the long drought had caused many fruit to fall. The budiegos and the manzanillos, which had especially suffered in the first misfortune, were even further punished, but now the zorzaleños and the reales and the hardy verdiales themselves were robbed of much of their burden. Each day Argote had walked through the most afflicted terraces sighing and cursing and not infrequently striking out at workers who offended him.

"Ah well, I knew the trees couldn't hold up that crop," he had said when he first noticed the undeveloped fruit with shriveled stems upon the soil. He had said this each day until at last he had been forced to admit that disaster looked like overtaking the terraces that faced directly into the sun and the hot wind that blew up from the south. The day the

verdiales, the green eating olives, had begun to drop, Argote
had barely spoken to anyone but to curse him.

"Hey you, get up into that tree and shake it," he had
ordered a worker. The man had shaken down a few green fruit,
a warning of the evil to come.

"Why the hell didn't you tell me about this?" he demanded.

"How the hell was I to know? We're so shorthanded on this
Skirt that we've no time for everything."

"Shorthanded, are you? God's teeth."

"Besides, what can you do about it?" At this retort the mayordomo had flung the fruit down and had given the man a terrific
backhanded blow; the man's mates, brought rushing to the
terrace by the shouts, had encircled Argote. Silently he had
glared at them while he had mounted, and then without
warning he had ridden straight at the nearest couple.

Argote had done everything possible to cope with the
drought; the ground had received double the number of disk-
harrowings so that the broken soil should lose its capillary
nature. Latterly he had been ordering the most drastic removal of all the small boughs possible in order to economize
the sap, yet against that tindering July sun nothing was of
any avail. That it was purely the drought afflicting the trees
the flourishing state of the lechins and dulzars in the watered
terraces proved. Morning after morning the sky showed hard
and clear save for the rim of dust gradually mounting into
the air. The atmosphere of Los Olivares became charged with
the rancor and ill temper of drought. Many workers were embittered with the loss of crops in their own little patches;
small and large tenant alike were feeling the strain, the latter
because the water supply was rapidly becoming dearer, the
former because their crops daily wilted. Upon the 2nd of
July one of the fountains in Cuestas Abajo had to be cut
off, and the natural irritation was increased when the inhabitants of that part of the town began to use the nearest fountain
of Villa Alta.

In addition to all this there was the anger caused by the discharge of hands, which this year did not respond to the trivial
crisis produced by the inactive months of July and August.
People said openly that Don Fadrique, who could spend 50,000

pesetas upon a book of old music, was saving money against the disaster likely to befall him as the result of the land reforms.

The bill now passing through the Cortes, denounced by the Anarchists and Left elements such as Robledo, was upheld by the Socialists and Radical Republicans in Los Olivares. It would transform the whole basis of Spanish life, these latter said. The power of the great landowners was to be broken at last.

The greatest bitterness was caused by the curiously knowing selection of workers for dismissal. Capacity was clearly not the criterion for retention as it had always been hitherto. García, an unusually able man trained in Jaén, the principal olive-producing province of Spain, was among the first to go. Gradually the more significant Anarchists, Socialists and Left elements were dismissed, then followed one or two Radicals distinguished by their anticlerical fervor rather than their social revolutionary zeal. Along with these were others, who soon received the name of "maskers." Clearly the dismissals were being planned by someone with close knowledge of the political life of the town. Daily Argote's temper became even worse under the strain of constant embittered inquiry from discharged workers. This policy, if policy it was, was not so successful as might have been supposed. The greater part of the men hung on, living upon their families; only a few moved to other districts. The result was, for the while at least, a rapid heightening of the political tension. This tension was noticeable in even the smallest events. When Father Martínez returned from his second appearance before the provincial prosecutor there was little demonstration of welcome even from the most faithful of his parishioners, despite the contrast his administration made with the unsympathetic and officious business of the assistant priest, who had now recovered from his sickness.

When Caro returned home upon the night of his dismissal there was a long and anxious conference.

"Ah, son," Pascual said at last, "I know you have been thinking of marriage—you will have to put that by for a while."

"We must all get to work," Ana Caro said. "Tonight the water will be going down to the olive-pressers' fields."

"Woman!" Pascual rebuked her tenderly.

"Why not," Marcial interjected, "do you want to see your last beds die off?"

"There'll be no theft by this family, sons."

Joaquín Caro spoke for the first time. "Father, this is all nonsense; every one of us can see that it is useless to hang on any longer. I had a letter from Ojeda last week, asking me to sell their olive field."

Marcial's laughter was stopped short by an attack of coughing.

"He says there is still work to be got in Asturias."

"Ah, son," the father murmured. Ursula began to weep.

"Well, what's the good of starving here?"

"You may go, Joaquín. I shall stay here till I die." The mother's flat opposition was expected, for in all things she sided with her husband. "Besides, Marcial . . ."

"Yes, Marcial!" said the sick man bitterly.

"Stay awhile and work with me and perhaps the good God will be merciful, son." No one replied, yet they understood that Joaquín would stay; he himself was not resolved.

Upon the Broad Skirt the following day he heard the swishing of a cleaning tool above him upon a terrace he could not see; it was a skilled worker evidently from the neatness the sounds implied. Dispiritedly he continued work until a movement behind him drew his attention. At the edge of the next terrace Mudarra was standing. Since that night when he had left the guitarist in his room, Caro had not seen him face to face.

"You've got the sack," Mudarra said dully.

"Yes."

"It's why I came to see you."

"Thank you."

"You'll be going away . . . you'll be going away?" There was an urgency like anger in the repetition.

"Perhaps."

"You'll have to go away; how can you live? That's why I came, I had to come." Mudarra leaped down and shuffled over to Caro.

"Joaquín, you think I was false to you."

"Think?"

"My God, I didn't mean it; it happened, I never planned it."

"No?"

"Ah, Jesus, no, I tried to keep away from her, I've always kept away as much as I could, why didn't you come to the pilgrimage?" Mudarra's voice was bitter.

"It began before then."

"No . . . at least I . . ." The monotonous chirring of the cigarras seemed to become distant.

"She, too—it was more than a week before that that she refused to sit at the window."

"Joaquín, I can explain that, that *was* my fault, yes. You've got her all wrong, all wrong, and me, too. We were mad, Joaquín. I could not resist her, she loved you, yes, man, but . . . she was easy for me, ah, what's the good, Joaquín . . ."

Caro paled. "You say," he began, but the complicated mood changed as he spoke. Before, this man had been beyond the range even of an enmity that only the habits of speech had sustained. But now as understanding flooded into him hatred came with it. Mudarra saw it and his face lightened with relief; he stepped back and drew his knife. Caro raced to the fork in which his coat was hanging and dragged out his knife also.

Twenty paces separated them as they stood upon that corridor of soft powdery earth bordered by olive boughs; behind Caro was the drop of a man's length to the next terrace, behind Mudarra the wall that shouldered up the field above. Each man waited, thinking how the other would cross that space. If he rushes shall I throw and close? If he advances slowly shall I meet him? The great body of the guitarist crouched slightly and he moved out into the open, but Caro did not meet him. Upon the hard ground at the edge of the field his quickness would count, the blade slips between the ribs of the strongest man with no more effort than into the weakest. Speed and a quick blow would serve him better than closing with that powerful enemy; besides, there was another strategy to use at this side of the field. Mudarra halted and shortened his hold on the knife; where will he throw, thought Caro coldly, straight to the throat or at the body? He balanced himself on the balls of his feet, the earth was not good, ah! it gave beneath his feet and he felt that he could not fling himself down or twist aside, he almost saw the white-flashing line of steel reach out from his enemy's hand and rip out his throat; the sweat cooled on his forehead and then his nerve broke for a moment and he dashed aside into the branches of an olive tree and at once knew his folly. Below the branches his legs and loins were open to the hissing blade should Mudarra throw and he could not see his enemy clearly unless he stood motionless; his hate came back from the man in the open and curled round the ashen leaves and the twigs that shut out his vision and threatened him with death if he but moved his head.

As he watched, Mudarra began to slip off his coat. Caro saw the foremost leg lose its weight and the right sink a little into the powder as his enemy prepared to defend himself with his foot should he rush at the moment when the coat would be over his antagonist's elbows. So that was the reason he had shortened his grip then, that the blade might not entangle in the sleeve, and yet, surely he would have reversed it; no, not reverse it, in a scuffle on the floor one must push a blade, not raise the hand to strike, no, reverse it, no, not reverse it. He shook off the nervous speculation and stood out upon the edge of the wall. With a rush Mudarra was upon him; he leaped forward to be inside the blow that the uplifted arm would deliver, and then his half-closed eyes saw in a flash that the handle of the knife was in his enemy's palm and not in his clenched fingers; as the feinting arm swung back round the circle and upward towards his abdomen he twisted, thrust his leg between Mudarra's and caught the uprushing crook with a thudding grasp upon the inside of the forearm. Yet the feint had been so good that he had no time to prepare a counter blow. As he now drew up his right arm he did not keep his elbow down against his body and there was no strength in it; the left hand of the guitarist snapped round his wrist, the powerful fingers settling into place like a flexible clamp. Desperately, he locked on to his enemy's leg, trying to flatten his body against him.

Suddenly he was aware of the yielding of Mudarra's body and he clamped more fiercely to throw him off his balance.

With a gasp his enemy staggered, the knife hand wrenched free, and they were apart, and back again in another desperate lock. Now they went rocking and tugging over the patch of soft earth, digging deep into it to the outer roots of the olive trees, each trying to meet the other's surprise thrusts with a rally. The cigarras in the trees around were silent. Their faces came together and Mudarra's sweat was salt and foul upon Caro's lips. He felt his legs weaken upon that stamina-soaking earth and he knew he must break or the steel would bore into his vital organs; at that instant his enemy realized his advantage and his heavy weight suddenly hung upon Caro. Though his legs trembled with the effort of trying to thrust that bulk away from him, he could not do it. He tried the strategy he had determined upon should their fatal close-fighting reduce him, and, reversing his effort, he surprised Mudarra and dragged him to the wall. Mudarra broke rather than be dragged over, knowing his heavy unprepared fall would hurt him more than Caro's prepared one. In an instant Caro pounced; the first blow missed but the reverse struck his enemy above the right nipple and sharply met the bone; he leaped back to avoid the sickle-curved stroke that would have torn out the flesh and muscle of his knife arm. His feet met the churned-up earth, he staggered, his hands came up and in that instant the flashing rod of light shot out from Mudarra's hand. Caro's eyes shut as he jerked sideways, and the blade hissed out into the air above the lower terrace; he opened his eyes and Mudarra was leaping at him with his right foot raised to stamp him down over the drop. He twisted again and clumsily grasped the body, and they rocked, shook violently and fell the seven feet to the hard earth at the wall's base, Mudarra beneath, upon his back. As they fell, Caro's right elbow caught the stepping-stone and the knife jerked from his hand. Before Mudarra could recover from the fall he seized a large smooth stone and beat him twice upon the forehead so that the bone rang clear; before a sickening knee blow made his grasp on the stone relax, and it slipped from his hand. In the same instant his enemy weakened. With a fresh burst of energy Caro reached for his knife and secured it. Now Mudarra's arms were weakening; he wrenched free from them and, kneeling astride, he got the knife haft into both hands and lunged down, turning the blade that it should incise deeply through the ribs. The guitarist's hands shot up and caught his wrists but there was no strength in them. Leaning his weight upon the knife, Caro forced the blade point down inch by inch; now it was above the right nipple, now an inch below; his lips parted as he prepared the final thrust. Below him the man lay still with no movement in his body save the cramped breathing and the trembling of his arms. The great black eyes opened and he gazed up into the intent, thinking eyes of the man above him.

"Adios . . . is it worth it?" he gasped.

Before the will had decided, Caro felt his thrust weaken, and then he bore down again.

"Adios . . ." whispered the guitarist again. Against one half of his will, or his yielding to something other than will, Caro hung still, and then the major forces within him revived and dragged the rest of his mind with them.

"No," he muttered. "No!"

He stood up, and slowly and wearily Mudarra stood up also and leaned against the wall and retched. Seeing the livid wounds on the man's forehead and the blood streaming down among the black hair of his body, and remembering what they had been fighting about, he said coldly, "No, no woman on God's earth is worth it."

He laid his left hand upon the guitarist's arm, finding no words to express the perplexity within him. Suddenly Mudarra turned and seized his knife wrist with feeble violence, but Caro did not flinch, he twisted his hand free and put the knife away, and Mudarra nodded and was sick again.

In silence they returned to the town, and then Mudarra sent Caro ahead to see whether the entry was safe. Caro saw no one who might be dangerous, yet upon their entry Captain Montaña stopped them.

"What's happened?" he snapped curtly.

"Nothing," replied Caro, and Montaña stood aside though he followed them at a distance. They parted without words and without a backward glance.

The same night about ten o'clock Diego rose and asked

Señora Pérez to prepare him a lower and cooler room, and while she and Conchita were doing this, he took off the bandages from his forehead and went out. A few minutes later he knocked at the rectory door; at last La Cándida opened it. "What do you want?" she said suspiciously, seeing his excitement. "You cannot see Father Martínez."

"The other," he said, and, hesitating, she let him pass.

La Cándida knocked upon Father Soriano's door. At his command she opened it and said, "A señor to see you, señor," and motioned to Mudarra to enter. The priest was sitting at a table upon which papers and books were neatly arranged; the light was pulled down low over a large book, upon which lay a pencil.

"What assistance can I give you, señor?"

"I came about my friend."

"Your friend, señor?" Soriano pushed up the light and looked at Mudarra; as he did so an expression of fear and suffering came into his eyes and he lowered himself in his chair; presently he shuddered and covered his face with his hands.

"I am sorry if my forehead is an ugly sight," Mudarra said.

The priest did not look up, and when Mudarra laid his hand upon his shoulder he shrank from his touch.

"I shan't hurt you, man, I came about my friend. Don Fadrique gave him the sack this week."

At last the priest stared at his visitor, making a minute sign of the cross upon his chest.

"What can I do for your friend, señor?" he said with immense effort.

Mudarra lurched forward and, taking the priest by the shoulders, thrust his face into Father Soriano's. "Listen, Pascual the old man, you remember? and his wife, Ursula and the brother, all of them will starve." The knees against his leg shook violently, and he released the priest and regarded him in bewilderment before leaving.

That night Father Martínez sent for the doctor to calm Soriano's fever.

12

Nocturne

On Sunday and at the spot called Six Olives the small tenant
Florez committed suicide with a shotgun. To one of the olives
which overhung a nearly vertical bank a rope was attached.
Florez had been one of the volunteers for the dynamiting of
the dam which had been planned for the Monday and that
enterprise was therefore postponed. At the F.A.I. meeting the
following day, when Mudarra, who had arrived late, announced that he would take the dead man's place, Florez's
fellow dynamiter withdrew. It was seen that the man had
lost his nerve.

"Well, any volunteers?" asked Mudarra, spitting in the direction of the frightened man.

There were several halfhearted replies

"All right, I'll find my own man."

"Who'll you find?"

Mudarra hesitated before answering, "Caro."

"Ca, not reliable," ejaculated Aguiló's companion from
Seville.

"Reliable as any man in the movement or out of it," and
the Sevillian suppressed his reply after a moment's reflection.

"Why hasn't he been to any of the meetings lately?" another
put in. "He should have plenty of time on his hands now."

"He started work this morning."

"Where?" Mudarra exclaimed.

"Back on the old job, round on White Hill."

At last Mudarra said, "All right, I'll ask him and make my
own arrangements. Have the guards found Florez's dynamite?"

There was a long pause, during which Soriano acquired an enemy. His guess had been right, Mudarra decided, that Soriano was responsible for the selection of workers for dismissal. Very probably the priest was being guided by spies within the movement. It was likely, too, that the womenfolk were unwittingly betraying their men.

"Doesn't anyone know about the dynamite?" Mudarra demanded fiercely. That impotent musicologist Peral should pay and the meddling fool Soriano should be humiliated.

"It's hidden under the altar at Mater Purissima."

"I shall pray there . . ." Mudarra muttered. But Soriano's spy might indeed be present and so he continued, "We'll let everything rest for two full weeks. Agreed?"

"Agreed."

After the depressed and short meeting Mudarra went to his new room, took down an instrument and tuned it, and then, laying it upon the bed, wandered out to the balcony. From the other balcony Conchita was making scoffing replies to a youth who was paying her the traditional compliments. As Mudarra appeared he ceased to reply to Conchita's equally traditional sallies, and presently moved off.

"Hola," he said to the girl with a yawn. "A suitor?"

"He presumes."

"How presumes?"

"Oh, he said he had a great passion for me."

"What d'you say?"

"You heard."

Mudarra shook his head and searched for a cigarette.

"Well, I told him that if he turned himself into a bull he mustn't expect to put it right in my bed."

Mudarra yawned and said, "Go and make me some coffee, girl," and she went in promptly.

After coffee, Mudarra found no comfort in the conversation of the Pérezes and left the house, strolling without purpose about the smaller streets of Villa Alta, brooding over Caro and Lucía and sometimes Soriano. The fight had not brought Caro and himself much nearer in understanding, though the old feeling of intolerable bondage had gone. He had fought without hate, finding in his fighting the keen, intelligent and almost

purely intellectual exhilaration which good fighters experience,
yet aware that he was exerting himself to the utmost out of
fairness to Caro. Defeatism or a morbid surrender would have
helped nothing, he had realized, for it would have been a decision without the rigors of the case and Caro would have been
further embittered by it. Even when his knife passing beneath
Caro's uplifted chin had lost him the fight he had felt no desire
to surrender, for that also would have prevented . . . Joaquín
returning. Returning, that was what he needed, and at the
thought he realized that had he not missed that straining
throat the three of them . . . well, in his case that would have
been the result of the State's interference, the State which was
the resort of cowards and thieves, *their* knife. But the ease
which the fight and its dissolution of an unwholesome bond
had brought had been momentary. It was the limit of the
movement of separation. Now that the deeper necessities of
their conflict had been cleared out of the way it was a desire
to reason with Caro which he felt. Surely an Anarchist like
Caro would be able to ignore such a thing as Lucía had
done. . . .

The fierce quarreling of a man and woman in a house at
the top of Rosas Street broke the sequence of his thoughts and
he turned down the hills through the narrow and airless streets
off Poniente, the poorest quarter of all. Here Mudarra usually
felt a strange contentment possess him, for in Poniente people
had no disguises. Now, however, he was disturbed by the frank
hostilities and derisive self-assertion of these compañeros. A
nasal voice with a recitative accompaniment of pulled strings
made him stand at the lower fountain awhile, but when two
bare-legged big-breasted girls squirted water over him it was
his tongue alone that jeered at them; a brawl of muleteers in
the Sevilla Inn and the hot smell of hay and locust bean and
rotting manure pleased him for a moment, and then it was but
obscene words in a stable. At the urinal beside the carbon-
seller's shop he stopped for a moment to read the scribbled
inscription, "Viva la F.A.I., Death to Christ the King," and
then the stench of alcoholic urine turned him away and he
moved on with a quickened gait towards the Rincón.

Acorín was playing when he entered and he took a chair and

sat astride it and listened. Soon the guitarist stopped and stared at Mudarra gloomily. "Ah, go on playing, man," Mudarra exclaimed. El Chino began a display of tricks and grace notes and his rival rose and left the Rincón with a feeling like disappointment.

Without thought he turned along the Travesía of Rosas Street and with a flush of pleasure decided to call on Bonifacio Tàrrega, the guitar-maker. The old man was still working in his dark cavelike shop when Mudarra arrived; around him were white-tabled guitars and lengths of gut, glue pots, cheap aluminum tailpieces, ebony bridges and the side chogs of mahogany. In Bonifacio's shop one picked one's way through the litter of wood waste, patterns, clamps and broken instruments, to a chair from which one removed tools or materials before sitting down. From poles slung across the ceiling hung the new instruments, looking like hams in the yellow light of the speckled globe.

"Hola, maestro," Bonifacio said, and pointed first to one chair, then another and then another. "Bueno," he added with a general wave, seeing that they were all taken up with gear.

"Anything worth handling lately?" Mudarra asked.

"Well, well, well, I've four of the best models I'd thank you to try, Dieguito, my son."

"Hand them over."

"They're up there on the pole, *chico*. Hey, Filharmónica, send for the apprentices and say Señor Mudarra is here." No one knew why Bonifacio addressed his wife so; with a screamed "Buenas, señor," the deaf old woman hobbled quickly out of the glass-paned door and drew it behind her. Bonifacio zealously watched her shut the door and then, protest being unnecessary, reached down behind his seat and passed over the wine flask. "Ah," he said, "here I've got an instrument you'll like, my boy. Don Fadrique sent it down for repair a while ago, somebody seemed to have dropped it, you haven't been in since it came or I'd have liked to hear it." He drew out of a piece of blanket the instrument Don Fadrique had bought at Easter.

"Presently," said Mudarra as Carlos and José, the apprentices, came in. While José climbed the stepladder, without invitation Carlos turned to a cupboard for music and, rubbing his thick glasses, sat down upon gut, tools and a bundle of pegs, which he angrily swept from under him.

"No music, thanks," said Mudarra. He took the first instrument and played a chromatic scale from the bottom E to the top fret of the upper E string, and then nodded.

"They don't set 'em right nowadays, eh?" Bonifacio laughed. "Listen to this one: factory article, good for a bedpan perhaps."

When all the instruments had been tried, Carlos said eagerly, "Yes, maestro?"

At that moment Justo Robledo rolled by; not drunk, but unsteady as usual. Mudarra knew where he would be going to in the Travesía at this hour.

"The Strauss waltzes?" José questioned

"Right then," and the three began with the "Morgenblatter." Such music is never heard at its best with the unsuggestive coloring of the piano, but now it received its full beauty from the glittering skeleton sounds of the three guitars, extravagantly played by the apprentices instinctively taking their cue from the older player thrumming the bass. Mudarra looked up suddenly at the third slow section, and Carlos quietened his tone to a whispered "tap-tap tap-tap" as the maestro played the simple conventional tune in the most thrilling of all tones, the upper harmonics of a guitar.

"Olé!" burst out Bonifacio, stamping his feet. Now the melody received a counterpoint of down-showering passages. José, at the bass, pulled softly and steadily at his E and A strings. Upon the guitar this music was not a ripple of water or a waving veil, but a shining movement of undulating brilliants, all clearly heard and with an ideal non-staccato detachment that would have filled that rarity, an intelligent pianist, with jealousy and a sudden vision. And then the two guitars hushed and left the melody to Mudarra. Slowly and with nostalgic irony, the E string gave out its bass, over which hovered the simple chords, enriched beyond their normal significance with melancholy and languor and something

more that was like cruelty. Above, the melody wavered and
hastened and was muffled and then rang out bitingly with
nail-plucked notes.

A woman, whose husband everyone knew to provide illicit
herb medicines, came down the stairs opposite and looked
about her; the electric light flickered. Then suddenly the music
became full of feeling and he was sad beyond bearing and
stopped in the middle of a phrase. Such music was somehow
not for his mood, though he could not imagine why. "Ah,"
sighed Carlos, taking his head out of the score.

"Play something more, maestro," José said, and he began a
fandango, an arrangement of Turina's "Malagueña," and a
suite in flamenco rhythms by Ponce the Mexican, yet finished
none of them. Catching sight of the old guitar, he commenced
the Narvaez Fantasia. Calmly, gravely, the ancient theme was
heard, and within a few bars it already sounded, not as if it were
being played, but as all such music must sound to contemporary
ears, as if it were being uncovered, as if the music were hung in
space and not in time. It was a music that was apprehended
not by the ears, or which did not seem to depend upon the
player even for its existence. The massive hand upon the fret-
board, for all its swift and complicated movement and knead-
ing strength, like the fingers of a lover upon his woman's spine,
was merely releasing the music from the instrument in which
it had been long shut away. The rising counterpoints which
carried up to the main structure their culminating notes of
clear sound were not voices with passion, as Diego had once
said, but were . . . what he could not say, but around him
there glowed a calm and cool framework of light. This music
for all its agility was not movement but a beautiful thing
suddenly perceptible, visible almost. It was a music effecting a
removal beyond the report and the concern of the present.
Carlos came over to watch the fingering of the difficult runs;
again the light flickered, and Mudarra saw a girl come out of
the door opposite, lean against the wall, pass her hand wearily
over her forehead and then walk droopingly away. And when
the old man clicked his tongue in admiration he heard and
smiled, yet none of this came within the music. Around
Mudarra was suspended a loveliness he had not perceived

before; he had forgotten his hands and they moved about their task remote from him; as each phrase closed to the continually changing identity of rhythm he recognized the beauty he had fragmentarily heard before, yet now he was caught far away by the sounds. He smiled as he gazed through the window to the empty street that was no more than light and shadow without substance, and his breast filled deep with peace. They listened, perplexed, yet recognizing that mastery, and were quiet. Then a man came to the door and pushed it open and shouted at the guitarist and the music ceased. It was as if a silvery vision had suddenly vanished.

Mudarra greeted the visitor without anger and then, as he turned to give the guitar to Carlos, he frowned in the effort of thought.

"Now try some of that aristocrat's music on this one," said Bonifacio, holding out the old guitar.

"Jesus Christ!" shouted Mudarra and, thrusting the visitor aside violently, he flung the door open and raced across the street. The apprentices saw him halt at the door opposite; without glancing round he knocked cautiously. The astonished apprentices and the visitor saw Mudarra charge against the door as it opened a few inches, and then the door slammed behind the guitarist and they heard the bolt flung over.

At the top of the stairs the woman's husband, an obese man of about forty, barred the way.

"Get into that room," said Mudarra, as the man tried to close the door.

"Here, this is my house . . ." the interceptor began, and then the breath was charged out of him and he was being forced back against the table.

"God . . . God!" he gasped as Mudarra's hand grasped him. "Don't, for the Virgin's sake."

"What have you given her, tell me?" Mudarra's left hand was at the man's throat and he shook him till the sweat of pain burst out of him.

"What have you given her?" he repeated fiercely, wrenching with his right hand.

"Nothing . . . nothing."

"Right, I give you half a minute before I start on you again."

Mudarra released the herbalist and he slowly straightened up, lurching with pain, his face gray and his lower lip hanging.

"I gave her nothing; she wanted a stomach medicine."

"A stomach medicine!"

"Yes, señor, for indigestion."

"Christ!" Mudarra grabbed at the man again and, jamming his sagging body against the table, thrust his head backwards and downwards.

"You gave her nothing though she only asked for a stomach medicine? Ca!"

"We hadn't got any, señor," wailed the woman.

Mudarra took out his knife and pulled off the sheath with his teeth. "Going to speak? . . . Going to speak? No? Well, see how you like this." Seizing the man's hair, he thrust the point of the knife hard into the herbalist's gums against the base of his upper teeth; a harsh choking scream like an idiot's burst from his throat as the knife blade bored through the gum into nerve and bone. The woman rushed at Mudarra and joined in her husband's feeble wrestling, trying to pull the great torturing hands away. The guitarist released the man and swung a heavy blow into her face. When he turned to the herbalist again his face showed surrender, blood was pumping freely from his torn gums.

"You gave her a mixture then?"

"For her periods, señor."

"Sit in that chair! You gave her an abortion mixture."

The man did not reply, and Mudarra approached him with the knife.

"Yes, señor," the herbalist screamed.

"Where's she gone?"

"I don't know . . . no, for Jesus' sake, señor, no . . . ah, ah! for Jesus' . . . sake . . . señor."

"We don't know, señor, we don't know, we don't know," wailed the woman, dragging at Mudarra's arm.

"All right . . . *God help you* if anything goes wrong with her."

He hurried along the street trying to think where Lucía could have gone. It was too late for her to be out alone with her parents' consent; surely she would not return to Miracle

Court, yet that was the only thing he could do to find her. He wheeled into the cooper's yard and, clambering on the stacked barrels, dropped over the wall into the court behind the Olive Oil Street barber's shop and hammered on the door. "Sorry, Miguel," he panted as the astonished barber opened, and hurried through the house and up the street into the court. Listening at the Robledos' window he could hear no voices within. It confirmed his belief that Lucía must have stolen out without her parents' knowledge or they would have been talking within. If she had returned then she must have entered undetected. Perhaps she had not returned. He went over to Gordito's café and ordered a coffee, ignoring the cries of recognition from the back of the room while Caravaca fussed round him, wiping the table top carefully and pouring out the coffee with exaggerated courtesy.

"Say, have you heard the news, Diego?" a voice shouted from behind him. He glanced round hurriedly and continued to watch the Robledos' house.

"No . . . no, what news?"

"The town council's decided to abolish the serenos; economy stunt."

"Christ," he ejaculated mechanically, "taking it in turns themselves?" Where could Lucía be? The girl must have been crazy with worry and fear to go to such desperate lengths. For a girl even to be out alone at night in Los Olivares meant the ruin of the most spotless reputation; to stay out all night and with such an object—even if no harm befell her! God, what a fool he had been to take her "no" for an answer upon that one night at her window when Escolástica had delivered his letter. He should have gone to her parents and told them the truth, he should have told Caro—"Ah, damn Caro," he muttered, and then without paying for his drink he hurried out of the café. At the steps he halted. He must find Caro and they must search for Lucía.

At the Rincón he was told that Caro was at the Republican Center, but he had already left there when Mudarra arrived. At the Gallows Rock he stood a moment and listened; the faint movement of air in the telephone wires going up to the Palacio was sufficient to throw him into doubt; he was not sure whether he could hear steps. He clattered down through the gleaming tins. At the threshing floor something white was moving and he whistled.

"Joaquín, you've got to help me," he blurted.

"Trouble? The civils?"

"No. . . . Christ in Heaven, Lucía's in trouble, she's got some stuff from that devil in the Travesía, I don't know where she's gone."

He could hear Caro breathe quickly and then say dully, "All right . . . we must find her." Mudarra told the little he knew.

"She must have gone crazy," Caro said. "If she has run away how the hell . . . they'll never . . . God, this is a bloody mess, she must be going to take that stuff tonight."

"Yes, she'll be gone to some place."

"Out here."

Each looked round at the dim hills and the immense broken slopes pitted and barred with black shadows; the sereno cried, "It is midnight and the night is clear," and both remembered the evening's news while thinking of the girl.

"The herbalist has got a vineyard down by the Jabalón," Caro said.

"I don't think he knew where she'd gone . . . no, he didn't know."

"I was thinking she'd be in the tool shed."

"She wouldn't have gone to her brother's?"

"He won't be back yet, I saw him drunk."

"That makes no difference; I saw him too; she'd speak to Celestina, you could trust her."

"Yes." They stood undecided and silent.

"Well, this is no good; would she have gone to Celestina?"

"No."

"No, she'd want to get rid of it alone. Try the tool shed. She's sure to go indoors somewhere," Mudarra said.

"No need to."

"Christ, of course she'd go in."

"Try the shed on the old Robledo grounds."

"All right." They hastened away over the goat pastures and

the fields to the abandoned track. Lucía was not in the tool shed when they broke the door in.

"In Ojeda's?" They doubled back and hastened down the slope till they saw the thin gleam of the Jabalón and they turned half right and slid down the bank to the tool shed. "The key's under the loose stone of the seat."

"What the hell . . . it's all right, a toad." The shed was empty.

"Who else does she know? God, this is a bloody mess; if any guards are about they'll just let drive."

"They won't be about; who else does she know?"

"I don't know. Try them all, those nearest the path, hell, she may be on the other side of the town."

"No, she'd think about tomorrow, they'd all be used to-morrow on the Huerta or on the other side of the town."

"Well . . ."

"Joaquín . . . water! She'd go where there's water, wouldn't she?"

"If she thought at all she might."

"Try all along the watercourse."

In a shed near the watercourse, at half-past one, they found Lucía; they were forced to smash in the chained door, and when it flew open it stuck against the foot of the moaning girl and they could not enter.

"Madre Santísima have mercy," Mudarra murmured, fumbling for his cigarette lighter; when he lit it he saw the girl upon her back rolling from side to side. Caro slipped through the opening and dragged her from the door.

As the two men touched her the girl thrust away their hands and screamed as they had not heard a woman scream before; it was of fear and agony, and of more than this, as if it had not been forced from her by pain but was the speech of hopeless loneliness. She did not hear their words but beat them, sometimes clutching at her belly and tearing at her clothes and then beating them, or the air again.

"See if there's anything for a light, for God's sake," Caro moaned through his tears, and Mudarra struck his lighter and looked round. "Nothing . . . nothing at all . . . here's the bottle.

God, she's drunk three-quarters of it." He put his hands firmly on the girl and tried to caress her, calling to her desperately, repeating his name and Caro's. She only screamed the more loudly.

"Hold her, Joaquín," pleaded Mudarra, "perhaps she'll know your hands."

Before Caro could touch the girl she had struggled to her feet and flung herself free from him. She fell at once, and they heard her head strike the wall, yet though her screams ceased she continued to struggle feebly.

"Strike a light," commanded Mudarra suddenly, and laying the girl's body, drenched with urine and sweat, in the middle of the floor, he knelt and examined her.

"No, nothing's happened," he muttered. Presently when Lucía began to scream again, her body was suddenly possessed of a beast's strength, and he was compelled to use great force to keep her from injuring herself. As he pinned her thrashing feet, Mudarra could feel the violent tremors running down to him, like fierce jerkings at the nerves. Suddenly Caro began to moan aloud.

"For Christ's sake keep hold of yourself," Mudarra pleaded. "You've got to for her sake."

Now the pain was like an impassioned beast within the girl, it flung her body from the floor, and then twisted it aside like a released spring, and then again her legs tried to thrash. Suddenly a piercing scream terrified them both, and though it was dark, Mudarra shut his eyes tightly and bore down upon the girl; her wet face brushed his hands and her teeth fastened into his thumb and were gone again at once.

"Lucía . . . Lucía," wailed Caro when a hour of this suffering had passed, and Mudarra shouted fiercely to him to be silent. The girl began to beat him again, and he knew that Caro had removed his hands.

"What's the matter?" he demanded. Caro did not reply, but Mudarra could hear him shifting nervously in the dark.

"What's the matter?" he repeated with anger; and again there was no answer, though Caro's arm struck his face as once more he wrestled with the girl. Suddenly her writhings became less violent and rapid, alarming Mudarra; she became quiet.

"Are you all right?" the guitarist questioned his companion. "God damn you, why can't you answer?" He leaned over the girl; she was moaning faintly with her mouth closed. Mudarra searched feverishly for his lighter and could not find it; he remembered placing it upon the floor the last time he had ignited it. His hands sweeping the floor encountered one of Caro's, and it darted away from his touch. "Give me your lighter," he ordered.

"No . . . don't," breathed Caro.

"God in hell, what's come over you?" In the dark he looked up. "Say, are you afraid . . . afraid of what's coming to you if she dies?" There was cold scorn in his voice, yet when he repeated the question it had softened. At last Caro murmured, "Yes . . . I was . . . it has gone . . ," The man's hands were feeling up his arm to his face, then he leaned over the girl and his lips were upon her cheek.

Slowly the gray light came over the Sierra del Jabalón, and evenly filled the immense valley; below near the river a bird called and was silent. Before the sun rose the girl was again in pain and they were compelled to restrain her. But now she was less disturbed by their presence and even gazed at them with recognition; her face, upon which the lines had deepened, tired and empty of life, dirty with the dust that her sweat had retained, seemed to grow more human as the smoldering edge of light crept down the golden-brown sierras across the river, setting them aflame. They laid her head upon some sacking and placed a coat over her; she seemed to sleep though at times her face disclosed pain. A rush of wings passed; over the tool shed and in the town across the Huerta hollow they could hear cocks crowing. To neither of them was there menace in that reminder of the town. It was comfort, and more.

To Mudarra, his hands resting lightly upon the girl's body, there was nothing even for pity in the tremors that shook her still. They sat there quietly, without speaking, sometimes watching the girl's gray face or peering through the door.

"Ah," murmured Caro at last, and Mudarra leaned forward again; the yellow light was streaming down the slopes from the crest behind them, the grains of the soil glittered upon the steep sides of hummocks, a stack of old and rotted *juncal* canes glowed like a tall sheaf of new barley and the long shadow of the untended olive trees above the shed lay blue-gray upon the field. The gurgling of the water in the course seemed to grow quieter. A little later Lucía opened her eyes for a few moments and looked at them both, then turning upon her side she fell asleep.

"We must fetch Justo and Celestina," Mudarra said. "Shall I go?" Caro answered, "Yes," but afterwards shook his head.

Neither spoke their thoughts, but they knew it would be better for Caro to tell the brother what had happened. "All right," whispered Mudarra and his companion rose stiffy to his feet, yet did not leave the shed; but stood regarding the sleeping girl. It seemed as if something or somebody unseen was present with them in the shed, someone who brought the stillness and peace and freshness of the morning. A hush seemed to fall upon the world. Caro remained standing until Mudarra said, "Get a move on . . . now," and then he tiptoed slowly from the shed; the drumming of his racing feet died away quickly beneath the whirring of the cigarras.

13

Aubade

UPSTAIRS he could hear Celestina trying to awaken her husband; first she called his name quietly, with long pauses between the repetitions, and then she spoke more loudly. He heard her step creep over the boards, and again her voice was very quiet; presently he heard Robledo answer gruffly. There followed a long conversation which he could not hear clearly, chiefly in Celestina's voice, and then silence. Slowly Celestina came downstairs.

"He says he won't come down, Señor Caro," she sighed, and stood nervously folding a napkin that had lain upon the table.

"Señora . . . Celestina . . . if he is drunk . . ."

"Yes, he came home drunk."

"Tell him I will come up then, I must see him."

The woman's bearing towards Caro changed at once; she went upstairs again and louder creakings followed.

When Robledo came in he was still lurching, his face swollen as if he had been crying, his eyes also were red and his uncombed hair dull and lifeless. He nodded gloomily to Caro and, stooping unsteadily, took out a bottle of aguardiente and poured out a liberal drink which he drank in silence.

"What have you come here for at this time?" he said truculently.

"I had to see you."

"Ca! . . . Fine sight; you're pleased, no doubt."

"No, man."

"Ah, ———," blurted Robledo. "You came to see me like this, wanted to see me all hot and sticky from the Black House."

"Justo," pleaded Celestina.

"Well, what else would he come for at this time? But you're right, Caro, you're right." Robledo belched and lowered his head upon his hand and closed his eyes. "Ah, Christ," he muttered. "Well, what do you want?"

"Your sister, she's in trouble."

"Eh?" Robledo stared blearily at him. He braced himself for the effort.

"Lucía has run away from home, she is ill, she's taken some stuff. She's pregnant."

Robledo staggered to his feet and clenched his fists, the drunken look in his eyes disappeared as if squeezed out of them by the hate pressing in from his brain. Trying to thrust his chair from him he stumbled, Celestina seized him, his weight came heavily upon her and his clutching hand tore open her blouse. Hastily she closed it.

"Justo," she said sharply, "pull yourself together."

"Good Christ," he shouted, turning upon his wife, who did not flinch. "You want me to be calm with this bastard here . . ."

Celestina clasped her hands and threw her head back and a greater sorrow came into her eyes. As Justo gazed at her Caro saw his anger change into anguish, and then shame. Flushing, he sat down and regarded Caro with entreaty though there was no question in the words when he said:

"You'll marry her, Caro."

"It was Mudarra."

"Mudarra . . . yes, it would have been, ah, God." Justo put his head upon the table and his shoulders shook. "She's ill, where is she?" he exclaimed suddenly. Caro told him what had happened during the night and how Mudarra had by chance seen Lucía leave the herbalist's house.

"He's at the shed now," he concluded.

Robledo burst into an obscene tirade, swearing violence against both the guitarist and the herbalist. Celestina made no attempt to interfere.

"He saw her come out of the house . . . why didn't he fetch me?"

Caro shrugged his shoulders. "He saw you also in the Travesía, he was in Bonifacio's shop when you went by."

When Celestina had wrapped a change of clothes in a blanket they set out at once for the old fields. Robledo followed closely behind Caro, going quickly but with difficulty. Mounting the rough slopes from the Huerta path he stopped momentarily to retch, and at once continued, calling Celestina to drag him up by the hand over the crumbling edge of the last bank. Mudarra, sitting against the wall, was asleep when they arrived, and, shaking him, Robledo pointed to the door; the guitarist ignored the gesture and, though for a moment it appeared that Justo would strike him, he refrained, obeying Celestina's command to lift the girl from the floor. Lucía shrank from her brother as he touched her, but he kneeled down and, spreading his arms over her, kissed her upon the temple and called her by name. Between them Robledo and his wife and Caro carried her to the latter's house, while Mudarra followed them silently. Several times, seeing Robledo stumble or Caro tire, Mudarra ran forward as if about to offer to take the girl, yet always the impulse was restrained by something obscure but invincible. No one spoke to him. At the bottom of the slope he ceased to accompany them, standing among the bushes long after they had entered the house; afterwards he climbed towards the town, frequently looking back at the white house against the cliff. At the last turn from which it was visible he sat upon a heap of burning rubble in the sun until he saw the Robledos coming up the path.

Pascual was leading out the mule when the party arrived; they shouted and he called to Ana within and mother and daughter ran out shouting to them.

"Poor little thing, poor little thing," wailed Ana, hovering round them as they hurried exhausted to the house. When they entered, the pot containing the beans, potatoes and pieces of sausage cooking for the dinner was boiling over and, still wailing, she ran and pulled some of the carbon out of the fire; Marcial ran into the kitchen and ordered her upstairs after Ursula. Pascual went out to the mule, which was being tormented by flies and was kicking its belly. When Robledo descended he looked indecisively from Marcial to Joaquín, who brought a chair and invited him to sit down. Ursula, sent

down for warm water, hurriedly placed a bottle of wine upon
the table, and took a pitcher of cold water and the small pot
from the fire. The three men watched her place the bottle of
wine on the table, watched her go to the pitcher rack and
select the black pitcher, and stared at her as she removed the
pot from the fire. No one spoke until Justo leaned forward in
his chair, and then the three Caros spoke simultaneously:

"Don't disturb yourself, man, don't move."

"Don't molest yourself so much, señor, there's no need."

"Many thanks, señor, but don't trouble yourself, I can
manage," Ursula protested, and Robledo leaned back in his
chair. Then there was silence again; everyone listened to the
sounds upstairs.

"How are the fields down this part?" Justo asked, and the
brothers at once stood up.

"Perhaps you would like to take a look over them."

"I should indeed," Justo replied. "May I have a drink of
water?" and he reached for a pitcher in the rack.

"Ah no, señor," exclaimed Marcial, and hurried to the cupboard in an angle of the wall and placed a glass on the table
and filled it; Robledo drank from the glass while Joaquín
tipped water down his throat from the pitcher.

Outside Marcial led the way to the upper fields, upon which
a thin and irregular crop of barley was standing. "This year
we have only half the usual yield, I'm afraid; though as the
donkey feeds herself on the slopes yonder it won't be quite so
bad."

"We had two mules until recently," added Joaquín.

"The drought, I suppose?" Robledo said.

"The drought, of course."

"How much do you expect to get off this field?"

"Oh, I don't know, I should say forty measures."

"And you planted ten, eh?" Robledo followed up rapidly,
"A four times yield, that is." He shook his head, they all
shook their heads.

As they moved on the vegetable plots near the watercourse where the father was working, Pascual greeted them
with a quiet "buenas," lifted his hand in salute and bent over
his beds again.

"This year the onions have done badly; a half of them have gone to seed already though there's nothing underneath, see." He pulled a root and gave it to Robledo. "That's not due to the drought, of course."

As they approached the field of the Well, which was planted with wheat, Ursula came out of the house and they all ceased their conversation and watched her.

"This we call the field of the Well," Marcial said when the girl had entered again.

"The well is at the far end to the right of the figs," added Joaquín.

"And this is your plow?" Robledo pointed to the plow before them.

"One of them. We have a smaller one for opening up under the olives and in the little plots up on the slopes." Justo nodded and tapped the share with his foot. "That's the cause of half the trouble, you know."

"Yes," the brothers assented.

"What's your yield in a good year of this field—about eight measures to one of seed?"

"That'd be a good year; about seven to one as a rule."

"Ha, I thought so. Now I'm not going to say this kind of plow is the only cause, but these fields with a better share and a heavier frame would easily yield twelve to one. It would break a furrow deep enough to resist this drought."

"Twelve to one!"

"Easily; why in England they get nineteen to one and in Germany more; of course they've better lands and they're more scientific, but you see what could be done. This is practically the same kind of plow the ancient Romans used."

"You mean to say the English get as much as that!" broke in Marcial and an excited discussion broke out.

"Yes, but man alive, how are we going to work a plow like that," Joaquín objected, when Robledo had described a modern share. "You couldn't get a mule and a donkey to pull that through the earth, nor yet two mules."

"That's it, it's a question of money; you can't afford a couple of horses, nor yet a yoke of oxen now, therefore you can't ever hope to afford them. Mules are cheaper, but don't pull deep enough, of course; that's why they're the ruin of Spain."

"It's all a question of silver; you can't pay rent out of this yield and buy horses and manure, so you can't improve the yield," Marcial said savagely.

"And then we had to sell one mule," Joaquín interjected. "But still, the donkey will have a foal next year. Here, that girl's been calling me for the last two minutes."

Ursula, who had now attracted their attention, came out to the field to meet them; gravely she said:

"Mother invites Señor Robledo to stay to dinner."

"How is my sister now?" Justo exclaimed.

"She is sleeping again, señor," the girl replied, hanging her head, and Marcial asked:

"What is the matter with her; it looked like sunstroke, but it couldn't have been, so early in the day."

Ursula at once said, "Adios," and returned to the house.

"Poor little thing," Marcial murmured when Joaquín had told him, and afterwards he avoided his brother's gaze.

"You will stay to dinner, of course," began Joaquín, and both brothers continued to press Robledo.

"Very many thanks indeed," he answered, "but you see, Lucía will be missed by now and . . ."

"I've been thinking about that; won't her father make trouble with the police?"

"He's sure to have raised hell," Marcial exclaimed. "The town will be on fire."

"He may have done." Robledo's gaze turned away towards the blazing hills.

"But surely . . ." began Joaquín, but watching Robledo's face he said no more; though both brothers were perplexed by Justo's answer.

They followed Ursula to the house, and presently Celestina and Ana came down to the kitchen, sweet wine and biscuits were handed round with compliments and then the conversation died away.

"Put the almonds on the table, Ursula," Ana said after a while. "Ursula, Ursula," sang Celestina, laughing uneasily. Ana nodded. "Yes . . .

> *Ursula, Ursula, what are you doing*
> *So long in the kitchen below?*

"Señora, señora." Ursula nervously took up the song:

> *You know I am plucking*
> *The small hen white as snow.*

Then mother and daughter sang:

> *The good little wine*
> *The blessed bread*
> *The heavenly food,*

and Celestina joined in with the last line:

> *On which God's angels are fed.*

"First she used to like that song and then she used to be very angry if we sang it," Ana said to Robledo. "Now I think she likes it again."

Outside Pascual began to shout and they heard him running past the end of the house; Joaquín glanced through the window and at once made for the door. "Ursula, Mother, Justo," he shouted. "Birds, outside, everybody."

Over the olive grove a dense flock of birds was circling with eccentric motion, like a black disk-shaped net. They ran to join Pascual, who was waving his arms and leaping about between the trees. "Out there," he shouted to Celestina. Robledo ran to the other side; Joaquín and Ursula climbed into the trees and shook the branches, and they all screamed and shouted, but still the birds whirred round the olive field, at each swerve sinking lower and packing more closely; a few birds seemed to collide and, tumbling out of the flock, flew out to the rim of the disk and joined the outer birds. Pascual's voice was cracking, and the fruit was dropping from the shaken boughs when Marcial, panting, arrived with a shotgun and discharged it into the flock; at the second cartridge they swerved and suddenly darkened the sun as they rose like a flapping sail and flew off towards the upper olivars. Ana was supporting Marcial when Joaquín jumped out of the tree. He stooped at once and examined the fruit.

"Not so bad," he said quietly. "We shan't lose too many."

"One year the birds took all our fruit," Ursula said to Robledo, "the day before we were going to pick them." They stayed talking of the birds and the vicissitudes of olive trees for a few minutes and then, as shotgun fire was heard on the great olivars, Justo and Celestina, fixing the hour for the evening visit, took leave of the Caros.

When Mudarra left the ricino bushes it was Justo alone who saw him. He said nothing to Celestina, but a minute later he drew her fiercely into his arms and kissed her upon the lips and face and ran his fingers through her hair.

"Ah, cowherd," she protested when he released her and said nothing more till they entered the town, when he invited her to have dinner at the fonda; she left him there with repeated promises not to be long, and hurried home. When she returned, she had changed her dress and her earrings. Seeing them, Robledo flushed and gave nervous orders to the waiter.

The following day Lucía walked between Celestina and her husband to their house in Villa Alta. The Robledos occupied a small house in Mendizabal Street, which ran from the Plaza de la República to the smaller Plaza de Hernández y Galán. It stood between two much taller houses and was conspicuous in that white street by its ever-white limewash and the viridian-green paint of its door and windows and the fresh black paint of its iron grille, and by the absence of balconies. Within, Celestina had submitted to several modernizations of which she had not approved, but Justo's pride in the exterior of his house she rejoiced in. She was glad to be able to make a brave show, for Mendizabal Street esteemed itself as highly as any community of horse dealers, cloth merchants, provincial lawyers and grocers. In the Lower Town, Mendizabal Street was known as "Tengan Ustedes"—"May You Have"—Street. "Good days" or "Good afternoons" were the accepted greetings in Los Olivares, but the residents of Mendizabal Street, it was said, affected the ceremonious courtesy of replying "May you have good days." When Justo had moved into the house there had been much comment on the furniture which he had brought. Especially remarked upon was the absence of images and plaster or bronze plaques of da Vinci's "Last Supper," which in the other houses of this street even had little rows of electric bulbs in their frames, guaranteed by the sacred-necessities dealer, also of Mendizabal Street, only to consume five centimes' worth of current a night.

Also worthy of comment were Robledo's four boxes of paper-covered books; books should be few, and leather covered, or, more safely, absent. When Robledo's irregular living became obvious, the three scandals were linked together so that it appeared, according to the more spontaneous remarks of Mendizabal Street, that if one desired to possess vices it was better to have many statues and no books. By the same logic, it was ruled that if one were profligate it was better to have many children, or conversely—and Mendizabal Street itself never got the proposition clear—if one were afflicted with the scandalous misfortune of childlessness then it was improper to be profligate. These precepts, however, were not the expression of Mendizabal Street's secret wishes, as Robledo had cynically remarked; in their hearts they made their double-entry compromise with Almighty God by desiring that their sins should be punished, or their virtues rewarded, with barrenness after the second child.

At one o'clock upon the day of Lucía's arrival at Justo's house, her parents visited them. Little anxious to see them, the son took them into the room he had furnished as a study, but without ceremony Juan Robledo forced himself into the kitchen where Celestina and Lucía were eating. The daughter started and looked towards the door.

"If you would like . . ." Celestina said, formally indicating the food.

"Many thanks, may it profit you," replied the father, observing the proper courtesy and advancing upon the girl, white with hate and anger.

"So this is my daughter, my virtuous daughter!"

"That will do, father, speak to her decently . . . or get out." The last words were not spoken with Justo's usual truculence.

"Get out! My son orders me out of his house! and protects his fornicating sister, ah, pretty, pretty . . ."

"And what kind of a sight are you making, may I ask?"

"I have come here to know . . ."

"Ah, the hell you have," shouted Robledo, and at once both men lost control of their tempers; Lucía and Celestina retreated into a corner while Señora Robledo stood gripping a rosary tightly, with no apparent share in the excitement.

"Well, I might have expected it of you, adulterer, drunkard," said the father, when they had given up trying to shout one another down.

"And I of you, Christian." Justo poured loathing into the word.

"And I might have expected it of her, though God knows what I have done to deserve the third . . ."

"That will do, say nothing of that."

"I shall say what I have a mind to say." The father's eyes narrowed and he leaned over the table.

"Say it and you go out of this house, for good, and by God I swear it . . . do you hear, I swear it! Say it and you go out of this town."

"Ha, my official son! And what could you do? What could you do?"

"Juan," interjected the mother.

"Be silent, woman," he shouted, turning upon her. "Isn't it enough that first my son should be a waster and a profligate and then Gloria . . ."

Justo sprang at his father and forced him back towards the door, Celestina ran to them and indiscriminately pulled at them both, with clenched teeth, saying nothing.

"See here," the father shouted over Justo's arm, "do you know how you'll finish? You'll finish like your sister Gloria, in a brothel, a common whore in a common brothel."

The son released the father, who crossed to the other side of the table and screamed hysterically.

"You thought she was in service, didn't you? Well, do you hear, she's in a brothel, a good municipal brothel, the sort of house your kind brother likes to visit, in Córdova . . ." The father began to laugh dementedly. "Oh, he's been in Córdova, too, oh, yes, to Córdova; I shouldn't wonder, oh, no, I shouldn't wonder if the brother has gone to bed with his sister . . ." He threw his head back and reeled over the table as Celestina beat his face. The mother angrily tried to drag him away from the daughter-in-law. Eventually Juan began to sob, but in an interval he lifted his head and said:

"Take two bloods and pour them together, and you have poison."

"Yes, poison," repeated the son and anger vanished, though hate remained.

When the parents had gone, Justo went into his study and lay down while his wife and the girl cleared away the uneaten food. Lucía had shown strangely little emotion during her father's final outburst, but that night they heard unusual noises in her room. They found the girl apparently trying to escape, her face and neck shining with perspiration. For a long time she would not be quieted and then suddenly she seized Celestina's arm and kissed it frantically. When she grew calmer the wife undressed and got into bed with the girl, who shortly fell asleep holding the elder woman's arm.

14

Introduction to Dynamite

AFTER his Saturday afternoon siesta Mudarra went down to the Posada de Sevilla to await the six-o'clock bus from Puente Nuevo, on which Aguiló would arrive; there was still an hour to wait, but the business of the inn yard always pleased him.

The Posada de Sevilla was the largest of the two original inns of the town and was situated immediately within the Lower or Sevilla Gate, and at one side. Before it lay a small plaza which military necessities of a bygone age had planned and which nowadays ensured that the posada would be the stopping place of the bus service and such motor traffic as came to Los Olivares. It was also the muleteers' inn, the drovers', the packmen's, the traveling craftsman's, the visiting peasant's, the market quack's and the small commercial traveler's inn. In short, it was the inn of all those who did not object to their inn being an exact replica of the violent and moving world in which they lived, and in addition, could support the petty discomfort of being eaten alive by bugs. It was a quadrangle of two stories, the inner yard being reached by a large rectangular doorway in the massive stone lintel of which was engraved a crude Paschal Lamb and the date 1512. At night the gateway was closed by a single massive wooden door, now held together with bolts and rivets, the former and beautiful nailheads of the four- and six-petaled type having been sold one by one to collectors of early ironwork. In the front wall there was only one window and that of the seventeenth century, belonging to the principal kitchen above the doorway. It was provided with a shallow nineteenth-century balcony of flat wood slats sawn so that the space between them had the shape of a turned baluster. La Gorda, wife of Vicente Molinos, the innkeeper, was usually to be seen seated on this balcony at the times when travelers might be expected. At these times she could also be heard, from well inside the town, as far as the Plaza of San Salvador.

The portal of the posada was tall enough to admit a man on horseback and wide enough to take the mule-drawn carts which arrived on market and fair days. It was paved with small oval stones set edgeways and arranged in a paneled pattern, which threw up sparks as the tall, straight-backed, blue-faced Andaluz muleteers galloped in with fierce explosive cries and violent wrenchings of the bit, the hard flesh of their flanks straining against the tight cloth and the black hairy hands smacking the animals' necks, or hanging loose by their sides. The yard was paved with coarser stones, upon which the beasts scuffled and slipped, and in the crevices of which the dung and dust collected and became fecund with rottenness, harboring the hordes of flies which monotonously hummed over the open drain in the center. Around the yard upon the ground floor were the stables, the harness rooms and the cart houses. In these the junior members of a mule team often slept or the shriveled peasant, who, with the wisdom of his grandfather and of his grandsons to come, trusted no man and neither expected nor wanted to be trusted by any. In one corner was the drinking-water tap and in the other the original well, with a pulley rope and bucket and stone troughs at each side.

Around the yard at the second story ran a gallery, railed in part with square-bar ironwork and in part with sawn slatwood, and over which a roof of red and yellow tiles, two deep, was supported by bleached and creviced wooden posts, carved with initials and chipped by the knives of idlers. Between these posts hung clotheslines, and from many of them hung flowerpots containing geraniums or carnations. It was in the unventilated rooms opening from this gallery that the ordinary traveler slept. There was no weakling need of privacy among these men and women, so that many of the rooms were divided into alcoves with a common table before them and a few rickety chairs. At night these rooms might harbor in one alcove an old peasant and his wife, a traveling carpenter and his young wife on their left and a team of ribald muleteers on their right. Nor was there shame; a creaking bed in the dark would be greeted with a snore, a nightdressed woman would not shrink from the chattering, brawling, drunkenly singing muleteers who burst in at one in the morning and flung their belts and boots about the floor, and the curtains before the alcoves were rarely drawn. And there was wisdom in these people; they slept with their money under the pillow and their goods under the bed. And they praised the clean sheets and cursed the bugs, but did nothing about them.

Within, the center of all interest was the great kitchen, but this La Gorda would permit none to enter and would thrust out an enormous leg to trip the intruder or repel him with a long scouring blast of descriptive remarks, so that from the doorway the muleteers and the hucksters roared and cursed and laughed at the cooks, but almost always preserved their good humor.

Beyond the family rooms were several large storerooms, which ran along the town wall; in these goats and sheep belonging to Molinos were kept at night. Beyond these rooms were more alcoves, so that the traveler's metal bedstead might be pushed forward into the room by a curved wall of rough masonry, a defensive tower of the late fourteenth-century wall of Los Olivares against which the Posada de Sevilla was built. The whole of this second floor was reached by two staircases, one in the archway and another in the yard, rising to the gallery along which ran the kitchen and the Molinos' rooms. It was true there was another. Opposite the archway stairs was a small wooden doorway thickly encrusted with whitewash like the masonry. If any asked what this door might be, Vicente would reply curtly, "A door," or "A door to a lumber room," and walk away. Indeed, it gave on to a narrow stone staircase which mounted steeply to a vaulted room filled with household odds and ends.

This room, to be entered from Molinos' bedroom, was the former chamber of the Santa Hermandad, the body of knights founded by the Catholic kings to put down banditry upon the royal paths, and murder, theft and violence in inns, and to preserve peace upon feudal fields. Fortified by knightly honor, rewarded with kingly approbation, sustained by Holy Church, and guided by Her quickly through the scorching mazes of Purgatory, the Santa Hermandad had once meted a hard justice to baron and peasant and wayside thief alike. The lumber room of the Posada de Sevilla was the only relic of that Holy Brotherhood remaining in the town. Across the square was the barrack house of the Civil Guard, concerned only with the pursuit of common criminals and in suppressing the revolt of the desperate hungry. They were rarely called to the inn, for there it was chiefly the cowardice of some weakling which provoked trouble. Cheerful aggression was the inn's ceremony of approach, and this might easily be converted into domination if a man shrank from it. Such disputes solved themselves, and sufficient for most others were Vicente, lean, mustached and staccato; La Gorda, obese, hard and scurrilous; Carlos, the second son, and Asunción, the eldest daughter, who might drain the life out of any man, said the muleteers approvingly.

As Mudarra was loitering in the square he was hailed from the balcony by Carlos, who had received guitar lessons from him, and he therefore ascended to the kitchen. They remained talking for a few minutes and then, at the sound of hoofs on the fine cobbles, Carlos invited him to descend.

"There's a mare to be covered by our donkey, you might lend a hand if you're waiting for the bus."

"Right," said Mudarra and they went down.

A bay mare belonging to the olive oil merchant Pedro Barrera was standing in the yard, held by a boy. Asunción Molinos was inspecting the animal while Molinos was un-stabling the donkey.

"Hola, maestro," La Gorda greeted him, from where she was seated at the foot of the steps.

"Buenas, how about throwing a song, Señora?" replied Diego, for even now La Gorda was esteemed as quite a good *cante hondo* singer, perhaps too much given to *granadinas* and half *granadinas* to be considered a stylist.

"This troubles me too much, señor," she answered with a sigh, glancing at her bulk.

"The Señorita, then?" María, the youngest daughter, of twenty years, tossed her head.

"Ah, they can't sing nowadays, the young ones," La Gorda continued, folding her immense arms over her bosom. "Carlos wants you, Dieguito."

"You stand this side, Diego, and father, the other, that's right. If she swerves round or tries any tricks keep her straight, see?"

"Right."

"Asunción, is that halter tight enough?"

"Yes, I think so."

"Right, let's begin then."

"*Suba, suba, suba,*" hissed Carlos, encouragingly, using the courteous subjunctive imperative of the verb *to ascend.* "*Suba, suba, suba,*" and urged the donkey towards the mare; all of them began to murmur softly, "*Suba, suba,*" with frequent acceleration and crescendos to give the donkey spirit. At the end of five minutes Molinos said, "This donkey has got the least will of any donkey I've ever had. Let me try, Carlos."

"*Suba, suba, suba la burra,*" purred Molinos with encouraging gestures; the mare as if bridling at being called a she-donkey became restive.

"Here, María, come and help your sister," Molinos called softly not to disturb the animals, and the girl took hold of the halter by the mare's neck.

"*Suba, suba, suba la burra,*" Molinos began again, placing the accent more heavily on the first syllable, and caressed the donkey and gave him little shoves in the direction of the mare; his ears stood up and fell down again, but he made no important movement and at last Molinos said:

"Try pretending to take the mare away, just about a foot, that's all."

The two daughters tried to drag the animal forward, but she resisted. It was then that someone laughed sniggeringly from the balcony above. Molinos, Carlos, Mudarra, Asunción and María all ceased to hiss and stared at the man above, a flashily dressed commercial traveler from Madrid. "Be quiet," growled Molinos, and the man continued to grin for a moment and then slunk into his room.

"*Suba, suba, suba,*" they all began again very quietly, with tense rhythm and encouraging tone and after a few minutes the donkey became restless. "*Suba, suba, suba,*" they whispered tensely.

"Now," ejaculated Carlos, and Molinos urged the donkey forward. Mudarra grasped the donkey's off forefoot as it came down and Carlos the other, and for a moment there was silence.

"Right," said Molinos, "take her away. God, I'll get a donkey with more will in him at once; that's too much like work."

Asunción mounted the stairs and María returned to her sewing, and a few minutes later the paintless, rattling, oil-dripping bus drew up and Mudarra ran outside. Aguiló was not on the bus; instead Captain Montaña and a large white-faced gentleman got out. Behind them was an elderly and nervous man carrying two portfolios. Montaña whispered something to his companion and they both approached the guitarist. "Come here, Mudarra," ordered the captain and the guitarist advanced from the wall.

"This is the man Mudarra you wanted to meet last time you were here, Señor Prosecutor."

"Indeed, perhaps you would be kind enough to visit me tomorrow," said the Prosecutor. "See that he is brought to the court tomorrow, Captain. Make a note of that, Jiménez," he added, without turning to the man with the portfolios, his secretary. The two men commenced to walk to the fonda in the High Town and on the way occurred the incident which set the casino laughing as Montaña told it. As they were passing the lower farrier's yard, Rosich pointed to the four panels of the gate, in which were four curious patterns, burned into the wood.

"How interesting," he said to Montana, "and how beautiful. I wonder who did them?"

"Ramos, the farrier, I expect," replied the captain. "Hey, Ramos, come here."

"What excellent patterns, señor," Rosich remarked to the astonished blacksmith. "Did you do them yourself?"

"Why . . . yes, yes," he replied, looking from Montaña to the prosecutor.

"Allow me to compliment you on your skill; it is good to see someone keeping vigil for beauty in this age; do you do much of this?"

"God bless my soul," the farrier replied, "that's the patterns we burn on donkeys' rumps. It's dying out nowadays, sir."

"Yes, it's dying out," said Montaña gravely, without a trace of a smile.

"Why, sir, there's some that don't even have bells on their harness nowadays."

Mudarra at once returned to the Pérez' house, thinking over the Prosecutor's words. He did not wonder at Aguiló's absence; the fact of Rosich's presence would have been sufficient to keep him away; very probably he was waiting for information at Puente Nuevo. But his remark about the courthouse was disquieting, though had they meant to arrest him surely they would have done so there and then; besides, the inquiry into Father Martínez's conduct could not very well implicate him, nor had there been any other arrests in connection with the Good Friday affair. Nevertheless there was still the possibility that tomorrow he would not be a free man, and that would frustrate the dynamiting project for the second time. He resolved to find Caro and urge him to join him in destroying the dam that night.

At once joyful excitement flooded into him; ah, this was going to be great, this was life and the fulfillment of the will, Action. He pictured themselves working at the dam, laying the fuse, already spliced for the previous attempt, and then the quick stealthy retreat over the terraces and the crouching in the shadow of Mater Purissima until the deep boom and the roar of released waters were heard. Ah, the Deed, the joy of unfettered defiant Action. The image of the explosion grew larger, he saw the great fan of orange-hued light soar up simultaneously against the background of boulders and tree branches and whirling trunks streaming up into the black night, the shadows of the olivars leaped fantastically like a black-dressed army from behind cover, the valley gleamed luridly and the roaring shook the mountainside and the walls of Los Olivares. Then there would be the handshakes, the pats upon the back of his companion and the joyful cautious return and the mingling with the awakened townsfolk pouring out of the gate. Gradually a deep calm came over him, the calm of nerves strung to a high tension and withstanding it. He called Conchita and told her that he was going to the Rincón and would be home late; that she was to tell only reliable friends his whereabouts.

"But won't you have supper before you go, Diego?" Conchita asked.

"No, I've a lot to do, I shall have something at the Rincón."

"Oh, but let me get you something . . ."

"No, no, I tell you."

"A bowl of soup and an omelet. I can make it while you eat the soup, and that's ready now."

"Oh, all right, woman," Mudarra said testily, looking at his watch.

When after a short search Mudarra found Caro he did not waste time in approach.

"We've got to blow up the dam tonight," he said vehemently.

"Why tonight? There'll be a moon."

"There are clouds. I've got to appear at the courthouse tomorrow."

Caro was silent.

"I can find someone else if you don't want to take it on, there's plenty won't want persuasion, but I'd rather have you than anybody else."

"All right, I'll come, Diego." Caro gripped Mudarra's forearm and his eyes shone. "Where shall we meet?"

"Mater Purissima."

"When?"

"First heavy cloud after eleven; we'll have to do it quickly so that there will be plenty of people still out of bed to rush out after the explosion and give us cover, otherwise the guard will just block the gates and search all the F.A.I. houses to see who's away, or even if they don't do that we'll not get back, they'll see who doesn't go out to work Monday morning."

"Right, the stuff's in the usual place, isn't it?"

"No, it's been moved to Mater Purissima, it's in that box where they keep the cleaners' brushes and things under the altar. I've got duplicates of both keys; the caretaker's son stole them for an evening. She won't go there until the day before the feast."

At half-past ten Mudarra strolled through the Sevilla Gate and down the road in the direction of the little tavern that stood at the bend where the road came out of the gully. In the ruins of an ancient hostel for late travelers shut out by the closed gates, he received word that three of the Civil Guard were on the walls above the Upper Gate, but that they were not on patrol. His informant also handed over a Star automatic pistol and a spare magazine.

At once Mudarra ran along the vineyard slope to above the level of the road; the air struck warm in the gully and he was soon perspiring freely as he clambered up through the boulders and the slipping rubble towards the matted briars and bushes that choked the gully head. Thence, skirting the fair ground by the broken hillocks, he doubled to the first terraces to rise out of the waste lands. As he did so the moon emerged from behind the slowly moving clouds and he climbed quickly into an olive. In the trees around him the cigarras whirred, and then suddenly an insect began its ear-splitting drone in the foliage above his head. "Stop it, you little devil," he muttered, and shook the branch a little; the leaves shivered slightly and the insect was quiet. No sooner had he made himself more comfortable in the triple fork than the cigarra once more whirred. "Oh hell," he ejaculated, and slowly stood up and commenced to climb the branch. Still the insect sawed away as he mounted. "I'll get you, you little devil," he murmured, and then as the whirring ceased again the moon went in and he slid to earth and ran directly to Mater Purissima, thinking with a quick surge of feeling of the man hidden there. To his disappointment Joaquín was not at the chapel, so he carefully slipped the key into the lock of the ironwork gate; it turned easily, for one of the workers had blown oil into it with his bicycle pump the day the copied keys were tried. For a moment he thought he heard steps upon the terrace in front, and then closing the gate behind him he stood to one side of the door; within a minute the clouds slid away from the moon again, so he retreated farther into the chapel and sat down to await Caro. The clear moonlight shone through the apertures of the whitewashed shelter and the bars and scrolls of the door were silhouetted blackly against the sharp-edged beams of light; beyond, the cactus blades faintly glimmered. Turning round he saw that the light was also shining through the ventilation hole high in the sanctuary wall, laying a white handkerchief of light before the altar, and as he watched it quickly faded and was gone. It was like a conjuring trick, and he laughed quietly. In imagination he watched the appearing and disappearing handkerchief of light and he thought that as it appeared a faint reflection of light shone upon the altar, the white cloths and the figure of Nuestra Señora, and then, surprising him, the patch of moonlight again appeared in reality and looking at the reredos he found that it was indeed illuminated. During the next darkness soft steps upon the hard ground before the shelter made him creep to the grille.

Caro set out from his home soon after ten o'clock, planning to mount by the goat pastures which began from the Field of the Well. At the foot he found that the donkey had pulled her tether pin and he was compelled to spend several minutes driving the pin into a crevice of the rocks. He had no sooner reached the crest of the slope than the moonlight crept up from behind him and he had to take shelter among the ricino bushes. He began at once to think of Diego, whom he had been unable to meet with warmth after all. For a while they had seemed to be at ease with one another again in the tool-shed, there had been something . . . mysterious . . . strange . . . he did not know how to define it, about those final moments before he had gone to fetch Robledo. He had determined not to let his dejection at losing Lucía influence him after that, yet anger and at times hate still ruled him, and when these were in abeyance he felt cold and impulseless. Yet, longing to restore that former warmth he had without irresolution consented to share in this enterprise, though he had not often mixed with the compañeros recently. By the time the moon was once more hidden he had forgotten the dam, though behind his thoughts there was something large and even more disturbing.

Caro had just attained the level of the terrace out of which rose the cactus-guarded bluff of the sanctuary when the moon came out and he pressed himself against an olive tree. His hands touched the trunk, from which the unwanted shoots had just been cut, and he found himself feeling round the bark in search of the trimmed shoots. How badly the work had been done! It was inconceivable that a worker could so maltreat the trees or that Argote's eye should have missed such brutal hacking; the downward blow of the hoe-shaped blade had scarred deeply into the bark in three places on this one trunk. He looked around carefully; he darted to the next tree, that also had been barbarously cleaned. Then the earth went dark and he hurried from tree to tree; "All naked and gashed. God, what a botcher!" he muttered. His disgust made him desist, and he raced up the slope and across the hard flat to the shelter and at once flung himself into cover as he saw something move in the doorway.

"*Tierra,*" he whispered.

"*Libertad,*" answered the man in the sanctuary. "Right, Joaquín, come and help me with the stuff."

"Three bars," said Caro as they moved away from the chapel. "How many have you got?"

"Three bars, hey, there's one left behind."

"I thought you said take three bars."

"I said I'd *got* three bars."

"Christ! That's a good start. I'll go back, give me the keys." When Caro returned with the stick of dynamite the moon came out and they stood close to a low terrace wall.

"Say, the wind up there must be freshening."

"No, it's smaller clouds; it's a bloody nuisance."

They stood facing the sanctuary of Mater Purissima, Caro thinking of the stick of dynamite and Mudarra gazing abstractedly at the chapel. They would have to pack the seven sticks closely together, so that the percussion cap should detonate them all. He thought of the white dam gleaming in the moonlight, like the sanctuary, which might have been carved snow in the white blaze. Upon its walls a branch's shadow carved Moorish scrolls. The cactus challenged the night fantastically, like something awake, save where shadows of the olive trunks thrust black voids through their transformed reality. He looked around at the hills now rising black to the clouds or to the needling stars in the awful gulf of uncovered sky towards the south. About all the trees there was a faint crepitation of sound, like a memory of sound, though the olives themselves stood as motionless and silent as on the sea's floor a sunken forest might stand. A little beyond them the white seat of the fountain gleamed and, looking for it, Mudarra saw the fallen olive of the Infanta like a prostrate dragon before the leaning crucifix. And then the moonlight moving on towards the crest of Jabalón illuminated the cliff that rose above Broad Skirt while yet the mountain behind remained dark. Thinking of the stones that sometimes fell from it, it seemed that the cliff was a great dike that barely stemmed back the black hill from overwhelming the sleeping olivars. Ah, it was like life itself, he thought, that awful thrusting darkness, the stemming cliff and the beautiful trees. They were the things of bravery, like music, like friendship, which man makes for himself, from which he gathers fruit, for a while only. And there were those who supposed that the trees might last forever, because beauty was too good to be destroyed, or that they would enjoy these things forever, as if they were gods upon some legendary hill over which the endless years passed light as the shadow of clouds. And then, thinking of the fall of rock that had occurred three years ago, he imagined that someday the dark mountain of eternity would burst through its yielding precipices and man and trees and the loveliness he reasoned by would lie forever, whelmed over in eternal darkness. It was a darkness of peace, though far off it seemed that agonized voices wailed the bleak desolation of the Dies Irae . . . and down the corridor of eternal desuetude processed the drooping banners and the wry-borne symbols of once-glorious faith. Ah, men did well, such men as he, to suffer nothing to limit their individuality if all at the last were to lie like this. Neither State nor Church, nor law must crush out individuality.

Caro was tugging at his arm, and with his interior vision still filled with the image of the moonlit cliff he hurried on over the black terraces. When next the moon emerged Caro said:

"Over here there will be no danger, let's get a move on," and abandoning caution, they doubled across the olivars. Suddenly Caro dropped in his steps and Mudarra, without thought, did the same and crept behind Caro to the shadow of the bank.

"Look over the top," whispered Caro. "I saw someone on the terraces down yonder." Mudarra laid down the dynamite and peered over; below, a figure in white was standing in the middle of a terrace. He recognized the poise of the body at once, even before the man moved away in the direction of Mater Purissima. "Don Fadrique," he whispered to Caro.

"Christ, what's he doing out here?"

"They say at the Palace that he walks about the estate at night sometimes, goes to the fountain and the other places Doña Inés had built. . . . He'll be coming back from that seat, the Mirador, over yonder."

"Well, what shall we do? Go on with it?"

"Yes, if he gets in the way . . ." began Mudarra and was silent. During the next darkness they reached the gully and climbed to the base of the dam.

Upon the Los Olivares side of the dam and a little below middle height the rock upon which the dam abutted was split by a deep crack of about a knee's width. There had always been some talk about cementing in this fissure into which they now were to insert the dynamite. It was while Mudarra was packing stones in the crack to form a platform for the explosive that Caro first felt dismay.

"God, this will lift the damn thing right out of the gully," chuckled Mudarra with glee.

"Yes."

"Can't you hear it? Hell, I can see the water going down this and out over the fields down there by the river. Say, that'll water old Montañas' trees right enough; I can see 'em going over like ninepins."

"Diego!" cried Caro.

"Yes, what's up?"

"We can't do it!"

"Can't we, by hell!"

"I mean, it's trees, it's crops, wheat, barley, potatoes, and all that; you can't do it, man." He wrenched at Mudarra's shoulder and the guitarist scrambled to his feet.

"What d'you mean—you're backing out!" he said fiercely.

"Yes, God damn it all, I'm backing out."

"Are you, by Christ!" Rushing at the crack, Caro seized the

dynamite and dragged it out; the stick with the cap and fuse remained in his hand.

"Joaquín! You can't back out, man, you can't now," Mudarra said, and caught at Caro's arm. Wrenching himself free, Joaquín drew back his arm and sweeping it round in an arc, hurled the dynamite down the gully. Both held their breath, and for a moment Mudarra was thinking desperately whether the dynamite at their feet would also explode with the detonation. Then with a deep boom a red-and-yellow glare shot up in the gully below them and the air was full of cracking and whirring stones; a moment later a cloud of hot and choking dust blew over them as the echoes rolled out and cracked along the slopes of the Jabalón. Afterwards they heard the slow trickle of stones and a few heavy thuds, and then all was silent.

"Come on, you bloody fool," whispered Mudarra, and raced up the bank and over the first moonlit fields. Rushing up a slope of soft earth, Mudarra swerved aside and took cover.

"God strike him," he cursed. "He's coming back." Quickly the white figure bore down on them, halted for a moment upon the terrace wall two fields away, and then slowly felt his way down the steppingstones and hurried on towards them, then half hidden by the low branches, Caro watched Don Fadrique with tense nerves, holding his breath painfully. "Come out into the open, into the open," Mudarra was muttering fiercely, and turning, Caro saw the pistol leveled at the white figure. Mudarra was trembling and cursing and trying to take aim.

"None of that," Caro said quietly.

"Shut your mouth," Mudarra snapped, and the barrel followed Don Fadrique as he moved behind the trees.

"You're going to take it out of him because *I* backed out," he said bitterly, rising to his feet. Mudarra dropped the pistol and dragged him to earth and held him down.

"Do you want to give us away?" he muttered.

"Better that than kill him."

"Oh, God strike you, too." Mudarra swore and crouched low beside Caro, gazing at the Marquis, who was climbing down the wall of the terrace beyond them. In a few moments they saw him through the branches moving like a white owl over the ground, running towards the gully.

"Go your own way, I'm going mine," said Caro and turned, down the terraces towards the goat pasture that descended to his home. Mudarra ran at full speed across the slopes below the sanctuary path, ignoring cover, and concerned only with reaching the gate before the Civil Guard might post sentries.

Upon the waste land before the Gallows Rock a small noisily conversing crowd was gathered, composed principally of the all-night casino patrons and the riffraff of gypsies, beggars and down-and-outs who inhabited the hovels against the walls. Among them were two guards. Retreating among the first trees he hurried round to the down valley side and, creeping along in the shadow of the walls, came up behind the crowd and joined them, and demanded information. Then disappointment, anger, and rage possessed him, but chiefly a sickening disappointment.

15

Homage to Justice

IT was the Posada de Sevilla which provided the relief in Sunday's excitement concerning the explosion and the forthcoming inquiry into the Good Friday incident in general and Father Martínez's conduct in particular. Señor Jiménez, the district judge's secretary, had been offered one of the superior rooms next to the family room, and after timid protest at the lockless door he had consented to occupy it. He had taken his meals after the manner of the inn, discontentedly buying his meat and vegetables at the extortionate prices the merchants of Los Olivares promptly placed upon them, and bringing them to the kitchen to be cooked. When at last his mutton chops were served, Señor Jiménez again weakly protested.

"Is there something wrong, Señor Lawyer?" asked La Gorda, emphasizing his offensive profession.

"There is something very wrong, Señora. I am accustomed to eat a precisely measured quantity of meat for my supper."

"Ah, señor, but an instructed man such as yourself must surely know that meat shrinks in the cooking."

"Quite so, señora, but my instruction is inadequate to explain how four chops can shrink into two."

La Gorda at once challenged Jiménez. Did he insinuate that any of her cooks could possibly steal two little chops?

Jiménez did not doubt the moral excellence of the cooks.

"Then do you suppose that I would permit thieves to rest under my roof, Señor Lawyer?" exclaimed La Gorda, knitting her brows and staring hard at the little man. Señor Jiménez likewise had no hesitation in saying that all her clients were of singular honesty in the matter of little mutton chops.

"Well, what then?" La Gorda asked triumphantly, waving at his plate.

"Nevertheless, all that still does not prejudice the fact that I am short of two mutton chops," said the secretary, pointing to the vacant space. At which a tall muleteer from Cazorla, with a face as black as an Indian and his clothing the color of dust, broke into a peal of macabre laughter which put an end to Señor Jiménez's objections.

Then about midnight, a terrible yell was heard from Jiménez's room, followed by one heavy bump and a scuffling series of little bumps, and a noise like that of a sack being dragged round the room, accompanied by protesting blasphemies. Señor Jiménez was found upon the gallery floor sprawled upon his face with his nightshirt round his waist, which prompted one of the cooks, none of whom had retired, to say that while Señor Jiménez was the only naked lawyer she had ever seen she nevertheless hoped that the good God would find her a husband of another profession. From subsequent reconstruction it appeared that the secretary had been awakened, first by suspicious noises and then by two violent and simultaneous blows upon his shins. Scared in all his being, he had yet shot upright in bed and, yelling lustily, had lunged forward and clutched hard with both hands and, having got a sound hold of the intruding goat, had been dragged out of bed and finally shaken off in the place of his discovery. By Sunday night, rapidly hardening tradition had already added another peal of macabre laughter from across the quadrangle at the moment when Señor Jiménez had emerged onto the gallery, but in this there was no truth. False, too, was the story that afterwards one of the cooks had offered to share her bed with the lawyer on the grounds that it was not the same as if he were a man. On Sunday, however, the secretary transferred to the Fonda, and so confirmed the numerous variants of his myth for all time.

But far outweighing this, and even the reservoir affair, was the inquiry. There were few public seats at the Court House, but these were filled by councilors and friends of councilors and important persons long before the court was opened, but that was partly because the law was honored with a very small temple at Los Olivares, and that built against the side of San Andrés. Within, a wooden partition in the corner provided the judge and his officials with the little privacy they were afforded; a worm-eaten pulpit-like erection served as judge's seat, and above this on the discolored wall the outline of the crucifix which the Republic had deposed could be seen. The prevailing colors were a purplish and muddy brown and a dull sap green long obscured by dust. Colloquially the Court House was known as the Tomato Store, because of a peculiar spermy smell which hung about it. Nor was there glamour or dignity about the proceedings of the court; only the pettiest of miscreants received sentence in it and the only counsel who had ever distinguished himself there was the Los Olivares lawyer, Don Blasco Ortega, and that in his own interests. Don Blasco, two years before the Republic, had incurred a debt for three hundred pesetas with Señora Pérez, then running a little wine merchant's business. All requests for payment having been futile, Señora Pérez had gone to law, and Don Blasco had immediately begun to resort to every obstructive device a modern and equitable judiciary system provides. First he had lodged an appeal for postponement of the case in order that witnesses to signatures should be produced, and this had naturally been granted. Two months later, when the judge had next been about to visit Los Olivares, Don Blasco had suggested to the only defendant besides himself that if he amended his plea he could be tried with more expedition at the provincial capital. The man had done so, and the judge had written congratulating Los Olivares on having a clean case list and Señora Pérez had perforce to wait another month. Don Blasco's next device was to apologize for the unavoidable nonappearance of his elected witness and ask for an adjournment, which was again granted. Following this he had discovered nine other expedients for delay, the result being that Señora Pérez was still without her money after three years of litigation, during which the Republic, described in its constitution as an equal union of workers of all classes, had been instituted. Another result had been that a small extramural property of Don Blasco's had been destroyed by fire, though the lawyer himself stoutly maintained at the Casino that despite the petrol can among the ruins, this had nothing to do with the Pérez case. The skill he had displayed had certainly brought Don Blasco a little increased business, but it had only enhanced his reputation in limited circles. Among the workers he had always been known by a cloacal nickname, because during a public lecture upon the superiority of modern law to medieval he had laid emphasis on the barbarous crudity of the medieval penal system. The instance he had given had been the punishment prescribed for the theft of a sheep bell in the early thirteenth-century redaction of the Chained Book of Jaca. By that statute the thief was condemned to the alternative of thrusting his hand into the bell as far as it would enter and of having it lopped off at that point, or of publicly eating as much human excrement as the bell would hold. That was, said Don Blasco, an indecency against the very spirit of law.

When Rosich and his secretary emerged from the official cubicle the Court House was full. On the front bench sat Fathers Martínez and Soriano and the two priests of San Salvador; behind them and alone on his bench was the ex-mayor, Señor Ricardo Castro. Don Blasco Ortega, appearing to be enjoying himself intensely, sat in a chair apart. Upon the first witnesses' form sat Justo Robledo, representing the town secretary, who was ill, and the present mayor, while uncomfortably crowded upon the second sat Indalecio Argote, Mudarra, and a half dozen other witnesses. Behind them sat Captain Montaña and a couple of the Civil Guard.

The judge, as gossip ranked him, opened the inquiry by ordering Jiménez to read the terms and conditions under which it was being held.

Then Father Martínez's letter of application to the mayor was read out. In it he pleaded for liberty, as senior priest of Los Olivares upon behalf of Christ's church, saying that it was a manifest injustice that so peaceful and redemptory a ceremony should be prohibited. Next the ex-mayor's letter was read. He had courteously invited Father Martínez to discuss the matter with him at the Town Hall. Both correspondents were asked to acknowledge the authenticity of these letters, the only ones remaining of the correspondence upon the subject, and then Jiménez called for the first witness, who was promptly dismissed by Rosich as having no evidence to contribute. Two more witnesses were rapidly questioned and then the casual mention of Soriano's name awakened Mudarra's interest. The whole business of the inquiry itself had bored and disgusted him; it seemed as if it were being conducted by a State anxious to injure the priest yet timidly desiring to justify itself before the public. Had Castro's letter granting permission been discoverable, no doubt the inquiry would have been a trial. But the mention of Soriano had stirred his hatred of the priest and he found himself obsessed with thoughts of the curate of San Andrés.

"Don Indalecio Argote," called Jiménez, and the mayordomo slowly got upon his feet and took the oath and sat down.

"You may be seated during your evidence," Rosich said acidly. Argote stared back at him and nodded.

"Señor Argote, I understand you to be the mayordomo of Don Fadrique Guevara."

"I am the Marquis's mayordomo and superintendent of his estate."

"You know that the ranks and titles of the former nobility have been abolished by the Republic?"

"Yes, but we don't take any notice of that in Los Olivares."

Rosich's white face became inflamed at once at Argote's deliberate effrontery, his plump hands stiffened and pressed the desk in front of him.

"Señor Argote, let me warn you that insolence of that kind will have serious consequences for you." The mayordomo sat up straight and put his fists upon his thighs and returned the judge's angry gaze. The Court House watched the two men in silence; it was Argote who abandoned that curious struggle; Rosich's voice was hard and firm when next he spoke.

"Get upon your feet and answer me." The mayordomo's knuckles jerked into his thighs, his eyes goggled from his head, and he sat back with a deliberate gesture of refusal. Montaña leaned forward and whispered to him, and at the judge's repetition he stood up sharply and thrust his thumbs into his belt.

"Thank you, señor," said Rosich quietly, "and thank you,

Captain, for assisting me." The eyes of the court were turned upon the captain, but Mudarra, recognizing the real strength of the man behind the power of his office, watched Rosich's flabby face. It disturbingly reawakened his alarm at the turn the inquiry might take, and then almost at once he smiled and collected himself for what might happen.

"So far we have settled that you are Señor Guevara's mayordomo. Do I also understand that you represent your employer in the Good Friday processions, Señor Argote?"

"I took his place last Good Friday."

"Then it is not the rule for you to represent your employer; he must have given you a special command to take his place."

"No . . . yes, he did command me."

"And no doubt he . . . perhaps you will tell us the reasons he gave you for his refusal."

"He didn't give me any."

"But he refused?"

"No."

"Well then, I take it that you yourself advised Don Fadrique not to take part."

"Yes," replied Argote.

Again Rosich considered, and Mudarra saw that he had grasped that Argote normally disposed of the Marquis as he wished.

"Did you accept your place in the procession with any sense of honor, or shall we say pleasure?"

"About as much as I take in being here."

"You may decline to answer the next question, Señor Argote, if you wish. May I ask whether you are a Catholic?"

The mayordomo shrugged his shoulders, and after a pause said, "Yes."

"Your employer is a Catholic, I mean a practicing Catholic?"

"Of course."

"It has been his custom to subscribe towards the Holy Week processions?"

"Yes; he didn't this year."

"So that sending you in his place was a compromise."

"I suppose so."

"Did your employer *at once* tell you to substitute for him?"

The mayordomo was puzzled for a moment and then he seemed to bridle and replied, "No."

"I see, then after you had, as you thought, persuaded Don Fadrique that it was unwise, shall we say, almost criminally foolish to celebrate these processions, and certainly inadvisable for him to take part, his Catholicism, his piety, impelled him to reverse his decision."

"No, no," replied Argote, obviously defending his master.

Rosich paused and wrote something upon paper and then appeared to draw a line through it; some of the audience began to fidget, wondering where the judge was leading, when the next question was put.

"Then you, a powerful adviser, Señor Argote, had dissuaded Don Fadrique from taking part, and afterwards someone over-ruled you. Who was that someone?"

"That you must ask his lordship."

Mudarra grinned, but something in the tone of Argote's voice made him look up; the mayordomo was uneasy.

"His lordship — Señor Guevera, I regret to say, has declined to be present, or rather he has declined to answer any questions whatever. Who was the person who overruled you?"

Mudarra saw the thick lips twitch and then compress, and his mind leaped at once to its conclusion.

"His lordship is sick," Argote muttered.

"Were you overruled, was your advice set aside?"

Argote stared at the judge, who said, "Come now, Señor Argote, with all solemnity I wish to put this question to you. Did Father Martinez overrule you?"

"No." There was a hint of exasperation in Argote's tone.

"Ah," smiled Rosich, motioning to Jiménez. "About that we may have to talk later. Did you wish to ask the witness a question, Señor Ortega?"

"No, no, Señor Judge, thank you." The lawyer rose and bowed in confusion.

"I thought from your movements you wished to cross-examine," said Rosich.

Mudarra's hate for Soriano now had fresh fuel. Clearly it was the curate who had persuaded the marquis at least to appoint a representative. He fell to wondering what had enabled Soriano to establish such an ascendancy over him; perhaps it lay in the character of the two men; between the cold and unhappy mind of the lord of Los Olivares and the strange, tortured personality of the priest with his keen intelligence and mingled courage and cowardice there was, he felt, some subtle affinity. But ascendancy there clearly was; Caro's return to work had proved that he was responsible for the dismissals, and had also shown the man to be weak.

"Very good, Señor Argote, you may sit down. The next witness."

"Señor Ricardo Castro."

"Señor Castro, from the previous inquiries into this affair I understand that you sent to Father Martínez a second letter granting him permission to hold the processions?"

"That is so."

"Why is there no copy of that letter at the Town Hall?"

"May I ask my client a question, Señor Judge?" said Don Blasco Ortega, rising from the counsel's chair and bowing to the judge.

"You may do so."

"Thank you. Don Ricardo, is it the custom for letters to be copied?"

"Notices to that effect have repeatedly been issued to the clerks."

"Ah, I see, but I understand that this letter is in your handwriting."

"Yes, the staff was heavily engaged with work upon the land statistics required by the Government and I wrote the letter myself."

"How did you come to forget that a copy would be necessary?"

"I cannot say, I just forgot to copy it. I am very sorry, it was a serious error."

"Thank you, Señor Judge." Ortega bowed and seated himself, and the ex-mayor's wife and daughter smiled at him with nervous gratitude. It seemed to Mudarra that Rosich was now puzzled and at a loss to proceed; he made several notes and again appeared to draw a line through them.

"What was your impression upon receiving Father Martínez's letter?"

"Señor Judge, I really think that is too difficult, too complex a question for my client to answer at this remove of time."

"Very well, did you at first refuse Father Martínez's request?"

"Yes."

"That would be at his first visit."

"Father Martínez only . . ."

"Señor Ortega, I must ask you to contain yourself. Did Father Martínez visit you more than once, Señor Castro?"

"Once."

"So that afterwards you changed your mind?" Rosich spoke sarcastically.

"Yes," faltered Castro, and Ortega writhed in his seat and then stood up.

"You may question your client."

"Thank you. Was your decision taken in view of the definite feeling that you had that Los Olivares was in a tranquil state, in a *tranquil* state?" Ortega repeated himself nervously and opened his file of papers.

"Yes."

Mudarra was amused at the lawyer's extreme discomfort, for which he could see no reason, and leaning forward to watch him the better, was sharply rebuked by the judge, who then said:

"When you received no reply to your letter to the Civil Governor, why did you not write again?" Both Castro and his counsel were too astonished to reply and gazed at one another with blank expressions. So the letter which Robledo had told Caro about had been written in Castro's name, Mudarra realized, and neither the ex-mayor nor his lawyer had had the slightest idea such a letter existed.

"It is a question of dates, Señor Judge," the bewildered counsel said, struggling to grasp the point. "As my client has had no opportunity of examining the papers since his removal from office I ask for the letter to be shown to me."

"Very good." Jiménez took the letter to Ortega, who bowed both to the secretary and to the judge, and then read through the letter, which trembled in his hand.

"Don Ricardo, after your letter of March 10th addressed to the Civil Governor did you have any opportunity of giving serious thought to Father Martinez's request?"

"I was very busy, the Government's exigencies . . ."

"Precisely, so that as the Governor had not replied by the end of the week, you supposed that he deemed the matter unimportant and within your competence to handle?"

Ortega's wide-opened eyes appealed with anguish to Castro; Soriano was gazing at Ortega with a triumphant expression. Why was he so interested in Castro's defense?

"Yes," replied Castro.

"I hope there is no doubt that my client gave the matter his careful attention and that he gave his assent because of the week's delay upon the part of the Civil Governor, a delay which in point of fact was prolonged beyond the 16th. The Civil Governor did not reply. That delay was interpreted in the manner Don Ricardo has explained."

"Thank you, Señor Ortega." Rosich spoke angrily, though he had not attempted to interrupt the counsel's remarks. The Civil Governor has told the prosecutor to keep him out of it, thought Mudarra. Ortega's quick seizure of the strong argument which the letter to the Governor had provided had excited him greatly, but it was at once forgotten when Rosich called upon Robledo.

"You are at present acting as secretary of Los Olivares, Señor Robledo?"

"I am."

"You were assistant secretary at the time to which this inquiry refers?"

"I was."

"You remember Father Martínez's visit to the Town Hall after the ex-mayor's invitation?"

"It occurred on Wednesday, March the 9th; at about five in the afternoon, the usual hour for such visits."

"The priest made no further visits?"

"None that I observed or know about. I should have been present."

The lawyer jumped to his feet and said eagerly:

"So that it was upon the following day my client wrote to the Civil Governor?"

"Señor Ortega, I have had before to ask you to contain yourself; please do not interrupt proceedings again."

"I am sorry, Señor Judge."

"Do you remember which day Señor Castro wrote to Father Martínez?"

"Señor Judge, I protest — in the absence of the copy . . ."

"Be seated, Señor Ortega," the prosecutor rapped out.

"I do not know," Robledo replied.

"Very good. Did Señor Castro express any doubts to you about the advisability of these processions?"

"Yes. I also expressed my fears."

"Very good. You may sit down. I should like to take this opportunity of stating that the Civil Governor has decided to grant Señor Robledo liberal compensation for the injury he sustained in doing his civic duty. I congratulate you, Señor Robledo. Swear Father Martínez."

"You are honorary chaplain to Señor Guevara?"

"Yes."

"Did you attempt to persuade him to be present at the Good Friday processions?"

"No."

"At your interview with the former mayor did you press him to grant permission?"

Father Martínez hesitated before replying and then he said, "No."

"You did not!"

"No, I had expressed my reason in the letter."

"You visited the mayor once only?"

"Yes, at the time Señor Robledo said he was present."

"When did you receive the letter granting you permission?"

"On March the 16th."

"How are you able to be so certain?"

"I returned from a journey to Puente Nuevo with Dr. Torres at about a quarter to five. A former penitent of mine died there that afternoon. He had been my penitent for thirty years before leaving the town. I found the letter upon the dining-room table when I returned."

"Very good. That will be all I shall need from you just now, Señor Martínez."

At this point Jiménez rose and announced that the inquiry would be adjourned for a quarter of an hour and that witnesses might go outside if they wished, but under surveillance of the guards. The minor witnesses and Mudarra, Argote, Martínez and the two priests of San Salvador at once left the Court House and stood outside in the sun, most of them talking of other things than the evidence. Mudarra's attention, however, was held by the rector's last remark, and then he was suddenly filled with the joy of exultant hate, for it was clearly evident that it was Soriano who had persuaded the ex-mayor, and that for some reason or other Castro did not wish to disclose the fact. With a leap of the imagination he realized that the word "penitent" which Martínez had just used had been occupying his mind, because Soriano was known to be Castro's confessor. That in itself might be some reason for Castro's desire to suppress knowledge of the younger priest's visit, though perhaps, and this was much more credible, it was Soriano who had insisted upon the suppression. Perhaps Soriano was also Ortega's confessor; his subtle intelligence would appeal to the lawyer. But the facts themselves certainly led in the direction of Soriano's guilt. "Guilt," Mudarra exclaimed to himself: well, it might serve to ruin the priest, though the action of the Republic in persecuting Martínez was contemptible, even though he had once made foolish attacks upon the young Republic; even though the Church was the inveterate and ineluctable enemy of liberty and any change in society which might profit the workers. But in Soriano's case, what were the facts? Robledo had said that five o'clock was the usual time for interviews and that he was always present. He had not seen Martínez a second time, nor by implication had he interviewed Soriano, and the letter itself had been delivered by, say, half-past four, at which hour there was certainly no postal delivery in Los Olivares. Upon that afternoon Soriano's superior was out of town and he had no doubt returned with the letter and laid it upon the table and Father Martínez was loyally keeping the young priest out of the case by not mentioning his delivery of the letter or his visit to the mayor. Well, the old boy was like that, of course, and the younger priest was like that, too, but what were his motives? Piety, Mudarra supposed, had made him anxious to have the processions, piety of the kind that makes of everything about the Church, even its pettiest of tinsel ornaments or most macabre speculation, a peculiar fascination for a certain type of devotee. Calasparra's nephew, for instance: he gloated over the least rite, or the latest rosary he had had blessed. He kept a list of indulgences to be gained from day to day, and he wore little red scapularies to work. And about Soriano's piety Los Olivares had no doubt; "He's the very symbol of mortification" was the common phrase about him. Zeal, in the defense of Holy Church, had surely motivated him in the case of the dismissals, in which he had been able to take profit of Don Fadrique's desire to save money.

Zeal for the glory of the Church had surely influenced him in the second case; the glory of dignified associations with the house of Guevara, for it was not only that the Church, the Crown and the landowners were natural allies upon the material plane, but the hierarchy of Prince of the Church, bishop, priest, deacon, acolyte and lay folk was but the doctrinal reflection of a pattern for the hierarchical society, and in opposing equality the Church was defending her more intimate being. She was a pattern, a fixed and rigid pattern, dying because of her rigidity. . . . Soriano, poor devil . . . and then hate thrust out pity. Zeal for the glory of Holy Church in that trumpery drama! Yet he delayed his imagination and for a moment he felt what that drama of the Church might be to such as Soriano. There had been one instant during that Good Friday scene when he had glimpsed the magic of such things, and that was when, just before fleeing, he had seen the abandoned statues standing silent and gaudy in the street. It had for a moment fascinated him, it was magic, a strange enchantment that had taken hold of him, very different from the joyful lust of swinging the iron bar— Ah, perhaps it was the stillness, yes, the stillness. It was the very essence of God, it would be disastrous for a believer if his god moved; at first he would be frightened, yes, if the Sacred Heart in San Salvador got down from its altar and walked about — the Indian before

his immense idols would scream and tear madly from his
temple or immolate himself — but after a while one would become familiar with such a god, one would desire to walk with
him, one would pat him on the back or see him from behind,
and no image was for long venerable from behind, because the
magic lay in the stare of those fixed and hypnotic eyes. Ah! of
course the Church's statues would never become realistic, nor
even be good art in the usual sense of the word; their power
seemed almost to reside in their tawdry splendor and staring
faces. The Holy Child which that old fellow Menudo brought
round to be kissed for his pence—there was something disturbing, appealing in that chubby face and chipped nose, a quality
in the eyes that moved him in a way that a living child did
not move him. It was an illusion not destroyed by the image
being carried about by a beggar who scratched for fleas while
one kissed the image he held out in the crook of his arm and
who got drunk at nine in the morning. The cries and the
bowings, the animosities and fierce excitements, the tears,
the breast-beatings and the fouling with dust, all of this did
not come from belief in the remote and mystical Trinity
but from a close blood-pulsing, heart-stirring magic. When
I was young, he thought, I remember now those tears as Christ
went by with blood streaming from his wounds; were those
tears of pity for the suffering Redeemer? They were the tears
of tremendous excitement, of secret powers within one, of
obeisance before—no, not of obeisance but of one's own
transfiguration. A Church which abolished its images or its
pictures would abolish itself. Soriano came out of the Court
House and stood in the shade regarding the three other priests.
Mudarra watched the pale, almost yellow face with the sunken
eyes and sensitive yet thin-lipped mouth. It seemed that the
priest was one of the kind he loathed and longed to destroy:
the tortuous, tormented and brooding mystic with a laby-
rinthine system of beliefs, suspensions of belief, qualifications,
scruples and learning and ignorance.

Captain Montaña announced that the interval was at an end
and they entered the court again, and waited ten minutes for
Rosich to take his seat.

"Swear Father Soriano," he said, and after formal questions

went on, "I understand that you are also a chaplain to Señor Guevara?"

"I say Mass at the Palacio upon alternate Fridays."

"Is that your only duty?"

Soriano hesitated and then said hurriedly:

"I am not Don Fadrique's confessor."

"I see, but I understand that you are at the palace more often than once a fortnight."

"I do sometimes visit the Palacio."

"You need not answer this question if you so desire. Did Father Martínez to your knowledge attempt to persuade Don Fadrique to take part in the procession?"

"No. Not to my knowledge."

"Thank you. Now have you any recollection of the date upon which the former mayor's letter was delivered to Father Martínez? Take a moment to consider that."

It was some time before Soriano's reply was given and then he said almost inaudibly, "Father Martínez's account is the correct one."

It was, Mudarra saw, an evasive answer; what was he trying to hide?

"You are sure. Father Martínez was away; did you receive the letter?"

"No . . ." and then he repeated more loudly in a lightened tone, "No."

Laughter pressed up within Mudarra, for the implication of Soriano's replies had suddenly struck him.

"Did Father Martínez discuss the letter with you?"

"Yes."

"Did he express approval? Perhaps more than approval?"

"I decline to answer that question. It is improper."

"Very good, my dear sir, you need not answer the next two questions if they offend your conscience. Father Martínez is Don Fadrique's father confessor, is he not?"

"No, señor," Soriano replied in a conciliatory tone.

"Then who is?"

"A doctor of the cathedral chapter," Soriano replied nervously after turning an appealing gaze to Martínez and the other clergy.

"Thank you, you need give no further details." Rosich pursed his lips and slowly drew a line through something written on the paper before him, while Jiménez stared at the curate.

The rector of San Salvador was sworn and then the prosecutor asked:

"When did Father Martínez inform you that he had received permission?"

"He did not; Father Soriano told me on the Friday of that week."

"The Friday?"

"Yes, señor, he delivered the Lenten sermons at San Salvador every Friday evening."

"Thank you."

"Swear Mudarra."

"I decline to be sworn."

"You decline? Your reasons?" Jiménez passed up a piece of paper and Rosich said, "Your Anarchism prevents you swearing? Very good; I warn you that if you answer, your replies will nonetheless be considered to be given under oath. You were formerly at the Palacio with some frequency, Señor Mudarra?"

"Once or twice a week, upon Wednesday and Friday afternoons."

"Have you any reason to suppose that Father Martínez has ever exercised great influence over Don Fadrique?"

"Not Father Martínez."

"Not Father Martínez; who then?"

"Father Soriano."

There was a murmur in the Court Room, which the judge suppressed with a lift of his head. A slow-witted worker said, "That's right," to Mudarra's charge after the suppression, and was promptly ejected.

"How do you know this?"

"I do not *know* it, but I am convinced of it. Just as I am convinced you are trying to blame Father Martínez for what his enemies did."

"Indeed?" Rosich replied sarcastically. "Is there anything else you are convinced of?"

"Yes, that Señor Soriano visited Señor Castro at the Town

Hall, obtained from him a letter and delivered it to the rectory."

"And why, may I ask, are you convinced of this?"

"Because between four and half-past four, as far as I can remember, on the afternoon of May the 16th, I saw Father Soriano leave the Town Hall with a letter. I passed him and, being of an inquisitive nature"—Mudarra grinned as he uttered the lie—"I glanced at the letter and saw that the envelope was addressed in Señor Castro's hand; at least, when I looked at an announcement on the notice board it seemed the same hand."

"Very good; remain standing."

"Father Soriano, you have heard the witness's statement; did you visit Señor Castro on the afternoon of May the 16th?"

As Soriano rose he turned towards Mudarra as if to challenge him, his face became paler than ever and he trembled visibly; it was long before he could murmur a reply and then it was, "No."

There was a profound silence in the courtroom. Captain Montaña was heard to whisper, "Christ!"

"Very good; sit down," said Rosich.

"Father Martínez, did Father Soriano deliver a letter from Señor Castro?"

Martínez's face slowly flushed as he stared at the curate, an expression of anger appeared in his eyes and then he answered, "No . . . I mean, I was away."

It was difficult for the old priest to perjure himself, Mudarra saw. It was not merely that the guitarist's hatred of Soriano gave him leave to pity Martínez. He did so naturally, and in smiling warmly at the old man, confused and embarrassed him the more.

Rosich gazed from one priest to the other and made a note and then drew a line though it and commenced to write again. For over a minute he left the three witnesses standing while he wrote. It seemed to Mudarra that Rosich was deliberately trying to break the nerve of the two priests. He ceased writing and regarded first Mudarra and then the younger priest.

"It is a great misfortune that the letter is missing," the judge commented, looking in the direction of Soriano.

The cold tones made no accusation, but Mudarra had a sense that Rosich believed that Soriano had obtained the letter; and more, it seemed that he suspected the priest of having ensured that the letter should now be missing. Ortega was biting his lips.

"Señor Argote, you need not trouble yourself to stand; the witness Mudarra is employed on the estate of Don Fadrique, isn't he?"

Mudarra grinned; he had thought of that before committing his perjury.

"Yes."

"Do you remember whether he was working on the afternoon of the 16th?"

"I don't know without the book; he comes when he likes and it would also depend on the day."

"The 16th was what day, Señor Jiménez?"

"Good Friday was the 25th," murmured Jiménez, and then counting quietly said, "A Wednesday, señor."

'On a Wednesday the witness would have left the Palacio early, after playing to the Marquis, and the same on Friday."

The readiness and the malice in the mayordomo's voice amused Mudarra, and it confirmed his belief that Soriano had been interfering with the administration of the estate.

"Thank you, that is all, Señor Argote, and thank you all, gentlemen. I am sorry to say that the evidence is rapidly becoming unreliable. Someone, I fear, is committing perjury."

Again he engaged himself with writing, leaving the three witnesses standing, Father Martínez, his shoulders bowed, Soriano, distracted and ill, and Mudarra, watching Argote's expressive face as he regarded the curate. The midday Angelus rang from San Andrés and the four priests crossed themselves, Soriano first, then the clergy of San Salvador and finally and slowly Father Martínez. A minute later the judge announced that the present inquiry was at an end, but that no witness must leave town without giving information of his address to the secretary at the Town Hall. As they filed out into the plaza, the children playing upon the steps of the church came over and silently watched them move away.

16

Hailstorm

SOME time after the inquiry into Father Martínez's conduct, Justo Robledo was invited by a group of workers, among them Caro, to lead a discussion on the situation in Los Olivares. To the dismay of many, Robledo arrived at the Rincón, not drunk, but certainly not sober. The discussion which followed was nonetheless dominated by the acting secretary. The failure of the dynamiting attempt had been the passing over without breaking of a wave of revolt which had been slowly approaching throughout April, May and June. In a sense, Robledo declared, it predated even the March iconoclasm, for as that affair had resulted in neither the formally necessary prosecutions nor the vastly more important and psychologically necessary persecutions, it had been counted a victory by the Anarchists and their followers. The impetus of the preceding months had been carried over almost undiminished. The drought and the unemployment had merely given it another direction, and this, he said, had been reinforced by a habitual shifting of attention. For the Spanish workers had always fought upon a revolving base, aiming their blows first at Rent and then at its instrument, the State, or its moralist, the Church, as if exhausted by the concepts and passions involved, or deceived by the hope that the other enemy would be easier of defeat. The summer heat, too, making labor and its discipline more severe, encouraged dreams of fewer hours and these dreams were often more embittering than hunger itself. And always there was the inflaming drama of harvest ahead when the crops were gathered for another, or were paid away in rent to the moneylenders.

Perhaps it was for this reason, Robledo said, that church burnings and image destruction usually occurred in the spring. And then, pushing aside his glass and tossing his cigar away, he began a wild and passionate speech that most of his hearers could not follow.

"It's not only that man is restless after a period of thinking about bread and rent and the brats coming along after the winter's play, but that in the spring man's impulses are at their strongest and also at their most religious phase."

"What religion is there in me?" questioned Mudarra.

"Ca! you'll full of it—your Anarchism is a sort of Christianity without God."

"What has the Catholicism of the people to do with God? It's older than that."

"But what I mean is that the Church puts over this drama, and a fine drama it is, of agony and death, and draws all the guts of man tight—I mean, all the nerves and cords of your inner being."

"Yes, I get you."

"Oh, shut your mouth—and that fixes the attention of people upon her and in a dangerous way, too. For there's an inner logic which the Church, nowadays blind and uncreative, no more understands than Father Martínez. The sufferings of Christ in the wilderness are a symbol of the hunger of winter and the unrest of brooding days. And though the symbols are remote from the first realities nowadays and the externals of belief are thrown off, down in here," said Robledo, hammering his body, "there's an older rhythm that goes on. Easter is the spring festivity, of fertility, of seed that germinates and spunk that comes to life and blinks at the sun—and men feel a new hunger. And here is this Church taking hold of all this rhythm and saying it belongs to Jesus Christ—and down in his heart man knows it's a lie. It belongs to his labor and to his fields and to the womb of his woman, it's something that's the salts of his blood—and he rebels against the lie and then churches smoke in the sun. God, I dream sometimes of what the Church might have been had she been true to Man instead

of to God. Can you imagine a Human Easter, a town like this
with its walls covered with the cloths and banners of every
house—I'd hang the cradle out as a song of joy—and the
bells tumbling over and over and the town shaking with their
noise, and then the singing as the people poured out of San
Andrés Gate, dressed in red and white for the blood throbbing
in your loins and the whiteness of bread. And the priests, the
old man, in gold and scarlet and silver and black, and the
incense smoking up and the music getting right down into you
and sending fire up and down your spine—do you get that?—
no, God blast you, you don't—and then the chosen field and
the oxen yoked and the naked men at their heads and the
women stripped to guide the plow—and the sun upon their
breasts and their bellies and their legs white like bread, and
then the shout as the earth turns over red like blood from the
share and the priests throw in the ritual seed—ah, what does
God have to do with all this—is it not beautiful enough?
Would it not stir music, and would not the plow and the field,
the ox and the olive, the sound-limbed maddening body of
woman and the sweating heavy-swung body of man, and the
sun, its light and the blessing of water and storms and lightning tearing up the sky, stir your poets and your painters . . .
and it's all gone into the sufferings of a Jew in a stinking
village—ah, Jesus, robber of mankind . . ." Caro and Baeza
took hold of Robledo and compelled him to be seated.

"You'll have the whole place over here, man."

"See here, you wonder why I drink? When I am sober I
think what ought to be done with life, but when I drink I can
see pictures and I hear music and I make dreams for myself—
and I half remember them, God, *that's* what's killing me, I see
their shadows and hear their echoes when I am sober, and I
look round and I see this place—and all your Church is some
sniveling priest and all your revolution is some yelling blas-
phemer and all your fertility magic is a moneylending ape
counting debts—isn't that hell enough to see? Don't you see?
There was a time when a man scratched bulls in a cave and
men rejoiced and danced and took hold of their women because of it—and there was a time not so long ago when a painter
painted even a Christ and the people streamed through the

streets shouting Hosannas for joy of it . . . Giotto in Italy . . . and it happened here in Sevilla, too . . . and it's all gone, all gone." Robledo was silent awhile, and then he poured out aguardiente into a tumbler and no one tried to stop him as he drank. "The gates of hell shall not prevail against the Church," he said, "because she has swallowed them up and built them into herself—when she took those two poisons, a philosophy which made man's soul something other than his body, and when she took over an empire and a power instead of building a new one, like a blasted Reformist. The only angelical doctor who might have saved the Church was born too late. *Ora pro nobis* San Carlos Marx, and God have mercy on the Holy Liberal Church in the day of his judgment."

"And the Black House?" There was no taunt in the question.

"The brothel is death, there ought to be a crucifix over every brothel door—I feel that. We Spaniards are mystics of the body, I suppose; we make our dying Christs more horrible than a man upon the Church's rack—and we've tried to make a mysticism of lust, too. It's the nearest I can get to immolation, I suppose, though I'm talking nonsense . . . but the brothel is death, death." He lowered his head upon his arms and grew incoherent and later four of them took him to Mendizabal Street. For a while the conversation at the Rincón, led by Mudarra, turned upon the question of whether such a ritual as Robledo had described could adapt itself to tractors and machine cultivators, and then Acorín entered with a guitar and it was at an end.

Only a slight lowering of tension resulted from the failure to blow up the dam, and that because one of the principal figures of the F.A.I. had defected in a moment of action. That defection and failure only caused the urge of revolt to grow sour and bitter, it did not depress it. The inquiry into Father Martínez's conduct merely raised the level of public excitement; it satisfied many in Los Olivares, but as it promised no real attack upon the Church the extreme left had no interest in it. And its absurdity was therefore all the more evident. All these events, and one which began upon the following day, were only the circumstances of an insurgent period.

About three in the afternoon small arrow-shaped clouds

appeared behind the hills across the Jabalón, traveling at a low altitude and at great speed. Behind them came an army of small clouds, at first thin and silvery and then without any slackening of speed, packing together and shutting out the sun so that dusk came an hour earlier. All night the clouds noiselessly slid over the town, for though they were low no wind moved at the level of the earth. Argote would not go to bed that night and at last, cursing the choking heat, he went out of the Palacio and mounted to the middle slopes of Broad Skirt. The air was lifeless and hot so that it barely fed the heaving lungs and his heart hammered irregularly. The olive trees stood utterly still in the darkness which barely allowed them to be seen, even less when he stooped to outline their branches against the sky than when he searched for their trunks. Not the least whispering of sound came from the trees themselves, though above on the blunt aretes and crumpled planes of the sierra he heard the whining and hissing of a gale, and the occasional echoing thud of gusts that swerved and battered against the hills. Without warning he tripped and fell into a mass of olive foliage which lay across the path. Rapidly feeling along the bark he had judged it to be a zorzaleño before he decided to fetch a lantern from one of the nearby tool sheds. It was not only one zorzaleño but three, and all the ground around was strewn with torn branches which gradually drew together and occupied a corridor across four terraces and then stopped abruptly. "*Ráfaga*," muttered the mayordomo, listening to the slamming and banging on the sierra. A terrific gust; no doubt there would be more shattered trees upon the terraces. His clothes soaked in sweat, he rapidly climbed to the very limits of Broad Skirt, and there the air was hotter than at the Palacio and moving slowly but irregularly towards the coast. The olives were rustling quietly, but with that appearance of stillness which they always have. In the yellow light of the lantern they seemed to stand like warriors of an ancient and noble tradition, samurai, impassively awaiting a peril from out of the hot blackness.

Out of the uppermost terraces a narrow path zigzagged up the bare slopes and into a gully by which it ascended to a saddle upon a ridge where in the spring of the previous year

Argote had made a field, meaning to plant *estacas* of wild olive, into which later he would graft some hardy species. The field had been a favorite with him, partly because from its sharply cut edge he could gaze over all the olivars upon that side of the Palacio as far as Little Skirt, and he had had a small tool house built upon it, though tools would rarely be kept there. He decided to climb to the new field to see if the wind was stronger there, and pressing his way through the bushes he walked across the bank of slat-shaped stones to the path. While he was still in the gully he heard the *ráfaga* approaching, roaring down the gully above him, like an avalanche of stones. It struck him before he was ready, pressing upon his chest and forcing the breath out of him and he flung himself to his knees and covered his head and face with his arms. It was as if an enormous fist reached out of the sky wielding a solid beam of rushing air, cudgeling from side to side of the gully down which swept torn-up bushes and a dense cloud of dust that choked all the more for being invisible. The blows became more violent and at the moment of their utmost violence ceased altogether and Argote pitched forward into a steadily declining stream of air. A few seconds later and only a gentle stirring upon the stripped gully walls was to be heard. The mayordomo rolled over onto his haunches and, sitting up, spat the dust from his lips and shouted a stream of blasphemous oaths against the *ráfaga*. Suddenly he stopped and listened; below he could hear the muffled cracking of boughs and the roar of the gust. A moment later a shrill whining passed far overhead.

When dawn broke he and Calasparra made an inspection of the estate. The net of foliage spread over the hills had been ripped through in six places, twenty-one trees had been uprooted and about sixty had had one or more mother branches torn out of the fork. Returning to the Palacio they encountered Soriano leaving the Chapel of the Olive, his eyes shining with the light of ecstasy. To Calasparra's amazement Argote wheeled about and savagely cursed the priest, who hurried out of the yard without protest at the mayordomo's obscenities.

Hourly the clouds grew denser and became slower and lower, and so for the rest of the day and the night they ballooned about the hills, monstrous indigo domes tinged with yellow and green-gray that at last became the color of weed smoke. Sometimes their edges seemed to slip and black wisps fell down as fronds of bluish-white horses charged up their crests, yet always they sank lower and became more sulphurous and the air more suffocating. At midday a deputation of Villa Alta cultivators called upon Father Martínez and asked for prayers against the storm. The rector nodded and muttered something to himself and went into the church. The major bell began to boom and soon the bell of San Salvador and the smaller bells of Nuestra Señora del Carmén and Mater Purissima were beating steadily. A few black-dressed women hurried to the gate of the Carmén and shrilly scolded the caretaker, who had run out without her key; then falling upon their knees they commenced to pray. Out upon the terraces near the grove an old worker heard them and scrambled frantically over the walls and set the bell in motion. Down at the bridge over the nearly empty Jabalón the bell of San Antonio's chapel shortly answered. Father Soriano went up to the San Andrés tower roof and read the ancient office for the conjuration of lightning and flood, which he prayed might fall upon the deathly hills across the valley. Meanwhile the rector panted up the track to Mater Purissima and conversed in a low voice with Calasparra about the trees. Here and there upon the fields, seeing the cassocked figure, a worker paused a moment and muttered a prayer. Then the smaller bells ceased to sound though until half-past two the great bell of San Andrés continued to boom. Above the town and its bay of hills the clouds slowly pitched over, their electrically charged nodules of vapor growing larger as they sank till they reached the limiting half-inch of diameter which the laws of their matter imposed. As each drop broke apart into smaller drops the snapping of their straining skins of surface tension increased their charge, and though they became minute vapor the cloud became more evil and menacing to the little green-brown and gray-green patches below. Then a solid mass of air slowly shoveled under the clouds and they lifted a few hundred feet and the hordes of charged drops commenced to sink again, running together like a people filled with the bitterness of revolt, and again were dispersed by rigid laws which only increased their charge. And now, at a quarter-past two by the time of the mites below on the patched and hutted earth, the fresh wind that came stealing over the valley floor prised up the towering mass of vapor into the colder air and the movement of drops became more violent moment by moment.

And then the enormous macabre machine of the storm began a fresh acceleration, for the heavily charged molecules were attracted to their neighbors more quickly and held together longer. Then as an icy wind struck through from above, the machine awoke and became a god; the yellow-green body of the sky shook, staggered, and with cataclysmic roar three blazing shafts shot down to the earth and stabbed into the net of trees. And after them raced the harsh whining hail, a column of wounding flails—the hate of heaven, stabbing and lashing, rod after rod flashing hate—stabbing and flashing— flashing. The hills dipped beneath the rolling crashes of thunder. Soriano on the tower top saw the black and spinning horde of hail swooping down upon him and he ran for the trap door and closed it as it struck the tower; a few stones tapped their way down the steps. He shivered. At the Palace, Argote stood long in the open, shielding his eyes until the pain of the hissing stones became unbearable, then, speechless, he went indoors and ascended to the arched upper floor. Los Olivares was invisible behind the hail, which, at first a single column, had now spread out over the hills, covering them with a white cape two inches deep, then three, then four. Argote said nothing, but gazed at the storm, now stationary over Los Olivares. At twenty to three the hail ceased and rain followed, its drops as large as grapes and a cold light in them; the hail upon the ground became a compact mass which endured for twenty minutes and then slowly melted. By three o'clock the lower slopes were glowing brown-red, though here and there a heap of hailstones lay against a wall or in the fork of a tree. Upon the unscourged hills across the valley a few patches of sunlight were smoldering.

That afternoon the mayordomo rode silently about the olivars, the truculence and the cheer drained out of him at the disaster. Half the verdial and all the gordal fruit were bruised beyond profit. These were the olives which, "killed" with salt, or sweetened by passing through many changes of water, were finally bottled and kegged for export or sale to northern towns. Grown for the table of discerning eaters, they could never hope for more than local sale, that principal insurance of the cultivator, even supposing they ripened without rotting. True, the mayordomo had as usual insured the crop against hail, but this year for far less than the damage inflicted, since Don Fadrique had insisted upon economies. Even had it covered the loss Argote would not have been comforted. It was not only the lacerated fruit and those now reddening upon the ground which grieved him, nor yet the three struck by lightning, but the plight of all the trees. The tender bark of the younger trunks had been gashed and torn by the storm and that, he knew, meant that the upper and tenderer wood of all the trees would be in an equal state. The sap might crystallize and heal the wound, but still the gash would give access to hordes of noxious insects which would infect the trees and lay their eggs in them. The winter pruning would have to be very severe. Next year might conceivably bring a plague of blight and disease; in any case the trees would be sickened and feeble, many would give no fruit the following year. At last, observing the fallen riches of the dulzar olives, Argote jumped off his horse and listened to the laments of the worker who had hailed him, the oaths seething to the mouth. The laborer also cursed, blaspheming against the Great "Virgin Puta" until, remembering his own four trees, he was silent and the tears came.

"God's testicles, you're a bloody woman," the mayordomo muttered, openly blaspheming, and, climbing into the saddle, drummed away to the far edge of the plantation known by the curious name of the Skirt of Beyond. There he was embittered by a contrary phenomenon; the storm appeared to have possessed a clearly defined edge, beyond which only rain had fallen, so that trees but half a chain from ruined trees were entirely untouched. These would profit by the rain and would now bear a good crop, but at the thought the mayordomo was filled with anger; he did not know why.

In the Huerta every crop had been ruined save those towards the dead lands; there would be no good wine and little wine at

all in Los Olivares that year; the almonds were beaten from
the trees. Only the figs, too advanced to be damaged, were untouched, and some of the grain. The mayor at once telegraphed
to Madrid and begged for assistance; this winter the Government would have to undertake works such as the widening of
the road, along which half a dozen vehicles a day passed, in
order to succor those ruined by the storm. On the other hand,
this drawing tight of the nerves was balanced by a reaction on
the olivars. The mayordomo openly insulted Soriano before a
group of olive workers and would have flung him out of the
Palacio yard had not three of the men grappled with him; that
evening Argote's voice was heard shouting in Don Fadrique's
music room, and though he emerged downcast and sheepish,
there was a great change on the olive fields next day. From
daybreak the mayordomo went round the houses of dismissed
workers, ordering them up to Mater Purissima at once, to dress
and disinfect the trees. During the days which followed he was
seen everywhere about the estate, riding hard, cursing and
encouraging the workers, extravagant with praise and letting
nothing slip by. The trees neglected all the summer once more
disclosed to the knowing eye that love and skill were caring for
them. And then the mayordomo himself unwittingly set the
tide of revolt in motion again. Seeing a worker stand talking to
Soriano for a quarter of an hour, he waited until the priest had
gone and then strode over and savagely dismissed the man.
Revenge gave him a taste for revenge and there followed a
fortnight's sacking, less severe than that of June, but just as
selective. A partisan of Soriano needed to be a very good
craftsman to be retained, and Argote received correct information, given him by anticlerical workers and by the old
machinery of the political boss, still standing intact beneath
the Republican heaps of paper.

On the Saturday afternoon after the storm Caro called at
Robledo's house and was at once cordially admitted by
Celestina, who ran upstairs to fetch her husband. Robledo's
manner had changed considerably; he spoke courteously and
briskly and did not question why Caro had called upon them.

"Come on in to my little office," he said. "No, let's stay here.

Celestina, bring out my cigars will you, the *brevas*. How are
your trees and the crops?"

"The crops are not too bad, we've chiefly planted potatoes
and the barley has stood it pretty well. The trees are bad, of
course, but we shall get some sort of a crop."

"Christ, it's good to hear someone talk cheerfully; this week's
been hell at the office. The tenants have just smothered us with
requests for aid, telegraph this, telegraph that, telegraph any
damn thing, we exhort and we appeal, we trust and we implore; telegrams to the deputy to Cortes, telegrams to the Civil
Governor, to the Minister, to the President, to every damned
person they think of up at the Casino. That's what the State
is for . . . but you'll have had enough of my ideas, I expect."

"No, that's chiefly what I came about."

"Yes?"

"I want some books and I may as well tell you that I've left
the F.A.I."

Robledo made no comment for a moment and then he
jumped from his seat and began to pull book after book from
his shelves, explaining their contents; finally he brought a few
to the table and pushed them over to Caro.

"When you've done with those, you can help yourself, man,
call any time. Celestina will let you in. But tell me, why have
you left the F.A.I.?"

"Well, I can see it's no good; of course, you can't make a
revolution the way we've set about it, you want a party and
a State, or at least a Workers' Government. I've got that far
anyway. I've been thinking over things that have happened
here." Robledo did not speak and so Caro went on.

"I was in that attempt on the dam."

"Well, you've covered yourself up pretty nicely—someone
else is getting the blame. You know, 'Acting upon information received, the Civil Guard . . .'"

"Well, I've told you I was in it; who *is* getting the blame?"

"They're watching the electrician Villado and a friend of
his. Is that right?"

"No, you know who was with me."

"Yes? . . . Well, the informant's getting his fifty pesetas

cheaply then. I shouldn't be surprised if he didn't spot the dynamite being brought in, and seeing that length of fuse imagined it to be wire."

"Very likely; anyhow, I've done with that kind of thing."

"Any good asking you what happened? You blew a bloody good hole in the gully."

"I just couldn't do it, that's all."

"But what about . . ."

"He couldn't either, he wanted to, but somehow . . ." Caro could not explain it to himself; his companion had wrestled with him for the percussion cap, but there had been no life in his efforts and he constantly carried about with him the impression that Mudarra had not possessed much determination after he had backed out.

Robledo nodded and said, "Yes, I see."

Steps were heard descending the stairs and the secretary went hurriedly to their foot and looked up; then, gazing anxiously at Caro, he lifted his hands nervously. Caro stood up and the steps stopped on the stairs.

"Come on down, *chica*," Robledo murmured at last. Lucía descended and, averting her face, hurried through to the high-walled square of garden beyond the house. For a while her brother toyed with the books on the table, and then, taking one from the pile, turned over its leaves and gloomily replaced it. Again he took the book and glanced at one or two pages, and finally tossed it on the pile before the bookshelf.

"I don't think that one is quite so good as the others," he said, taking another from those on the table.

"You know best," Caro managed to say and with a sigh Robledo tossed the book he was examining back on the table. "Well, I expect you'll be wanting to go, Caro; I was forgetting you're usually busy."

"Oh . . . no . . . which of these ought I to read first, I mean . . . which . . ."

"This is a general introduction to Marxism." Robledo dropped the book and Caro, retrieving it, opened its pages and turned them.

"Caro, what . . ." Robledo burst out and looked appealingly

at him. The olive worker rose and glanced at the door.

"I've talked to her, man, I've dragged it out of her, she wouldn't speak to me at first but Celestina told me some of it and I let her see I knew." Robledo approached Caro and spoke vehemently. "I've dragged it out of her, she's better now and she can stand it, but there's something I can't get at, night after night she's been trying to tell me. I know—I've spent hours with her . . . Ah, God in heaven bless her . . . my sister . . . God in heaven bless her."

"What is it?"

"Caro . . . One day she saw Mudarra crossing the square and I felt her arm drag on mine—she was tired and Celestina and I were helping her home, yet the next day she saw you."

"I've not seen her."

"No . . . Celestina took her for a walk . . . a way down the Huerta path, but she was ill and had to come back. My wife says it was you they saw. You were doing something among the olive trees, so it wouldn't have been Marcial or your father."

It seemed to Caro that Robledo was striving to convince him that it had been he who had been working at the grove; his voice was urgent and he made thrusting gestures with his hands.

"Have you seen Mudarra, Justo?"

"No." There was no bitterness in the reply. "She has told me how it happened."

"Yes."

There was nothing else to be said and, without permitting Celestina to wrap them as she desired, Caro took the books and prepared to leave the house. As he turned away he was moved by a sudden impulse to say:

"Perhaps we could meet and talk about these?"

"I'd be glad to indeed."

"Tomorrow?"

"Yes, tomorrow; what time?"

"Early? I'd like it to be early, say ten in the morning, will that do?"

"Yes, yes, I'd like that best of all."

"Right then." They shook hands again and when Joaquín was halfway along Mendizabal Street Robledo shouted that they had not fixed the place.

"Oh, come on down to our place, will you? You might like to look at the fields."

"Yes, I'd like to do that." Robledo entered and, hearing the sound of the well pulley, he dismissed the image of a plow which had been haunting his thoughts since Caro had suggested they should meet, and joined the two women in the garden.

"Two more buckets," Celestina said, and he took the bucket from her and poured the water into the earthenware bowls in which they were washing linen.

"How long will this job take you, all night?" Robledo said.

"Yes, there'll be no supper this evening."

"Well then, supposing we all go out for a stroll; there's a nice breeze blowing." He knew by his wife's hesitation that there had been other plans, yet she accepted eagerly.

"No, better than that," he said. "There's a little concert at the Town Hall after dinner; I can get the mayor's seats right up at the front."

Celestina nodded, and after glancing at the girl by her side nodded again.

"It won't be much of a show, of course, woman, not like that one we went to in Sevilla."

The wife looked up in astonishment and then nodded again and commenced to pound the linen.

At seven the two women dressed to go out, and hearing the knife-grinder's wheel whirring in the street as they departed, she told Justo to have the bread knife sharpened. All the way to the church Lucía conversed quietly with Celestina, from whom she separated as they entered, the wife going to the chapel of San Antonio where Father Soriano's confessional box was situated and Lucía's to a seat below the pulpit, near which the rector heard confessions.

The comfortable anticipation of the priest's absolution had given her some peace all day, and after the first shock it had even vanquished the sorrow which seeing Caro had caused. Now they knelt facing the high altar, about which the sacristan was moving, perfunctorily bobbing as he passed in front of the tabernacle. The little serving boy who had been hurrying about the sanctuary disappeared and she heard the clink of brass vessels and the dragging of a form and then a tall wobbling candle appeared behind the altar and was lifted into place behind the tabernacle, and after it another. The form on which the boy had stood fell over with a crash and one of the women in the crowd before Father Soriano's box screamed. There were only a few old peasant and worker men and women around her, and she saw that soon her turn would arrive, so she opened her manual and began her preparatory exercises. She had no fear of the confessional; that had disappeared when she had gone giddy with fear and sickness into the rector's box after the pilgrimage. He had given her the penance of three Hail Marys and a Paternoster for her sin. "Ay de mi," she read from the book she had received before her first communion. "What have I done? I have offended a God who has created me . . . who has redeemed me and is loading me with good things. How great is my ingratitude, to behave so against all reason, what recklessness! to sin with so much knowledge of the truth, what evil for a vile pleasure or interest to lose my peace of soul and convert myself into a denizen of hell, what madness! And is there no remedy for me? . . . Shall I not confess? Yes, of course I am going to confess. . . ."

There were now only two penitents between her and the confessional box and Lucía began to look through the Laments of Hell to see which she might read. There was the lament of the blasphemous Sennacherib and of the rancorous Cain, and the laments of the glutton and the lustful man and of the thief and the sacrilegious Judas. Once these cries of hell had seemed terrible to her and she had been unable to keep her eyes upon the Judgment painted over the sanctuary arch. Father Martínez had pointed out the burning sinners to her each by his vice; there was Lust with a face upon his belly, and beside him, thrust back into hell by a devil with a fork, was thin writhing Envy. . . . It was her turn to enter.

"In the name of the Father, the Son and the Holy Ghost," she began humbly.

"Is that all, my daughter?" Father Martínez was saying when she had finished.

"Yes, Father."

"Are you sure you have not consented to sin in others?"

She had not the least idea of whom the rector might be thinking, but she replied, "No, Father."

"And you haven't read any forbidden books, books against the Church, or the truth she teaches, or her ministers, or newspapers of that kind?"

"No, Father."

"You are sure, no Republican newspapers or other improper papers?"

"No, Father."

"You must beware of the temptation of forbidden reading, my daughter."

"Father, I wish to accuse myself of another sin."

"That is good, my child, you must always pray for strength to search your conscience."

"I accuse myself that I have read a novel, a part of one."

"Bless my soul! That's not a very terrible sin."

"But Sister . . . a nun told me it was a sin to read novels."

"What kind of a novel was it, my child?"

"In a magazine Celestina buys, it's a pattern magazine, she makes clothes," Lucía hastened to say. Father Martínez's quiet laugh could be heard by the kneeling penitents outside, one of whom crossed herself and frowned as she stared at the serving boy who was quietly whistling to himself.

"I shall have to talk to that nun," the rector said with mock severity. "We won't call that a sin, there are too many in the world already. Now bow your head, my daughter, and for your penance you may say three Hail Marys and a Paternoster and I shall give you a special blessing." Eagerly she listened to the priest, and though he spoke very rapidly and ran all his words together she thought she heard *"I absolve thee,"* and at once she was at peace, a deep cool peace that ran through every vein and into every part of her body, a peace like spring water upon hot weary hands and which endured long as she knelt before the Sacrament, repeating her Hail Marys and her Paternoster again and again. Everything in the church was kindly and beautiful; even the little weathervane which she heard creaking in the wind above the sanctuary creaked comfortingly. And then, as an old woman slowly led her young married daughter upon her arm to the confessional box, a knifelike grief and a shaking terror ran through her and she cowered down, and all she heard was the knife-grinder's wheel filling every vault and corner of the echoing church with its long, tortured and ululating wail.

17

Of Liturgy

"Those prayers of yours didn't do much good, Father," one of the workers called, as the rector of San Andrés shambled by Mater Purissima.

"Hombre, no, nor anything you could do," he replied with mild exasperation. "But you've got to take such things as mysteries of God's will."

"That's right, Father."

"Besides, haven't you ever heard the saying, 'If it rained only when it pleased everyone we should die of thirst'?"

"And when was hail good for anybody or anything?"

"Once it fell on a plague of locusts," Mudarra said, "but they were dying of hunger and drowning in the middle of the sea."

Father Martínez shook his head at the laughter and walked off by a side path.

"It was God who drowned the locusts," a worker laughed.

"Poor old bastard, he looks about twice as old as he did."

"He likes to hang about here."

"It's the trees," Mudarra added. "He likes to say his bloody prayers up here, and now he doesn't say Mass any longer at the Palacio, he comes up more than ever."

"I'd rather have him than the other bastard, anyway."

The hailstorm had had severer consequences than Indalecio Argote or any of them had first thought, and for days the talk of Mater Purissima had been solely of the trees. It had been expected that the soft-wooded trees such as the zorzaleños and the manzanillos would be damaged but not to the extent they had been. By the end of the week the wounds had begun to show signs of spore diseases, and tuberculosis was feared; the leaves also began to fall.

"Well, it's a good thing it's the manzanillos," a worker said. "Yes."

He was understood to mean that the manzanillo, which suffers extremely from excessive heat or drought, had already lost the greater part of its burden. With the added castigation of the hail there would be none of its brilliant, purple-black, apple-shaped fruit to gather.

"That's right, but next year!" exclaimed another, and all of them ceased to think of the symmetrical little manzanillos, good alike for oil or table, and commenced to imagine the trees as they would be in the following March. This year's shoots had been largely destroyed or would die off very soon, and this meant that the following year the trees would be barren, for it is two-year-old wood which bears in the olive.

Besides the trees the cessation of the serenos also was discussed. "The nights don't seem the same nowadays," was the general opinion, though nobody cared much about the matter. More exciting was the decision of the Government to build a school as part of the relief works. In Los Olivares the only schools had been the small municipal school with one master aided by the clergy, the smaller school of the Hermanas Terciarias, the Carmelite Sisters, and a private college for the children of Villa Alta. There was also a dress-cutting school run by the Sisters, much criticized by its pupils because the nuns refused to deal with any dress which did not satisfy Papal requirements in the matter of sleeve length. There was another criticism; Escolástica herself had been persuaded to enter the order by the directresses of this school, and four years ago an abandoned *novio* had created a violent scene in the hall of the convent. Although allowed to speak with the young man from behind a door, the girl had elected for the convent. Nevertheless, the man's arrest and six months' sentence had not diminished the attendance. Father Soriano had also provided free instruction for about sixty children for three hours a day until recently, when the Town Council had forbidden him. In Los Olivares the official statistics returned fifty-four percent of the population as illiterate, though it was nearer seventy percent.

Father Soriano had been reported as in opposition to the project of the school, from which, he said, religion would be shut out, and it was this that principally occupied the group at Mater Purissima. Beneath that excitement there was really indifference, save in a few, and for this there were complicated reasons. A two-day interest was the arrest of the electrician Villado and his release upon an unusually perfect alibi. Another and more suggestive theme was the appearance of Don Fadrique upon the olivars.

Upon the evening of the storm, when the mayordomo had finally obeyed his order to leave the music room, Don Fadrique worked for a while upon his monograph upon the vihuelistas, the lutenists of Spain, which he had lately begun, and then locking the manuscript away, went into the chapel and prayed. Presently he lit the altar candles and switched off the electric light and returned to his seat.

It was not the Virgin of the altar piece he now gazed at, but the Christ which his chaplain had required might be brought from the chapel below the olive on the wall, and it was Soriano's extraordinary meditation on that crucifix which he now remembered. One Friday before he had appointed him, the younger priest had very timidly laid upon his table a beautifully written document with the request that the Marquis might read it. It was the language of this meditation that had first impressed Don Fadrique, and then he had seen that its level, cold and stately prose was expressing subtle and searching thought. That Soriano was a brilliant theologian he discovered one evening when his brother the bishop had been staying with him. Bored by too much talk of music, Ubaldo Guevara had that afternoon asked him if any of the Los Olivares clergy might care to dine with them. The consequent discussion upon the nature of God had startled him. "Very able," Ubaldo had said when Soriano had gone away, "very very able and very daring."

"You think so?" he had questioned.

"The man may claim that that doctrine of number can be brought under the scholastic discipline, but . . ." Ubaldo had shaken his head, "How did he define number? As the class of all classes of the same . . . I've forgotten it already. That shows

you how dangerous it is, brother. What are we bishops to do
if philosophy becomes so difficult?"

"I thought he subsumed the doctrine very well. I'm sure St.
Thomas Aquinas would have been delighted to hear him."

"Oh, no doubt about that. St. Thomas, I fear, would have
been frightfully bored in the absence of heresy."

"Well, I thought he did it successfully."

"Music may be a short path to experience, brother, but it is
not necessarily a high road to God."

"Perhaps experience may be that high road."

"II'm, but to argue from that theory of number that God
must exist to be the necessary sustaining principle of the class
of all classes of supernumerical unity is daring indeed, though
extraordinarily exciting, I admit. I'll have him brought down
to talk with our chapter philosophers, whom, I confess, I find
invincibly boring. Yes, I must certainly give Canon Gutierrez
a surprise. Nothing, Fadrique, is more amusing than the
spectacle of infallibility confronted with an error it had not
foreseen. Can the man preach?"

The meditation, however, showed yet another side of the
man's mind; its poetry of Love as Death was even more interesting than his theology.

Yet before long it was not the meditation of which he was
thinking but of the mayordomo and his furious outburst when
he had refused him leave to buy manures.

"But, man, the trees will *need* it now," he had pleaded.

"You must manage without it, Señor Argote," he had replied.

"The trees, the *trees*," the mayordomo had repeated before
his outbreak.

Don Fadrique's memory repeated the words so often that at
last he rose and, without extinguishing the candles, went out
of the Palacio and made his way towards the fountain near
Mater Purissima. A dim light still hung over the opposite hills,
the ground beneath the trees was sprinkled with leaves and
fruit as Argote had said; these then must be the manzanillos, or
were they zorzaleños? He approached a tree and took a spray
of the leaves in his hand and searched for the fruit; there were
none, and he remained thinking about the mayordomo's warning of disaster until a blundering cockchafer collided with his

forehead. He had somehow thought of the olivars as something natural and abiding, something as eternal and changeless as the light droning of the cigarras in the olive boughs. There seemed to be less noise that night and he supposed it was because the hail had killed the insects. The olivars were—they were—they seemed more than possessions of the family, throughout whose history they had provided its revenue. They were almost *of* the family—he remembered his father's constant concern with the estate and his own in former years, far less profound than his father's, but still real. It hurt him suddenly to think he might have to leave this place. His economies, the books he had bought and the money saved sufficient for a living in one room near a great library, all of it seemed like the digging of ditches against an advancing sea. What was the book *El Maestro* of Luis Milan against these olivars, in their solemnity now a reproach, even if his copy of that lovely book was from the press of that great printer Francisco Diaz Romano and of the first edition of 1536? He thought of his joy at receiving it, again at a low price, and how its dedication to John III of Portugal had filled him with the nostalgic longing which to him was one of the purest joys of scholarship. What was his *Orphenica Lyra* of old Miguel Fuenllana against these thousands of trees? Or his recent extraordinary discovery in his own library of three unknown hymns of Pedro de Hotz in his own hand, obviously a continuation of the two he had written for the Grand Prior of Malta? He thought now of the things he had had conveyed to Paris, of his bundle of Domenico Scarlatti's letters—and though he imagined clearly the beautiful firm handwriting of old Scarlatti, Paris was now incredibly remote. Even his crowning fortune, the discovery among a chest of books his brother Ubaldo had once borrowed of the missing lute books of Narvaez, now seemed cold and insignificant. A little bundle of leather and inked paper, a few phrases of curious and beautiful language, a day of exquisite music against this enduring, accusing army of trees in which was the gravity of God himself.

He returned to the chapel haunted by strange thoughts. As he stood before the altar the yellow light poured softly over the linen, and his thoughts became anguish at the remembrance of the woman whose frail body had once warmed it, and he understood why the olives had never interested him. His line was dead, his seed had been evil in the womb of Inés, or she herself had been too exhausted of line to bear. With Ubaldo a bishop, there was no one to whom the olive fields might have passed save the second cousin whom he had never seen, living in Paris with the group of exiles around Don Carlos. His wife's name, like something suspended, hung motionless in his mind and he tried to recall the arguments that Soriano had expounded to him concerning his wife's death. The priest had assured him that there was no justification for the sense of guilt which ever cast a gloom over him. They were learned and emphatic arguments, and when he had first heard them he had gone with a lighter heart through the wearying days, but now they had lost their force, he could not even remember the important steps in that subtle chain of reasoning. They now seemed nothing more than the assertion that a believer was justified in trusting God to suspend the laws of nature as Dr. Torres had interpreted them. Yet the doctor had been right and Inés had died, and it was remorse rather than his grief which had prevented him marrying again to provide an heir to the olivars. These hills were a foundry of death and his line was sentenced to extirpation.

Nevertheless during that week he had found himself thinking about the olive trees again and again, and at last, in the first days of August, he went out and searched for Argote.

It was near the reservoir that he found the mayordomo, standing in the stirrups shouting at some workers across the gully.

"Buenos días," he said.

"Buenos . . . ah, buenos días."

"How are the trees on this side, Señor Argote?"

"Bad, damn bad."

"Perhaps you would care to show me?" Sulkily the mayordomo led the way to a grove and pointed out the bruises upon the new wood. "They'll be dead before a month is out," he said, "and about a quarter of the trees are like that."

From this the conversation led to the means of cure and so to the whole treatment and care of olives, at which the mayordomo put his fingers to his lips and whistled piercingly. He sent the worker who answered to the stable for a saddled horse.

"Take this one, my lord, we'll have a look round the estate."

Don Fadrique accepted the invitation and the workers upon Narrow and Broad Skirt and the Skirt of Beyond were astonished to see the mayordomo ride up with the Marquis beside him. Argote had to show Don Fadrique everything appertaining to the olive trees, and it was half-past two before the lord of Los Olivares remarked:

"Perhaps you will lunch with me today, Argote?"

"Ah, God's wounds—I'd forgotten that; yes, my lord, I should be pleased."

That afternoon they had ridden about the hills again, and now the mayordomo invited him to try his hand with the tools. There was a curious pleasure in watching the strong firm pressure of the knife as the grafters made their shield insertions, and he at last consented to try his hand at the task. He drew a letter T upon the bark.

"This is a job that can only be done when the sap is still. March or August is the best."

"But isn't the sap still in winter? Oh, I see, of course. It's still now, but it will move again when the autumn rains come and so the wood will grow."

"That's right—now take the knife and cut along your T."

There was something almost uncanny in the operation the Marquis felt, as he stopped before the smooth and tender bark; it was a sensation too vague for analysis; though fascinating, yet it was definitely unpleasant. Silently he accepted the little triangular-shaped graft and placed it between his lips as he had seen the worker do. The curious sensation of significance disappeared and he was tempted to laugh as Argote and the worker also took hold of grafts in their lips and stooped with him before imaginary trees. Then suddenly the worker laughed uproariously and Don Fadrique dropped his graft and laughed with him, and finally Argote bellowed and all three stood shaking with laughter at the comical figures they had presented.

Again he placed his graft between his lips and, getting upon his knees, slid the shield into place; once more the indefinable sensation of significance returned.

Half an hour later the mayordomo announced that he would

have to ride to the Skirt of Beyond and Don Fadrique immediately replied that he would stay with the worker and graft
a few more trees. By five o'clock the Marquis was trembling
with fatigue and the nauseating discomfort of sweat, and when
the worker suggested that they climb down the wall to the
fountain and drink he gladly accepted.

"Can you whistle?" he asked.

"Sure," the man answered in perplexity.

"Whistle for another worker then; we'll send him for something to eat and drink and we'll rest there till six."

He stayed talking until a quarter-past six and then wearily
walked back to the Palacio, bathed and ate his supper, worked
for a contented hour and a half upon his monograph, and then
wandered by the long path to the fountain and sat there awhile
trying to remember whether to find the Pole Star one produced
the two hind stars of the Plow's rectangle or the two front
points. Unexpectedly he also found himself wondering what
the worker's name might be.

This interest, however, did not endure long; by the end of
the following week its novelty had disappeared and, more
importantly, Argote began to press him again for money for
manures. Then one day, when he had made a significant
discovery concerning the text of a sixteenth-century song, he
chanced to remark to the mayordomo:

"By the way, where is that girl who used to sing 'Ay de mi'?
I haven't seen her lately."

"I sacked her."

"Why?"

"Father Soriano . . ." began the olivero. "She's in the family
way and she's not married."

The Marquis of Peral was silent awhile and then he said
with faint bitterness, "Quite right," and returned to the Palacio
shortly afterwards. Indalecio Argote made one or two more
attempts to persuade the lord of Los Olivares to accompany
him but soon gave it up with disgust, and he ceased even to
inform Don Fadrique of the state of the work, latterly his
practice. Yet the episode was not wholly without impression
on the mayordomo, for when the Marquis next visited the
Fountain of Doña Inés he found that the place had been

cleaned, repaired and whitewashed and the crucifix set upright; the Olive of the Infanta had also been removed. This he
regretted, but he thanked Argote the same evening.

On the Friday, Father Soriano very deferentially told the
Marquis at lunch that he had been invited by the bishop of
the diocese to preach at the cathedral upon a Sunday, in the
near future.

"Indeed, I congratulate you," Don Fadrique said. "I wish it
were possible for me to hear you."

"If your lordship would care, I have my sermon prepared
and I shall deliver it at the parish church on Sunday, at the
parochial Mass."

"Very good, I shall hear Mass at the church and you may tell
Father Martínez he need not celebrate here."

At the rectory supper table that night the atmosphere was
more than usually strained, and since the inquiry it had been
at times almost intolerable. Soriano knew that it had been
caused by his announcement that Don Fadrique would not re-
quire Father Martínez to celebrate at the Palacio that Sunday,
and this had so embarrassed him that he could make no conversation at all. La Cándida made things far worse by noisily
laying the plates and cutlery before them, behavior which
always exasperated the rector and exhausted the curate. Eventually he could stand the silence no longer, and he stammered
that Don Fadrique would be present "to hear me preach,"
whereupon the housekeeper sharply put down a dish and
stared at Father Martínez.

"Well, what do you want, woman?" he shouted suddenly,
and Soriano started and upset his glass of water. For a moment
the rector was obviously struggling with emotion and then
he blurted, "You're not preaching on Sunday morning, you're
singing Mass."

"But you announced that I should preach."

"Yes, I did . . ." Father Martínez crossed himself and Soriano
said quietly, "Very well, may I preach on Sunday afternoon?"

"As you wish . . . Leave the room, woman, leave the room at
once."

When La Cándida had angrily marched out, the rector said
quietly but with determination:

"You know what people are saying about you, brother?"

"What are they saying?" asked the terrified curate.

"They say you have ambition, to turn me out of this living—they say you are working behind my back. I am dismissed from my chaplaincy, you force me to perjure myself at the inquiry because you lied, and now . . ."

"Quiet, man, quiet," Soriano urged, crossing himself swiftly three times.

"I'll not be quiet—you come into this house with my blessing, I do my best to make you comfortable and content, I try to be friendly to you, you draw back and distrust me and you never speak to me. Then you begin to set yourself up before the parishioners, you visit them without informing me, you turn Don Fadrique against me, you endanger me at that inquiry when every bit of trouble was your fault—and then you have the insolence to tell me to be quiet when I protest."

Soriano, staring at the rector, interrupted him wildly: "Brother, I am sorry I lied . . ." but Father Martínez rose from his seat and leaned across the table, struck the priest across the face, and in doing so overreached himself and fell across the table.

There was a long silence, which the rector broke by saying sadly yet with anger, "And now I have sinned in striking a priest of God."

"That is nothing," Soriano whispered, grieving and sick.

"Tell me, brother, have you ambition to turn me out?" Martínez said chokingly.

"No . . ." he dully replied, "no, I swear I have not." His voice rapidly rose and he stood up, and holding his crucifix before him exclaimed loudly, "I swear it, brother, by the Virgin and her Blessed Son, that I have no ambition to turn you out of this living and God be my judge." There was an excitement like ecstasy in his voice and his face shone, his right hand fumbled in his breast and he withdrew a letter. "It came this morning, I wanted to ask your permission and blessing before going to the capital. I was going to preach the sermon here first on Sunday."

The rector read the letter and then, laying it on the table before him, said, "Forgive me, brother . . . ah, man, it's I who should ask your blessing." He bowed his head and with shining face Soriano gave his blessing in clear but faltering Latin, slowly spoken. When he retired to his room shortly afterwards Father Soriano experienced in all his being deep and generous love for the old man; and behind the gothic image of San Andrés towered the great baroque miter-shaped front of the cathedral. The cathedral—ah, how his voice would resound throughout the cathedral! Most certainly he no longer coveted the good Martínez's place.

That Don Fadrique had been seen to enter the church was itself sufficient reason for a number of last-minute entrances and these were pleased when the rector emerged vested for celebration, for Soriano's preaching was at least better than Father Martínez's. It would mean a badly sung Mass, of course, and old Dr. Torres at the organ would probably exhibit one of his humors; sometimes, when Father Martínez grew flatter and flatter, he would stop playing until the parish priest turned round and lifted his face to the organ, and then he would repeatedly sound the pitch note before commencing again. Or he would attack the response before the last syllable had left the priest's mouth, loudly producing a musical expostulation which confused the choir much more than the rector's flatness.

"In the beginning was the Word, and the Word was made flesh." Father Soriano had accustomed his hearers to that text; he had preached upon "In the beginning" and upon "the Word," upon "and was made flesh," and whatever text he chose or whatever the theme, the beginning and the Word and the Flesh were sure to appear regularly. Having announced his text he at once surprised the burghers of Villa Alta by saying that his theme was really "Life as Liturgy and Liturgy as Life," and straightway began with a description of savage man, his instinctive following of the seasons and of the greater significances of his primitive rites. These were all of them of the earth and the flesh of man, to which he was striving to give significance, and the essence of them was that they were not still and rhythmless but that they followed the cycle of nature itself. "The vegetation grows out of the earth and the rains refresh it, it dries and rots and its corruption enriches the earth, the earth is labored by the sun and the rain and then it lies at rest and is broken and cleared by frost. Even the thunderstorms, with their rich downpourings of dissolved acid necessary for vegetation, have their place in this revolving, eternally passing and changing, eternally the same drama.

"Yet behind this there is a God who is still, the mover who is not moved. This is the great liturgical rhythm which God has imposed upon life, upon the dumb salts and the blind waters of this earth. And man's mental life, however far it climb from the superstitions of ignorance, must remain in contact with this liturgical necessity. Whatever patterns he make for society, whatever philosophies he embody, unless they possess this revolving dramatic rhythm he will languish and grow sterile. And this because even in its details life follows a liturgical plan. Consider the Liturgy of the Mass, the supremest drama man has been given, consider the marrying of man and woman for the fruitful multiplication which pleases God. The Introit, the confession—the meeting and coming to be known. The first shout of triumph in the Gloria and the Gospel the first awakening of love and the deliberate recounting of how it came to be. The Credo—the simple talk of marriage, humbly accepting the disciplines of God's revelation and of civilized use. Then the fresh glory of the Sanctus and the consecration, the consorting in love.

"And if we move our attention to the most mental and spiritual of man's arts, to music, we shall see how music is all of it liturgy. Those of you who have heard a symphony will know how the music changes from movement to movement, and if it is to be good it is a disciplined and logical sequence of emotion it arouses. And within the movement, the entry of the themes, the relaxation, the gathering impetus, the first shout of Gloria, the hush, the reappearance of the themes and then the close, often formal, like the Ite Missa Est which is, I often think, a piece of divine courtesy or a sanctified convenience."

Don Fadrique smiled throughout this passage; it was not only that it pleased him but that he understood now why Soriano had borrowed so many books on musical form.

"That is why religion can never be a purely mystical act, of contemplation alone, for man is a dramatic being, he must

have this liturgical basis for his life. And that is why the heresy
of Protestantism carried to its conclusion leads to a polar chill
of the heart and mind, because being rhythmless—I mean that
man is provided with no varied forms of grace or with less,
and so tires, for he is never nourished by that change, that
development, that permitting to exult and then to lie fallow
which the great Catholic drama gently imposes. It is eternally
the same effort its unfortunate deceived must make, and a
lonely effort, for the society of a drama-less civilization must
ever be a surging mob, an inert crowd or an archipelago of
isolated individuals thrust into an inane and tideless sea.

"But it is not only that life must be a drama, a liturgical
drama, but that this drama of Holy Church is itself so perfect.
Let us consider the entry into the Church's year through the
initiation, the discipline, the sublime agony of Lent. Throughout a month there is an accumulation of desire and of anticipation; the shutting out of color and the subduing of our music
of worship to a pleading sadness. But, and you see here the
immense genius of our Faith, the dramatic apparatus of relief,
of liberation from grief, is so different yet so complementary of
Holy Week. All the love, all the passion of man's sympathy
with his Redeemer stand out in that week of terrible drama—
it is for that reason that her enemies recently tried to destroy
that drama. Every device of the living theater of God's revelation has been used, and so Easter is a white, still splendor and
its rites are confined to the sanctuary, made golden and frag-
rant with incense and flowers, or spread over the homes of a
relieved and resting people. Or see how when the corn first
ripens and the first sheaves lie upon the ground—and, children of God, yesterday by the river I saw the golden sheaves
lying prostrate before the image of Life Crucified—in that
time the Church has placed Corpus Christi, the mystery of
Bread, the dramatic and spiritual apotheosis of the material
basis of life.

"Then the secular feasts blessed by the Church throughout
the summer and so to the darkening days. But in these man is
still strong and nourished from the summer and so this Advent
culminates in the birth of innocence and love. . . . It has no
disturbing drama, it is as it were God's gracious comedy for His

children. The Word is made Flesh. And we may smile at Him
before whom, in the rhythm of this Drama, we shortly must
bow in shame and fear. Thus we see that the strains and con-
flicts set up by this drama resolve themselves and enrich the
soul.

"But more than this, that bringing in of the emotions into
this drama—this drama of controlled but not thwarted expression—is also a sign of genius. It is good to hate Iscariot
as he is borne through the streets — it is good to love the
Blessed Mother of us all. For there is a special genius in this use
of symbols.

"There are those, children of God, who scorn the symbol.
Yet to the spiritual man is not this body, this vesture, these acts
which he performs, all symbols? They are matter used to por-
tray this mighty drama of redemption." Father Soriano leaned
over the pulpit and his eyes were narrowed and his brow contracted and it seemed to the Marquis that many shrank from
him.

"Psychologists tell us . . . would have us believe that whatever
the mind of man may do merely to repress desires and passions,
it will still express them. It will express them, not openly and
with the check and discipline of society and of the Church, but
in bizarre and trivial symbols, manipulating them with miserable, tormented ingenuity into a sin-haunted and pernicious
drama. What a descent, my children! From the peace and
serenity of the divinely disposed rhythm, from the glory, the
banners of triumph and the uplifted and luminous travail of
the Cross to the squalor of introspection fumbling with the
poor tatters of deceit! Yet, oh, bitter irony for the Prince of
Evil, even this deceit is witness to the truth. Men cannot escape
the symbol, he is himself a symbol, a religion without symbols
or drama would yet leave him perpetually in a fallow and
twilight desuetude over which he would stalk, the solitary
symbol of his own declining into a skeleton death.

"Then again, a liturgy demands the disciplined relationship
of interior worship and external rite. And this is, as I have
argued, a pattern of our life. And that balance between the interior and the exterior discipline of life is profoundly necessary.
It is only within the Church that the great mystics will arise.

Mysticism, that adventurous searching for God in the soul, would again involve the same bizarre fantasies if it were not for the constraining drama of the Church. So for the humbler soul. As daydreaming or reveries debilitate the mind because they use its passions and impulses without the discipline of exterior fact, so introspection weakens the mind if it is not checked and confined with rigor, as in the sacrament of penance. For this reason an interior, individual religion can never be satisfactory, because it denies the dramatic nature of man. . . ."

Father Soriano, as usual, tired his hearers long before he reached the end of his sermon and upon this occasion before he had reached its central argument. With the exception of Don Fadrique no one had understood the priest's pragmatic defense of northern hemispherical Catholicism, and to the rector it was a fantastic and utterly unreal performance, the like of which he had never heard or read. Sermons should be about Heaven and Hell, the Church and her enemy the Devil, the Seven Sacraments and the Virgin in her principal titles, or they should be about Charity. But neither Don Fadrique nor the rector knew whom Soriano was answering, though the Marquis might have guessed how he came to hear of the challenge. The challenger was not a churchgoer.

When the congregation emerged from the church, many of them dipped their hands into the stoup with deliberation instead of habit, many had a feeling of pride in the building itself, through which Dr. Torres was trying to send reverberating diapason peals. Some were vaguely comforted, some vaguely distressed, but most of them screwed up their eyes against the light, greeted a few friends and hurried in a habitual manner in a habitual direction and then, finding themselves at home, set about preparing their midday meal.

Father Soriano, invited by Don Fadrique to dine that night at the Palacio, hesitated and then declined. "I think Father Martínez is a little lonely, your lordship," he added.

"In that case kindly invite him, too, and if you would permit it, I should be pleased to read the manuscript of your sermon."

18

Fiesta

As a consequence of his secession from the F.A.I., Joaquín Caro
had now much more time to devote to the holding, the appearance of which rapidly improved. He had intended first to
break the ground upon the goat pastures in order to set a few
apricot trees, but a fortunate opportunity caused him to repair
the corral wall instead. The base of the footbridge over the
Jabalón having rested in a dangerous condition for four years,
the civil engineers of the province had at last been ordered to
repair it. It was thus easy to come by two bags of cement, and,
though it meant all-night work, the job was well worth the
labor. Then he cleaned the well and relaid the broken tiles
of the threshing floor, and at Pascual's request slung all the
tubs and vessels they possessed on the mule and the donkey
and he and Marcial went twice nightly to the Jabalón and
carried up water to the vegetable plots. This was an exhausting
labor and needed patience, for the Jabalón was now but a
sluggish thread running through pebbles and dust and they
had to bail water into the tubs with small aluminum pots
borrowed from the kitchen. Once the tubs were three-quarters
filled the return was even more trying, for the beasts had now
to be steadied over the chaotic Jabalón path in which ruts had
been worn to knee depth, and it was useless to fill the tubs,
although Pascual made a couple of rough lids which had some
use. Once the sure-footed donkey slipped, and though Caro
leaped at her and, getting her head under his arm, twisted her
neck in the opposite direction, she fell upon her side and the
water was wasted.

It was Marcial who eased the labor most; wandering gloomily up the hot-stoned bed about two hundred yards, he found a deep trough in the rocks of the winter bed, and borrowing a pickax from a bridge worker placed on guard over the nightly vanishing materials, they succeeded in diverting a trickle of water into the trough. Marcial insisted on aiding his brother in this channel clearing, but a bout of blood coughing put an end to that. The reservoir now made required three hours to fill, but it provided two journeys without effort of bailing, so that now they were able to fetch three loads of water. Upon the fourth night they were watched by a worker belonging to one of the larger holdings and the following night they found the trough empty.

"Well, there's nothing for it but to bail," Joaquín said, and so they returned to the bridge. Despite the danger to Marcial, both brothers waited that night until the other irrigator came. At half-past twelve, as the hot air of the bed was first penetrated by the cold earthy puffs from the watered lands, two black figures were silhouetted on the bank top; with a clanking of buckets one of them slid down the bank into the bushes at its base. As he approached the basin Joaquín stood up. The man halted and then came on.

"Ah, it's you, Bruno," Joaquín said and the man on the bank top shouted and called down to them.

"It's me, Caro," Bruno answered, when his companion arrived and dipped his bucket into the water. Caro stepped over the trough and grappled with him, the spilled water made the rocks slippery and they fell and broke apart. Bruno's helper, having downed Marcial, left him choking on the river bed and tripped up Joaquín from behind, and this ended the fight, for both men stood over him and kicked him in the ribs till he said, "All right—take it." The following night Marcial borrowed a revolver and spent two hours filling in the trough, after which the bridge worker showed them how to siphon water through a narrow hose into a bucket placed in the first pit dug for the new pier base, and for two nights they again made three journeys. Then the pit was cemented in and they were reduced to one journey, as the Jabalón had now dwindled even more.

The result of this labor was that Marcial again suffered a serious collapse, and Joaquín alone could make one journey only. Nevertheless, the green stuffs prospered and, being in good condition, sold readily; life was bettered, they ate meat twice a week for a fortnight and Ana bought her daughter a new dress length and a pair of earrings. One night, while returning from the Jabalón, Caro turned sick and giddy and lay down till the attack should pass off. The beasts returned alone, and Pascual and Ursula, searching in alarm, for the daughter had been told of the trough incident, found him lying amidst vomit fast asleep with his coat drawn over his head. After that the sister accompanied him to the river and even made one journey with the donkey in the late afternoon before Joaquín returned from work on the olivars. On a Saturday, two days before the feast of the Assumption of Our Lady, the Jabalón dried up, and the price of water rose immediately by three pesetas the *hilo*. The Caros reverted to their one fresh meat meal a week, as Pascual had always argued they should.

The Feast of the Assumption was the major feast of Los Olivares, although neither of the churches was dedicated to the Virgin. San Andrés' day unfortunately fell at the end of November when the days were short, and, much more importantly, the work of the olive harvest was at its height and the three days of feast could not be afforded. The 15th, 16th and 17th of August had been the days of *fiesta mayor* for two centuries. At the time of the change there had been some protest, but nowadays the Lower Town workers were well content to rest during the burdensome heat of August.

Several days before the feast, Argote, cursing the while about this interference with the olive-field labors, selected two of the older workers.

"Now look here, you bloody wasters," he said, "this chapel has got to be whitewashed and the goddamned cactus hedge cleaned up, and you can tidy up the path and dig a hole for rubbish and put a basket for paper by the fountain, and listen —if you leave so much as a stick of wood lying about you'll be for it. There's going to be no fires up here."

At every return to the Palacio the mayordomo halted at Mater Purissima to inspect the work, never failing to express his displeasure with the interruption. On the Saturday afternoon the disk harrows were run carefully over the olive fields around the chapel and the fountain; the steppingstones were pulled out where possible, and the walls and the younger tree trunks were whitewashed. Upon the Sunday morning he sent for a party of workers and, when they arrived, said:

"You'll work today at trimming up the bypaths—though what the hell all this is wanted for I don't know."

"Sunday rates?" Baeza asked.

"Sunday pay! God, what a grasping lot of bastards you are."

"Offends my conscience," a worker said.

"The Sunday rest regulations," another added.

"God's sacred teeth!" Argote shouted. "Do you think I give a damn for your conscience or your Sunday rest regulations or the confounded chapel?"

"Sunday pay?"

"Christ, yes, Sunday pay."

"That's the only time you can win a strike," a worker said reflectively, "when the boss wants something bad."

On Saturday the caravans arrived, a procession of colored wagons trailing over the dazzling lunar lands above the Huerta, and behind them with motley equipages of mules and donkeys came the gypsies, full-skirted, many-petticoated women moving with bare blackened feet and beautiful gait over the scorching dusts, young girls with disarrayed hair and faces of primitive paintings, faces at once sad and cunning, of the professionals of sorrow; little boys eager as birds and knowing the weaknesses of house-dwelling mankind, little boys with black beautiful faces and little lovely bodies, and all of them filthy and none more so than the hard, implacable liars, the good-tempered warmhearted crafty and stinking men. And behind them at three hours' distance a solitary gypsy woman with a day-old baby. The miller at Puente Nuevo had a tale to tell when he attended the feast, of how a gypsy had knocked at his door and asked for shelter in which to bear her child. The miller's wife, childless, had offered the woman a room, which she had refused in favor of an empty corner of the straw barn. There she delivered herself and, having swept the floor, continued her march before five in the morning, when the miller's wife had descended.

These gypsies were an intolerable nuisance which everyone at Los Olivares tolerated, Justo Robledo being the only person to lose his temper with them. Not only was he compelled to endorse all the passes without which a gypsy may not move in Spain and which must be given afresh in every town, but a mass of petty litigation passed through his hands. On the Sunday morning an infuriated peasant presented himself, accompanied by a Civil Guard and an indignant and injured innocent of a gypsy, known in northern Andalucía as "El Guiño."

"Well, what's your complaint?" Robledo asked the peasant, and at once El Guiño broke into a rapid lament punctuated with staccato protests. It appeared at last that the peasant, "this caballero," had bought a donkey from El Guiño.

"Be quiet," shouted Robledo. "You, what did you want to buy a donkey from a gypsy for?" Doggedly the peasant stuck to his point; he had been sold a lame and nearly dying donkey and he wanted his money back. Half an hour of fierce controversy had been sifted and noted down, when Robledo suddenly asked:

"How much did you pay for the donkey?"

"Fifty pesetas," replied the peasant.

"Lord Christ and his blessed Mother," shouted Robledo. "Get out of here before I have you locked up as a raving lunatic; what kind of a donkey do you expect to get for fifty pesetas?"

El Guiño immediately drew himself up and swaggered before the peasant.

"Make that the first question to answer in future," Robledo said to the clerk. "See here, Guiño. Have the goodness to warn your people to go slow here; if there's another case of this in Los Olivares I'll mark every damn pass in gypsydom. Get me?"

"Ah, caballero, caballero," whined the gypsy. "Don't be so hard on a man who just, just knows how to sell a little beastie."

"You're warning them?"

"Ah yes, caballero, of course. *I* always do as the señores secretarios command."

"Then get out."

El Guiño departed quickly, and the next day the same tricks were practiced and the same deferential insolence displayed. As he had threatened, Robledo marked all the gypsy passes, with the result that they were harassed all down their route for weeks, and two eventually went to jail. This made no difference to the gypsies; that was their life, the life of the arrogant cringers.

On the morning of the Assumption the fair ground was covered with booths selling paste fritters, ground nut drink, fruit, ties, pictures, statues, herb water, wine, syrups, song sheets and books of model correspondence and the meaning of dreams; there were three carrousels equipped with green and yellow fish, black and yellow lions, pink pigs and scarlet cocks; there were sideshows of conjurors with purple-clothed tables, beautiful dancers who racketed about the stage for fifteen centimes a performance, to please male appetites with grotesque and suggestive posturings. The heavy, blue fumes of boiling olive oil hung around the fritter stalls. Blind beggars with images of saints moaned through the crowd, gypsies whined and the quacks shouted, here and there a guitar sounded through the blare and the rattle, and above the colored swinging and whirling of the fairground the tricolor floated against the blazing sky from every turret of the brown walls.

When the organ began to blare in San Andrés and the doors were thrust open, a peal of acclamation went up, though this year there would be no procession. Father Martínez and the three priests came to the steps and solemnly blessed the people, while the Civil Guard, heavily reinforced, closely scrutinized the young men standing on the outskirts of the crowd.

The priests withdrew, and immediately there was a clatter of hoofs and two horses pranced into the square. Upon their backs were couples dressed in flamenco style. In the saddle of a bay horse sat a young man, known at the casino as Elegantito, wearing a black broad-brimmed hat with chin strap, a short-cut coat of black velvet with silver buttons and wide-bottomed trousers of a similar stuff with scrolled leather boots thrust into stirrups of burnished steel. Before him was slung a red blanket and behind him sat his fiancée with shawl and fan and crinkled dress of white silk. The rider was the Hermano Mayor of the Guild, the leading Brother. Upon the other, a black horse, the rider wore a coatee of white velvet and his fiancée was dressed entirely in white, the Hermana Mayor. Urging the horses to make them restless, the horsemen moved quickly through the crowd, causing the scurrying people to break a way for them, as was their right, disdain upon their faces. Behind them the people followed in confusion up the swept track between the somber trees to Mater Purissima, stark white against red-brown hills and defended by aloe blades of venomed copper.

The horses were taken by attendant brothers and led to the rear of the chapel, and the leaders waited upon the flattened bluff for the crowd to close up. It was now that, in other years, the track would have been alive with the colored movement of banner and emblem, of cross and draped oxen chariot with its awning of silk and flowers, and its silk-draped beasts, bearing flowers on their horns, trundling slowly up to the sanctuary to bear the star-haloed, golden-rayed Mother in her cobalt robe and golden stole back to the incense-filled square where a terrific shout of adoration would have gone up. The religious procession had been forbidden both by the mayor and by the civil governor, and the only color that lined the track was the red-and-white awnings of refreshment stalls and the shawls of two young girls, one of whom was wrestling with a broken high heel.

The Brother led his fiancée to the bench of the mayoress and with a proud movement offered her the seat. She glanced at it and haughtily replied, "It is dusty." This was not tradition, for the seat had escaped the caretaker's duster and was thick with dust. With explosive peremptoriness the Hermano Mayor demanded that the seat be cleaned, and two young men, one the brother of his fiancée, rushed to the caretaker's box and prised it open. As they pulled out the cloths something fell to the floor, and before Captain Montaña could snatch up the percussion cap, one of the escort had trodden upon it. The explosion caused the lad to stagger into the doorway, where he was seen by the startled watchers on the flat. Shrieks of women mingled with the shouts of men, and at once the crowd began to surge down the slope, some trying to fight a way through the cactus and ripping their clothing on the fish-hooked blades. Montaña ran outside and shouted sharply, and with hysterical laughter the panic was stayed. Many slowly returned from the foot-pocked olive fields, climbing up the walls with angry questions, one or two young men returned from the direction of the fountain, whither they had fled.

"It is nothing, a mere practical joke," Captain Montaña said quietly, after holding up his hand. "I warn any other humorists I shall arrest them if they attempt anything of the kind." He entered the chapel again and, searching the box, found two more percussion caps, which he sent back to the barracks at once. A minute later Father Martínez began the Mass, throughout which the crowd without whispered and muttered of dynamite and the dam of Don Fadrique.

When the Office was concluded the Hermano Mayor and the feast committee prepared the decorated tray on which stood a statue of the Virgin and upon which the generous would lay their offerings. The Brother himself, an olive oil merchant's son, laid upon the tray a hundred-peseta note and his fiancée emptied a purse of silver onto it. The Hermana Mayor, daughter of a former petty manufacturer of Puente Nuevo, also laid down a hundred-peseta note and with a flush of pleasure watched her fiancée toss onto the tray two one-hundred-peseta notes.

"Now then, to the Palace!"

There was some comment at this, but following the tray-bearers the four flamencos mounted the path to the Palacio. The gates were flung open by a servant and the horsemen cantered in and reined violently, while an escort ran to the door and hammered loudly.

"Good day, Señor Mayordomo," the Brother called as Argote appeared.

"May you have good days."

"We desire to speak with his lordship if it pleases him to come out."

"Very good, have the kindness to wait."

As the Marquis appeared at the door the Hermano Mayor dismounted and, handing down his fiancée, led her to the steps, where she curtsied and said:

"If your lordship pleases we should be grateful to receive a contribution."

"Very good, Señorita," Don Fadrique replied and, taking out his case withdrew a note. The Brother flushed as he perceived its color; the Marquis of Peral was giving fifty pesetas in place of the customary thousand. With a checked exclamation, the Hermano Mayor picked up the note from the extended tray and, taking out his wallet, wrapped Don Fadrique's contribution in a thousand-peseta note and tossed it back to the tray-bearer. He mounted, received his novia on the cruppers and with a single "Thanks, adios" rode away, followed by the excited escort, leaving Argote fuming beside his silent master

The very Andaluz gesture of the Hermano Mayor ensured that the incident should be talked about for days. The Brother was popularly saluted in the streets, and to fling down a note with a disdainful expression was for weeks a notable hit. Don Fadrique, in saving nine hundred and fifty pesetas, had lost a great volume of sympathy in Los Olivares. It was said of him that he could spend seventy thousand pesetas on a book of old music and offer a handful of coppers to God's own Mother.

That night the plaza was bright with strings of electric lights, with flares and with wide-flung balcony windows, from which bedspreads and bright-hued carpets had been hung. Upon a plank patform the band blared into a pasodoble, and after that came a modern dance and the crowd crystallized and couples began to creep about beneath the network of lights. Señor Pérez led out his wife, and Diego Mudarra, bowing before Conchita, begged for a dance and was given it with a laugh. As he swiftly maneuvered the girl through the couples, there were cries of admiration from the onlookers and he responded to them with increased panache and preciser and more varied steps; it was a musician's or a painter's dancing, with form and line about it, and Conchita awakened to it and took the least signal of his body without hesitation.

"Like this dance, Concepción?" Mudarra asked quietly but proudly.

"Yes," she replied, and said no more till he led her to her parents.

Upon the third day of the feast, surprised that he had not seen Justo Robledo and Celestina at the dancing, for they were nowadays sometimes seen together at the Republican Dances, Caro called at Mendizabal Street.

"I'd expected to see you at the dancing, Justo," he said after formalities.

"No," he replied hesitatingly, and Caro was suddenly embarrassed, for he remembered that it was at a feast dance that Lucía had given way to Mudarra.

"Please stay to dinner . . . it will only be a dog's meal but we should like you to stay," Robledo said hurriedly.

"Please stay," Celestina added; glancing at her, he perceived an intensity of questioning melancholy in her eyes and consented, without conscious thought. When Lucía came in he joined in the Robledos' salutations and after a while said to her:

"Have you heard the story about Justo and the gypsy Guiño?"

"No," she replied, staring at her plate, "tell me it."

"Why didn't you tell me that?" Celestina asked her husband. "You've got the manners of a cowherd."

"Woman," he protested, "if I told you all the business of the Town Hall I'd be talking all day."

"What else do you know about him?" Lucía said, and from thence onwards she occasionally joined in the conversation.

That night Robledo and Caro went to the Republican Center and the latter began to learn the rudiments of chess. Afterwards he accompanied the acting secretary to Mendizabal Street before going out of the San Andrés Gate and down the Huerta path to his home. As he descended the first steps he was astonished to hear the sereno cry, "Midnight, señores, and the night is calm and fine." He stood wondering whether the council had rescinded their order, and then continued his walk home.

Red Dance

THE Rincón was crowded when Justo Robledo flung aside the chain curtain and forced his way into the debate on the Land Act.

"Uncultivated lands are to be expropriated also, paragraph 7 of Section 5," Mudarra was shouting. "Ca! The Dead Lands out there beyond the Huerta, the lands that Christ himself refused for his Passion in the wilderness, the Government will take it and turn it into a garden of figs and flowers and bee-autiful waving corn; with a little watering can. You can have it, García, and give your blasted party leaders a May Day bouquet."

"I tell you," began García, waving the *Gazette* in Mudarra's face.

"The Dead Lands!" everyone shouted in chorus, and García swept the *Gazette* round in a half circle of angry disgust and sat down. "Well, do you want me to talk or not?" he said, when the uproar subsided.

Cries of "Yes" and "No" answered him.

"Well then," he continued, "it doesn't say all uncultivated lands will be expropriated, but only those that can be used profitably . . . for God's sake shut your mouth," he shouted at Baeza before the latter could interrupt, but a moment later there was a fresh storm of protest.

"I don't give a damn about other towns, it's Los Olivares I'm thinking about. . . ."

"Yes, what uncultivated lands are there here for us to take over?"

"Christ, do you want an Act all to yourselves, and there's the old fields below the Reservoir," García replied.

"We want an Act that will do something for us," Baeza shouted. "See here, this and this," and he banged first his pocket and then his stomach and turned to yell at the waiter who was forcing his way through with Robledo's coffee.

In every part of the Rincón, as at the Republican Center and the Casino, as daily at Mater Purissima, all interests had gone down before the excitement provoked by the Agrarian Reform Act of September 15th, which contained the basis for the manner of land expropriation. This debate was the third Robledo had entered; at the Casino the controversy had been terminated by Don Bartolomé's tirade of insult, in which he had declared Robledo to be a partisan of the nationalization of women as practiced in Russia, and otherwise a propagator of Black House politics. At the Republican Center he had been howled down, while in the streets on the way to the Rincón he had been delayed by a group of small tenants anxious to know their position.

"That's all you can think of," García replied. "You've no idea of how a new order can be built up."

"I've got as much ideas as you; are you going to tell me the Civil Service can do it?" Baeza said.

"Here, let me have a say," Robledo shouted, rattling his glass on the table top.

"We all know what you're going to say," Mudarra sneered.

"And we never know what you'll say," Robledo flung back, and both men stood up and glared at one another.

"I say it's all the damn same either way, Act or no Act."

"Bloody useful remark."

"It might be if you understood it."

"Oh, for Christ's sake shut your blasted mouth, Robledo," Mudarra said. "Section II, the persons and groups who are to be settled on expropriated land by the government fall into four categories. Number one, workers without land at all, that's me, that's you, that's Baeza, that's old Robledo. Number two, peasant societies more than two years old, small owners who pay less than fifty pesetas cultivation tax or twenty-five in rent

of land tax. Lovely, isn't it? Any landless worker here got the
capital to work a holding? Like to buy me a nice pair of mules,
Robledo, and a couple of plows, or run me up a decent house?"

"The Government will create banks to grant loans," García
contested.

"Anyone care to take up ten thousand pesetas at six percent?" There was a shout of laughter.

"It doesn't say the percentage."

"No, but what kind of percentage do you expect from a
Spanish bank?"

"It's likely enough to be two and a half percent."

"Two and a half, my foot," Robledo put in, "and even at
that, with stamp duties and so on, it would be four and a half.
The Bank of Spain always makes its greatest profit in times of
greatest crisis. In 1920 it paid sixteen percent dividend; in
1921, time of the smash-up in Morocco, fifty-four percent. Same
thing last year; on a paid-up capital of one hundred and fifty
million pesetas the Bank of Spain paid one hundred and
twenty millions in dividend. How's it done? You ought to
know. You're proposing to give the bank another fifty percent."

"Nevertheless, I think it might easily be fixed at two and a
half percent."

"What the hell does it matter what the percentage is as long
as the debt is over my head. . . . Christ almighty, man,"
Mudarra yelled, *"Christ in heaven,* think of it, you're taking
over land and you've got difficulties enough with that alone
supposing you started in a year like this, and then with a
bloodsucking Government and a horde of officials all demanding this return and that, and the Bank and the Town Secretary and all the rest . . . Can't you see, you *bloody* idiot, you'd
go stark raving *mad.* Say, you Bernardo, can you read? Or
write?"

The man addressed, a long and lean-faced worker of middle
age with a bald patch like a tonsure, shook his head.

"No . . . you'd like a loan from Madrid, Bernardo? The hell
you would."

"Well, what's your point?" Robledo jabbed in quickly.

"The point is it's no damn good pulling that trick."

"And supposing the workers took the land for themselves, could they work it without capital, and who's to give it to them?"

Mudarra faltered before replying to Robledo's attack, and then said, "We're asking for a revolution, just as much as you . . . we want the land, and the workshops, and when we get them we'll trust the workers to make plows and build houses. Got that?"

"Ah, you'll conjure them up with a guitar, I suppose. Where do you think you'll get the materials, say, cement?"

"The Puente Nuevo cement workers."

"And pipes?"

"The Sevilla workers."

"And tiles?"

"The Cazorla men."

"Christ, you're going for a tour round Spain; can't you see you'll want an organization to buy and sell for you?"

The worker Bernardo kept on repeating, "The fair, the fair."

"See here, Robledo, we know you're coming to that State idea, or some damned network of Soviets. Well, cut it out; we know your views and they don't go here. We want *free* associations, that's why group number two is a washout. Anybody here want to join a farming society with the Government as a nurse? Russian collectives, I suppose; we've read about them; there wouldn't be a rabbit or a rat left in Los Olivares by next week. Now let's take group three, phrase two, persons paying less than twenty-five pesetas a year let-land tax; anyone know such a person?"

A peal of laughter followed the question.

"Don Blasco," they shouted. "Don Blasco, he of the Shitty Sheep Bell."

The town lawyer was known to pay less, though his lands were worth at least a hundred pesetas a year tax.

"Right, we'll invite Señor Ortega to join a farming society; perhaps on second thought, I'll lend him the capital myself, like Señora Pérez."

"Listen," Robledo shouted, standing up; cries of "Sit down, sit down," resounded from all sides.

"Government societies and free associations are all one,

they're all moonshine with the land worker as he is. Does any worker in Los Olivares *want* to enter a free association yet? Do you, Bernardo?"

"No," he replied in some embarrassment.

"Well, there's an example of your bloody free associations, Mudarra. . . . I tell you it's all very well for historians and cranks like Costa to rake up examples of primitive Communism still surviving in Spain, and it's damned silly of you Anarchists to argue from them that the worker is ready to behave like a man. It's a lie, he isn't. Christ, there are places in Spain where the man still goes to bed and groans when his wife's having a kid . . . but that's no proof that we'll be breeding out of bottles next spring. What the worker wants right now is land, and no rent to pay and a good market, a woman to mount and children to drive. He's got to be taught and kicked up the rear till he'll want something better."

"Processions round the fields and naked women with plows," Bernardo said.

"Ca! I was drunk then, though you'd never get the sense of anything, sober or drunk."

"And what does it all boil down to then?" García asked.

"To this: Spain needs a party to make a revolution that'll give the workers the land first in any way and form they take it."

"You don't belong to a party yourself," Mudarra sneered.

"Small owners," shouted García. "You want to create a mass of small owners and turn them into Socialist collectives afterwards. Why not start straight away. . . ."

"Because the Republic'll go down first while you're arguing about how to do it, because your enemies will get back their wind. Hell, can't you see? You attack the Church while a third of the workers still believe in it, and to make it worse you give the women the vote while ninety percent of them are Catholics . . . you're playing into your enemies' hands. Land first, and then you can do what you like with the Church."

"Amen, amen and amen," Mudarra intoned, "the same old litany."

"Yes, the same today as tomorrow," Robledo said, with the sudden weariness that always seized him in political disputes.

These men would never be convinced; ah, what was the use of faith, supposing . . . yes, supposing one really had it? He rose and pushed his way through the crowded tables to the door, whence the smoke was wreathing into the street. Slowly, and swaying as if he were intoxicated, he returned to Mendizabal Street. By the time he arrived there he was trembling as if he were physically weary, and with a sensation of sickness at the top of his stomach. He searched for his key and then, still holding it in his hand, turned and indecisively walked a few paces away. The Upper Town sereno passed along the street, and he began to muse over the stupid controversy the Council had tabled. Shortly before the *fiesta mayor* the inhabitants of Villa Alta had adopted a suggestion of Don Bartolomé's that they themselves engage and pay the vigilants as formally they had done. The Upper Town sereno had been ordered by the householders to cry the hours according to tradition, and within two days Cuestas Abajo did the same. The Council, however, offended at this lack of respect, had by a special bylaw forbidding the serenos to cry, whereupon a few of the Villa Alta inhabitants refused to pay their quota when next the sereno knocked at the door. The unfortunate man had gone to the Town Hall and claimed redress, with no other result than that Robledo had been requested to draw up a resolution decreeing that householders should not themselves employ vigilants without the Council's consent. Cuestas Abajo was now proposing to defy the Council, which a few humorists had already done by crying the hours upon their return from the tavern.

The sereno tried a door at the corner of the street and vanished into the gloom of the plaza arcade, and again he felt sick and restless. Robledo retraced his steps and entered the house; he found a parcel upon the table with a letter beneath the string, at which he began to tug. It was too strong to break, so he opened the letter; it was from Caro, thanking him for the loan of the books, three of which he had read with great interest. The other two he was compelled to return, because his responsibilities towards, and labor upon, the land gave him no leisure for reading. With a strange dejection he put the letter down and mixed himself a cognac and soda water and drank it down. After a while he read the letter again and began to brood over Lucía.

It was natural enough that Caro should so break off their relations, for no one could expect a man to continue to visit the house in such circumstances. He would have been willing to meet Caro at any place, however, glad to have met him, he realized, for it was not only that he had encouraged an absurd hope that Caro might forgive Lucía, but that he liked the man with a curious intensity that he had barely remarked to himself. But now the knowledge of Caro's withdrawal from politics disturbed him greatly, and he saw that it was the man's apparently invincible belief that had attracted him. "He's only a peasant at heart, like the rest," he said aloud, reading the letter again, and then a sharp emotion like anger arose in him, without person or thing for objective. He poured out a tumblerful of cognac and drank half of it, tore the letter up and flung the books into a corner and finished the drink. As he was opening the front door he heard Celestina moving above, and he hastened to get out of the house before she should come down. The sickness and trembling had disappeared now, and a burning sensation in the base of his spine had taken its place, his knees were aching, and his heart thumping, and there was a keen exaltation in his mind as of a glowing lamp that grew brighter and illumined all his being. His pace quickened as he drew near to the Black House.

As he descended the steep gully-like alley to enter by the rear door, the shutter of the window above rapped upon the wall and looking up he saw the haggard face and white hair of old Góngora peering out. "Buenas noches," the old man said, and Justo waved his hand and returned the greeting and was at once filled with a sense of desolation; he returned to the street and broodingly lit a cigarette. Enrique Góngora, now eighty-four years of age, had spent the last four years of his life in that tiny cell which his daughter the proprietor allowed him above the floor to which the girls took their men. The old bullfighter's life had been a curious and saddening one. At the age of eighteen he had been given "the alternative" by El Frascuelo. That early distinction had been at first belied, however, and

Góngora had gone from second-class ring to ring with no more
than the reputation of a good honest fighter who never shirked
either the dullest bull or one with superabundant *brio*. Then
his form unexpectedly returned and before long he was declining to appear without the guarantee of good bulls, or with
a poor alternative; and this period of triumph endured for
ten spendthrift years, until one day he trod upon the fallen
pole from which fireworks had been discharged at the beginning of the *corrida*. The bull's horn traversed Góngora's leg
from front to back. After a year's idleness and utmost poverty
he again returned to the Madrid ring and secured a resounding
success with his brilliant and daring *muleta* work of the natural
style, cutting ears and tails from two of his three bulls and
being carried round the ring by enthusiastic youths. With a
sudden tactical instinct he straightway departed for Mexico,
where he shortly became the leading *espada*. However, a
Mexican of some ability had popularized a method of horseback fighting and, finding himself losing ground before
Góngora's brilliant work in the classical tradition, discovered
an excellent retort in bribing the president to prohibit the
Spanish *corrida*. Fierce riots of protest took place and in one
of these a newspaper vendor was killed, and Góngora, standing nearby, was arrested, charged with the crime and flung into
prison. Thence he escaped by teaching the warder's little son
to manage the *muleta* and so delighting the father. Returned
to Spain, Góngora became a Republican and suffered persecu-
tion for several years until he recanted, and then in his next
fight he was caught by a bull and laid by for three months.
Again he went to Mexico and southern America, returned with
a fortune and a wife and lost both, the second to another
fighter's charms. Four years he spent in prison for the murder
of the rival, in whose body he embedded the spiked firework
of the bullring, the sign of an unworthy enemy. Emerging, he
found his fame undiminished, but his six-year-old daughter not
recognizing him and not wishing to live with him, he relinquished her to professional guardians to whom he gave an
enormous sum, and for the future lived only for the ring. At
seventy he was still fighting, and at seventy-nine, half-blinded,
dragging his feet behind him with varicose legs, he was re-

duced to beggary, occasionally earning a few duros by inspecting the bulls before *corridas*. Upon his eightieth birthday a column appeared giving some account of his life, and Concepción, the daughter, proprietor of the Black House in Los Olivares, journeyed to Madrid with money. Finding Góngora little equipped with judgment, she brought him back to Los Olivares and lodged him on the top floor, whence he was never allowed to emerge. A photograph of his daughter hung upon his wall, and this he had often told Robledo was the portrait of his wife. He had no idea what manner of a house it was in which he lived; escaping once, he had invited an olive oil merchant of Villa Alta to dine with him at his mansion. One thing alone remained to him, a sword given to him by a Mexican lady, and this he polished every day, though during the last years he had forgotten its use.

"Buenas," called the quavering voice again, and Robledo approached the window and replied softly:

"Buenas, Don Enrique."

"Buenas," the old fighter said again and remained smiling at Robledo, who was again swept by icy desolation, seeing that end to masculinity. He rushed down to the back door, rang in his private manner, and was admitted to a blaze of tawdry scarlet of paint and colored bulbs, by a half-naked girl whose unpainted lips and flat nipples were black in the lurid light.

The Black House was so called only because of its ill-kept exterior; within, it was decorated almost completely in red. The lower floor was divided into two salons, separated by arches of flimsy wood, roughly painted with a red of different tone with medallions of gold papier-mâché representing nudes. The rear salon was the bar, and around it ran a wooden settle with tattered red cushions, before which stood iron, marble-topped tables painted red also; the low ceiling was of the same color; a few of the girls wore red slips and brassieres and red chiffon dresses. In the fore salon was the cabaret and dancing floor. Beside a yard-high red-draped platform stood a piano, almost the only unpainted thing in the place, before which stood a red chair. About the floor, but leaving a space in the middle, were more painted chairs and tables; a staircase mounted from the bar to the upper floors, painted indiscriminately, though in the cubicle-like rooms were both red and white electric bulbs.

When Robledo entered, the cabaret was in progress, a girl of about twenty years of age was dancing to the music provided by the piano, a cornet and percussion. The girl was naked save for shoes, but carried a large shawl with which she successively covered or uncovered parts of her body. "Hola, Lolita," he called, and she smiled and dropped the shawl from her breast for an instant. Concepción knew Robledo's requirements, a bottle of brandy and frequent coffees, and these were brought at once by La Zaragozana, the girl he most favored. He had no illusions about Concepción's girls; many had been beautiful, in particular La Zaragozana, but unlike many he saw clearly their hideousness, and liked it. Out of hard masklike faces, beneath their paint weary and cramped with an eight-hour smile—he had seen La Zaragozana put on that smile in her sleep when he had touched her—carrion eyes searched the face of the customer. The dead hair, settling low over the brow, the loose and blackened breasts, the relaxed bellies and the hollow flanks and scarred shins of the girls of the Black House, all enforced that impression of inhumanity. This was another world, and he exulted in entering it, and the sign of entering was that the girl stood up and threw off all her clothes except her transparent muslin dress. Placing her leg over his thigh she poured out a drink. The rattling and bumping piano began a *fandango* and the hired artist of the evening entered and sang that love divided the heart with unalleviable sorrows.

In Robledo was that exalted yet mechanical serenity which the outside world can never know nor understand, nor believe to exist. Not burning of desire, nor excitement, nor reckless abandonment was the temper of the brothel, but a still, mechanical calm. There was no pleasure in this girl's contact, there would be no pleasure in her desperate professional services later on, but as she spoke to him, knowing herself that her words were barely heard, that her contact was awakening no thrill, the physical apparatus of nerve and tissue took hold of the brain and it became dead set in its course. The idiotic courtesies he was performing were mechanical but willed, it seemed. It was this deliberate setting in motion of the mechanism of body which provided the only thrill and that minute, though nonetheless macabre and fearful to his tingling brain. About the rest there was no horror, until thought came afterwards, and to not one in ten thousand brothel-goers does such ever come. That pulling of the lever was an act of faith, or an act of assertion. The body is a puppet of wire and wood and vibrating springs, and the brain a tangle of nerve and sensitive pulp; hot, irritated and anguished pulp. The hideousness of the faces and the worn, used bodies with their stereotyped dances of desire, their jerking simulations, their deliberate and earnest obscenities, their violent and squawking speech, all this asserted the same thing. And yet, within the aching pulp was still the mind, but this not now traitor to the flesh, and as he sat swallowing the brandy and the girl touched his ear and cheek the mind awakened, shook off the day-long torturing spirit, or turned its back upon the treacherous ambush of ideal, god or thought; the prancing writhing figures upon the stage, the guzzling fat-bellied men and the drained gray men, the hovering hawk-beaked, bird-eyed women were caught up in a fantastic red dance of mechanical serenity; this was the red mysticism of the pleasureless flesh, the peeling off of the deceits, yes, yes, not only the deceits of the emotions—all lies! all romanticism!—but the deceit of pleasure also, the desperate frenzied grappling search for something that should be unique, homogeneous, perfect—not mingled with spirit, nor thought, nor sensation, but the peace of the union of dust with dust and earth with the earth, yet possessing will. Far off his body was trembling—it seemed indeed his body was far off—then looming through the red whirl came a face he knew, the face of his own clerk.

The clerk sat down at the table and took a girl upon his knees and fondled her excitedly. "Hola, Justo," he shouted, "you're well out of it."

"Well out of what?" he was replying.

"The row up at the Town Hall; there's a crowd of tenants up there . . . at this time of night."

"Why the hell," he began, but the girl tugged at his shoulders and the sentences fell apart.

"They saw a light burning . . . someone must have left it on

. . . they were hammering the door when I passed . . . wanted Act . . . explained." The man's voice was receding. "I left 'em to it . . . told 'em they could form a society, some had been drinking."

"What size holdings had they got?" It was his own voice speaking though he had not meant to be dragged into this.

"Christ knows . . . here, get down, girl." The clerk slid the girl from his knees and scraped his chair across the floor. "Come and have a drink out here, Justo." Robledo felt sick as he rose, yet he followed the clerk to the bar, La Zaragozana behind him; the three sat down side by side upon the settle.

"I went down to the Rincón because they said you'd gone there; there's nearly a free fight there and I came away . . . no politics for me . . . administration is my line."

"All life's politics," Robledo said emphatically, and the clerk laughed and looked round with a grin.

"Well, young Caro was holding forth when I left. . . ." The clerk glanced at Robledo's face and said, "No, the other one, the sick one."

"Here, come on, *chato*," La Zaragozana said earnestly, "let's go and have some fun, see." She patted her muslin dress and gestured to him. The clerk slapped him on the back and said, "Come out here afterwards; there's a few points I'd like to ask you about the Act."

The man's cynicism revolted him yet, instead of anger, his brain was gripped by anguish and shame, for the name of Caro had brought another name into his mind and he shrank from it.

"Come and have some fun, *chato*," the girl idiotically repeated. Regarding her, something wedge-shaped seemed to thrust up from beneath his torment and the shame and the anguish were spilled apart like incompatible venoms and the old exultation rose through, yet without serenity.

"Fun! Ah . . ." he shouted, "you're not fun, little devil, you pitiable, gibbering little bitch of sweet mercy, you're the dust, the stones, the earth, you're the red dance, the red nerves off on their own, you're god the holy devil, you're the woman virgin of the jumping spirit . . ." His voice rose and the girl receded and he followed her with grasping hands. "Do you know what you are, do you know, you're wires, you're bones, and you're laughter inside the bones, you're a grinning dummy, you'd burst into flames, but you're dead, you're dead, ah, glory be to the flesh, you're dead! . . ."

The girl screamed hysterically and then, laughing at her laughter, he lunged and struck her across the face, another woman snatched her away and kicked at his crotch, and he struck her so heavily below the breast that the bones seemed to cave in. The waiter ran around the bar and rushed at him, and he threw a bottle which smashed the mirror behind the bar and brought down a tray of liqueur glasses. About him the tables were falling, and as the waiter drew near he lifted his fist and brought it down across the man's eyebrows and he fell, dashing his face against the table rim. Turning, he lowered his head as the pianist charged him and swept his assailant from his feet and fell over him. At the instant when his hands had reached the scraggy throat something struck him on the back of the head. . . .

When he recovered consciousness he was sitting in the rear doorway with Concepción bathing his head. He pushed her away and stumbled up the stinking alley. "Buenas noches," called Góngora as he turned into the street.

There was nothing to be done now. Slowly he walked along the Travesía, without even a stab of pain as he passed the herbalist's, mounted the hill to the plaza, clapped hands for the vigilant and entered the Town Hall. Opening his drawer, he took out the revolver and laid it on his desk, walked to the electric switch and turned off the light. Then quietly he returned to the desk and felt for the weapon and lifted it.

"No . . . can't die in the dark," he thought, and he turned towards the switch. "No," he muttered, and leaning over the desk, pulled up the blind. Below lay the plaza in a cold blaze of moonlight, the white houses standing over their black arches rising like bergs to the dusted sky and the gray mass of San Andrés ribbed with black. Faintly, at the bottom of the hill, the Cuestas Abajo sereno called, "One in the morning, señores, and a clear night."

Afterwards Robledo knew it was to that distant cry that he owed his life; to that ridiculous challenge to a ridiculous opposition, the faint, the idiotic spark of faith. The pulling of a trigger is but the twitching of a nerve and the stillness of the nerve is but a moment between twitchings. Again the Cuestas Abajo sereno called, and he looked out upon the silent plaza again; the Upper Town vigilant was standing at the far corner, his lantern upon the ground, waiting for him to descend.

Standing upon the steps, he clapped again, and the sereno came over and locked the door. "Good night, Señor Secretary," he said, and Robledo replied, "May you have good nights," and returned to Mendizabal Street. In the bedroom a light was burning and as he mounted the stairs Celestina opened the door; without a word he entered the room and sat down on the edge of the bed. "Come to bed," Celestina said and he barely heard her. "Come to bed, dear," she repeated, and sat by him and put her arm round his shoulders. Mechanically he pushed off his shoes and allowed his wife to help him remove his coat. As if startled, he turned to her and slid his hand beneath her nightdress and laid it upon her knee and stared at her, and she smiled and repeated her command. "My head," he muttered, and lay upon the bed while she scolded him and dressed the bruise, with something like contentment, until she began to plead with him and to weep, which she had rarely done during the last two years.

Suddenly he struggled into a sitting position and, gripping her fiercely, said, with awakened terror, "The sereno . . . the sereno," and hid his face against her shoulder. "Faith must be defended with lies" was the last thing he said before falling asleep, but there was in it neither bitterness nor relief.

Most Green, Most Purple

THE long days passed and the heats that blind the eyes with thin rancid sweat no more tormented the workers still laboring upon the Huerta, and the cigarras ceased to drown with hypnotic sound the men upon the olivars. The crazy brown dust storms of October fretted into every crevice of the walls of Los Olivares, lending their minute erosion to Time's genial labor of bringing all things low. The first rains came and upon the hills of nights, so men said with nods, the first frosts; distances summer-long invisible behind the shaking chains of the heat took shape. At the head of the valley the Cerro startlingly stood up as if it had taken its winter post a mile outside the town, and over the col at its side were seen the blue hills that look down upon Guadalquivir, rank upon rank of washed indigo and palest cyanine hard-drawn and cut in glass, and beyond the transparent light itself bore the rumor of hills. One morning, for the first hour of day only, the Cerro bore a fragile cape of white lace upon its shoulders.

In the town nothing had happened; the traveler came and sold his goods and paid his compliments and hurried away. One day there was a great noise of shouting, and through the hollow gloom of San Andrés echoed the brays and hoofbeats of the donkeys tethered to its walls, and then their owners untethered the she-donkeys upon the north side, and others untethered the male donkeys from the south, and they rode away and the fair was over; the new school was brought near to completion, a priest went down to the capital and stayed there many weeks, a girl at the Black House was murdered

239

by her lover whom she had been keeping in Sevilla. Don Blasco Ortega won another round of his battle against a tiresome shopkeeper, and the serenos cried some nights and were silent upon others and at last were silent altogether.

Then turning all eyes in one direction the slowly moving low-hanging pall of dust appeared in the shallow dip in the crest of the sprawling hills across the valley, and the sheep of distant hills and unknown masters went down to their winter pastures, and men felt strange emotions stirring obscurely within them at the sight of the dust and looked about them restlessly as the strength went out of their arms and the hoe or the spade lay idle against their legs. But the dust passed quickly, for the great days of transhumance are over and the countless flocks of the Mesta no longer bleat along the immemorial tracks that still link the vast light-foundered and fantastic cordilleras of Spain. And the transhumance shepherds, brown men with immensity in their gaze and strange gear and different knowledge, who knew every fountain, every resting place, every place where the malign spirits still haunt the stones and neither man nor beast may sleep but imagine broken macabre things, who know as they pass that here the earth is salt, or bitter, or that here a man died; these shepherds looked across the valley at the brown ring of stone and the towers and the white cubes dotted with black standing amidst the dark monotonous pattern of trees, and when the far-off Angelus rang and one of the shepherds whispered his prayer, the words of the Faith were still like a novel thing upon his lips.

And one of the girls of the Black House, sitting with her companions at the café outside the walls, watching the dust pall creep over the hills, suddenly lifted her northern face to the sun and shutting her eyes sang a strange and lovely song of the far-off Asturian hills. *"Ya se van los pastores,"* she sang, "The shepherds are going away," she sang, and they listened till one of them said, "Ah, be silent," and the singer obeyed and gazed away over the hills and her companions paid for her coffee and spoke loudly to her. And that was all the link that was between the clouded drama of the vanishing flocks, and the town of massive walls and red-tiled roofs.

At the end of September began the longest task which the olivar workers of Don Fadrique had to undertake, the gathering of the fruit. Many wise men of his line and the culminating care of Don Fadrique's father and his present mayordomo had resulted in olive crops perfectly "stepped," that is, so diversified in varieties that first one and then another ripened, or came to the maturity desired. From the first days of October when the first eating manzanillos and zorzaleños were being gathered, to March or April when the late eating verdials were picked, there was incessant and well-regulated labor upon the fields of Los Olivares, the principal oil crops forming the dramatic crisis in December.

One Friday evening in early October Justo Robledo was surprised to receive a visit from Joaquín Caro, whom he had seen the night before at the Republican Center, as usual lately. At his invitation Caro entered the house and ate a few olives and drank a glass of vermouth which Lucía placed before him.

"What I came to see you about is the Ojeda field. It's time something was done about the fruit."

"What do you mean—it's ripe?"

"Not all the varieties, there's some budiegos, but there are flocks of birds about and they'd best be gathered."

"Have you heard from Ojeda?"

"No, he's written only once since he started work in the mine. What do you think I ought to do? Am I in the right if I strip the trees and sell the crop?"

"Well, I don't see how any harm could come of it. He wrote asking if you would dress the trees, didn't he?"

"You don't think anyone will make trouble . . ."

"You mean Escolástica's family . . . and my people; no, I don't think so; anyway, leave that to me. If they want picking and you've got the decency to do it, nobody's likely to trouble you. You can leave the money with me if you like and I'll bank it in Ojeda's name after paying your labor costs, of course."

"All right then, I shall go out there tomorrow."

"Yes?"

"Ursula and my mother will come, I expect, and the old man

will bring the donkey with baskets. I was wondering whether you'd care to come out. I shall go straight round the slopes and they'll bring the dinner."

"Yes, I'd like to join you; what time are you going to eat?"

"One o'clock. If you've got some old cloths or sheets that it won't hurt to soil you might bring them out. All of us working together might get the job done in one afternoon."

At half-past one, when they began work on the olive gathering, Robledo was as excited and intent as the rest of them; he climbed into the trees and directed his wife and sister with the petulance of the enthusiast.

"No, no, no, bring the cloth a little more this way; *that's* right, ah, now you've carried it too far."

"A little dirt won't hurt the fruit," Celestina protested.

"No, no, but it won't do it any good either, woman."

"Well then, how's that?"

"And now we've put it to your liking you are going to strip another branch."

"Nonsense, woman, I was just looking at it."

In the other trees worked Ursula and Joaquín, while Ana and Celestina climbed the two ladders they had brought. Soon Ursula began to sing; as soon as she was silent Ana began, the same song, and after her Joaquín, then Celestina and Justo. The fruit began to rain down upon the cloths, green and red and purple-black.

"It's a good thing we came out, Justo," Caro shouted from a manzanillo.

"They're overripe?"

"Yes, the oil will be chock full of glycerin . . . though we can mix it with the others . . . but there's a few attacked by the olive fly."

"Ha, ha, any cure for that?"

"No, prevention only, spraying and disinfection."

"Ha, ha . . . Well, they say the maggot is the same fruit as the olive; a few won't hurt the belly."

Again the singing began, but now it was those in the boughs who sang, for the others were stooping and collecting the fruit that had fallen upon the soil and pouring it from sieve to sieve. And then the singing and even conversation gradually

died away, as the thoughts of all of them were filled only with
the small fruit, the stretching forth of the hand with the
wooden claw-toothed rake towards a spray and the downward
drag, the gentle resistance of one or two fruit, the fall and the
soft *plop* of the olives on the cloth below. The red hand
stretching out among the ashen green leaves fixed the rhythm
of the mind for those in the trees; the stooping, the swing to
the cloth, or the irregular rain made the rhythm for those on
the ground. Justo was the first to grow silent; his clumsy movements in the trees many trunks behind Joaquín and Ursula,
though they had begun together, were the only sounds they
heard from him; when Lucía or Celestina spoke to him he
replied briefly or absently and they soon left him alone, returning to his trees only when he called quietly for the cloths
to be moved; even this he often did for himself, when he
descended from the fork to pick the low outer fruit.

Then at the last tree of his row Caro shouted:

"How's it going, Justo?"

"Fine, boy," Robledo replied.

"I'll start on your row from this end."

"No, I'll finish it, there's no need for that."

"Oh, I don't mind, I may as well."

"No need at all," Robledo said, leaning forward from the
fork of a tree to peer at Caro. "I like picking."

"All right, I'll leave it to you, sing out if you want help."

"Right, I'll sing out if I do," he answered loudly and once
more reached out his white hand among the leaves and gently
showered a bunch of purple-black fruit upon the cloth and
shifted his feet cautiously along the mother branch. A little
farther and he would be able to reach some fine glistening
fruit, plump and unshriveled, in which would be rich sweet oil.
He stretched out his hand, but with the wooden claw held at its
extremist point he could not reach the bunches. With more
caution he slid his left foot along the bough and leaned forward
till his fingertips barely kept contact with the bough behind
him; still he could not draw the claw down even the nearest
burdened sprays, and beyond them were many purple-black
clusters. Bringing his right foot nearer his left he thrust with
his supporting hand and rocked safely forward and quietly

took hold of the slender bough in front. "Very good," he
whispered, praising his skill in getting so far out on the
bough. Momentarily he swayed, and his movement caused a
few fruit noiselessly to slip from their stems. "Ah," he said,
feeling minute but definite disappointment that the fruit had
fallen, and then deliberately reached out his hand and drew
the rake over the twig. The tiny rustle of the leaves, their
turning movement which disclosed their pale underside, his
careful adjustment of balance, all of this was pleasure to him
and so keen his senses were that he felt the round pressure, and
the barely perceptible knock of the fruit against the wood and
the slight resistance they made in parting from their stems.
His eyes were fastening on the claw and the fruit; the yellow
hills visible through the netlike foliage, the other people around
him, the voice of his sister and his wife—nothing was perceived, or only perceived through a calm monotony of purple-
black fruit falling to the white cloths. Now the sprays were
bare and he moved back to the fork and gazed along another
bough; out there was a ripe and lovely richness of olives and
a calm unemotional greed entered him, like a spreading out
of his own self to include the shining clusters, or to bring
them within him. Even when he looked down at his white-
shod feet it was through an imagery of fruit that he saw them
and shifted them along the green-gray rugose bark.

He was disappointed and sad when the last tree had been
stripped, and then suddenly he was invaded by a rush of
thoughts. He rejoined the others, and at once returned with
Ursula to carry over his last clothful of fruit; proudly he laid
them beside the others.

"Now we'll commence sorting them," Caro said, and Ana,
who had already begun, stood up and awaited instructions.

"I think we'll leave the women to it and have a smoke and
a talk, eh, Justo?"

"There's some coffee over there which only wants warming,"
Celestina said.

"Ah, good," Robledo replied. "I've brought some wine but
I'd rather have coffee; go and warm it, really hot, my dear."

"I'll come with you," Ana said, and the two wives went over
to the ruins.

"My sister's worth watching sorting olives."

"And so is Lucía, she's like a machine."

"We'll see; you're not to race though, girls," he shouted, and both of them looked up and Lucía called, "What did you say?"

"I said, don't race."

"That's right, you'd better not race," Robledo added.

"What's that?"

"I said . . . don't race."

"Oh, they say we mustn't race; I'm tired too," Ursula said.

She knelt down at one end of the row, and Lucía, at the other, regarding the cloths, laid her hands upon her swollen belly and gazed at the fruit; Ursula laid her hands upon her thighs and put her head on one side to regard the pile before her, and then laughed at Lucía, who smiled faintly in response.

"Shall we race, Lucía?"

"Yes. There's six piles, that'll be three each. There's more on that one of mine than on any of yours, but it doesn't matter. Are you ready? Ave María. Gratia plena! Off!"

The two girls worked in the same, the traditional way, the only way to sort olives. The green ones are kept for preparation with water and salt or herbs for the table, the wrinkled and the overripe yield dense gummy oil which sours easily, the ripe fruit sweet oil and the greatest yields, but the red-purple olive gives the finest-flavored oil. These, then, are the categories the small olive grower observes, and he does not much care to keep his varieties separate as the commercial producer must often do, though some green olives must be "killed" with salt and others with frequent changes of water, otherwise they are bitter and unpalatable.

At first Lucía went rapidly ahead. First of all she spread the fruit and then with a quick turn began to throw them out to right and left, Most Purples to the right and Most Greens to the left, leaving a multihued pile of red, purple and green fruit in the center. Then she moved to the next cloth and began the same operation. She reached the center a whole cloth ahead of Ursula.

"Bravo," called Robledo, but his sister did not look up, holding her belly to kneel down in order to put her Most Greens into one basket and her Most Purples into the other.

"No cheating, Lucía," Caro called, as Ursula began to work on her last cloth.

Again she began to sort the remaining piles into Most Purples and Most Greens, and now the remaining pile was composed of the Red-Purple fruit, the finest oil-givers.

"Hurry, Ursula," Caro shouted as she began her second sorting, and Robledo shouted encouragement to his sister, now working more slowly. The fruit showered out from both girls, but they came faster from the younger and she flung up her hands some twenty seconds before her rival. There is no great difference between any two olive sorters worthy of the name, as the "one hour" or "two hours" of the shepherd in speaking of distances will be "one hour" or "two hours" for all shepherds however young or old or short or long of leg.

"I've won," Ursula screamed, and flinging her arms round Lucía, kissed her repeatedly on the cheek; slowly Lucía's hands rose from her belly to the girl's shoulders and she accepted the kisses.

"Right, we'll judge the result," Caro called, and when they came over he put out his hand to help Lucía rise.

"Yes, that's fine work, both of you. The coffee's ready, to judge by the noise Mother and Señora Robledo are kicking up."

After coffee they sat talking for a while and then Caro and Robledo strolled off to look at the trees again.

"I don't know, I think I should have been a happier man if I'd been put to the land work," Robledo said.

"Happier? I know what you mean, but there's no living in it."

"Yes."

"It deadens the mind, Justo, and that makes you forget things. Do you know, I can't bear to think while I'm working."

"It spoils your work?"

"No, that's a question of my hands, but it hurts, upsets me, or the thinking is bad, do you know the sort, all turning over and over and twisting about?"

"Christ, do I not!"

"I have to stop to think, for the land, the trees and all that deaden the mind. That's why the landworker is so hard to move. If you don't think, you can forgive anything . . . anything."

At the unusual intonation Robledo glanced at Caro and said, "If you don't think, there isn't anything to forgive." He said this sadly and then put out his hand sharply and touched Caro and then withdrew it, for he had realized why Caro had been slaving on the fields to the limit of the body's power, and that was not to be spoken about. Instead he remarked, "It deadens the mind . . . but there's more in it than that."

Caro was a long time replying, and then he said:

"How so?"

"What I said at the Rincón, there's a magic in it . . . no, nothing so damn romantic, it's a natural flow of the lusts and the hates; thought is an unnatural flow, or a stick bobbing on the flow, to beat yourself with."

"You don't believe that thought is evil?"

"No. I'm explaining its pain."

"Well, it seems that either you've got to suffer poverty in quiet like my father, or suffer the same poverty and all the . . . trouble of thinking as well. I'm wondering whether we'd think if we had a better civilization."

"Oh, I think so . . . if we didn't it would mean that all our thought was trying to extinguish itself, or that man was doomed to torture himself for nothing . . . Christ!"

"What's the matter?"

"Say, that's astonishingly like an explanation of the Church's attitude. Don't think! Leave that to those specially protected by grace, just as science is left to those with special brains; it comes to naught and it disturbs the soul. Pray, trust in God and Holy Church and you'll arrive at the perfection of heaven, where thought is ruled out by knowledge. Contemplation, we call it, to use a better-flavored word, quiet experience of truth, and it's truth which matters, not thought. Jesus, that's a good argument to knock down." Robledo laughed.

"Why do you laugh?"

"Oh, that's the devil of honesty in me; I laughed because I took it for granted it must be false because the Church behaves as if it were true."

"I envy you; I'd think a lot better if I could see both sides of the case like that."

"You envy me . . . *ah, God, Caro!*"

When they set out for the town Robledo and his sister walked side by side, and then he hastened and allowed Caro to take his place. Lucía greeted him directly and they walked for a quarter of an hour or so till he turned to the girl and, delaying her march, called her by name.

"Won't you ever forgive me?" she said.

"My dear, my dear," he burst out, and took her hand and held it tightly. "I want to, I want to forgive you . . . you know I do, Lucía."

"Then you do," she whispered.

"How can I?" he said. "How can I forgive you when you're going to have his baby?"

For a moment before she fell, Lucía realized he was speaking of marriage, and then they were kneeling by her side at the well near the mayordomo's vineyard.

A week later Robledo again picked olives at the Caros' holding when he stayed to dinner. One of the consequences of this visit was that Pascual's dues to the Town Council were illegally lowered. Then, a fortnight before the great harvest, occurred an event which set the town talking of nothing else for several days.

In the first week of November Father Martínez celebrated his Golden Wedding to the priesthood. At the invitation of a committee of parishioners he was present at a celebration in the hall of the nuns' school. Special wines were opened and passed round, and even Soriano, returned from the capital for the occasion, drank wine. Then, responding to Don Blasco's toast, the rector began a speech which in the upshot was to have important consequences. After a period of review, in which he looked back over his long years in Los Olivares, he remarked, "You know, I am old enough to remember the First Republic . . . and, well, I have seen that Republic pass. . . ." There was a murmur at the back of the hall, and Don Blasco noted that there were several present who certainly were not Catholics.

"But often I think the world is tired, my children, it seems that the earth itself does not yield as once it did, though as to that there are diverse causes, I think." Father Soriano and the lawyer smiled, for that was how the rector always confronted his *bête noire*. "Latterly, being an old man, I have begun to write a book, my children, upon the notable defection of our country from the truth, and also upon the impoverishment of her economic life and its cause. It is not surprising to me to note that our wisest governors always foresaw the danger we should run in abandoning the horse and the ox. The Cortes of Madrid considered the danger of mules in 1534, and the Cortes of Valladolid requested their prohibition also, that was in 1542. But even before this, in 1494, the great Catholic kings prohibited, under rigorous pains, that anyone save women should ride mules in public. I ought to say I owe these points of legal history to my respected friend Don Blasco Ortega."

"You will pardon me, Don Bautista," Ortega said, smiling broadly. "But in that instance of Ferdinand and Isabella you have omitted an important fact."

"Have I, and what is that, Don Blasco?"

"In 1494 the public riding of mules was forbidden to all save women and ecclesiastics."

There was some affectionate chaff after this and Don Blasco even ventured the phrase "community of skirts," but this was not warmly received.

"I have heard all sorts of excuses about oxen," the rector continued, "such as that they are slow. This is a pure false-hood, for if the ox is taken while young it can be trained to go as fast as a mule. The Dutchmen of the Cape of Good Hope used to train their beasts so, and there used to be a posting master at Jerez whose oxen were actually preferred to his horses. And Buffon says that in the East Indies they are ridden with saddles and provide a gentle, swift, smooth and regular mode of progression. Also, I read in an old book that the Prior of the Cartuja, at Paular in the Sierra de Guadarrama, while on his way to Madrid, was overtaken by a nobleman whose postillions scorned the Prior's ox-drawn carriage. The Prior accepted the challenge and arrived at Madrid long before the nobleman.

"Wise agriculturists have always seen the danger, too.

Bachiller Juan de Arrieta in his *Awakener,* published in 1605, my children, writes thus: 'I say, then, that the cause of the total perdition of Spain has been and is the omission to plow and sow and carry with oxen and having introduced and invented the mule in their place, whose costs are excessive and whose work is bad, pestilential, useless and pernicious.' And López Deza in his *Eulogy* of 1608 praises Arrieta's condemnation. Why, it was Varro himself who said: 'Terram boves proscindere nisi viribus non possunt.' You cannot plow with mules, they pull too shallow, nor with donkeys. Why, I've even seen people plowing with an ox and a donkey, against the express prohibition of Deuteronomy 22:10.

"And this shameful inutility of the mule, dear children, is because in its very origin it is a shameful beast. Unlike the fruitful ox it *cannot* respond to God's command 'Be fruitful and multiply,' that moral law by which you yourselves have multiplied and produced offspring whose love you have enjoyed beneath God's blessing. But it is not only plowing that is better done by oxen or by horses, but carrying. There was once a great Condestable of Castilla for whose tomb a huge stone was being dragged up a hill by fifteen pairs of oxen. The wagon slipped back and dragged the oxen with it, yet one of them resisted so much that he bled from the nose and mouth. And the Condestable, who was himself directing the building of the tomb, made that ox free of labor for the rest of his life. . . ."

Father Soriano was still smiling when he rose to speak; in his first sentence he began an exposition of the Leo XIII encyclicals on labor, passing thence to a brief criticism of Socialism, Anarchism and Communism, and then devoted the rest of his speech to a eulogy of the rector. When they emerged from the school a crowd had collected, whose jostling led to sharp words and these to blows. Within a few seconds Don Blasco was down with a bleeding mouth and people were screaming for the Civil Guard.

The day after the "riot" Father Martínez was arrested by Captain Montaña at superior command and taken to the capital. There he was tried for anti-Republican agitation and sentenced to six months' imprisonment. The trial figured at a column's length in the Madrid newspapers, most of which reprinted an account of the Good Friday disturbances. A middle-aged priest, formerly a lawyer and now an amateur of electricity, replaced Martínez. He disliked garlic and quarreled with La Cándida about her use of it; for the rest he was a solid, sensible, unpious and unmystical priest, a practical Man of God. People began to talk affectionately of Father Soriano, now a non-chapter priest at the cathedral, who sometimes preached at San Andrés.

Harvest

ALL the afternoon the harvesters had been arriving, in motor-
buses, lorries, carts, wagons, and upon foot, sometimes with
the *hato,* the bundled equipment of pots, clothing, food and
bedding and things of no conceivable use in olive-gathering,
slung over shabby little donkeys, sometimes with hands full
and necks burdened with the same. All that evening the Puente
Nuevo bus made repeated journeys to and fro and, towards
midnight, long-distance lorries crowded with pickers roared
and detonated through the Sevilla Gate, to be greeted with
yells and cheers from the children permitted to witness the
annual arrival. Most of the visitors were old acquaintances who
yearly returned to Los Olivares for the harvest and these knew
where to seek such lodging as they needed. The Sevilla Inn
and Upper Inn were both thronged with people, families of
twelve and fourteen packing into one tiny room or alcove, or
occupying a chalked space in the long storeroom of the former.
About the yard that night coke devils were placed for the
poorer visitors to cook upon, and around these and upon the
dirty cobbles slept many who had wandered vainly about the
town looking for shelter. Neither La Gorda nor Molinos went
to bed that night and at five in the morning the hostess could
still be heard shrieking her commands to the shambling late
arrivals. An hour before daybreak Mater Purissima was surrounded by a quietly murmuring crowd. Before the shelter
itself stood a queue of those *banco* or group leaders who had
slept at Mater Purissima or in the tool houses and caves about
the mountainside. At daybreak Calasparra and the other

charge hands arrived from the palace, and a quarter of an hour later Argote rode down.

Now the mayordomo began to apportion the fields to the groups, mostly families.

"You there, Chiclero."

"Señor Argote!"

"Follow me," and the man scrambled on foot behind the mounted mayordomo, who shouted directions about a shortcut.

"You'll take this line of trees and that and that."

"Ah, one more, señor; I've brought two more children this year and a neighbor's girl, and my boy is old enough to pick now."

"All right . . . that row and the one beyond then, but listen, if I catch you beating the trees too hard do you know what I'll do?"

"Yes, sir."

"Oh, you do; what'll I do, then?" replied Argote, frowning.

"Cut off my teeth with a rusty sickle," Chiclero said, grinning, and Argote swore mildly.

"Well, what's it going to be?" Chiclero said suddenly, and their smiles disappeared.

"One peseta twenty-five the *fanega* of fifty kilograms," Argote answered firmly.

"One twenty-five—God preserve me, Señor Argote!"

"God's teeth, one twenty-five, I said."

"But, Jesus, this year the trees are only half burdened; we ought to be paid two fifty at the least; we shall have to work twice as hard for the *fanega*."

The mayordomo put his hands upon his thighs, stared down at the man and, giving his horse a single prod with the blind-side spur, caused the animal to rear up with pawing forefeet. Chiclero, however, stood his ground, for he knew the trick.

"One twenty-five, I said, señor mio."

"Two fifty."

"Ca, you'd take two twenty-five."

"Two twenty-five then, I'll take it."

"Sure you would; if I offered it. One twenty-five."

"Señor Argote, for the love of God, give us two pesetas; the trees are half bare."

"I might consider one seventy-five, but no, one twenty-five is enough."

"Ah, Jesus, one fifty, señor, one fifty or we might as well go home," cried Chiclero desperately. There was sweat on his forehead and his eyes were staring.

"One fifty then and clean fruit."

Within a few minutes the news had spread over the olivars that Chiclero, one of the toughest banco leaders, had secured only one fifty; it was the lowest price in living memory and silence fell upon the gatherers; with such a poor and scattered crop this harvest would give no relief to winter's poverty. A few Puente Nuevo people halfheartedly returned home. It seemed that the mayordomo knew the price was an unjust one, for his shout was seldom heard and he answered the uncordial salutations with a gruff voice.

Nevertheless, the busy cheer of olive harvest gradually restored itself and a shout went up as the first basket of fruit was brought in to Argote standing at the base of Broad Skirt. Within a few minutes there were gathered half a dozen impatient leaders, each with his basket and his tally stick. The olivar bookkeeping was of the simplest and was also infallible. A stick of olive wood or peeled nut was first parted in the middle, each half looped with string and then laid side by side and compared. Next a number was engraved on each half by Argote and the banco leaders, each of whom took a tally, examined it afresh and then exchanged it for the other half. A simple cut with a knife represented one *fanega,* a diagonal cut five *fanegas* and crossed cuts indicated ten. There never had been any case of fraudulence, and it was not even necessary to guard the poles upon which the estate tallies hung.

"Serene day, sweet oil," the pickers said to one another as they placed the broad-based tapering stepladders beside the trees, and though that was because wet fruit ferment and sour the oil and windy days put the bitter leaves of the tree among the fruit of the presses, it seemed as if the palest gold light filtered into the olives and gave the oil an added loveliness. "Serene day, sweet oil," they cried, drawing their hands down the rustling branches, "milking" the tree or stripping it "by the tress" as it is called in the Andaluz olivar language.

"It is the tree of peace," others said, sometimes ironically.

"Yes, of peace, which God grant you may enjoy," was the reply, or perhaps, "And no other tree gives so many eating days to the worker."

It was a ritual of greeting, this, and after it came the inquiries about the family, the new births, the recent deaths and then more hushed and with a secret embitterment the talk of pay.

"One and a half pesetas, ay!"

"Ay, one has to suffer in this world, ay!"

"Patience, man."

"And patience thou, woman."

"Ay!"

There was little external sign of discord all that morning; the joy of harvesting, the deeper-than-joy which man feels as the fruit of his trees are gathered soothed away the memory of hovel homes and poverty, and at last even the misery of many yielded to that medicine prime to the spirit. These were Man's trees, they were not of a man, and in Los Olivares this feeling was strengthened by the knowledge of Argote's devotion to them, a devotion which, it was said, had not prevented the mayordomo amassing a small fortune for himself out of ungranted perquisites, but which had nothing of proprietary pettiness about it. The still trees themselves were inviting the harvesters to strip them. The trees, whose immobility in the sapless winter had been a reproach to man's embitterment, whose sobriety of minute blossom had been a rebuke to license, whose stillness in the suffocating torment of August had been a doctrine of patience and whose harvest at its richest is ever a reproof to man avid of the yield from the meager tillages he apportions life, the trees now stood like naked women in the purest sunlight, with a woman's desire and gentle contempt awaiting the searching hands of her lover. Eyes which had glanced over olive trees without intent regard now peered closely and it seemed as if the trees willingly disclosed their fruit. The winter month had put on its paschal colors, and man crowded about the year's altar in festal-hued rags. Behind and above the trees rose the golden-brown sierra, scored with the vast baroque grooves and whorls of time, its crags and gullies shining with a washed clarity that disclosed every stone. The brown lands were dyed to a richer hue, the boughs were turned to candelabras of golden indwelling light, the sky softened from its harsh July assertion was the sky of an old reredos. Upon the floor the white cloths were spread and upon them the purple-black olives were raining.

There was an intensity about the labor which excluded all superficial thought of money. By careful jockeying of Argote, Caro had secured six fields of the very best trees, yet their superiority now meant to him only the greater joy of abundant fruit for the hands. Near the tree in which he was working Lucía was pouring from a sieve the soiled olives which had fallen beyond the cloths while Ursula winnowed with a cloth stretched over two sticks. Pascual and Ana and Joaquín were standing upon the ladders, the son reserving to himself the task of gently beating the upper branches with a short stick to dislodge the fruit; Marcial was slowly gathering the fruit into baskets, yet, for a while at least, the harvest was to all of them but the earth's joyful sacrifice to the God Man. In the afternoon Justo Robledo and Celestina joined the Caro party at about the hour when the singing began. The secretary immediately mounted the other leg of old Caro's ladder and the two men picked silently face to face for an hour. Beyond greetings they did not speak until Menudo, half-drunk, brought the Virgin of the Guild of Our Lady of Succor to the field and held the image out before Ursula, who ran to her heap of belongings for a five-cent piece and returned to kiss the feet of the Virgin. Then Lucía genuflected with difficulty, and putting a coin into the box, kissed the image. Robledo clicked his tongue softly. "Good girl," Pascual murmured, and Justo frowned and tugged at a branch, sending a shower of fruit over Menudo and the girl now painfully rising. Menudo looked up angrily at the picker and ostentatiously brushed a burst fruit from the Virgin. Unsteadily he held up the statue to Pascual, who rebuked him, saying, "Have you no respect for the Virgin that you bring Her here with drink in you?" and Menudo swore.

"Mother of God, I am not drunk. The offerings are for charity."

"Drunk, no, but this is no respectful state," Pascual said and, descending, kissed the image and placed a coin in the box.

"A bad man," he said to Robledo, who took no notice. For a long time they picked together silently. In the trees above them on Broad Skirt a woman singer was declaring that there was rage in all her songs, because as a woman she could not avenge her wrongs.

Now the singing became more widespread, from all quarters strong metallic voices began their *cante hondo,* sometimes breaking off because of incompetence or to reach for a distant bunch or to listen to a good singer. At the top of the Skirt where the yellow slope sank into a rubble of bloodstone, now darkly glowing like a wound turned evil, a hoarse tenor voice accompanied by Acorín, began a funeral soléa, beginning with a long-noted phrase, solemn and massive as the bough of an olive; bitterly sad as if sorrow brooded under a blinding sun, suddenly it flung itself high with sharp agony, like a gust tearing the boughs of the trees, and then sank through a wavering vibrating rain of notes, hard and individual as the leaves of an olive. At first it was like a rebellion of the heart and then it ceased to be mutinous, till it seemed like a tree of music growing out of the stone seams of the heart. What it had of treeness came from the singer and his listeners, whose lives grew to the same symmetry of hunger and desire and pleasure and despair. The monotonous singing, bitterly grieving in its beauty, lifted the same bough of song above the undiffering roots of their lives. There was in the music as much variation as there was in the clusters of olives; or as in men, hanging upon a common bough of life. Robledo descended the ladder and climbed to the singer's field and listened. The singer was a middle-aged man; his lean, blackened face and small blood shot eyes stared straight into Robledo's. His head slightly tilted; his mouth was twisted to one side also with the effort of singing; there was no recognition or acknowledgment in his gaze. When the singer had with an effort of his abdomen thrust out the last note Robledo nodded and the singer nodded and slowly came down the ladder. He limped slightly and across his face was a broad scar.

"You sing well, señor."

"My son sings better."

"I'd like to hear him."

"He's not come, he's in prison, señor," the singer replied with a shrug; "politics. It was he who first sang the song. We're from Puente Nuevo; are you of this town, señor?"

"Yes; how is the Señora, your wife, if it's not a bad question."

"Very well indeed, thank you. She has gone down with her daughter to have two fanegas marked up. And how is your wife, señor, supposing you to be married, and if it's not a bad question."

"Very well indeed, thank you. . . . Perhaps you would join us later, we're down there where you can hear the two girls singing."

"A sea of thanks, but I am sorry not to be able to come. Will you bring your folk up to drink a glass of something with us?"

"Many, many thanks, but I am afraid we have an engagement."

That night a group of Los Olivares people built an altar of trestles and planks at Mater Purissima and the Virgin was placed upon it, a few said their rosaries near it and a young girl from Jaén staying with García's family sang a song about "the little brown Virgin left alone on the sierra to watch her sheep all night." In the morning it was found that the altar had been thrown down and the unbroken image placed in one of the unoccupied toolhouses. A chance remark of Menudo's led to a fight between Puente Nuevo men and a few of Los Olivares.

"It was a Puente Nuevo man who did it," he said, after charging Mudarra.

"Meaning me?"

"I don't say you, but a Puente Nuevo man."

"Then me?"

"No, some other."

"Perhaps me?"

"Yes, perhaps you, you did it," shouted the now infuriated Menudo, and the Puente Nuevo man, a basket-maker seeking divorce under the new Act, struck the image-bearer with the

back of his hand, to be badly mauled by Mudarra in the free
fight which followed. In reality it had been a group of Socialists
led by García who had dismantled the altar. Overhearing a
significant remark, they had done this to avoid trouble. The
trestles and planks, neatly stacked, had been disturbed by
pickers seeking to make a bed. This traditional animosity received fresh stimulus that afternoon when it was heard that the
Provincial Government had ordered that unemployed Puente
Nuevo men should also be given work on the Los Olivares
school. First, two men began a clumsy squabble which Argote
brutally terminated with a kick for one and a blow for the
other, and this in itself was a violation of all the traditional
atmosphere of olive-gathering. The mayordomo had walked
about the olivars all that morning, but now he sent for a
horse and thereafter was rarely seen dismounted.

"First one thing then another with these blasted Puente
Nuevo men," Baeza shouted during a controversy about the
position of the tally poles, and at once the animosity was
revived.

"You want us to have the tally poles on our field all the
time," ejaculated a Puente Nuevo man. "You'd like us to put
up with people traipsing through our trees every minute, eh?"

It was the custom daily to change the place for receiving the
gathered fruit in order not unfairly to molest any one group,
and the failure to do this promptly had led to the argument.

"First you smash up an altar, then you sneak in on our
work, and now . . ."

"And now what?" the man said with sudden quietness,
squaring up to Baeza.

"If it weren't for you foreigners we'd be getting a decent
wage for this bloody picking," another Los Olivares man
shouted, and again there was fighting.

That afternoon Indalecio Argote rode down to the Civil
Guard barracks and demanded reinforcements for the couple
of guards on duty on the fields.

"There's going to be serious trouble between the Puente
Nuevo men and ours by the look of it."

"All right, I'll wire to the capital for a fresh company; in the meantime we will get a posse over from Puente Nuevo. They'll be able to pick out their ringleaders; the sergeant will do the same for ours," replied Captain Montaña.

After half an hour's telephone conversation with his superiors Montaña sent a guard to the casino, whither Argote had gone, to inform him that a company of guards was arriving from the capital; Argote, asleep in a chair, upon being awakened gruffly answered, "Very good, that'll put a stop to all this nonsense."

At night after the evening meal there was always music and dancing around Mater Purissima or upon the few open spaces such as the disused threshing floor near Argote's vineyard. It had been the custom for the Palacio yard to be thrown open for this purpose and formerly Don Fadrique himself had had a table placed upon a balcony and had watched the dancing from above. Occasionally he would send down a toast glass to the fiancé of some exceptionally good dancer and, rising, himself would drink to the couple. A worker so honored would boast proudly of it afterwards. However, the senior officer in command of the reinforced guard forbade the dancing in the palace yard after a minor incident which in reality had nothing to do with Puente Nuevo rivalry. This prohibition was naturally announced by the mayordomo, nor had the Marquis any knowledge of the affair, for he had gone overnight to the capital at his ailing brother's urgent invitation, but the result was that murmurings were directed against Don Fadrique.

"A bottle of champagne would cost him five pesetas."

"For a twenty-five-peseta note you could buy six bottles, for fifty an odd dozen."

"That's as much as he'd give God's own mother."

"It wouldn't buy a sheet of old music though."

At Mater Purissima that same evening occurred an event which caused the Civil Guard sergeant to clap a hand on his pistol butt. On the flat bluff a dance was in progress, Diego Mudarra and a violinist providing the modern music, while the guitarist played an occasional flamenco.

The chapel had rarely appeared so beautiful; chairs had been brought from the interior for the musicians and red shawls draped over them, upon the grille four lanterns hung,

outside a petrol-gas lamp threw a strange lurid light over the
dancing floor and the aloes beyond; behind the chapel another
lamp beneath the great dulzar olives threw upwards white and
black rods and made a reredos of light for the rite upon the
bluff around which the watchers sat, huddled together in
shawls and blankets, though the unmoving air was not cold.
The hills, seeming now even more enormous, rose blackly to
the sky trembling with quicksilver stars.

Near the musicians Acorín sat astride a chair, his guitar by
his side, covered by a case of baize-covered wood. At the
second flamenco Diego made a deliberate display of runs and
spread chords as a challenge to him, but he merely sighed profoundly and fingered his mustache. Then, during an interval,
a Puente Nuevo man engaged in a piece of horseplay tripped
in passing over Mudarra's chair, kicked the guitar and, falling, crushed in the sound board. The guitarist sprang to his
feet with an oath and swung a savage blow at the man, who,
apologizing the while, drew a knife and crouched.

"I'm sorry, man, I'll buy you another," he said fiercely, and
suddenly Mudarra laughed at the mingling of tempers. In that
instant the sergeant had blown his whistle and a pair of Civil
Guards patrolling the downtrack unslung their rifles and
wheeled towards the sanctuary.

"All right, buy me another then, though you're a bloody
fool, nonetheless," Mudarra said, and everyone felt the tension
relax, though their bodies were still held stiffly.

"That's finished the dance for tonight," the violinist exclaimed, though Pérez came forward and offered to fetch another instrument from the town. There were immediate offers
of guitars from several of the onlookers, whereupon Acorín,
picking up his instrument, approached Mudarra and said,
"Play on this one, it's a good guitar."

"No, you play, man," Mudarra replied, rising.

"No, you play, Mudarra."

"You play."

"You play."

"What about some music?" an onlooker shouted, but
Mudarra waved his hand.

"Man, you haven't played all the evening; they'll be wanting to hear you."

Acorín sighed and turned away with the guitar loosely held under his arm. "Hey, give me that instrument," Mudarra, said, and clapped the ex-sereno on the shoulder and both of them grabbed at the falling instrument, which Acorín saved from damage.

"That's right, you play, Mudarra . . . you're a better player than me," Acorín blurted gloomily.

"Christ," shouted Mudarra, "you play, come on, play to please me, man."

"Many thanks," El Chino replied, and seating himself, took out the guitar. It was the instrument Don Fadrique had first given to Mudarra.

"Where did you get that, friend?"

"I bought it from Bonifacio; it belonged to the Marquis but he had no use for it."

"It's got a new finger board." Acorín hesitated for a moment and then said, "Yes . . . Bonifacio told me all about it."

After Acorín had played he put the guitar into Mudarra's hands, and after striking a few preludial chords, he said:

"Let's go into the chapel and try it; the effects of the guitar will be lost out here," and the two men and a few followers entered the sanctuary, and sitting down with his back to the altar, Mudarra played first a flamenco rhythm and then the Narvaez Fantasia.

"God's daddy, you're a marvel," Acorín said when he had finished.

"Ah, nothing, man."

"It makes me want to give up the instrument."

"Oh, teeth, you're a good player," Diego said emphatically, but Acorín refused to be comforted and sat gazing at Mudarra in dejected admiration.

"It's your hand isn't big enough," the younger man said at last.

"Of course it's big enough," the other replied with heat. Mudarra saw that to have confessed its smallness would have meant giving up the instrument. Acorín's devotion pleased him and he said:

"Well, let's play together now and then; come round to my place tomorrow night, eh?"

El Chino nodded.

The following day Aguiló arrived, and within an hour was arrested; from that moment nerves began to grow taut; there were numerous outbreaks between the Puente Nuevo folk and the townspeople, who were now universally charged with lowering the piecework rates. At midday another turn of the screw was given by Argote. By custom the harvesters were allowed to gather the dulzar olives for themselves, but the commercial inutility of the variety, which will not keep and yields little fruit, prevented there being sufficient trees to satisfy the demand. The classical dish known as *remojón*, made by washing the fresh fruit and flavoring with oil, vinegar and onion, was so popular as a midday meal that by the fourth day the trees had been nearly stripped. As a result a quarrel broke out at the Fountain of Doña Inés about the fruit, between a Puente Nuevo woman and Joaquín Caro, who was pouring water over a bowl of olives held by Lucía Robledo. Hearing the shouting, the mayordomo rode over to the fountain and, in order to break up the disturbance, caused his mount to rear up. Lucía screamed and dropped the plate and the beast shied at the rush of women.

"There was a time when only virgins and married women were allowed to gather olives," Argote said when the commotion had ceased, at which Caro leaped at his leg and, hitting the box stirrup from his foot, essayed to drag him from the horse, ignoring the hail of blows with the stock butt on his head and neck. Though he tried fiercely for a "rabbit killer," Argote could not beat off Caro and at last he was pulled to the ground. Men and women dragged Caro from the cursing olivero and then, as the latter rushed at his adversary, closed between them with a menacing attitude.

"Get back on your horse, Argote," Baeza sneered.

"Enough from you, you're sacked, call at the Palacio and get your money tonight."

"Sacked, am I? It won't pay you."

"Won't it? We'll see."

"With a tale like that to put round and the low pay, you'd have every man on strike in an instant."

"The foreigners also, I suppose," said Argote with sudden cunning.

"The foreigners, too," Caro replied, but there was no conviction in the words.

The next morning Anarchist propaganda swept over the olive yards: the fruit belonged to the workers who worked the earth and nursed the trees, ownership was not a sacred right, it was the most trivial form of individualism, the Marquis had no function and did nothing for the crops. Someday the worker must arise and gather the crops for himself. That afternoon the first payments were made and people who had suffered patiently the knowledge of low rates were in the event sickened with despair or infuriated by the sum received. Puente Nuevo and other visitors were met with hostile regard, the very light seemed to lose its December purity, the machine of hatred was racing faster and faster every minute. Montaña telephoned urgently for reinforcements and the pairs of Civil Guards about the slopes drew together and conversed in whispers.

Then suddenly it began. In the gully below the fountain of Doña Inés a burst of shouting rang out, a tangle of angry voices without intonation, and then those round Mater Purissima were startled to see men running swiftly through the trees towards the town. Only their legs could be seen but there was something in their nervous excited pace which did not resemble the running of ordinary haste. Pickers stopped and gazed open-mouthed as another group came running up the hill, passing Mater Purissima with strained eager faces that saw nothing about them. As the runners, Los Olivares men, passed the queue of banco leaders waiting for pay, a chance collision provoked a vicious remark from a Puente Nuevo man and at once the runners and the foreigners in the queue were fighting. The uproar and the Civil Guards' warning shots brought those who had received their pay racing back to the tally field and the fight extended over the fields around; again the guards discharged their Mausers into the air without effect.

"Don't fire, men," shouted Montaña. "Keep your heads," and a moment later he ordered them to fall in around him.

"Make a wedge and force your way through, separate them, then break them up, defend yourselves if necessary; use your butts unless you're drawn upon."

The wedge commenced to force itself into the wrestling crowd of infuriated ineffectual men and women. A swirl of the crowd and the three men at the apex were swept away and the others pressing on could not hold together and their line was broken.

A shot cracked, muffled and distant, in the direction of the Palacio, and Montaña waved the guards to return. They did so, and then a shriek rang out of the crowd and a portion of it split and broke up, leaving a man motionless upon the ground. As if responding to command, silence fell upon the mob, and those nearest the wounded man encircled him and burst into loud lament. "Ay, ay," the women cried, and a frantic woman beat and tugged at the circle round the injured man. "Ay, ay," the crowd moaned and beneath the wails a muttering was heard.

"Clear a way," ordered Montaña, and the guards advanced into the crowd, rifles short-held at the waist.

"Get back, get back," they commanded, thrusting the muzzles into the stomachs of the men. "Ah, would you," shouted the sergeant, as a man tried to fend off his rifle, and clapped his hands smartly upon the bolt and jabbed the muzzle hard into the man's dirty flesh; he wilted and staggered away and fell upon his knees and flurried the soil with his hands, gibbering with fear. The prostrate man was carried away and the crowd stood about in silent remorse. From all parts of the olivars the harvesters were arriving. Far away on the Skirt of Beyond a powerful voice was ululating.

On the Mater Purissima track an isolated shout was heard and at once a fresh current of hatred ran through the crowd. The Marquis of Peral and Father Soriano, the latter carrying a suitcase, were hurrying towards the Palacio, escorted by a pair of guards.

"There's the workers' enemy," someone shouted, and there was a cry of "Both enemies." "They're all enemies," Baeza added, and out of a rapid crystallizing movement of the crowd Mudarra was lifted up.

"There's the enemy," he shouted, "the enemy of the workers and his priestly servant, Soriano, servant of God, who can put you in hell with a word or give you the sack and never did a day's work in his life." The Los Olivares men acclaimed the opening with a shout and Mudarra continued with an appeal to the harvesters to abandon their local feud. As he motioned to be lowered, Baeza scrambled up the wall of the higher field and began to address the pickers.

"The olives are yours, take them. Don't wait for the day that will never come when the Government will give you the crops. Don't wait for the day when the priest will bless you and beg you to take them in the name of the Lord. They are yours, you've got hands, there are ladders, there are the trees . . . what right has the Marquis of Peral to this fruit?"

Another orator ran to the edge of the lower wall and repeated the appeal. . . .

"To the Great Grove," a voice cried, and with a sudden breakaway a score of men raced towards the field of the Great Grove, as yet unharvested. Others snatched up cloths and baskets and followed them through the haze of dust.

"Down there, to the Grove, round by the well track," Montaña commanded, and the guards bunched together and moved off at the double. "Let them get into the trees first and then pick out the cowards," the sergeant shouted down the guards' line.

In the Grove the first pickers climbed straight into the trees and began to throw down fruit, not waiting for cloths or ladders. The neighboring pickers stopped in astonishment and one of them called out, "Eh, throw them clear of the 'drip' boy." When the cloth bearers arrived these fruit were at once covered up by the spreaders, too excited to remove them. The Grove was now filled with men and youths running to and fro and shouting orders and advice to one another.

On the far side of the Grove there was a sharp whistle, again the warning volley was fired into the air and the guards divided into couples and approached the nearest trees. At once Mudarra leaped down and, thrusting past the two guards, put his fingers to his lips, whistled piercingly and waved to the pickers to join him. Montaña shouted a command and the guards doubled up the slope to him and lined out facing the harvesters. There was a moment's silence, then Montaña spoke.

"The authorities have shown patience today, you can have no complaint. I shall not permit these trees to be touched; if you do touch them I warn you I shall order fire." A few pickers laughed and Montaña sharply mentioned one man by name and the laughter became an angry snarl.

"You won't have enough ammo; too many warning shots, Montana." Mudarra's sneer angered the captain and he shouted:

"Get outside of this field, all of you. I give you one minute to be out of it."

"Or you'll fire?"

"One minute to be out of it."

"Ca! See here. You couldn't miss at this range and there's a nice lot of us, we're not carrying arms because the olive is the symbol of peace, señor mio. Why don't you begin? It would be great fun for you and your —— crowd. We're not going and we're going to strip these trees, got that?"

"That talk will do you no good, Mudarra," the sergeant said.

"Ah, so you're not going to shoot! I'll tell you why. Do you hear all that shouting up on the Skirt and over yonder? Course you do. You'd have a lot of shooting to do, wouldn't you? And one or two out of all that might have a gun. Come on, brothers," and turning, Mudarra took a few paces towards a tree, and then, with a burst, he sprang to the tree and climbing swiftly into the fork, called for cloths, overjoyed that the guard had not opened fire as the pickers broke up and swarmed around the trees.

For a few minutes, though they picked the black shining fruit with trembling hands, their imagination was filled with the line of sullen guards, rifles lowered and the sun glinting on their black shining hats, and then thought of violence disappeared and a joy, a wild exultant joy of olive-picking filled them.

"Mother of God!" screamed a youth. "What a harvest, oh, Mother of God!"

Upon the Skirt of Beyond the wave of exaltation seemed to arrive almost simultaneously, and though there were a few protests from those who had picked well, the trees were soon being stripped irrespective of demarcation. It was on Broad Skirt that the first clash occurred. The foreigners attempted to defend their trees and took up sticks and stones and cooking utensils to drive off the raiders; a few drew knives. For a moment there promised to be trouble, and then the resisters were disheartened by the approach of fresh pickers racing down the slopes and dropping from wall to wall, often rolling over into the puffing dust. The submission of the foreigners on Broad Skirt was followed by that of the others. The majority sullenly withdrew from the fields and collected around Mater Purissima, a few joined the expropriators; of these, one named Ortíz became a leading spirit; others returned to Los Olivares and prepared to leave for their homes.

It was on Broad Skirt also that Argote surrendered. When the harvesters had raced away towards the Great Grove he had confided in the guards to deal with them and had ridden hard to the Palacio to close the gates and post the servants along the walls and on the roof with shotguns and pistols. He found, however, that Soriano and the Marquis had already begun this, and so, seizing a large-bored revolver from old Robledo, changed his mount and rode hard to the top of the Skirt and began to rally those of the men who had formed part of his political machine whom he found there. His plan was to mass the foreigners across the bottom of the Skirt; he arrived at the middle fields of Broad Skirt in time to see his plan rendered useless by the submission of the foreigners; the down-rushing party which effected this had been collected by Argote himself. Cursing incessantly, the mayordomo wrenched his mount's head towards the Palacio and, spurring hard, drove the animal at a group of harvesters approaching a line of verdials, leaning forward and slashing at the air with his stock. The workers darted beneath the boughs of the olives and, reining hard, Argote flung himself forward in the saddle as the horse reared and then came down upon four feet, its head and shoulders splintering the brittle boughs.

"What's the good, Argote?" a worker yelled from beneath the "drip" of a neighboring tree. "We've got you down." At that moment and at the other end of the verdials there was another splintering of boughs.

"Ah, Mother of God, what in Christ's hell are you *doing*?" bellowed the mayordomo, backing his horse away from the tree. There were cloths beneath the trees at the end of the row and upon them hard green fruit. "Don't you know they're not ready till February?" Argote shouted. A round of hysterical laughter answered him from the trees.

"Ah, Jesus of my life!" the mayordomo said, and there was defeat in his voice. Between one sentence and another he had surrendered. Slowly he rode away, caring not to attempt to prevent the raiding nor even watching it, his stock hanging down in his left hand, the reins over the saddle peak. Before the palace gate were hundreds of baskets filled with fruit, a guard of workers over them; mechanically he noticed that it was ill-picked and mixed with soil and leaves, and then he called dully to old Robledo to open the gate. The stableman hesitated and said, "Be careful, señor, they've been trying to get in."

"Open," Argote repeated, and when the gate closed behind him he waited for Robledo to take the reins, staring the while through the iron bars at the workers bringing in the baskets of olives. Suddenly he lifted his whip and brought it down viciously across the stableman's back and shoulders, threw the whip to the floor and dismounted, and walked without acknowledgment past Soriano, who had emerged from the Chapel of the Olive at Robledo's scream.

22

Christmas Tale

THE men who had attempted to break into the Palacio had been possessed of one idea only, that of burning all the documents they might find, so to destroy the legal basis of Peral's claims to his lands. The same thing was attempted at the Town Hall that afternoon. Justo Robledo had dictated the last letter to go by the afternoon post, when the hall below was filled with clamoring men, a few of whom displayed weapons. There were no documents of land tenures in the Town Hall but the tenants refused to believe this and, thrusting Robledo aside, trampled into the clerks' office and broke open a cupboard. Within were several files and books of carbon copies and these were burned in the hall before a pair of the Civil Guards arrived and cowed the intruders. The burned copies consisted of copies of assessments of municipal advertisement taxes and carbons of the gypsy "guides." The intruders were marched to the Civil Guard barrack house and the arms bearers and one arbitrarily dubbed the ringleader were taken to the prison, which occupied one of the towers beside the Sevilla Gate.

The end of the rising was as sudden as its beginning. The next morning a commission of harvesters brought the olives to the town and, surprised and secretly dismayed to meet no opposition, took them to the press house owned by Pedro Barrera. Barrera, sternly adhering to the most elevated of moralities, refused to admit the fruit and at once the commission began to drift away. One or two decided to appeal to the press workers and, entering the factory, discovered the Civil Guard standing about in the press room.

The news of the fiasco was carried back to the olivars, where desultory picking was in progress. By midday the fields were silent; near the last tally field a few baskets of fruit were standing, and these were shortly carried away by the workers to their houses, where they were pressed with household technique. As a result of this more arrests were made, and people anxiously tried to dispose of fruit and oil. A basket of rotting olives was found near the Sevilla Gate and a small keg of oil was discovered on the Huerta path. One or two hung on to their spoils and buried the badly made, rapidly souring oil, and lived in fear all that winter.

One of the more important consequences of the rising occurred the following evening. Darkness had barely fallen when one of the indrafted guards strolling on the walls near San Andrés noticed a point of red fire upon the olivars near the Palacio track. It did not grow in size and he had already continued his walk when, glancing back, he perceived that the point had become much brighter. It might be a weed fire or something of the kind, he decided, when a lateral column of flame shot out of the fire, a thick beamlike tongue spitting at the hills across the valley; the light was strong enough to illuminate a great volume of smoke. Whistling loudly, the puzzled guard continued to watch. Suddenly an orange glow shot out of the point. The trees around were clearly visible for a second, then an explosion of sparks fountained out of the fire, flames appeared and were torn from side to side by the fitful wind. Again the glow was sucked back into the fire and once more an explosion threw a shower of sparks and isolated flaming points about the hillside. In response to the whistling a Los Olivares guard panted up the steps and stared through the crenellations.

"My God, Mater Purissima!" he exclaimed. "The captain's at the casino. I'm going to the Town Hall for the firemen; telephone the barracks."

"Mater Purissima, that's the sanctuary on the track, isn't it?"

"Yes, hurry, man."

"Christ, it'll be over long before you get there." The Los Olivares guard was out of hearing.

The Town Hall was closed; the guard therefore rushed to

the church, the doors of which were still open. The sacristan was not to be seen, and the daily bell rope was not hanging in the tower porch. The guard ran up the pitch-dark spiral steps that led to the chamber whence the one-roped bell was rung; the iron gate was locked. "Jesus, Mary and Joseph," he muttered and turned to descend. Someone was mounting the steps rumblingly muttering; hearing one another's movement in the impenetrable darkness both men stopped and shouted, "Who's there?" Neither answered the other and both moved; again the guard called, "Who's there?" and stood still. The other was descending. "Who is it?" the guard shouted, and the descending steps quickened and the noise of hard breathing ascended the spiral. "Mother of God, halt or I fire!" he yelled and drew his Mauser and hurried down the stairs, pointing the muzzle round the central column of the spiral so that a bullet would have embedded in nearly six feet of fourteenth-century masonry. A moment later his groping left hand collided with something soft and, grasping a shoulder, the guard held the descender firmly. "Christ Jesus, it's you, Menguillo, why didn't you say?" he burst out angrily, feeling the torn cassock. "It's me, Hernández. Come on, man, open the bell chamber."

"God be praised, what's the matter? What are you doing here?" the sacristan replied.

"Come on, man, Mater Purissima's on fire."

"Holy Virgin," the sacristan said slowly and, as if gathering his forces, hesitated a moment and then pressed forward, his head meeting Hernández's stomach; the guard hurriedly turned round in the shoulder-broad spiral, trod on the inner edge of the step, missed his footing and fell, kicking the sacristan's legs from beneath him.

"God burden me," Menguillo swore, his bunch of keys rattling upon the stone.

When they got the chamber door open Hernández hurried across the floor in the direction of the rope, his hands extended before him. Menguillo yelled at the top of his voice, "Don't move, man, you'll go through, the boards are up," and Hernández swore and stood giddily, still swaying as if standing on a pinpoint. "Jesus, Mary and Joseph," he muttered, the sweat prickling on his forehead. "What in God's name am I doing here? Haven't you got a light, man?"

"I've taken the bulb away to the sacristy," Menguillo replied. "Haven't you got any matches or a pipe lighter?"

Hernández cautiously moved to feel in his pockets, his giddiness increasing as he did so. "I'm falling, Menguillo," he shouted hoarsely, and with an oath the sacristan came forward and took his arm. "God's Daddy, man, you're nowhere near the hole, it's underneath the ropes."

"Why the hell did you tell me, then?" Hernández exploded and pulled out his lighter and ignited it. Remembering the burning sanctuary, he grasped the bell rope and began to tug, at which Menguillo protested that it was his task to ring the bell.

"I know how to pull a bell," answered the guard, continuing to tug ineffectually.

"I get paid a peseta for ringing for a fire," muttered the sacristan grimly, and the other flung the rope from him and ejaculated, "Oh, all right, man, ring the bloody bell yourself."

"Ah, carai! It's the wrong bell, of course," Menguillo exclaimed after a few strokes. He raced up the next section of the spiral and, seizing the clappers, began furiously to hammer the great and the third bell alternately. The electrifying sound hurtled out over the dark town like solid bolts of noise streaming out of the tower; women stopped work in the kitchen, men rushed out of the cafés and turned round in the street and cocked their heads, the better to hear the noise that was shaking every pane of glass in the neighborhood.

"Fire, fire," they shouted to one another. "Do you hear? The fire bell, the fire bell," and pointed into the sky, towards the throbbing tower where the bells were bombarding the darkness like a mass of audibly discharged radium. "Yes, the fire bell." In the plaza a cheer went up as the firemen arrived. When the hand engine pressed through the crowd at Mater Purissima nothing but the blackened walls remained and a thick bed of red ashes within, and the only thing to be done was to fell a dulzar olive whose tindery *peana,* the domed juncture of the roots, was glowing brightly. This they did with tools from one of the neighboring tool sheds.

The incendiaries were never discovered. "If the town gates still had doors, we could have caught them," argued Don Bartolomé. "If the doors had been closed at once they wouldn't have been able to sneak in without detection."

"In the Middle Ages the laws concerning usury were stricter than at present," Señor Ortega commented acidly when this opinion was reported to him, and this reference to Don Bartolomé's profession of banking was much quoted at the casino, where the lawyer's defense of the ex-mayor had increased the reputation he had already augmented with the Pérez affair.

Desultorily the work of harvesting was continued, supervised by Calasparra, for Argote was now rarely seen upon the fields. The mayordomo's character appeared completely to have changed; he wandered gloomily about the Palacio, finding fault in sour tones, doing nothing in particular in the house and never concerning himself with the trees. Don Fadrique fregently urged him to take a complete rest. "You have worked too hard, Argote, the harvest will be safe enough in the hands of Calasparra"; but this advice the mayordomo invariably rejected with ill humor.

In the Caro household the rising had one immediate consequence. When the surge of revolt had reached Broad Skirt, Marcial had climbed into a tree and begun to pick feverishly. Suddenly Joaquín and Pascual, who had attempted to dissuade him and had drawn aside anxiously to consider removing him by force, were startled to hear him weeping among the leaves. A moment later Marcial fell headlong from the fork of the tree and lay senseless. Frantically they hurried him to the town to Dr. Torres' house, whence three hours later they removed him to his home, prostrate in a grave crisis. During the next few days the Caros picked the remaining fruit in their own grove, pressing out the oil, silently. Sometimes Ursula wept at her task and once Ana threw herself upon the baskets of fruit and screamed. Then Pascual left the turning pole of the press and went over to her and tried to lift her, but in her frenzy she thrust her hands into the black olives, spilling them over the dusty earth, and he desisted. "Our Lord and his Blessed Mother comfort you, wife," he murmured, making the sign of the cross upon his breast; for a moment he stood over her in silence and then returned to his place at the press, where Ursula remained gazing at the blurred hills across the Jabalón until he spoke sharply to her.

In that week Señor and Señora Pérez celebrated the anniversary of their marriage and many friends were invited to the dinner, among them Baeza, Acorín and Caro. At first Caro declined, but pressed by Pérez, he accepted. That evening the dinner was served in the stockroom in which Señora Pérez had formerly kept her wine. Throughout the later afternoon guests arrived; first came three of Señora Pérez's friends, one of them the wife of the headwaiter at the Republican Center, another the former caretaker of Mater Purissima. Then came Caro and with him his mother and sister, the Calasparras, Baeza and his mother and several relatives of the Pérezes from Puente Nuevo. Soon the noisy storeroom was dense with smoke and for a while Pérez opened the double doors that led to the street behind the house. After a while the guitarists were asked for music and protesting they yielded. Pérez especially was delighted for now his former and his present master were playing together. Miguel Pérez, of Puente Nuevo, known as "the lame card," "*el tio cojo*," was called upon for a tale and responded with a chain of derisive stories about Cortijos, the village that neighbored Puente Nuevo on the down-valley side.

Again pressed, he began a series of popular anticlerical jests.

"Have you heard this one about the parish priest of Cortijos? It's a poor and very paltry place, you know, and though he was fat the cura chiefly fed on brotherly love. There were, of course, many who said that the love was not only brotherly, and so at last His Most Illustriousness the Bishop decided to pay a pastoral visit to Cortijos. 'I am afraid, your illustriousness, that I can offer only a wretched hospitality, I am very poor.'

" 'The apostles themselves were poor,' replied his lordship with considerable unction, and so after many hours of interrogation the cura led the way into the bedroom.

" 'Your illustriousness will have to share my bed, I am afraid, as I have only one, being poor.'

" 'But, son, how is this? You have only one bed? Where, then, does your housekeeper sleep? She is, I observe, young and not unpleasant in appearance.'

" 'We share this bed, though of course we always sleep with this plank between us, reverend father.'

" 'I see, but suppose you are visited by an evil temptation?'

" 'Oh, in that case,' said the cura of Cortijos, making the sign of the cross and yawning, 'in that case we kick the plank out of bed and pray for strength to resist temptation.' "

"Shameless one," said Luisa, the former caretaker, laughing. Miguel's next story was of an innkeeper's donkey, and then Luisa recounted a tale of the Sierra del Jabalón.

"There is a town over the hills," she began, "where once upon a time they resolved to purchase a new statue of the Virgin and a half of the cost was to be paid by a rich man in memory of his mother, whem he had loved greatly. Now in those days there were painters and image-makers who traveled from town to town, and in each town they came to they inquired of the priests and the authorities if there was any holy work to be done in that place. Thus there came to that town many image-makers and to each of them the task was confided, but none of them could satisfy the rich man.

" 'That, indeed, is an excellent statue of a Virgin,' he said to them when they had finished, 'but it is not the statue of a mother. Take this money and go, carrying your statue with you.' And to one of them he said at last, 'Do you see this portrait; this woman was a mother; do you not see by her face she was a mother?'

" 'She is beautiful and good, I see, but that may be the work of God's grace, sire. How do you know she was a mother?' the image maker said.

" 'Should not a son know his own mother, Señor Image-maker?' the rich man replied, and the painter bowed and took his image away, and the rich man was saddened, for he had great devotion to the Virgin Mother.

"Now one day near the time of Christmas, a ragged child came to that town beyond the hills and demanded to see the rich man.

" 'What do you want with me?' the rich man said to the child.

" 'I am an image-maker and I have been told that you desire a statue of the Virgin Mother.'

" 'You an image-maker!' cried the rich man angrily. 'You are only a child and you have neither wood nor stone, neither chisels nor brushes, that I see.'

" 'Nevertheless, sir, I can make you the image that you need and if you will pay me one hundred pieces of gold now I will bring the image to you in the morning.' And the Angel of Evil on his left tempted him, and the rich man raged, and called for his servants to whip the ragged boy, but the Angel of Goodness on his right hand whispered to him and, staying his words, he said:

" 'Boy, you shall have your hundred gold pieces, but you shall be locked in that room that you may not escape. If by morning you have not made the statue you shall be whipped and cast into prison, for I am a powerful lord.' And the ragged boy smiled and went into the room and called for water and wine and bread, and putting these things on the table with the gold, they locked him in that bare chamber.

"In the morning the lord of the house commanded his servants to open the door, and taking with them the portrait of the rich man's mother, they entered and found the boy asleep and upon the table a most lovely image. And upon her head was a crown of gold and they were astonished greatly.

" 'There is your statue,' the boy said when they awakened him, and after a while the rich man said:

" 'Child, you have done well and I am humbled, but this, I see, is the statue of a Virgin who is not a mother.'

" 'That is so,' said all the servants.

" 'Bow your head and pray a Hail Mary,' the boy said, and the Angel of Evil on his left hand said to the rich man, 'Pray not,' and the Angel of Goodness upon his right hand said, 'Pray,' and because he was a good man he prayed and commanded his servants to do likewise and they prayed. 'Hail Mary, full of grace, the Lord is with thee and blessed is the fruit of thy womb, Jesus.'

" 'Now cast your eyes upon the statue again,' the boy commanded, and lo! they beheld the statue of the Virgin Mother.

" 'Her face has changed,' they exclaimed, marveling.

" 'But this Virgin Mother is like no other Mother of God,' the Angel of Evil said, and the rich man declared this to the ragged boy.

" 'That is because this is a real portrait of the Mother of God,' the child said.

" 'But how may I believe this to be a real portrait of the Mother of God?' the rich man said, and the boy commanded:

" 'Bow your head and pray to the Son of Mary.'

" 'Pray not,' said the evil angel, and 'Pray,' said the good, and the rich man hearkened to the good and ordered his servants to pray likewise. And when they lifted their eyes the boy was gone."

"The boy was the Christ Child," Señora Pérez said.

"He goes about the world disguised at Christmas time," Luisa added.

"That reminds me of the story of the carter of Cortijos," exclaimed Miguel, and Pérez said, "Tell it."

"Well, it runs like this. The town of Cortijos wanted a new Santo Cristo and so they ordered the carter, who was going to the capital, to bring back with him a Santo Cristo.

" 'Give me a Santo Cristo,' said the carter to the image-maker, laying down the money, and the merchant replied:

" 'But, man, what kind of a Cristo do you want? There are Christs in the cradle, Christs before Pilate, Christs living, and Christs dead.'

" 'Oh, to be on the safe side, you'd better give me a living Christ,' answered the carter, 'for the people of Cortijos can always kill Him themselves.' "

Then, as Mudarra began a story of the Jabalón hills, there was a knock at the door which Pérez answered!

"Barrera wants you to play at his house, Diego." The guitarist at first refused but when they told him that hard silver was not to be refused, he consented. He had been gone rather more than two hours when the door was suddenly flung open by a pair of body guards. Montaña and the sergeant came from the rear of the file and entered the house.

"Put up your hands, everybody," commanded the sergeant and came forward and held his Mauser against Caro's waist. "Up with them, Caro."

"Where is Mudarra?" Montaña said to Pérez.

"He's not here."

"Search the house," the captain ordered, and a file of guards hastened upstairs.

"He's playing in Córdova," Caro said to the sergeant.

"In Córdova . . . since when?" Montaña approached Caro and questioned him sharply.

"He left on the afternoon bus."

The sergeant's eyes narrowed and he said, "He used to be your friend, didn't he?"

"He *used* to be."

"He's not in the house, Señor Captain," the senior guard reported upon descending.

"Very good. Pérez, I'm not going to arrest you, but you understand that you must not leave the town."

"What have I done?" faltered Pérez.

"That is not your business; you're fortunate not to be spending the night with us."

The guards left the house and Señora Pérez fainted, and when they had assisted her to the bedroom Conchita descended and demanded that Caro go to Barrera's house to warn Diego.

"No good me going; someone's sure to split if I'm seen moving about."

The girl thought a moment and then, coloring, asked for money from her father, and he and Miguel and Baeza emptied their pockets and gave her the money. She was heard moving about in the next room for a few moments and then she ran upstairs to her own bedroom and shortly left the house.

"Good luck to her," murmured Miguel, and Luisa crossed herself.

"Don't tell her mother, for the love of God," Pérez faltered and burst into tears. In the midst of the consequent confusion Señora Pérez entered the storeroom, and became hysterical when they confessed the truth about Conchita's absence.

"My wedding day!" she screamed, and the men drew to one side of the room shamefacedly and left her to the women. In the midst of this scene Mudarra walked in, rattling his pockets ostentatiously.

"Well, ten duros . . . hey, in Christ's name, what's up?"

"No, I've not seen her," he answered, when they questioned him about Conchita.

"She'll be all right," said Miguel. "You'll have to get out of this at once."

"The girl's got it all, we're cleaned out."

"Christ! I've got a bit upstairs. I'll run up for it."

As he turned there was a loud banging upon the rear door, he wheeled to face it and at that moment footsteps were heard in the passage and a sharp command.

"Put up your hands, Mudarra," the sergeant ordered. "You, too, Caro; you thought we swallowed that kid's bluff, didn't you?"

Caro suddenly felt sick as he realized that it was his story that had ensured Mudarra's arrest; a more probable tale might have given them a few minutes' respite.

"He told me he was going to Córdova," he said.

"That's right," Mudarra said, his gaze fixed upon Caro.

"Go on, talk away," the sergeant laughed. "When you and your —— crowd talk you help me quite a lot."

Silently the two men filed out between the guards; then, as Montaña watched them, he remarked quietly to the sergeant: "Pérez also; he'll like to see his daughter's being well treated."

23

The Gates of Hell

Upon the morning of the general arrests Pérez, Caro and Conchita were released, Caro being told that his public disapproval of violence had earned him absolution for his offense.

"You mean you know you wouldn't get a conviction," Caro replied, to which Montaña said:

"I shouldn't be too daring, if I were you; we can always reconsider the matter."

"Sure you can reconsider; that's why I'm going out."

The sergeant slowly turned his trunk without moving his feet and, glancing at the captain, wheeled round and struck Caro across the face, whereupon the guard on his left, flinging up his rifle, hit him upon the flank with the butt; the third guard lifted him by the chin and threw him against the wall. "Another round," Montaña said quietly, and the three guards took hold of him and, two of them pinning his arms, the third slung his rifle butt against hips and ribs. "Enough," called Montaña. "You may go now, Caro, and remember you are being absolved from your offense."

Silently he moved towards the passage, each breath sucking the same blade of pain farther and farther into his body; as he laid his hand upon the door handle, Montaña, seating himself before a marbled log book, ordered, "Another round," and commenced to make a suitable entry against the date.

That same evening flybills were posted all over the town. "There is hunger and want, more Civil Guard," and below these words, inspired by a famous essay of Azorín, was the cry,

Queremos los presos, "We want the prisoners." By nightfall, eighty had been arrested and, the town prison being full, the cells at the barracks and the one cell at the Town Hall also, the more inoffensive of the prisoners were shut up in the new schoolhouse cellar, to await removal to the capital. Throughout the night the guards were making their calls in Cuestas Abajo, in one street of which a band of women were nearly responsible for a disorderly scene.

At midday, when the prisoners were to be fed, a queue of women stood before the prisons carrying meals for their men and, watching the queue, hundreds of silent and hating towns-people. During half an hour the file moved slowly forward, only one woman being allowed in the building at a time; those who came out did not move away. Once, as a woman emerged weeping, a sudden moan from the crowd swelled loudly, as if a great bird flung up its wings and lifted into the air, a cry of rage burst out and the square was filled with beating waves of sorrow. A sharp command, rifle magazines were slapped, and the crowd was silent in a few moments. "The soup is already cold," a woman cried hysterically, and her words were heard by La Gorda upon the inn balcony. With Andaluz romanticism she ordered a coke devil to be placed in the inn archway for the warming of the evening soup. Montaña sauntered over to see what was happening, pursed his lips and nodded approval. Everyone sighed with relief as he walked away.

Mudarra in the gate tower was more fortunate. Before the lower chamber became nearly full the indrafted sergeant called him to the iron gate, and between four guards he was removed to a small cell with a slit window above the gate itself, whence the officer of the walls for the week had once sat glancing down over the old track towards the crook of the hills which shut out Guadalquivir and the amethyst-hazed plains of nostalgia.

"That box stays with me for luck, eh, sergeant?" Mudarra exclaimed on entering.

"That's right, boy."

"Good, now send for my guitar and I'll be like a prisoner in a bloody song sheet."

"Sorry, I am completely at your feet, of course, but no guitars for you, sonny."

This upper room was certainly colder than the packed chamber in the tower, but the window was more than compensation. The Sevilla Gate was the one which offered the most varied interest and in these days the least embittering. In the summer months Mudarra had often stood upon the wall above, having borrowed the tower key from Montaña or one of his subordinates, watching the late return of the Huerta workers and the small herds of goats, their huge dusty udders bumping the ground, or the slow oxcarts, or laughing at the hurrying gait of beggars, unaware of the prompt ejection to which Montaña would subject them, or amiably jeering at the protected gypsies. The modern road unfortunately bent sharply to the left and was hidden for a long stretch by the brown belly of the left tower, so that the Puente Nuevo bus was first seen small and faintly buzzing as it skirted the head of the Huerta hollow, and then was unseen until it appeared large and rattling and snorting like a bull emerging from the *toril*. But most of the local traffic still went by the old track, the wide, ever dividing, ever reuniting track worn deep into the soft places, showing light over the scarred and powdered rocks, straying down to the Jabalón like a thin stream over a rocky bed, only to climb by terraced zigzags the impassable Bluff of the Moors, where it crossed the new road to traverse the Dead Lands at a higher level. The red-caparisoned mules with their quick nonchalant stride, as if they were experienced performers rather than beasts of burden, the few horsemen and the ox wagons from the Huerta all came by this track, and gypsies who preferred it to monotonous walking by the new. There was something about the old track more appealing than its traffic, however. The modern high road aroused no nostalgia in Mudarra, it suggested no travel, no adventure, it was too sure, too self-willed a thing, it imposed itself too determinedly upon the bruised land. A caravan of mules going down the old path resembled a small ship pulling out over the surface of a rocking sea; it rose over the billow of yellow rock that swept round from the cliff top, it sank into the deep trough where the watercourses talk to themselves, it wavered and then curved and tacked about the floor of the Huerta. Regarding, and saluting every accident of the earth, any section of the old path might stand as a symbol of all voyages over earth, and a man in gazing along it was stirred, at once made uneasy and comforted by its strange rapport with his experience of his own life. The new road carried a man, conducted him; the old path was a companion who counseled with grave words. The things that were seen from the new road were half-seen things, things shorn of their significance by the arbitrary view it gave of a life planned before it. Following the path one saw things whole and with their purpose—the washing pool, the fountain, the wells, the gardens, the press house and the open space where traveling flocks might rest—and by these things the wayfarer was refreshed. And always the nostalgia and allurements of lands far off. For remembering all the old paths of the Jabalón hills Mudarra saw that they ever suggested the way they would lead on, but to lands fabulous and renowned whither the mind ran and was lost upon the plains where amid blue mists and beside glassy rivers anything might happen. More, as if the spirit of man had been quicker in those days, the landscape which the traveler on the old tracks perceived was inevitably dramatic, as if man had chosen to be guided even through hills and valleys by some dramatic sense rather than by the guide of easeful reason. It was surely unnecessary for the old path to loop so low into the Huerta; by keeping higher that steep assault of the Moors Bluff would have been avoided. Yet had it been so the traveler arriving at evening would never have had the heart-swelling magical perception of Los Olivares upon its red, cliff-walled promontory, its walls and towers glowing redly in the declining day, against the vast screen of the green-barred Jabalón. Seen thus the town was a symbol of the City of God, set upon the high bluff of heaven. Would not a man see this city in the painting in the Chapel of San Benedict in San Andrés, pennons hanging from its masts, black birds encircling its towers with olive sprigs in their beaks and ranks of trumpeting angels surmounting the walls?

Yet as he gazed upon the path little by little a deep longing possessed him, and he wanted to see the town behind him and it was then he saw that a similar window had been boarded up and covered with whitewash. An hour of piercing at the wood with a nail pulled from the box did not loosen the boards, and then the indrafted sergeant mounted to the chamber and took the box away without a word; leaving Mudarra a copy of the Madrid A.B.C.

Mudarra's meals were brought by Conchita Pérez, and he began to look forward to her visits with uneasy excitement, listening for the San Andrés clock to strike and picturing her descending the hill street by street. It was she who brought the copy of the paper which had so many consequences for at least one person in Los Olivares. An hour after she had gone he sat against the wall to read the paper, still disturbed by the plain longings of the body which the girl now aroused in him, longing which often exasperated him and at rare intervals disgusted him. Remembering the sickening glimpse of Conchita's bosom as she bent before him, the warm smell of her body and roundness of her knees as she stooped to pick up the dirty plates, he could not read the paper with interest. "Christ, only two days in here," he muttered savagely, "and I'm like this already." Outside he had rarely had any necessity of going to the Los Olivares brothels, but had relieved himself only when on visits to neighboring towns. Turning over the smudged leaves, a name suddenly caught his eye and he read:

"We understand that after Christmas the Reverend Father Soriano, formerly of the major church of Los Olivares, will return to the capital to occupy a stall as canon of the chapter. We are informed by our correspondent that the above-mentioned cleric's sermons have awakened much interest in the cathedral congregation and that it is to this and to his reputed distinction as a theologian he owes his advancement. Recently Father Soriano gave a much discussed lecture on Music and the Spiritual Life before a distinguished audience, receiving much applause."

The cold note liberated an upsurge of hate in Mudarra, and this flooded refreshingly through all his thought, sweeping out all uneasy desire. It was the word "music" which gave him an exciting focus for his hate, calling to mind a forgotten scene in the library of Guevara. When Conchita came at eight o'clock of the evening he eagerly asked her to smuggle in pencil and paper.

All that morning he sat at the window slit watching the

racing clouds go down their foundering courses from the hills
he knew to be screaming in the snow-flinging wind, phrasing
and rephrasing a message to the members of the F.A.I. remaining in liberty. At midday he rose to meet Conchita and,
putting out his hands to welcome her, drew her away from the
door. She nodded and took out of her breast a stub of pencil
around which was rolled half a sheet of notepaper secured
with a rubber band.

"I'll give you a note tonight, *chica*," he said and set about
his meal hungrily, while the girl chatted to him until the guard
called to her to descend.

That evening Mudarra returned the paper rolled into a thin
spill, and the girl at once carefully slid it into her hair and
pressed it to the curve of her head.

"Deliver it to Acorín," he said, and added, "Will it be safe
there?"

"Yes, I have practiced it this afternoon."

"You practiced?"

"Yes, the guard felt all over my breast when I went out at
lunchtime. He's young. Said he was searching." She laughed
contemptuously.

The blood rushed to Mudarra's face and he lifted his hands
and clenched them.

"Ah, don't fret yourself, boy, I can stand that," Conchita
explained. "If he likes to give himself a bad quarter of an hour,
more's his misfortune." The girl playfully pushed his clenched
hands down. "It doesn't matter, Diego, don't say anything to
him about it. . . ."

Staring at her breast he saw the swelling nipples pressing
more tightly against her blouse. "Conchita," he burst out, and
placing his crooked hand on the nape of her neck, pressed her
breast and kissed her hair.

"Ah, don't be silly, son," she said.

"God, I'm going to be put away, Conchita, my dear," he
muttered, and she looked up at his face and watched it pale.

"All right then," she whispered, and laid her body against
him while his hand caressed tremblingly downwards to her
withdrawn loins, and as it paused she yielded her body to

his touch and lifted her face again and kissed him. "Diego, my dear, I shall have done you harm, you'll be upset."

"Ah, no, my little star," he whispered fiercely, and as the guard mounted the stairs she turned away and, flinging down her dress, stood back.

"Ah, like that, is it?" the guard laughed with a vicious undertone. "Well, none of that there; out of it, woman, and quick." The girl ran out, hiding her face from the guard, who turned and, picking up the paper with a flourish, said, "Good taste you've got, Mudarra, she carries a nice balcony, eh?"

Leaving his dinner untouched, he watched the girl as she stood near the light bracketed to the tower wall, a great gale blowing dust and paper and refuse of the road against her legs, yet nothing she said could he hear, yet he thought he could hear her weeping as she leaned against the wall. It could not have been so, he reasoned against the half-longing to believe she had wept, for when suddenly she ran away into the darkness he could not hear her steps. "It must have been so," he argued against his half-hope that he had not committed himself, for she had covered her face.

During the three remaining days of his confinement in the gate chamber he did not see Conchita again, though once he heard her call his name up the stairs. The guard, or one of his colleagues, always brought him his meals. Nevertheless fugitive but vivid images of the girl came before his mind even when the guards cleaned out his nails with alcohol that there might be no telltale infection and thrust sterilized thorns beneath his fingernails in the attempt to find out who had caused to be posted the flybills which appeared the next day. And he thought sometimes of the girl below in the stupid yellow light, when they harnessed him with a folded blanket that the thick corded tourniquet crushing in ribs against heart and lungs should leave no scars, and only when with grim ceremonial they whipped the soles of his feet with thin canes the images of the girl faded into darkness. In the year that followed, endlessly making straw hats for export, confined in the castle of Figueras in the far north, or starving below ground in the fortress of San Cristóbal, it was not the years of daily association, of banter and courtesy in Pérez's house that he remembered, but that minute in the gate chamber, Conchita's voice and the smell of her olive-oiled hair and the smooth skin of stomach and thighs and the zigzagging gale blowing paper and the road's refuse over the girl's legs and the empty yellow light after she had disappeared in the darkness. And towards the end of that year, body feebled by hunger and cold, and the mind inwardly raging at torment with gathering venom, it was only the empty light and the darkness he remembered.

The serious dolphin swam on and the rapt musician saw neither the stately ship nor the serrated shining sea. The dolphin regarded the water as if measuring his progress by the little thorn-shaped waves, or perhaps his grave expression had to do with the harnessed ship so proudly pennoned for a ceremonial victory. The musician was rapt in an inner vision of music, or he gazed at the City of God, or it was an empty light? Or he sang a song to bourdon thrummings, for the thick cords of his lute were not strung for sweet sounding, a song perhaps of slow, painted cattle, gentle beasts to be tended in moist pastures where the whipping stalks of grass were thin canes of green honey and a northern Love sat in a breeze-tossed willow and sang to a nymph below in the yellow light of the sun, regarding her white hands and rose-hued fingernails. What was the significance of the dolphin that Narvaez should have named his book after the beast? Don Fadrique rose from his table, went into the library, and searched in old encyclopedias for information about the dolphin. He read several paragraphs about its classification—absurd, one doesn't need to classify dolphins, he thought, they cannot be confined behind the iron bars and stone walls of systems; and then he found a paragraph about its habits, its mode of swimming, which would have unseated the rapt musician, and the hatred the Mediterranean fishers bear the problematic beast. "It plunges through their nets as if it saw them not in its lust for the prize of escaping fish or if the nets be passing stout it leaps into the air and falls upon the fish gathered within the net as the fishers draw it closer and closer, and oftentimes it happens that a score of dolphins will so bespoil the fisher who for the darkness of night may not easily slay them."

And now he stood holding the pleasantly smelling volume with its yellow paper brittle as a moth's wings, and dusted like them, imagining the smooth-swelling sea speared with stars and the phosphorescent thorn-shaped plumes of water blossoming out of it, and the dolphins crowning them with laughing faces as they turned over, to plunge upon the black-headed fish, splashing the water into quicksilver scribbles. And smiling at the pleasant beast, he returned to his table and pulled the book towards him, and the morning became suddenly golden.

Argote knocked and entered, carrying the morning's post, and he motioned to the mayordomo to sit down.

"What news is there from the town?" the Marquis asked.

"Things are all right, my lord, they have arrested nearly all they are going to arrest."

"How many have been arrested?"

"Montaña was not at the barracks when I rang up, but I understand about a hundred and ten."

"Cristina! One hundred and ten." Peral moved nervously in his seat and Argote shrugged his shoulders.

"It's no good interfering, su señoría, they've orders from the Government in Madrid to make a clean job of it."

"From the Government!"

"Yes, the sergeant read me out the civil governor's letter; the Government are determined to maintain order while the reforms are being made. He says in his letter that they have evidence of an anarchist plot extending over all the south of Spain."

"He calls that a plot! Contemporary governors appear to lack the precision of language once expected of their office."

"That's what he says."

"What do you think, Argote; is this affair likely to attract much Governmental attention?"

"I don't know, who can tell with this Government? They are going to dispossess all the grandees of Spain, I understand; what they can do with the olive fields I don't know, but olive fields are in the Act right enough."

"Well, I don't like these arrests; they can do no good now the revolt is over."

"The Government is going to put down Anarchism, su señoría; they've arrested nearly all the F.A.I. in this town. Mudarra is for trial."

"H'm, a dangerous man, no doubt."

"Not so dangerous as others."

"Who, for instance?"

"The man Caro."

"Caro, I don't know him; has he been arrested?"

"No, su señoría, but he understands politics. I mean he's a practical-minded man. He's begun agitating lately."

"H'm, well, can I leave it to you to watch the ways of affairs?"

"Yes, su señoría, but there's something I wish to talk about, if you can spare the time."

"Of course."

"Well, sir, I don't like to say it, but I'd like to give up the trees."

"You mean surrender your post as . . . I mean, you wish me to engage a bailiff?"

"Yes, sir; I don't know what's the matter with me, but they want someone more . . . more . . ."

"But, man, who else knows so much about olives in Los Olivares, or in all the province indeed?"

"Thank you, sir, but I hope you'll release me."

"No, I am not sure that I shall release you. Why don't you take an assistant as I have suggested? You are letting this revolt unbalance you."

"May be." The mayordomo's voice was full of bitterness.

"Well now. Why not advance Calasparra; he . . ."

"No, sir."

"Why not? You say he's doing well and he could surely be taught the business side of the estate. Why don't you like the man?"

"There's nothing wrong with Calasparra, but I couldn't work with him."

The Marquis of Peral watched Argote for several moments and then he nodded and said quietly, "I see; is there anyone else you can suggest? I am determined not to lose you."

"I wanted to stay on in the house, señor."

"I am glad to hear that, but I want you on the Skirts."

"Perhaps Morcillo might be taken back as my assistant."

Don Fadrique smiled faintly; though Morcillo had not worked upon the olivars for many years his knowledge was still likely to be sound. But it was not this which had caused Argote to suggest him. Rather than struggle with a powerful and younger man like Calasparra he preferred to resign; compelled to stay on, he was selecting an already defeated enemy for assistant.

"That is agreed upon then," Don Fadrique said. "Please wait a minute while I look through the letters."

As he opened his letters, placing those which were within the mayordomo's department on one side, the Marquis watched Argote. He seemed to have taken heart at receiving permission to engage Morcillo. Well, the man had worked hard, he was to be humored, he thought, as he opened an envelope and took out a paper of unusual appearance. Glancing mechanically at the letter, his body grew rigid. Above a printed flybill was written in block letters:

BY TOMORROW ALL LOS OLIVARES WILL HAVE READ THIS.

And the printed matter said:

Farewell to Don Mamerto Soriano. We thank him for his services. He prayed for us. He dominated the mind of a weakling and seedless aristocrat and oppressed us. He was false to his chosen master in that he told Villa Alta that Guevara had bought a music book for twenty thousand pesetas. His people's blessing goes with him.

For a moment he hesitated and then thrust the flybill towards Argote and sprang to his feet; white fists turned knuckles to the table and pressed hard upon the wood. Reading the bill Argote flushed red and also rose to his feet.

"Where is he?" Don Fadrique said through his teeth.

"He'll be in one of the chapels."

"Bring him here, do you understand? Bring him here."

"Su señoría!"

Argote strode to the door, and while he was gone Peral stood motionless by the table, his gaze fixed upon the door. When Soriano entered, he shrank immediately from the sight of the man at the table, and was roughly impelled forward by the body of the mayordomo.

"Read this . . . is this true?"

"Su señoría, I . . ."

"Is it true?" Don Fadrique thrust the question forward like something solid. "Answer me."

"Answer his lordship," shouted Argote, and Peral without glancing at him said with cold ferocity, "Be silent."

"Su señoría!" Argote assented, in the same fierce tone, glaring at Soriano.

"Yes," whispered the priest.

"You will stay here, in this house, until I return."

"Your lordship, I must return to the capital . . . his lordship the bishop . . . Holy Church . . ."

"Your bishop is my . . ." began Don Fadrique, and then the man in him withdrew behind the grandee, the extinguished grandeur of Spain. "I am going to the capital, I shall talk with his lordship the bishop."

"My lord, I beg you . . ."

"Be silent. Argote, ring to the town for a car and see that this man does not leave the house. Does not leave the house, do you understand?"

"Su señoría."

"You will manage all affairs while I am away."

"Su señoría."

An hour later, seated behind Dr. Torres, in his car, Don Fadrique, brooding over the scene in the library, remembered more clearly than the priest's collapse the grinding and triumphant hate in the mayordomo's voice.

As Leaves to the Fire

"HE'LL be nearly dressed now," Celestina said to herself listening to Justo's movements above, and taking his shoes from the corner beneath the icebox, she went into the yard. Opening the hanging cupboard, she took out the tin of polish and the rags and laid them upon the bench. The tin would not open to her fingers and she laid it upon its side and commenced to strike it with the brush, whereupon it spilled the dried and broken polish upon the paving. At the sound of the blows Justo opened the balcony door and said:

"Don't clean them, I'm going to drop in at the Republican Center and have them done."

"You won't have time," she replied, picking up a piece of polish with the brush.

"Of course I shall have time."

"You won't; besides, what do you want to spend the money for; anyone would think you were . . ."

"Woman, I tell you I am going to call at the Republican Center!"

Celestina applied the polish to the toe of the shoe and rubbed it vigorously.

"Don't *do* it," Justo shouted, but his wife pursed her lips as if she heard through them, and took a fresh quantity of polish; he swore and withdrew from the balcony.

"You won't have time, Justo," she called after him, listening to his behavior in the room.

"I told you not to do it," he said, coming suddenly to the door, and returned before she could answer him; her hands moved more slowly and at last she called: "They'll look just as good when I've done with them; and the delegation arrives at three and it's two thirty-five now."

"And it'll take me half an hour to walk round to the Town Hall, I suppose; do you think I'm a triumphal procession, woman?"

"No, you're not," she shouted, losing her temper, and Justo ran out onto the balcony and shouted in return. When he came downstairs he put on his shoes with angry movements.

As he opened the street door he turned to Celestina and said, "After the procession is over you must persuade Lucía to lie down, she'll be tired and excited."

"She shouldn't have gone to the meeting. I'll come up to the Square after the delegation and find her before they start another."

"That's right; well, you may as well come to the end of the street with me."

"I'm not dressed."

"Christ, does that matter? Town Secretary's wife seen in Mendizabal Street wearing apron, grave scandal, protests, neighborhood indignant."

"I'll take it off."

At the end of the street the couple stood a moment and then, looking at his watch, Robledo remarked, "I must be getting along, it's twenty to. I've one or two things to do before the delegation arrives."

"Are you going to the Center?" Celestina asked, nodding at the building across the Square, and he said curtly, "Yes."

"They're as bright as a guard's hat," she answered, nodding at the company of guards drawn up before San Andrés.

He grunted "H'm" and hurried away; nevertheless, though he knew she was watching him, he went straight to the Town Hall. She returned to the house and, finding the cleaning materials upon the bench, began to polish her own and Lucía's shoes.

At five minutes to three there was a violent knock upon the street door and opening it she was addressed without formality by the mayor, Señor Luis Carrasco.

"Is Señor Robledo at home?" he blurted, breathing quickly.

"No, señor, he's gone to the Town Hall to receive the delegation with you."

"Ah . . . Jesus . . . I hoped to catch him, the delegation is not to be received; he really must have the telephone put in here now he's been promoted."

"He's going to, señor," Celestina exclaimed.

"Yes, of course. You must go to the Town Hall and tell him not to receive the delegation."

"But, señor, why . . ."

"God's truth, can't you see, Señora; I mustn't be seen near the Town Hall, the delegation's not to be received."

"I can't go, Señor Carrasco, how can I go? What am I to tell him?"

"Tell him I have received instructions . . . that the Governor advises me that it would be impolitic to receive the delegation."

"But," began Celestina, looking at her clothes and her polish-stained fingers.

"Señora, I beg you, if the telephone . . . upon this occasion it won't matter that you are not dressed for going out, I implore you."

"Very well," she muttered, drawing the street door closed.

"I'm to tell him that the Governor has forbidden you to receive the procession?"

"No, no no, that he says it is impolitic to receive the delegation, impolitic, tell him that."

"Impolitic," she said, and set out for the Town Hall.

Riding along the top of the Skirt of Beyond, Argote mounted to the unused plot known as Lightning Field. One August evening six years ago a bolt of lightning had broken the roof and destroyed some of the pipes of San Andrés. Another stroke had split two trees upon the high plot. *Estacas* had been planted in place of the destroyed trees and the following year, in the same month, another discharge of lightning had killed the remaining fruit-bearing trees and once more had damaged the roof of San Andrés. Since then the field had been allowed to lie derelict and was fast sinking back into the earth. Slate rubble from the slopes above had trickled down over the upper wall and was slowly spreading over the field; herbs and low bushes sprang up and a beaten path traversed its middle. To this field the mayordomo often mounted, to obtain a view over the slopes of the bay which here narrowed to a valley rising to a shallow gully that ran out to a bell-mouthed finish on soilless slopes. Now, arriving at Lightning Field, he saw to his surprise that someone had cleaned the field and broken its surface as if it were once more destined to bear wood. He sat for a while with knitted brows and then, hearing Calasparra's voice below, he rode down and found the charge hand directing the cutting of wood from a tree in which the sap was already immobile, wood which was to serve as planting-out material for *garrotes,* as the other method of propagating olives was known.

"Know anything about the field up yonder?" Argote asked Calasparra curtly.

"Field, which field?"

"Christ, which field would it be? Lightning Field, of course."

"What about it then?"

"Did you have it cleaned? I've just been up there."

"I had it cleaned a week ago; I thought you'd seen it."

"What's the idea?" The mayordomo frowned at Calasparra's reminder of his recent neglect.

"I'm going to put some arbequíns up there."

"Oh, you are, are you; well, you're not, not if I know it. Arbequíns resist the bloody lightning, do they?"

"That was only pure coincidence; it's not likely it'll happen again."

"Well, you listen to me, Calasparra, just leave that field alone and keep yourself to your own work. *I'll* say what has to be done on these olivars."

"Very good," Calasparra said sourly and glanced at the listeners. Argote rode away a few lengths of his mount and, turning, glared at the group conversing in low tones with the charge hand. Slowly they broke up and returned to their tasks; Calasparra pointed to the ground and gave orders in a loud voice. Meditating over the charge hand's cleaning of the field, the mayordomo became more sullen and bitter and, continually spurring his horse, eventually urged the beast into a gallop. Suddenly, remembering the Marquis of Peral's advice to him to take an assistant, he determined to offer Morcillo, the former olivar assistant, the post. Wheeling his horse, he hastened to the Palacio, dismounted, threw his whip to the ground before Robledo, and went down to Los Olivares on foot to visit Morcillo, who occupied a room in the second house on the left-hand side of Mendizabal Street.

Gruffly he saluted the guards stationed at the church, and was striding on, when Montaña hailed him.

"Well, many of your men absent from work this morning?"

"Yes, some blasted meeting or other, isn't it?" The captain stared with perplexity at the olivero, whose vagueness of reference seemed to disclose lack of interest, or relaxing grip on local affairs.

"That's the band," he ejaculated suddenly. "They'll have finished their oratory; you'll meet them if you're going downtown, Indalecio, they're coming in procession to the Town Hall. Are you taking part in this one?"

"Don't talk to me of processions," the mayordomo replied with a faint grin, glancing at the Town Hall, and with a farewell "Adios," left the guards.

His interview with Morcillo was brief. The ex-administrator coldly refused to return to the estate, and with an oath the mayordomo left the house. At two minutes to three, as the procession entered the Square from Olive Oil Street, Indalecio Argote turned to glance at a woman knocking upon the Town Hall door, and then halted to watch the delegation detach itself, wondering whether the man Caro could safely be advanced to a responsible post.

In the Square of Our Lady of Carmén the children ceased to watch the caretaker cleaning the chapel and begun to play around the dark patch which now served as the center for their ring games. "What shall we play?" "What shall we play?" they shouted after the leader and three or four cried simultaneously, "The Prince of France, Mariquita and Don Juan Pintado."

"Don Juan Pintado," the leader elected, and the girl who had called for the game pulled up her skirts in excitement and danced, disclosing a dusty pair of white knickers. An elder girl caressed her and took her hand and several others squabbled like sparrows for the other. "Luisita me, Luisita me," they claimed, grabbing at her dirty fist.

"Who do you think is going to be married?" began the leader in an artificial tone.

"Who is going to be married?" shrilly intoned the ring at once.

"Why, Don Juan Pintado."

"Don Juan Pintado!" The little girls were astonished at this and opened wide their eyes.

"And how do you think Don Juan Pintado goes to his wedding?" the leader declaimed, and the children began to fidget with mounting excitement. "And how does Don Juan Pintado go to his wedding?" they screamed.

"Why, hopping, dancing, laughing, weeping, hopping, dancing, laughing, weeping, *dancing*," sang the leader, and the ring began to dance with jumping steps, grasping hands suddenly.

"Hopping, dancing, laughing, weeping, *laughing*," shouted the leader, and all the little girls laughed save one who began to weep. "Out you go, María," they shouted, and the girl silently withdrew from the ring.

"Hopping, dancing, laughing, weeping, hopping, dancing, laughing, *weeping*," and a wail rose from the ring and fists were pushed into closed eyes and Don Juan Pintado wept.

"Out you go, Luisita," the leader screamed, and the laughing girl ran out of the ring. At that moment the band began to play at the bottom of the hill and the chorus of weepers broke up and ran to the middle of Olive Oil Street, where a few timid merchants had closed their shutters. A number of women emerged from the streets beyond the chapel and led their daughters indoors before the procession went by, with its paper placards demanding the release of the prisoners and justice and work and bread and similar abstractions of the revolutionary movement. The unclaimed girls joined with the convoy of children upon the pavements and with the procession entered the Square.

The speakers stood upon the wall of what had once been the hostel for benighted travelers shut out of the town, and all of the broken ground to the leeward of the walls was occupied by the crowd. The rising arête-like bank which swept round behind the hostel ruins was also occupied, and these people made a strange stairway into the windy sky like the angels of a visionary master. Beneath the arch of the Sevilla Gate stood a posse of the Civil Guard and in the Plaza de Armas another group was stationed; the indrafted captain stood upon the walls above. No guards were placed near the meeting, as information was better to be obtained by the Governmental spies.

Towards the end of the meeting passions took flame and the crowd was hardly to be kept under control. It was Baeza who was responsible for this. "In the prison yonder, locked behind those stone walls, are our brothers," he began. "Before we go to the authorities to demand their release let us give them a shout of encouragement. Here, give me that placard," he said to a bystander. "Do you see this, shout it out with all your heart, 'We want the prisoners.' " Part of the crowd began late and the cry was confused, and then as it was concluded a section repeated it feebly.

"No," shouted Baeza, "again, after I count three. One, two, three." Again the cry was indistinct, some pronouncing the syllables slowly and separately and others quickly delivering the whole sentence. At the third and fourth attempt no greater unanimity was achieved, and at the fifth a half of the meeting did not shout, their attention being distracted by the flight of a stork, one of the pair of birds rarely seen in those parts, which had recently begun to build a nest below the bell cage of San Salvador.

García spoke next. The arrests were arbitrary, he claimed, granting that there might be some justification for judicial procedure after the olivar stripping, nevertheless this should be conducted with some regard for the decencies of investigation. "That I assert is a moderate demand," he concluded. "Very moderate," a sarcastic voice called, and García appealed for unanimity upon this occasion; there was a little laughter from the center of the meeting.

"Nominations to the delegation," he announced, twisting a button on his coat till the thread parted and he put the button in his pocket. "Let them represent all sections of opinion. If there are any Catholic workers here let them not fear to put forward one of their number; upon this occasion at least we can all respect one another's ideas."

"I propose the delegation be restricted to members of Governmental parties," a worker on the arête called out.

"You're a Socialist, García," the placard bearer shouted. "Your party is in office."

"Yes, let the Socialists and the Radicals put up the petition," others cried, and voices added, "And the Radical Socialists." A wag interjected, "Any Catalans here?" and the laughter calmed the rising feeling.

"What about the Communists?" García said, and there was fresh laughter and the placard bearer again interposed with, "No, keep it to the Governmental parties."

"The Communists may not be a very numerous element in the meeting," García continued, "but they are an organized party and ought to be invited."

"Joaquín," a voice cried out, and Caro lifted his hand and accepted. Eventually two Radicals, a Radical Socialist, García as leader and two other Socialists, an Independent, a Catholic and Caro were elected; two women also volunteered and were acclaimed. No important Anarchist was forthcoming and their sympathizers declined to be associated with the protest. Playing the "Hymn of Riego," the Republican anthem, the dance band led the way through the Sevilla Gate. A shrill whistle resounded from the guard patrol.

When Ana Caro had cleared away the bowls and plates, Pascual took a stick of broken box from the corner of the room and cut himself a toothpick, with great care laying it upon the edge of the table to scrape it smooth. While he was doing so, Marcial came downstairs and moved towards the door. "Where are you going, son?" Pascual said, and Marcial shrugged his shoulders. The father rose, and pressing the point of the knife upon the table, said:

"I think you'd better not go to the meeting, it will be bad for you," and the son replied:

"I was going to the Square to hear if the mayor makes any reply."

"Joaquín will be there."

"He's not coming back tonight."

"Not coming back, son?"

"No, some business of his new . . ." The unfinished sentence was spoken with anger and sadness.

"I'll go up to the Square, Marcial," Ursula said. "I'll come straight back after the delegation comes out." And the old man made no comment.

Ana returned to the kitchen carrying a large earthenware bowl of olives buried in discolored salt and this she laid upon the table. "We'll help you, Mother, this afternoon," the father remarked, and crossed to the cupboard in the angle of the wall and took out a basket of dried herbs.

"I'll go to the rocks at the bottom of the Well Field," he said, "and pick those herbs we marked down; your mother always likes that sort to be put in fresh."

"These dry," Ana assented, picking up a handful of rosemary, "but the others living from the earth; that way the fruit have a finer flavor."

Pascual left the house and together the mother and son washed the fruit and placed them in a clean bowl.

"Oh, how bitter," Ana exclaimed, tasting an olive. "We did not put enough salt, they aren't properly killed."

"Yes, they're bitter right enough," Marcial and Ursula agreed, and the daughter added, "But Father likes them bitter and Joaquín does, too; they'll be pleased."

"We must put less herbs," Marcial said, and Ana countered with, "Oh, no, the more bitter the olives the more herbs we must put into the water, or else we should not taste the herbs at all."

"But the herbs are bitter also."

"Of course, but two bitternesses go well together."

"We did not put enough salt," the son repeated as Ursula departed.

"We put the salt of other years; perhaps the salt was weak or the fruit not quite ready."

"Oh, they were ready. Neither Father nor Joaquín would make any mistake."

"The salt was weak, then."

Pascual entered bearing a bunch of herbs from which he was shaking the particles of soil, and Ana greeted him with:

"The olives are bitter."

"Ah, good for me," he said with a smile, "but in that case we shall need more of this grass; send Ursula."

"She's gone to the Square."

"Ah, she ought not to have gone; I've been thinking it over."

For ten minutes father and son watched the mother put the fruit and herbs into jars, and then Pascual said quietly:

"I am going up to the Square, too, I shall go into San Andrés after; help your mother, boy," and taking his rosary from the nail beside the settle and thinking of the Five Triumphant Mysteries of Christ's Passion, he went out of the house. Approaching the Gate of San Andrés, he suddenly stood as if gripped by an electric current, listened, and then, whimpering with horror, raced to the Square, his body draining of strength with fear and effort. He arrived there at five minutes past three.

Robledo glanced at his watch and saw that the time was one minute to three; cursing the mayor for his habitual lateness, he stepped back from the window as the procession entered the Square, considering whether to descend and see who was hammering upon the door. Then as a solitary voice began to sing he heard a noise against the church steps that caused him to wheel. Incredulous, utterly rejecting the evidence of his eyes, he leaped to the window and gripped the sill; the blood spurted from his lips where his teeth bit into them; his stomach retched like a mechanical thing . . . far away . . . below his eyes . . . eyes . . . staring at the church steps. Then all of his body swept up into his brain and he was helpless and terrified as a falling babe.

Hammering upon the door with the great ring knocker engraved with olive leaves, Celestina turned her head in the direction of the procession. A man began to sing the "Internationale" and a metallic sound from the church steps and a cry of "They're coming" made her spin around. She flung up her hands and screamed, her legs weakened and she fell to her knees, screaming with choking throat.

"They're coming, the bastards," shouted the sergeant of the Civil Guard from the second step of San Andrés, and Montaña wrenched his pistol from its holster and shouted, "Fire." Rifles fled up and the muzzles came down to the waistline of the advancing fours of the procession and the first volley cracked like lightning before the sounding board of San Andrés front. The leading ranks crumpled and blew apart as if a terrific *ráfaga* had whirled among them, an uplifted placard spun round and the paper was torn away by an invisible thong which whipped fragments of wood into the air. The screams of the procession and the thundering of the rifles drowned Montaña's cracking voice as he yelled, "Fire, fire." One of the guards could not jam the cartridge clip into the magazine and, cursing and whimpering, tried to close the bolt, the rifle jammed and, wrenching the bolt back, he snatched at the cartridge in the barrel, removed it and flung both cartridge and rifle away and shouted hysterically as he dragged at his Mauser. The quicker, steady hammering of the guards' pistols at once ran through the irregular cracking of the rifles.

Those protestors behind the head of the column broke away and dashed frantically for the colonnade of the Republican Café; Montaña's bullets followed them and bodies writhed about the Square as he picked the runners off. . . .

Robledo flung himself back as the window before his assistant's table was shattered, and then with frenzied movements he tore at the drawer of his desk. It was locked and he felt madly for his keys. . . .

Baeza clutched at his stomach at the first volley and fell upon his back, his head straining back away from the agony in his abdomen, his feet jerking like those of a naked baby . . . then, as a child was flung across him by a bullet, he lay still.

For a moment Argote stood facing the shattered procession, uncomprehendingly watching the falling bodies, and then, as the woman before the Town Hall door pitched forward and slid down the steps, he turned and shouted at the guards; as he did so an immense and stunning blow struck him in the chest and he staggered back. "No," he roared. "You God . . ." and then there was a sudden thundering in his ears and the sight went from his eyes and he lifted his fists and pressed them over his breast.

"No, no," he shouted again, and lurching forward, he suddenly realized that he was wounded. Yet he could not *believe* that he had been shot, and though something within his mind told him that this was mortal he was filled with a rage of indignation. Pressing his breast he rocked forward towards the guards, and one of them, fumbling at the bolt, flung his rifle down and pulled out his pistol and fired it crazily at Argote as he advanced. None of the bullets struck him and at each shot he felt more exultant—missed, missed, missed! Missed!! It was absurd, ridiculous, it was madly, blazingly *funny* and Indalecio Argote burst into crackling laughter. The guard threw his empty pistol down and tried to draw the bayonet at his side as the bearlike man flung forward his bloodied fists and caught him by the throat, and he screamed once before the great fingers crumpled up the delicate bones in his throat. The laughing Argote hung his weight upon the choking guard and as he fell drew the knife at his belt and thrust it into the belly beneath him and rested his weight upon it. The guard flung about like a chained beast for a second and with a harsh sigh closed his eyes and Argote laughed more madly at the ridiculous sound the guard made in dying. Slowly he raised his body upon his arms and gazed through a red-and-green cloud at the guard upon the steps. His laughter ceased as another tremendous blow struck him in the back, mechanically his hands returned to the throat of the dead guard and his fingers began to fumble at it like the feet of a cat treading a woman's lap. Then an immense white hate burst in his brain and he roared out an obscene oath and struggled to rise and grapple with the taunting, flickering figure in the olive-green uniform dancing like a showman's monkey upon the steps beneath the olive tree full of stabbing flames. "Mush in his throat," his brain shouted, and tugged to get away from his body caught among the bloodied olive branches that littered the path. His fingers still fumbled at the throat beneath him as his brain put out an arm to drag himself up by the olive bough bending over him from the walls of Vallodolid, and then the bough broke and white Mater' Purissima sailed away like a kite and bells in the blue water. . . .

The drawer came out of the desk and papers fell to the floor, but the revolver slid to the corner of the drawer and he grabbed it and started towards the broken window. At that instant his own window flew to pieces. He would fire from his own, he decided, it would be better to fire from his own, and stamping over the glass as if it were a danger to be crushed down—it would trip him if he did not tread resolutely—he lifted the weapon and aimed it at a guard pointing his Mauser at the back of a man kneeling upon a uniformed body. Grinding his teeth, Robledo fired and the guard flung up his hands and fell sideways and lay still. "Good, oh good, good, good," he repeated again and again and mechanically withdrew to the desk. Suddenly the firing outside ceased and he returned to the window, where he stood picking out the glass from the putty with bleeding fingers, gazing at the dead below until the clock struck a quarter-past three, when he went downstairs and opened the door.

During the firing Caro stood still; Garcia beside him was down, blood pouring from his calf, Baeza lay dead with a little girl stretched across him, the dimpled skin behind the knees and the young virginal legs exposed. He could not tear his gaze away from the dimpled back of the girl's knee joints; they were so beautiful, so perfect; he could see the delicate molding of the muscles beneath the unwrinkled, tender skin; it was absurd, it was useless to leave so much beauty in a dead thing, it was too beautiful to be dead, the girl was not dead. Then a woman who had been screaming behind him fell against his legs and he stooped to lift her and her head had no face. Behind the first rank, men were scrambling like frightened seals among the bodies, upon the steps lay the inverted body of a woman, her head touching the pavement. He stood and waited. After a while the thunderous crackling ceased and he moved to sit down and get his breath, pushing his fountain pen deeper into his pocket and pressing the clip which ineffectually secured it. Suddenly, as he was stooping, he realized there were things to be done, and he looked around him desperately and ran to the side of a sitting man spouting blood in the groin and felt frantically for the torn artery. Before the Red Cross men arrived he remembered Lucía, and though four of the ten first aid men collapsed at the sight of the Square, he began to search for her. He found her in a house at the top of Olive Oil Street and Ursula tending her; he kissed her first with lifeless lips and then hungrily and with huge relief of tears and returned to the Square, where he saw his father kneeling by a groaning man, holding the cross of his rosary before the man's eyes. The man was gazing at it with graying face. "Thanks be to God," ejaculated Pascual as Joaquín approached, and lifted his face to the son, who flung his arms around him and kissed his cheek.

"Hold it farther away, Father," he said; "he can't see it properly there," and pulled his father's hand backwards. "Ursula is safe," he said, and went to the aid of a Red Cross man struggling to bandage a raving boy. The Square began to fill with weeping, hysterical people who hindered the doctors and the ambulance men, until the Civil Guard from Cuestas Abajo arrived and with drawn pistols cleared them back under the colonnades.

That night the twenty-four bodies were laid side by side in San Andrés and the people of Los Olivares filed through the church, about the floor of which were camped the families of the dead. All that night the building was full of wailing that rose from the floor beneath the great candles burning beside the dead. All night a silent crowd stood in the plaza before the barracks of the guards, drawing more closely hour by hour to the barred windows from which rifle barrels peered with round black eyes. When the Civil Governor arrived in the early hours of the morning with reinforcements of guards behind him, the officers within the barracks refused to open the doors until the plaza had been cleared of people. Straightway the Governor began a formal and documented inquiry. The abandoned placards were collected and their inscriptions recorded, witnesses were sworn and their accounts typed out, and a carefully worded note was issued to the swarming journalists, who were expelled from Los Olivares de Don Fadrique at eleven o'clock by the Governor at the demand of many citizens. One of the journalists discovered, with the aid of a flash light, that the hands of one of the victims were stained with shoe polish, and upon this he wrote three moving paragraphs. The fact was also mentioned at the inquiry and several times during the subsequent procedures. It was a detail somehow irritating to Montaña, and its mention continued to exasperate him even several months later, when he had been transferred to a new command in a fishing port of the Biscay coast.

Sideshow

AFTER the first silent accusation before the barracks house Los Olivares made no judgments. At the burial of the dead a voice had cried, "Death to the Civil Guards," and a hiss of condemnation put immediate end to the irreverence; and all that grinding and in-boring silence in the cemetery became a monstrous force to thrust down trivial anger. All that day, as the black, round-backed procession had moved out of the Sevilla Gate to the cemetery above the Huerta, and as the rioters' coffins had been slid into their white-painted pigeonholes in the cemetery wall, it had seemed as if the townspeople, or a mystical entity that included all the past, present and the future of Los Olivares had willed this. That day the quick passionless chanting of the Dies Irae disclosed its real and quelling horror that escapes recognition at a private and trivial death, when it is but a little black flag fluttering in a sleet wind. It was a chant of sacrifice, a cold chant of enforced submission before the god of death, for all the gods of life, declared the silence around the chant and its own passionless singing, had died long ago. And the death of these men and women and children was a ritual death which aroused no wild and plunging hate. The tawdry yellow of candle flames in the clear morning light and the ministrations of the priests in their trumpery black vestments and their trifling manual gestures gave this corporate death a new and monstrous significance. It was the tawdriness and the littleness which was effectual in this, the copes and the flames and the fussing hands were things of fantastic ineffectuality before the vast hills and beneath the flooding Christmas light. They were vain conjurations with which to confront the icy cordillera of death, and because men did these ineffectual things, their ineffectualness became more than an assertion that the dead are dead, but was strangley converted into assent, and life sacrificed itself dumbly to the god of death.

And though no one attended the funeral of the slain guards, people regarded the olive-green uniforms with awe that was neither hate nor quelled rebelliousness. The black cope and the biretta, the tricorne and the green cloth were symbols of a ritual, habiliments of a fatal liturgy.

The press, however, occupied itself greatly with blame. The Republican papers declared the tragedy to be the result of the barbarous neglect of culture by the clerical monarchy, the Socialist organs spoke of the system of land tenure, the center press deplored it and wrote weightily about the danger of extremism, and the Catholic journals said it was the natural work of a Socialist Radical and atheist Government. Cartoons were published about Los Olivares.

For several days the town lay under a stupor more profound than that of unvocable grief.

Upon the third day after the burial, Acorín, seeing that the fire-station door was wide open, entered the station and slowly collected some of the parts of the Gate Clock in a sack and took them to his home. He was observed to do this by a guard, who questioned him about his right to the parts. "No, I've got no right," he replied dully, but made no motion to put down the sack and stood dully gazing at the guard, who, after a few moments, strolled away. Arriving at his home, he threw the sack in a corner of his workroom and sat upon his leather-topped seat for half an hour with his hands folded upon his knees. Later he emptied the battered wheels and pinions upon his bench and toyed with them for a while before throwing his apron over them and going out. Two days later the mayor called him by name in the Street of Olive Oil and the two men stood side by side on the curb.

"You've taken the clock parts," Carrasco said, and Acorín replied, "Yes."

"Are you going to repair the clock?" the mayor continued, and first shrugging his shoulders, El Chino answered:

"You'd have to rebuild it."

"I'd put through a resolution in the Council if you'd care to rebuild it," Carrasco muttered, but Acorín pursed his lips and shook his head, and the mayor walked away. Having descended half the length of the street Carrasco turned and hastened after Acorín, whom he found standing before the Chapel of Our Lady of Carmén as if awaiting him.

"Why don't you undertake the job, Acorín?" he said, and the clock repairer said, "I might."

"I'll get a resolution through for you at once, with a money grant." The mayor's voice expressed a faint eagerness and the guitarist nodded and went back to his workroom, but did nothing except lay the wheels on the floor in the order of their trains. At the end of that week the mayor resigned office and with him the whole of the Council.

Before this, Don Blasco Ortega announced to his friends at the Casino that he proposed to defend the man Mudarra. He appeared to be shocked when one of them expressed his belief that Mudarra possessed no money.

"Ah," Ortega exclaimed, "this is different," and he drew himself up in his seat with that air of forensic nobility which his associates knew to signify a coming speech; yet he made no further reply. At the Casino the tragedy itself was rarely directly mentioned. During the World War several of its members had worn a button in their lapels reading, "Do not speak to me of the War." The fear that had possessed them then was in them now; when they mentioned recent events it was always of Don Fadrique they spoke. "What will the Marquis do now?" was their question, but they meant, "What shall we do if the olivars collapse?" Therefore they were chiefly silent.

Don Blasco indeed went to the capital and obtained leave to visit Mudarra, but the Anarchist did not wish to be defended; his sole desire was for information about the shooting of the rioters, which he had heard from the gate chamber but about which the guards would tell him nothing. He was more moved at hearing that Argote was dead than that Pérez was wounded. At his trial Mudarra broke into a passionate and unreasonable outburst and Don Blasco, present in court upon another case, asked leave to speak and without permission announced that the Marquis of Peral did not wish the charge of theft to be proceeded with. For this interruption the Los Olivares lawyer was severely reprimanded by the judge. Mudarra received the trifling sentence of one year's imprisonment, half of which was to correspond to the charge of offensive remarks to the Civil Guard and of hindering them in the performance of their duty on the olivars. The judge ignored Mudarra's vicious remark that they had since performed it in the town.

Christmas went by with no more festivities than the corresponding ecclesiastical rites; the plaster Babe was placed in the cradle in both churches and the midnight Mass was sung, but in a few homes only were the vigil customs observed.

Upon the Wednesday after Christmas Juan Robledo and his wife visited their son's house dressed in black and bearing a basket of presents of food and wine. Lucía answered their knock, and upon the threshold her mother kissed her upon the cheeks and they went together to Robledo's room. The secretary had been too ill to attend the funeral, yet he had astonished Mendizabal Street by paying for a Mass to be said for Celestina at San Andrés. Once only he had left the house and then had returned drunk to weep against the door. Alternatively he returned to Lucía with passionate need of her presence, and raved and cursed at her with uncontrolled violence. Now he consented readily to his sister returning home, though he told them he had written to the Caros asking them to take responsibility for her against the cost of her keep which he would allow them. When Juan commenced to condole with him in the loss of his wife he sat up suddenly and swung his legs to the edge of the bed and stared at his father without audible speech, whereupon Señora Robledo scolded her daughter for not attending to Justo's meals and invited him to return home with Lucía. With profound dejection he consented. A few nights later he became drunk again and ran wildly through the streets and tried to incite the neighbors to set fire to the Black House. Many who witnessed this were sympathetic with Robledo, though he had never won public affection, being too hard and unbending and too scrupulous in his duties, and a few bystanders tried to calm him. Finally he broke down and, leaning upon his constrainers, wept, saying again and again, "My poor girl, my poor girl." The quiet attention of the father to his son was noticed by many, though the comment this formerly would have aroused was missing. Slowly Justo recovered and took up his duties again, but he no longer displayed that alertness which had secured him his post without any political or personal influence.

On the olivars work slowly went on under Calasparra; the only crop to be gathered was the verdiales and these had been so damaged by the hailstorm of July that it was unprofitable to spend much labor upon them. Calasparra against his will was forced to discharge a quarter of the men, nor would Don Fadrique consent to fresh land being broken. In this he was peremptory. It seemed that impulse and energy had disappeared from Los Olivares, men went listlessly about their work under the trees, and Calasparra himself had lost heart. In the old days Don Indalecio, as he was now always called, would have stormed if the plows had not left a straight furrow between the trees or if the breaking irons had not reduced every clod to pigeon's egg size. Now the fields were allowed to take on a different aspect, and though the work was really quite as effective, the men were further depressed by its apparent slovenliness. The trees themselves, standing patiently through the sapless months, seemed to reflect the general dejection and their silence became morbid to the workers; the more so because that January was a month of crystalline sunlight. And when at length Pérez died of his wounds that single death recast the common shadow of death over everyone.

The day following Pérez's burial a motor lorry approached the Sevilla Gate. The driver then backed along the road, directed by a woman who descended from the rear of the lorry, until the spot where the road ran level with the wasteland was reached; when with a terrific jolting that threatened to shake the lorry to pieces, the driver backed in onto the fair ground. A few children watched this done and presently the women gave them a few handbills to distribute in the town.

They announced the arrival of the Spanish giant, Martin
Luengo of Extremadura, who could be seen for twenty-five
cents. That night a wooden shack was erected and over its
front were hung a few placards representing an enormous
male in tights with bursting muscles and indications of massive
sexual organs; from the body electric sparks were indicated as
springing; a purple curtain hid the door and a raised platform
with a handbell upon it. A sad-faced individual of fidgety
behavior who normally thrust his chin well down into a filthy
scarf stood outside the shack and when anyone passed withdrew
his chin and announced the presence of the Spanish giant.
No one entered upon the first day and the price was reduced to
twenty cents. A few passed in and out on the next day.

On that Saturday afternoon Caro called at Miracle Court
at the moment when Justo Robledo was about to take Lucía
for a short walk. The girl, seeing Caro, did not wish to go, but
Justo insisted, whereupon the olive worker offered to accompany her. Conversing little, they descended the hill to the
Plaza de las Armas, where, as Caro sighed, Lucía said, "You
seem more sad today, Joaquín." He replied, "The walls make
me think of Diego." It was the first time he had mentioned
Mudarra to the girl and he felt her wince. "Yes," she murmured, and after a pause added, "They say the guards
tortured him."

"I expect they did," he said, and made no further reference
to Mudarra but presently she seemed about to cry. It irritated
him and he said roughly, "He can stand that," and a sudden
antipathy held them apart as they passed out of the Sevilla
Gate, threading through the knot of people gathered there;
his grip on her arm relaxed and he felt hers grow lifeless.
A motor approached the Gate, and as he drew the girl aside
he heard a woman say to her husband, "They say they both
had her." Whether or not the girl heard the remark he was
not sure but a surge of disgust and repulsion from her swept
through him, and everything about her pregnancy, her swollen
body, pale unhealthy face and ringed eyes, and her balanced
and waddling gait, became nauseous to him. It was not shame,
but fear and disgust, she was in an unclean state, and for a
moment his nostrils were deceived into reporting that she

poisoned the air around her; his fear was of the obscene. This revulsion soon began to pass, but she was aware of his shrinking and withdrew from him into herself in fear and humility; and then he saw her face set and an indignant anger burn in her eyes, and he was at once eased. They were walking side by side like two individuals and it seemed that his breath came more freely; there was something he must tell her; it was perfectly clear now what he must tell her. He felt more love for her because its day was to be put off, now that this absurd effort to conform to a moral doctrine was relinquished, and he took her arm again. But Lucía recognized through his obvious affection that he was now farther from her, less imprisoned in the ideas that might make him her support and defense, and though she accepted his touch it was with distrust. And then with increased weight the sorrow that overlaid Los Olivares oppressed them again and they were confined in the gloom of death that would not be dispersed. Black-dressed people were moving about silently or conversing in low voices; the very refuse of the road, the yellow papers flapping lightly against the base of the tower beneath the electric lamp, the straws and scraps and the battered tins seemed to him to deliver the same doctrine of gloom.

As they passed the shack the spieler took his chin out of his scarf and commenced to whine, "Pass inside, señores, and contemplate with amazement the extraordinary work of nature, the Spanish giant, pass inside, at once a . . ." As they walked by, the spieler's voice trailed away and was silent. "Let's go in and see the giant," said Caro, and impelled the girl towards the shack; as they approached the door the spieler recommenced to shout for their benefit, continuing while he took the forty cents. His breath was hot on Caro's hands as he took up his change.

They entered and contemplated the giant. Seated in an arm-chair was a frail and consumptive man with stooping shoulders and the gaze of a doomed animal. The lower half of his legs seemed to be disproportionately long, or the chair was too low, and his fleshless thighs ran up to big misshapen knees upon which rested the long waxen hands with their little babylike thumbs. Out of the white face peered eyes that despite their dullness disclosed boredom and hate. The spieler put his head into the shack and said, "Stand up, giant," and the tottering skeleton slowly obeyed; upon its tall body the small head seemed obscene.

"You may touch the giant, señores," the spieler announced in the same professional voice he used outside. "Feel his limbs or any part of his body you care to be sure there is no deception." Caro listlessly touched the exhibit's forearm and sunken stomach The showman went on to give particulars of the freak's birth, native town, measurements and so forth, and while he was doing so Dr. Torres entered the shack.

"I should like to measure the exhibit, I am a doctor," he said after a few moments, and the spieler at once placed a chair beside the giant and, standing upon it, winked at Caro.

"I should be pleased to have your reading, Señor Doctor," the showman said. "It will interest you to know that Dr. Jiménez of Madrid has already bought the giant's skeleton, which after his death will be included in his famous collection of mummies and skeletons. My little friend here receives three pesetas a day from the doctor" —he gave the exhibit a smack with the back of his hand as he spoke—"three pesetas a day as long as he lives, as long as he lives, eh?"

The dull eyes were turned first upon the spieler and then pleadingly upon Torres, who made no remark but was obviously estimating the giant's probable length of life. Caro and Lucía went out of the shack; the showman followed them and as Conchita Pérez passed, supported on the arm of Calasparra, began to rap with a stick on the placard of the electrical Hercules, whining with an absurd mixture of appeal and command.

"Let's go down to the café, there's something I want to say," Caro said, and the girl obeyed readily. When the proprietor had gone to the rear of the house he began.

"It's no good going on like this, Lucía. I've been trying to do the impossible, and it is impossible. It just comes to this; when it's all over I'm going to ask you to marry me. But you'll have to put the child away with someone."

The girl showed no anger but her answer was as immediate as anger:

"That's as I thought. No . . . I've gone so far alone, and as for the child . . ."

"Have you?" he interjected quickly, and with a desire to hurt that derived from his disappointment that she should have said alone; but determining to keep to the point he said:

"You can't expect me to keep another man's child."

She broke in with unsteady voice:

"Yes, you've been good, Joaquín, I know, but it's really been alone, worse than alone. You'll not see that."

"All right, it's finished then."

"If that's how it is, yes." She stood up, but he motioned that the coffees were not paid for, and she sat down.

"Yes, you've been good," Lucía said suddenly, "but, well, you don't understand this either. I like Diego's attitude better than yours just now."

He made no reply but flushed deeply, and she continued with cold anger:

"He had what he wanted and when I wouldn't marry him he cleared off and forgot me like a man. You don't know what you want and you've been wanting me to tell you. If that medicine had worked you'd have asked me before this."

He had begun by admitting this, he saw, but it hurt, though with an effort he ignored the thrust; he had been going to say Mudarra had not known what he wanted.

"I didn't, perhaps, but I do now," he said clearly, and Lucía saw that though he was troubled this was costing him less than she had supposed.

"Well, you're not the only one to have learned things. I've changed too; I wanted to marry you and I would have been happy . . . O Christ . . . O Mother Mary," she moaned and burst into tears.

"Well, it's all I've got to say. You needn't give any answer now. Come round to it if you can," he said, putting a peseta on the table and rising.

"Mother of God . . . and you haven't even the decency to wait to tell me till it's over," she screamed through her tears as he left the café. He heard the proprietor enter the room behind him.

After that it was not easy to return for the girl to escort her home as he felt bound to do; fortunately she childishly refused to return with him. Because she spoke quietly he thought at first it was a childish refusal. Recognizing him as already a patron, the spieler cut his appeal short.

Giant Again

THE thought, somehow shameful, wandered into his soft haze of melancholy like a boorish intruder and the candle flames, which had run together into one comforting yellow suffusion above the cold linen, became separate and hard; and, rising, Don Fadrique extinguished the candles and went out of the chapel. The housekeeper took several minutes to detach the key of Argote's room from her heavy bunch, and he turned away to avoid watching her erratic fleshless hands.

He closed the door behind him. It was strange that in all these years since he had given the keys to the mayordomo he had never entered this room. Indefinitely he began to look round at the tidy but overcrowded contents of the room. Over the absurdly small desk was the stuffed boar's head of which Argote had once been so proud and which he had seen carried into the room after it had been exhibited in the servants' eating room. Near it was the stag's head mounted upon a split shield of olive wood, the head which had caused Argote to be absent from the olive harvest of ten years ago. One December morning, when the exhilarating crop of 1922 was being gathered, the mayordomo had not appeared upon the Skirts. The festivities of the preceding night and Don Indalecio's unhidden liking for a flamenco singer, whose caprice it had been to take harvest employment, had made his nonappearance a matter for jest among the workers, though the Marquis had not known this. At the middle hour of the morning's labor one of the charge hands had inquired at the Palacio; the housekeeper's scream had brought the servants rushing to the mayordomo's room. His papers covered with darkened blood, Argote lay sprawled upon the floor, the fallen stag's head beside him, its broken cord telling them what had happened. Don Fadrique remembered that day and its strange tension in the palace; he himself had watched the housekeeper and two of her assistants strip the massive figure and wash the blood from his neck and the black clots from the hair of his chest. He remembered clearly the whispering young women's sudden silence and their reverent sighs of admiration as they peeled down his tight-fitting trousers and disclosed the enormous thighs and matted loins. Until the evening Argote had remained motionless upon his bed while the servants had tiptoed about their duties. A little before supper a bawled oath from the mayordomo's room had lit everyone's face with smiles, the shaken table clattered and hands quickly made the sign of the cross as the housekeeper rushed to the room; everyone repeated her fervent "Thanks be to God" from the corridor above. Two days later Don Indalecio was riding about the olivars as before. The flamenco singer, everyone in the town knew, had hung about Los Olivares for six weeks, and then had suddenly disappeared.

Yet the mayordomo's passion for hunting had waned slowly and was now forgotten; the servants no more jested about him lovingly brushing the boar's head once a week. It had been a curious religious passion. The bearskin still hung upon the door as Peral had been told, and he remembered the day when Argote had asked him for an advance upon his next month's salary in order to spend his leave in far-off Asturias, bear-hunting. And when a visiting relative of one of the servants had told a ribald story of a bear, who had seized a priest, and had been outwitted by the cleric's tongue, the mayordomo had frowned angrily at the slighting reference to the noble animal. The incident had since been recounted as an anticlerical jest. In the corner of the room the rifle with which the bear had been killed still stood, beside two shotguns, one a fine and expensive English double-barreled weapon, specially ordered from London.

Wondering why the mayordomo had grown indifferent to his former delight, Don Fadrique moved to the desk and took out the ledgers. Among them was Argote's private account book. The shame he had felt in the chapel returned strongly as he opened it.

So . . . it was true, the rumor which had deviously reached him. There could be no doubt about the meaning of the figures. This then was the service and the devotion which the mayordomo had given him; the estate had prospered and with it Argote. Traditional enough, Don Fadrique thought cynically, yet the sneer was uncomfortable and somehow, thinking of the drained body lying wreathed and still in San Andrés, he could not maintain it. Dully his eyes returned to the figures, their meaning clear on every page of the book. Well, it was natural, he supposed; if one permitted a servant such enjoyment of liberty, dishonesty was inevitable. That the judgment was incorrect Don Fadrique knew, and he smiled as he confessed that he had not permitted the mayordomo to exercise complete control, Argote had taken control, and that because he himself had been too indifferent to the olivars to concern himself with them. Nevertheless, though it might almost be considered as justifiable reward for unsparing service, the man's continuous and unfearing dishonesty hurt Peral greatly. The thought that he had even given up his passion for hunting the better to plunder the estate was somehow even more embittering. And as he turned the leaves and noted how the mayordomo's daring increased, Don Fadrique was moved with indignation.

Closing the book he turned away from the desk to the bookshelf and idly withdrew a volume. It was a French treatise on the insect pests most to be feared by the olive-grower; he replaced it and took out another whose binding interested him. "Friar Francisco Baeza," he read aloud, "Memoir upon the planting of *garrotes* . . . for the augmenting of olives, 1799." He had heard of the Friar Francisco from a few bibliophiles and he laid the book aside and glanced along the shelves again. How many treatises upon olive-growing the mayordomo possessed, he commented, and noted that many of them were annotated in the olivero's surprisingly small hand. There were other books in foreign languages, too, recent French treatises embodying the latest research in the chemistry of manures and pest extermination, and the Italian Bracci's *Manuale*. What

curious collector's obsession had prompted Argote to acquire
these books, certainly incomprehensible to the mayordomo,
whose schooling was that afforded by Los Olivares. Another
binding attracted him and he spent several minutes examining
a delightful book of the Portuguese, Coelho de Saabra, issued
from the press of Coimbra in 1792. And then, his interest in
the mayordomo's library thoroughly awakened, he began to
search methodically. A splendid and unknown seventeenth-
century translation of Varro and Friar Francisco's most important and highly prized work were his reward; he placed
them with the other two volumes and returned to the desk
to examine the papers.

Opening the topmost of a collection of school exercise books,
he found it was filled with figures in cheap faded ink; the
books were clearly those used by the mayordomo to master the
devices of arithmetic. The exercises were dated, he noticed, and
between the first and the last there was a difference of five
years. He certainly profited by his study, the Marquis thought,
glancing at the olivero's account book and then, turning to
the bookshelves to look for the arithmetic primer, his gaze
caught the pile of books he had selected. Flushing, he returned
them to the shelves. Beside a ready reckoner he discovered a
French and an Italian grammar, much thumbed. "*Caramba!*"
he whispered, and stood pondering awhile before returning to
the desk. Argote had certainly possessed great zeal in his
plundering in desiring to master foreign olivicultural treatises.

Turning over a bundle of papers, Don Fadrique next found
a mass of correspondence dealing with a lawsuit between Don
Indalecio Argote and a company of oil refiners, in which it
appeared that after lengthy litigation the mayordomo had been
compelled to forfeit five thousand pesetas in addition to the
costs. This is strange, thought the Marquis of Peral, I have
never heard of this action, and examining the papers afresh,
he perceived that the action should properly have been
brought against the estate, himself. Could the man have been
impelled by the desire to serve after all, then? Or was it some
form of retribution for dishonesty? The date of the action
annulled that hypothesis, however, and he continued to turn
over a set of papers of whose meaning he could make nothing

at all; vaguely they seemed to have political significance. The name Lorca figured in many of them and then at the foot of a letter in which the name occurred twice he found a calculation in Argote's handwriting; it appeared to be a computation of what a sum in French francs would equal in Spanish currency. Lorca, Lorca, Don Fadrique muttered, the name seemed disturbingly familiar. Suddenly he stood upright, before his shrinking imagination the vision of a world he had never entered. Lorca was the name of one who had been tried for the murder of two Socialists in Los Olivares in the year preceding the dictatorship of Primo de Rivera; he had been acquitted a week later, and had gone to France. His hands trembling the Marquis laid down the letter, the name Lorca ringing in his brain; fearfully he looked round the room, at the boar's and the stag's heads, at the weapon in the rack and the account book upon the desk, his gaze shrinking from the letter beside it. And then his horror passed and with still shaking hands he picked up the letter and reread it.

So Argote's avarice had determined this; he had known that the mayordomo had maintained a political organization, that for many years he had prevented the holding of elections in Los Olivares—his mind added with special force the word "de Don Fadrique"—that Socialist agitation had been barred out of the town. All that he had quietly approved, for what but evil had this demented movement against the eternal necessity and sanction of property ever brought the workman? and this political activity was general upon all the estates of Andalucía, too—but this black thing, that his own mayordomo should have been a party to it, perhaps—should have removed these men in this manner—he was indignant, and at once ashamed, and then suddenly the voice of his indignation and the whisper of his shame were hushed and a curious silence took possession of his mind. He seemed to be on the edge of some understanding, or a door was to be opened upon a landscape. The figure of Indalecio Argote stood before him, the great body filled with hot strong blood, the bursting lips and the heavy, starting eyes, the flushed face, and the pulsing neck with its black hair showing above the collar band. He heard the ferocious blasphemies and the drum of hoofs, and yet also he heard the hushed voices of the servant maids stripping the sweat-stained trousers from the great swarthy legs. Argote's laugh rang in his memory as the mayordomo sat astride his bay mount and gazed down the quivering slopes lined with a gray-green army of trees that shimmered silently beneath the arching sky. Why had Indalecio Argote removed these men? The grammar book upon the floor caught his eye and he crossed the room and with a hint of reverence stooped and placed it upon the shelf.

Perhaps he had private reasons—impossible; he could not have hated these men, they would have avoided meeting the mayordomo in person, and the man was too simple to hate an idea. Yet he had removed them—for the sake of his thefts from the estate? Argote had been dishonest, that was certain, yet there was something incredible in this extreme, as if passion had entered into it, a richer and less calculating thing than greed. Service then, beneath the dishonesty no, beneath the old and glowing tradition of service he had been dishonest. The image of the mayordomo persisted, standing by the chapel of Mater Purissima, gazing over the fields where the workers were cleaning the silent sapless trees; Don Fadrique shook his head in perplexity.

A bundle of letters in the back of a pigeon-hole suggested that there might be another reason for Argote's incomprehensible life, but this he rejected while he was still glancing through the packet. The postmark Valladolid was upon them all and the handwriting was of a woman; hesitantly he withdrew a letter from its envelope—and without reading it returned it and replaced the packet. Later, when he found the mayordomo's will, he knew that he was reading it with the name Valladolid in his mind, but the document threw no light on the letters. For a while he puzzled over the odd bequest of two sums of a thousand duros to Father Martínez; why had he so insisted upon its being two separate quantities? The bequest to a woman of Los Olivares or in the event of her previous death to her son occupied his thought for a while, sadly. There was no explanation here; the woman had been well recompensed for her misfortune and she had her son—and the mayordomo appeared to have taken no sustained interest in his child.

Half an hour later a sheet of paper gave him the under-standing he had felt to be imminent. Upon it were written various texts from Holy Scripture in which the olive tree was mentioned and beneath them a quotation from a nineteenth-century work of shoddy scholarship upon the religious customs of the Ancient Romans. "Virgins and married women alone were permitted to gather the fruit of the olive in Ancient Rome" it read. Even as he perceived the real passion of Argote's life he felt a curious pity for the mayordomo with his pathetic lack of scholarship searching for all that referred to the tree to which he had given his life. And then swiftly all the details of the room swung themselves into place around this passion, and Don Fadrique understood the abandoned sport, the laborious studies, the primitive life, the two dead Socialists —he found he had risen to his feet as he thought of the mayordomo's life; the persistent image of the man had dis-appeared, and Don Fadrique walked quietly out of the room and entered the library.

Again it was the tale of old violence which he brooded upon; far off, a long way down the wall-less corridor of interior vision, was an uplifted platform of rock, veined and shaded with heightened earth colors. Around the platform the land fell into a haze of boughs, though beyond was the shining sea and a sierra with curious thorn-shaped serrations, like a regular swell of the sea blown to a sharp and overhanging crest. A group of olives stood upon the platform, their leaves visible at that great remove as if painted in enamels, and over the trees was bent a hoop of white curdled clouds. Two men stepped from the trees and moved their diverse ways and suddenly flung up their arms and fell and lay still; another figure crept over the rear edge of the platform and felt their bodies. It was all far off, beyond the communication of voice or any sound but the breathing of the stooping man—it was his own breathing, he realized, yet the interruption did not destroy the image. Music was sounding, faintly, the slow trill-ing of a note and a Picardian tierce which never completed its cadence but lifted the sweet nostalgic naïveté of the melody on to a fresh wave of sound. Then the plucked chords grew for a moment more resonant, a hint of passion sounded and the lute became a guitar and the platform disappeared, though the memory of it was like an image, an image which he compared with the former. How do we test accuracy of our memory images? Don Fadrique thought; we cannot in the act of memory have the reality by us with which to compare the image—and yet we say of our memory of a face that it is incorrect, that it does not give a good description of what we know to be a reality, yet that reality itself must be a memory— The face of Argote rose up; the mayordomo was standing somewhere to his left gazing at a tree; presently he put up his hand and drew his thick fingers down a tiny cluster of blossom—behind the tree was the silent sea and a dolphin swimming alone among the unmoving thorn-shaped waves, again the guitar was sounding and in some unseen place a man was groaning—he was groaning himself, he realized, and at once his reverie was broken; thought became hard and unpleasurable, the pain unmixed with beauty, the world he had made for himself fell away and only the broken, bouldery parts of another world remained.

How had the mayordomo handled this world? The question caused him to smile; he could not believe that Don Indalecio had ever felt the impact of pain, or the rotating knife of conscience—and if he had, when had the beauty arisen to sweeten pain? It was only a thing of beauty could present the truth about the world in one object, for the faint anguish in beauty and its remote tranquillity made a synthetic symbol of the world. How often he had comfortably arrived at this point and how restless and cold it now seemed. Could an olive tree, or seven thousand olive trees, do this for the man what the music of lutenists had done for him? Did such a man as the mayordomo need this? He was surely unaware of pain that he could remain so bluffly in the world. . . . Yet, men had made beauty of substance, they had made beautiful things to live amongst— the walls of Los Olivares were present before his imagination, the beauty of their towers and their gates. And the walls were a recognition of evil—and at once it became clear that this man had accepted this living world, and had taken his life into it, had poured it into trees and fruit, into the mountainside, into labor, domination, strife, and he was groaning again. One

may make an interior world, or one may go out to the world—
if one is mightily strong, he thought bitterly—bitterly. . . .

He tore up the letter to Morcillo, the former superintendent,
and stood up. Well, the town would say he had fled because he
could no longer live upon the strength of Don Indalecio; let
them say it. They would never know that it had become
impossible for him to employ another person in the place of
that man, it would be disrespect, irreverence—it hurt him to
think that he had considered selling Don Indalecio's four
books, stealing them.

In the early hours of the morning, when the music books had
been packed and the money hidden away in his clothes, Don
Fadrique Guevara y Muñaroz entered the chapel and switched
on the electric light. The picture above the altar glistened—he
smiled as he thought of the scholarship he had brought to the
capricious dream that Morales had once been the Guevara
music master. Dream? No, he knew now that he had never
believed it, the encouraged lie. Don Indalecio had used his
little learning to glorify a tree, a thing of living wood and
breathing leaves. . . . Mother of God, O Mother of God, it was
not merely his learning, it was the deeds of this man's hands,
the enthusiasm of his brain, the thrust of his loins, the plotting
of his hate, the tyranny and devotion of his love—which he had
given to the trees—he himself would never get through this
excluding veil to the solid world beyond. What was that
argument of Soriano's? That man only needed a liturgy to
hold him firm within the rhythm of life, to fuse the ideal and
the real into one, to mingle the mystical and the material—ah,
surely these men who labored among the trees, who accepted
the discipline of the soil, followed their unwritten liturgy. Once
he had watched two men examining each a handful of soil,
arguing about its value, gazing into the crumbled soil with
intent faces. When they had finished one of them had thrown
his handful to the ground, reverently, following it with his
eyes, as if it were something holy. Could Holy Church ever win
back these men, ever lift the world wholly into her? . . .
Somehow, not doubting his orthodox faith, Don Fadrique felt
that Holy Church herself was far removed from that world
which these men and Don Indalecio accepted. To escape the

evil and pain of the world might be to forsake life, to sap one's own life. For if one retreated into an interior world evil followed there also, and one must flee it anew; escape was an eternal and enfeebling regression. Upon what icy cordillera to gasp among what ghostly splendors would one arrive at last? There was no dodging this devil, the only thing to be done was to go out, down into the hot and reeking plains and meet it, wrestle with it, perhaps to remove it. . . . Strange and exciting territory opened before him! It appalled him, for was this not the doctrine of these men whom he had never known? The two men lying beneath the trees upon the platform beneath the hoop of curdled clouds. Ah, but there was dissension about the manner of removing evil, dissension was evil, or was it only pain? These men accepted that evil, they fled nothing. The man Mudarra also, he had had faith and had certainly loved music, also he had not fled the devil of pain. . . . Suddenly Don Fadrique laughed aloud at Soriano bending his curious mind with its terrific subtlety to straighten out every difficulty for him. Once, cold and bored, he had said to the priest, "If it is sinful to disbelieve in the existence of the devil, and the devil is the source of all temptation, who then tempts one to disbelieve in the devil. Satan himself?" And Soriano had pounced with grim zest to explain the devil's psychology—pathetic priest, poor devil.

The rain from which he had sheltered at the fountain of Doña Inés had stopped, and the moon, perilously skirting the edge of a dense cloud, disclosed the smoke-blackened ruins of Mater Purissima; a smell of wet charred wood still arose from within the walls. It was a pity the chapel had been burned, yet beauty existed to be destroyed, it seemed, otherwise, timeless and too serene it would be a thing without significance, it would be no symbol—and man might be content with old beauty so long that . . .

He was tiring already, the two heavy suitcases were numbing his upper arms, yet he could not risk a passage through the town, and turning through the olivars he skirted the fair ground, moving confusedly through the hummocks that bordered it. When he arrived at the sudden downward tilt of the earth he perceived the road far below him and knew his fear of detection had driven him too far to the left. From a tangle of thorn bushes a gully descended to the road; there would be a culvert at the bottom, he guessed, and he would have to climb with difficulty onto the road, yet he entered the gully and pressed through the bushes, into darkness. His breathing sounded like the respiration of a beast near him, the wet stones were cold to his touch and the wind whined above him as, dry-mouthed with fear, he picked his way down the gully, lowering the suitcases stage by stage. At the middle of the gully he slipped and a suitcase rolled over and came to a standstill a few yards below him upon a platform of brambled rubble. He could see nothing of the road, nor of the exit above. . . . But it was not with fear of the gully that he commenced to tremble violently. Shaking in all his body with a more than physical coldness in his flesh, Don Fadrique Guevara y Muñaroz stood facing the night. . . . He was late, he would not get past Puente Nuevo before dawn, he had better ask for assistance of the lorry that he heard rattling down the road from Los Olivares. He must pay well, buy silence. . . .

The lorry driver took the silver coins eagerly and opened the flap at the rear for him to enter and, climbing in behind him, struck a match to point out a long planklike ledge running down the side of the lorry. "The bedclothes are on the floor," the lorry driver said as the match went out. A warm human smell arose from the floor and there was a movement on the other side of the interior. When the man struck another match Don Fadrique peered at the floor. Beneath two overlapping blankets lay a man, his head inclined sideways to avoid the frontboard, a pair of feet protruding from the blanket at the tailboard. From the other ledge a woman gazed at him and began to speak and then the match was extinguished and she was silent. Rocking and sliding upon the narrow ledge, Don Fadrique jolted down the highroad away from Los Olivares. Sometimes he thought of Argote and sometimes of the estate and the trees, at other times he thought of Morales, amongst all the great masters of his age the most legendary still, and from time to time he wondered who this man of enormous length sleeping on the lorry floor could be.

27

Miracle Court

A few lance-shaped slips of clouds were moving over the Jabalón sky, though the straggling goat-bitten retama bushes that bordered the palace side of the Gallows Rock gully were flurrying in the running breeze. The breeze in its sudden galloping spurts flicked the dust from the top of the dried ruts and pushed the crumbled mortar from the summit of the sanctuary walls. The breeze even succeeded in stirring the olives to visible motion; the puddles near the fountain of Doña Inés opened their black-lidded eyes, but rarely to gaze at the blue sky. Yet the breeze was kindly, being warmed by the clear February sun, and scented as if the year's florescence had already begun. Here and there the wagging rosemary masts appeared to be dusted with dim violet, but there were no flowers; a few zorzaleños had put out new shoots upon the best-fed branches.

Lucía became tired soon after leaving the fountain and asked her brother to take her home.

"It is sheltered here, better have a rest," he replied and she sat upon a heap of stones that had fallen from the top of the wall which held up the soil of the right-hand field. Robledo looked around and, going a few paces up the path to make water, his gaze found a way through the trunks to the farthest head hills of the valley not visible from the town. It was a curious view, for the trunks formed a pillared corridor to the edge of a long undulation. The trees were old and their rather close setting had always been criticized by Don Indalecio because the sun and air could not freely enter. Their approaching branches left only a narrow space above and the sun laid a pattern of trunk shadows across the soil, here almost white, so that Justo appeared to be gazing down a latticed tube of light and shade.

"Come up here," he called after a while and the girl obeyed.

"What is it?" she asked as he drew her up the bank and steadied her, and pointed along the corridor.

"Yes," she said, "the hills," and he could see from her widening eyes that she liked the view. "I'd like to see more," she gasped, when she regained the floor of the deep-driven path.

"It was the trunks standing the way they do," he explained.

"No, it was the hills; they're all white, they shine."

"All right," he smiled, and smiling in return she repeated, "I'd like to see more, I'd like to see the hills."

"We shall have to go too far, to be clear of the trees."

"Can't we go up? There are paths," she said, turning away from him, and without reply he led her away from the town. Soon they came to a steep side path floored with hard-stepped layers of stone down which a broad film of water was trickling.

"This will take us above the trees, I expect," Justo remarked, "because the water must be coming from the slopes above. Walk on the side, because you mustn't catch cold."

Lucía shook her head. "No, it comes from the watercourse that takes the overflow of the reservoir," but nevertheless they commenced to climb the path. They had rested twice before they reached the red-bricked aqueduct which bore the overflow; a silver chain-veil of water was spilling from it onto the path and they could hear the stream bubbling along in the channel. Robledo regarded the shining spill and finally shook his head.

"No, you'll get wet," he said abruptly.

"That won't matter," she contested in scolding tones. "You are always talking about colds."

"Of course, woman."

"Colds, I never catch colds," but he merely grunted in reply and darted through the spill and turned to face her, brushing the water from his coat. "It's not so heavy here," he said, pointing to the other side of the path. "Give me your hand and I'll pull you through; put your foot forward."

The water fell on their hands as they joined and she grimaced and stepped through the spill before he pulled her.

Above, the path turned sharply to the left, and hurrying along ahead of her he found that it commenced to descend the slopes again. At its height the head hills were still invisible. "No good," he exclaimed upon his return, "you can't see through the trees."

"I'd forgotten the hills," Lucía confessed, "but I'd like to see them now nonetheless."

"Good God, what a woman, but you can't anyhow."

"Let's go up the fields then, the trees are arbequins, that means we're near the top."

"Nonsense, you can't climb this wall."

"I can, if you can find a place where there are stones."

He had no intention of letting her climb the wall even if he found the mounting stones, but setting his foot in a crevice of the wall he essayed to scramble up to the field; at the third attempt he succeeded and found himself upon a narrow terrace upon which, amongst smaller trees, stood one larger and much older tree, its branches propped with v-topped timbers. Behind this tree were steppingstones to the next terrace, and glancing back once, he climbed to the next field; the head hills were also climbing out of the boughs.

"Lucia," he called, and she answered, "Yes?" and hearing her voice, he mounted to the next field, bringing down in his clumsy scrambling several heavy stones which thudded upon the hard, unworked soil of the neglected terraces.

"Lucía," he shouted and her voice sounded unexpectedly close. "Where are you, you're not to move," he called quickly.

"I'm not moving."

"I can see the hills, there's snow on them right down to the pass."

"Yes," he heard her reply.

"You can see over the dip from here," Justo continued. "The hills beyond are all white and there are white clouds on them; you can't see which is hills and which is sky."

"Can't I come up?"

"No, you can't . . . the head hills on the other side of the valley are already clear of snow; perhaps they never had snow, though. What else do you want to know?" There was no answer and he called sharply; still Lucía did not reply, and he leaped down the wall. When he reached the path she was crouching down, her head resting against the wall, eyes shut.

"Mother of God, what's the matter," he shouted and caught her by the arm.

"Don't pull," she gasped, opening her eyes and staring at him.

"It's not that?" he answered wildly.

"I don't know, it hurts, it's a week too soon. No, let me stay, let me stay," she said frantically as he tried to lift her.

"You must come home at once, oh, Mother of God." She shook her head and gripped her dress with white knuckled hands. He stood waiting with dry mouth and racing heart. Suddenly she sighed deeply.

"There, I knew it would pass," she murmured, and he knelt down and put his arm around her and she laid her head against him.

"Have you had it before? Why did you come out so far then?"

"No," she whispered, "let me rest a minute first."

"Yes, yes," he answered fervently and closed his eyes. The breeze rustled in the trees over the wall top and a bird flew by; the noises frightened him and he opened his eyes.

As they were passing Mater Purissima the girl halted and said:

"We're silly, I forgot you can see the hills from just over there."

"God's daddy, of course, you can," he replied, hearing the curious longing in her voice. Then, looking about her a moment, the girl insisted on being allowed to cross the broad level field to the edge where the earth sank away to the river. She stood long gazing towards the head of the valley. . . .

Two days later, while Lucía was standing at the door of her home listening to the conversation of a group of women, she was again seized by pain. The women, some of whom belonged to the lower houses of Olive Oil Street, were waiting their turn to draw water from the well, the bursting of a pipe having caused the nearest public fountain to run dry. They were apathetically discussing the news which Juan the baker's assistant had given them.

"Why don't the nuns give something better than this fool's soup?"

"They've got the money."

"They've got six houses in Republican Square."

"No, they haven't." The baker had been emphatic and he put the wooden bin lid down with affirmative decision.

"Everybody knows they have."

"Everybody knows wrong then."

The man had gone into the shop and sullenly the women reasserted among themselves that the nuns certainly possessed the property for they collected the rent every month in advance. The "fool's soup," *sopa boba*, was that given in diminishing quantities to relieve the poverty caused by the dereliction of the olivars, which since Peral's departure had not been cultivated. The nuns had become the subject of much criticism for the inadequacy of this relief, and once or twice they had been shouted after, though such demonstrations were never forceful; the town still lay inert beneath the weight of the December tragedy.

"Explain yourself, man," Gordito's daughter snapped.

"Well, you thought the Sergeant went to Madrid to collect alms, didn't you? Well, she didn't. She went to the monastery of Chamartín to ask the Jesuits whether they would grant a month's rent to the relief fund."

The Sergeant was the nickname of the Mother Superior.

"The Jesuits, you've got Jesuits on the brain, like all you Republicans," Mercedes Caravaca said.

"Ah, ha . . . well, she went to Chamartín, she did, the Sergeant did, and she was so much ignorant of the world that she didn't know the special Government commission was in and the Jesuits were out."

"What have the Jesuits got to do with the Sergeant anyway, or with Los Olivares?"

"Well, those six houses belonged to the Jesuits, but they'd had the deeds made out in the name of the nuns so that when they were expropriated they could hang on to something. Knew it was coming right enough. They'd got a secret company to hold property, stocks and shares and all that."

"Nonsense, man, the Jesuits don't do that, they're men of God."

"Sure. Well, the police they tried to get the papers in Chamartín. Didn't get many but quite enough. . . . You'll hear about Father Villada's letters someday; that is, if you women hear about anything. Faked bookkeeping and all that. I'll bet they'll bell, book and candle the old Sergeant for letting the cat out of the bag."

It was a woman of Olive Oil Street who noticed Lucía clutching at the doorpost; the chair upon which she had been previously sitting was overturned. All the women ran over and two held the girl while the others screamed loudly for Señora Robledo to descend.

"Her time's nearly up," Mercedes said quietly afterwards.

"Whose is it, do you think, Mudarra's or Caro's?"

"Mudarra's," most of them replied, though several answered, "They say both of them had her."

Mercedes answered after a moment, "Disgraceful, if it's the truth."

"Or if it isn't."

"Yes, well, she's got her punishment, and it'll hang on to her a number of years."

"If God wills."

"Yes, if God wills. Ah."

It was Mercedes who next morning inquired at her home about Lucía's condition, and when Lucía descended and took up her place at the door of the house she crossed the Court and for a while exchanged trivial remarks with her. It was the first occasion upon which the five months' quarantine had been broken by a female resident of the Callejón del Milagro, though Juan the baker's assistant had talked to her for a while and had been very anxious to condone her offense, at every conversation. The women of the Court were willing to forgive, they loudly declared this, though they admitted it was not their business, but they would have been aided in the difficult task of forgiving had Lucía absented herself from Los Olivares; and

had she let it be known that she did not intend to return they
would have forgiven her generously. But not even entry of a
convent or the ranks of licensed prostitution, the two extremest
forms of expiation, would have secured the forgetting of her
offense. Nevertheless, though it had cost the lives of twenty-four
men, the administrative mishap of December had not been
without the spiritualizing effect so notably the justification for
pain and evil. Since December the women had been less persistent in their criticism of Lucía's conduct, though they maintained their aloofness. Scandal itself could not lift its head
against the lifeless apathy of Los Olivares. Now, Mercedes had
barely left the girl when she was moved with a sudden warmth,
and going to the room above she drew out of its place behind a
chest of drawers a deck chair which her father used in summer.
With this she descended, and crossing the Court, opened it
and invited Lucía to use it.

"It's more comfortable than that chair, it will rest your back."
Wondering what her father, a man observant of propriety,
would say, the pleasant glow quickly faded from Mercedes'
body, yet when the coffee had been made for the baker and his
man she took over a glass to the girl. The baker himself gave
Mercedes a few *bizcochos* for Lucía and when Justo arrived
after lunch he was greeted by several women who acknowledged
him again as he appeared in the Court with his sister on his
arm.

For the rest of the week the women of Miracle Court com-
peted with one another in their attention to Lucía. Mercedes
herself was thrust into the background by the mothers, anxious
to relate their experiences of labor and to proffer advice. A
bottle of herb tea was given her by the baker's wife with the
assurance that it would not only deliver the child quickly, but
ensure the immediate expulsion of the afterbirth. "It has never
failed me, though of course I am very broad in the body," she
said, faintly accenting the pronoun. The oil merchant's
married daughter also presented her with a bottle of water
of a different kind and urged its superiority, lending Lucía
also a rosary which had been blessed before Our Lady of
Guadalupe and which was treasured in her family for its comfort in labor. "We've had it in the family for little less than a

hundred years and it is known never to have failed; last year
mother lent it to my cousin's friend in Puente Nuevo and she
had the largest child the doctor had seen for many years. It was
a boy, a beautiful boy, I have seen him and I have never seen
such eyes, most beautiful they are, and lively, Mother of God,
you should see that boy."

"Did she . . . ?" began Lucía, gazing towards the Court
entrance, half fearing to see Justo enter, frown and interrupt
the woman.

"Yes, yes, girl," the woman replied hastily, "it never fails.
I told you, you take it; you don't have to wear it unless you
want to; hang it on the bedpost or round a statue."

Lucía slowly put out her hand for the rosary and then
withdrew it.

"Come, take it, daughter," the woman urged. "It was blessed
before Our Lady of Guadalupe." She shook the black beads
before Lucía and stooped over her. "Our Lady of Guadalupe—
my great grandmother went there with her first child big in
her body, they went in a cart and it took them three days."

"Your great-grandmother?"

"Yes, daughter, my great-grandmother, and it was her first
child; it is known she delivered well."

"Yes?"

The oil merchant's daughter stooped and opened her knees,
and her face became strained; with staring eyes she clenched
her fists as she said fervently, "Listen, child, every woman who
has held this rosary or has had it in her room has given good
birth, every woman, it never fails, do you hear me, take it,
take it, ah, sweet Mother of God have pity on her. . . ."

Lucía put out her hand and the woman feverishly hung the
rosary over her sweating fingers. "Take it, take it, take it," she
whispered fiercely.

Suddenly the girl's fingers closed tightly round the beads
and she dashed them to her lips. "It never fails?" she whispered
through the beads, tears appearing in her eyes.

"Never, never, never, ah, Mother of God be praised for ever
and ever, my daughter, my daughter."

Lucía flung her arms round the woman, who kissed her face,
her forehead, and her eyes repeatedly. "Do not fear, I have

given birth twice and the Virgin of Guadalupe has helped me each time. Listen, my dear, my husband took me to a bull-fight to help it on . . . my mother says it always helps . . . and I went home and the pains came on and in an hour and a half the baby was sucking and I was ready to sleep. Do you hear? An hour and a half after the bullfight I was through. That was my boy Martin. There, it's better to cry if you want to, my dear, though there's nothing to fear with the rosary in your room."

That Lucía was now thus protected the oil merchant's daughter told everyone, including the women of Olive Oil Street, who next day came to the well for water, their fountain having been put out of use by a burst pipe. Then one day there was a noisy controversy between the women of the outer street, which began in a piece of traditional banter. The fountain of Olive Oil Street was situated halfway down the hill, so that the women of the upper street descended with empty vessels and ascended with heavy ones, whereas the dwellers in the lower half were spared the labor of carrying filled pitchers uphill. There had always been a few stock wit-ticisms upon this inequality, mainly kept in use because of two bachelors, the stout and misanthropic Pablo of the lower half and the less stout and more genial Serafino of the upper; these two frequently fetched water for the households in which they lived and upon occasion they met and then Serafino would taunt Pablo with his girth and attribute it to the ease of his task. The stout bachelor's tongue was never at a loss for a variant of the old jests, though the cold fury he poured into his phrase made him more of a laughingstock than ever.

Now the jests were by habit brought into use again and the women, more full of pride and less able to release tension with a *guasa*, the redeeming Andalucian jest, were shortly quarreling, not openly but with venom.

"Pity *she* can't come down for water, then," a lower-street woman finally called, nodding towards the Robledos' house. The voices of the women of Miracle Court were suddenly raised and the two halves of the outer street answered them and one another. The upper-street women presently sided with those of the Court, and then the dispute as suddenly ended.

"Bueno, may God deliver her," a lower-street woman ejaculated, and adjusting the ring pad on her head, lifted a pitcher, took two pitchers in her hands from the hands of another, an upper-street woman, and walked stately towards the entrance. As she approached it a boy cried, *"Hola, Madre,"* and ran to her, holding out his cupped hands. Still balancing the pitcher upon her head, the mother lifted her left-hand vessel to the level of her waist and using her hip as a fulcrum, poured out a thin stream of water. The boy drank, and then nodding at his mother, threw the water remaining in his hands upon the pavement, wetting her feet. As the boy ran away she shouted a stream of abuse and slowly made her stately exit from the Court. While the women were watching this a wail was heard from the Robledos' house.

"She's begun," they all said in low eager voices, and their faces became full of urgency, all directed upon an upper window of the Robledos' house. There was no pity in their faces, but a determined urgency as if they were compelling the girl to approach her ordeal, thrusting her forward towards the blows from which she shrank. And then the impulsion died out of their faces and they became grave and impassive, and consciousness of dignity informed them. They stood silently, or softly conversing in groups about the Court, and many who went away returned later.

Within half an hour the two doctors arrived, for Justo had engaged them both; a woman help had already been in the house during the last two days. Midnight had passed when Justo telephoned hurriedly for the Puente Nuevo doctor, who possessed an unjustified reputation for skill in deliveries, and an hour later he arrived. The girl, terribly exhausted by her ten hours' labor, did not wish to be examined by yet another doctor.

"A perfectly normal case," the Puente Nuevo physician said when he had finished, and though Robledo desired him to remain in the house, he refused and at once departed. All the following morning the women stood in groups around the well, making isolated remarks and inquiries.

"She must try, she must try," the baker's wife said angrily, and many of the women tightened the muscles of their stomach and closed their jaws firmly as they stared at the house, as if it were a collective birth.

Hour by hour the faces of the women grew more grave, and as they became more grave the women drew closer together, and newcomers at once attached themselves to a group; those who left rarely looked back but entered the street as if dazed by long vigil, though there were some who had been there but half an hour. At midday, when the oil merchant approached the well with a saucer full of olive oil to silence the squeaking pulley wheel, there were many who did not turn their heads, though an old woman, pulling up her outer skirts, climbed onto the rim of the wellhead to brush the spindle with oil. At two o'clock a short, big-breasted and massive-bodied woman with a sullen face threw up her arms and cried, "O God, O my God, what is this woman doing?" and a dozen hands made rapid signs of the cross. Within the house the helping woman, hearing the cry, threw herself over the bed and, taking the girl's drawn up knees in her hands, kissed them frantically, and knelt down, weeping silently, her hands upon Lucía's knees. The girl allowed her legs to be pulled sideways, staring at the ceiling, until the doctor drew the kneeling woman away. Almost immediately the final labor began.

When at last the doctors descended to the Court they were surrounded by the watchers. "Yes, yes, yes," Dr. Torres answered peevishly, "quite all right, normal case, healthy boy, go away and do as well."

The women broke into excited talk for a few minutes, but before long they seemed suddenly to grow tired and the light left their eyes and many dragged their feet as they moved away. The oil merchant's daughter slowly climbed to her own alcove, her hands pressed into her own aching loins. "Ah, God," she murmured as she slowly drew her feet up, still thinking of the girl's labor. By and by the pain grew less, and she fell asleep, her left hand open, palm upwards, a little away from her body. After a while, awakened by her father's voice, she descended and watched Mercedes, the baker's assistant, and two women of Olive Oil Street assisting him to raise a barrel of oil from the storehouse to the Court.

"A good oil?" one of the women inquired, and the merchant

stood back, spat, and drawled, "No, it's a passable oil, but the fruit, you know, was badly gathered."

The group nodded, and he said, "It has a bitter taste, leaves must have got into the press," and they nodded again. "Here, wait a minute, I've got some of this already drawn, taste it for yourselves." He returned with a sample of oil in a measure, and each one tasted. "If you want a really cheap oil I can sell it to you for a peseta the liter .It tastes of the leaf."

"Yes, and something else, though I can't say what it is," Mercedes added.

"Something else, nor can I say, and now old Tomás is dead. . . ." The merchant gazed across the Court to Olive Oil Street, remembering the Tomás of whom he spoke.

"Yes, he could have told us," Mercedes assented and, though the merchant knew that all of them had heard the centuries-old tale, he commenced:

"One year, not so long ago, there had been a fine crop of olives, and that December the weather had been golden and serene and windless, and the oil therefore was of good color."

The women nodded and the baker's assistant said, "Serene weather, sweet oil."

"Yet when the fruit had been pressed and the oil was stored in the vat and they came to assess its quality there was something amiss with it though none dared declare what its fault could be. The vat had been cleaned with all conscience and the oil had been well made, yet an unusual taste there was and the owner was displeased. At last he sent for old Tomás. Tomás was then a very old man." The group nodded again. "With the face of a saint, bent of back and with a soft voice that barely could be heard. And when at last he came, for he lived far off to the north near Jaén," and the baker waved largely towards the west, "he climbed the ladder slowly, and leaning over the edge of the vat, sniffed at the oil, and descended straightway.

" 'Well, Don Tomás?' the owner asked, and the old man wiped his fingers and said: 'It tastes of iron.' The master wouldn't believe him, but Don Tomás merely smiled, bowed and went his way. Now, the thought that Don Tomás might be right rankled in the mind of the owner and at last at great cost he had the vat emptied. And there, at the bottom of the vat, they found a pin, of the old kind, about so long," and the merchant held out his little finger.

"Yes," they all said, and smiled contentedly, as if the story had comforted them.

28

In Exitu

ANGRY with his mother for recalling him to meet Father Martínez, who was spending his vacation in his former parish, Joaquín Caro returned to the olive grove and began to break the earth beneath the drip of an inner tree; but although he worked with fierce energy he felt no enthusiasm. The trees held him yet they awakened no impulse within him. The energy with which he drove the iron into the earth was coming from his own will. It was conscience which compelled him to smash the clods and the work tormented him; he wanted to do it less thoroughly but could not. As the iron clove through a clod he determined to break it no further and swung the tool to the next, but as his eyes returned obstinately to the abandoned clod conscience snapped and tugged at his will until he obeyed it.

He straightened up and his gaze rested upon the flowering boughs. The blossom was less abundant than in the previous years, but he saw that it was healthy and well distributed over the trees. The wood was healthy, too, and there was every sign of a good crop, given only favorable weather. He did not check his onward-running imagination, it checked itself, the eternal lure of the abounding harvest was dying within him. The name Asturias was now a name of hope; Ojeda's last letter still lay in his pocket, though it was a week old. Beyond the trees he saw Father Martínez returning to the town and he watched indifferently to see if the old man would hail him; his gaze followed him as he mounted towards the Gallows Rock. The ex-rector had changed greatly; his stoop, though not more

pronounced, was more the stoop of old age; he had been un-
shaven and his white hair had been dirty; his clothing showed
no signs of care. Ana had listened with interest to Father
Martínez's account. He had said nothing of prison life save
that his sentence had been reduced. The bishop had not
permitted him to return to a cure in Los Olivares and he was
now an assistant priest in an industrialized parish of the city of
Cartagena. He had told them this with the deepest dejection;
Ana's congratulation upon receiving Argote's legacies called
from him only brief and formal thanks. The priest disappeared
from view and again Caro bent over the earth. Presently he
threw the tools together and returned to the house, meaning
to call the family together to announce his determination to
abandon the holding. He found his mother lamenting that
Marcial had again gone out to work, however, and at her
request he went out to try to persuade his brother to desist.

"He's over at the watercourse," Ursula said.

"You'd do more good if you were to help with this course,"
Marcial muttered bitterly, continuing to work. Joaquín said
nothing, thinking of the labor needed to do what his brother
had planned. Now that the Peral estate was being slovenly ad-
ministered by the lawyer Guevara's brother had appointed,
Marcial had proposed that they tap the main watercourse
higher up so that the larger fields might be irrigated. Others
better placed than they had already done this.

"What's the use," Joaquín exclaimed with sudden anger.
"Is it likely we shall be allowed to draw water for long? You'll
just about get the job finished in time for the estate to be taken
over by the Government; likely as not you'll put the rent up."

"And likely as not the rents will be put down," flared
Marcial.

Joaquín turned away; it was useless to argue with his
brother. That evening he went into the town; upon his return his mother told him Marcial had again collapsed. He felt
little pity until he stood by his brother's bedside and then he
was moved to promise his assistance on the watercourse.

"Good man," Marcial gasped. "Put Ursula on with me to
build up the stones while you dig."

"No, I can't do that. Ursula must work in the garden."

"No, Joaquín, I beg you, put her to work with me," the brother pleaded, but Joaquín, now the acknowledged head of the family, steadily refused. Nevertheless that weekend the work advanced considerably, as Justo Robledo visited them and spent the whole of Sunday upon the course. A fresh source of life seemed to have been opened for Marcial now that his brother had consented to the scheme. He rose early each day and flung himself into the work with strength that amazed them, returning at night to speak of it with glowing eyes and inflamed face. Pascual, his scruples overridden, sometimes came up to the course and proffered advice, which the son listened to with respect. For several days this continued and then, after a day's rest and defying his brother, Marcial went up to the course upon a Saturday morning, saying that Robledo and another were coming down that afternoon to assist him. A little before two o'clock Joaquín Caro noticed his brother swinging the pickax wildly; he watched him for a moment intending to shout to him to stop, but carrying the tool, the digger climbed the bank and went towards the parent course and disappeared from view. Hesitating a moment, Joaquín decided to follow him.

When the pain hit him Marcial dropped the pickax and gasped for breath. His gaze traveled along the bed of the new watercourse and in astonishment he stared at the bend where it came level with the path. The amazement disappeared and a wild joy burst in his brain. "Water," he gasped, and half turned as if to point out the advancing flood to someone standing near. He was only conscious of the agony in his chest and the shining water which now was flooding over all the field below him, though it seemed to him that someone really had been standing by him. He rushed forward and swung the pickax madly at a boulder which blocked the bed of the course; someone was speaking to him from behind and though the work must be done and the water permitted to flow past the boulder he turned choking to see who it was. He clutched the haft of the pick as he turned; there was no one there. "Ah, ah, ah," he screamed, but the sounds were caught and drowned by the scalding flood surging about his chest—the water which he remembered to have been pouring over the

field was gone now—he rocked forward and touched the
boulder; it was as dry as the gully had always been. A voice
shouted inside his head, "Let the water run," and he staggered
towards the parent course to smash through the barrier, no
time to build a sluice, no time, the water must be let through,
the fields were starving, the corn upon them drooping, the
barley wasted with the sun's fire that scorched his temples and
thrust a hot bar through his chest. "Let the water run," he
gasped as he staggered up the slope. Standing over the edge
of the parent course he saw the water sliding rapidly by, going
down to the river through the Huerta—"Let it through, no
time, sluice, sluice," he screamed, and lifted the pick; the blow
seemed to strike him in the chest and all went dead.

He was looking up at the red sky, the water was behind him
roaring along the channel. Suddenly it sank to a thin thread
of buzzing sound, and then, as the dark figures approached,
burst into a roar again.

"I know, I know, I know," he screamed as the black figure
leaned over him. "Go away." There was a crucifix hanging
over him, white against the red sky, its face staring down into
his! The others were beating his heart. The crucifix came
nearer and its face pleaded, tears came into his eyes and the
mouth was curved downwards. "Love, love," a voice was saying
by his side and then the crucifix began to float about over his
face, while hands were behind it. "Go away, go away," he tried
to scream, but he knew that the words did not really get
beyond his chest where the hot flood was surging. Suddenly the
crucifix flew back and stood upright and its pleading face became clear, pleading to be loved. Come unto me. . . .

Marcial raised himself and his laughter broke through the
bubbling flood in his mouth; how comical, how despicable of
the face before him. His laughter broke and he was suddenly
reminded of something he had been going to say when his
laughter began; too late! too late! he would not have time to
say it before the laughter came back. . . . He raised himself
higher and said, *"This miserable Christ, who must be loved,"*
and laughing lay back. . . .

"Best to die alone," his own voice calmly remarked in his
brain and he waved back the black figures and they dis-

appeared . . . alone . . . as one lives . . . Water . . . water rocking . . . a—rocking. . . .

Justo and old Robledo raced up the slope to Joaquín and
both slowly took off their hats. After a while they stooped
and lifted the body and descended the slope.

Pascual stood by Ana as she sat upon the furrows; she did
not weep as the three burdened men went by to the house.
When they had gone in she turned her head aside and leaned
heavily upon her left arm, her face resting upon the thrust-up
shoulder, slowly taking soil in her right hand and letting it
trickle through her fingers. A purple-black beetle was scurrying
in the dust, trying to mount the edge of the furrow. A white
stone blocked its path and it stumbled and lost its way; again
it ascended the slope and rounding the stone blundered down
into the furrow again and essayed to climb out upon the other
side. It rolled over, showing the reddish-brown joints in its
abdomen, and righting itself scurried towards her along the
trench and she poured the reddish dust over its back, at which
it turned about and hurried back. Once more it reached the
white stone and rounding it descended into the furrow and
came towards her, its legs working frantically, the sheen upon
its back gleaming purple and green; minute ridges like those
of a child's nail ran down its back and these had red in them.
She poured dust over it and it met the white stone, dodged this
way and that and, circumventing the stone, blundered down
into the furrow again and scuffled in the dust she had poured.
Pascual's hand was upon her head, she clutched his leg, but
her gaze followed the beetle going round the white stone.

As the three men stumbled by, Pascual took off his hat,
stooped slightly and gazed at them, unmarveling. The hills,
too, they were always there.

When the body had been laid out, Justo offered to accompany Ana to the town, but she made no answer. She had not
yet spoken. Without a shawl she crossed the threshing floor
and ascended the path, and Ursula, meeting her as she returned with the Saturday purchases, was terrified at the expression of her face and ran whimpering to the house.

Ana entered the shop in the upper plaza and beat the
counter with her hand until the woman shuffled out of the

room beyond. "Buenas," the shopkeeper said, and laid her hands wide open upon the counter and waited for Ana to speak.

"I want twelve long candles," Ana said.

"How long do you want them to be?"

"So long, longer. So long."

The woman crossed herself and went into the gloom at the back of the shop, and placing a pair of stepladders against the shelves, climbed them insecurely and withdrew a package.

"How much are they?" Ana asked.

"The twelve will be five pesetas."

"That is too much, they are dear."

"Five pesetas is the price of these candles. They are of good wax."

"Yes. It is too much; I will pay three pesetas."

"No, they are long candles and of good color."

"They are yellow."

"They are of church wax."

"I will pay three pesetas."

"I might sell them for four and a half pesetas; their price is really five pesetas."

"I cannot pay more than three."

The woman behind the counter laid her hands upon the candles and pressed them together. "I will sell this one packet for four pesetas."

Ana took four pesetas from her purse and, gathering up the package, left the shop, holding the candles before her away from her body. The shopkeeper crossed herself again and muttered a Hail Mary.

When the mother had set four candles burning before the body she knelt by the bed for more than an hour, but she did not pray, nor did she weep. Pascual and her children became alarmed that she did not weep, and Justo advised Ursula to go into the room and speak to her.

"Perhaps she will weep then," Pascual said. "If her grief turns inwards and she does not weep it will be ill for her."

Ursula attempted to obey, but seeing the body lying upon the bed and the yellow light upon its sunken face, she was suddenly in terror of the dead thing and ran downstairs and out into the field, whence Justo fetched her in his arms.

When Marcial had been buried two days Ana still had not wept, and now, refusing food and drinking a little water only, she wandered about the house and the holding, sometimes going to the place where Marcial had died. Speech left her and she began to stare uncomprehensively at them. Lucía's mother advised them to bring her into the town to see whether that would bring tears to her. Sometimes Ana came to the town to make purchases, but she fell an easy prey to shopkeepers and returned with her money spent and few goods, so that Pascual with Joaquín's consent hid the money in the son's room. And now all the women of the town were talking of Ana, of how she had not wept and that her grief had turned inwards and she was going out of her reason. Some of them approached Father Martínez, and he consented to visit the Caro home.

Ana would not speak to the priest, and he decided to offer comfort to the father, who was plowing upon the Well field with the mule and the donkey harnessed, he noted, to the lighter of the Caros' plows. Pascual was singing quietly as the priest approached and he stopped to listen.

"The plow I sing and all its parts," the plowman's voice wavered, and though Father Martínez knew the words he waited to hear him sing, "And I shall tell forth the mysteries of Christ's Passion." Father Martínez crossed himself and watched the man climb the slope again as far as the white boulder; as he came down the field he heard him singing, "The plow and all its parts," and after a while he heard the words "The share and the oaken beam," sung to the same melody. I wonder why he is singing about the plow, thought Father Martínez. Then the singer was silent as he drew near the priest.

"God be with you, my son," Father Martínez said, and Pascual halted and bowed his head and faced him dumbly.

"God be with you in your distress," the priest began, and he meant to speak of Our Lady's succor to those who lose their sons, but seeing Pascual's face and the depth in his gaze he could not find words. He considered blessing the plowman, but that also he did not do. At the end of a minute the priest bowed, and going to the corner of the field and seeing a spade, took off his cassock and commenced to dig the corner square.

For several days longer Ana continued to be silent, grieving always but never wailing or weeping after the manner of the women who advised her, nor working, nor eating nor drinking. The mule kicked a gap in the yard wall and she took to sitting for hours at a time upon the stones. At evening they had sometimes to fetch her in from the fields or from the heap. One night Ursula heard her mother blundering into her alcove, and found her toying vacantly with the Virgin and Child from the niche at the foot of the bed. The daughter urged her to pray, but this she could not, yet next day the mother hurried up the path and after lingering awhile by the smithy, visited the church of San Andrés, where she knelt. But still she did not weep, and when a group of women who had been watching began to advise her afresh, she turned away sharply and went out of the church, carrying the votive candle which she had meant to light before the Virgin. In the plaza the playing children made way for her and stared as she crossed quickly to the head of Olive Oil Street and went down to Our Lady of Carmen.

As Ana Caro crossed the little plaza, she heard shouting in one of the poor streets leading out of it and along with others she stood to watch what was happening. A Civil Guard emerged from a house and cleared a space before the door and then a handcuffed lad was violently thrust out of the house; a sergeant of the Civil Guard followed him. The lad, of about eighteen years of age, was coatless and blood was threading down his white face from a cut among the hairs of his right brow. A third guard came out of the house and stood in front of it with drawn pistol to prevent people entering or leaving, and then the two guards led the prisoner away. The women around Ana stood back to let them pass, muttering among themselves at the conduct of the guard sergeant, who directed the lad by striking him upon the side of the head. At a second blow the lad wheeled and appeared to be about to shout at his captor, but Ana, recognizing him, screamed his name, "Juan," and he desisted. The guard nonetheless struck the prisoner in the mouth, drawing blood; a drawn pistol covered the snarling women.

"You can thank your friends for that," the sergeant said as the lad lifted his hands to his mouth. Ana's temper was suddenly inflamed, and shouting at the sergeant, she rushed at him, waving the votive candle, reviling him for his brutality. The guard thrust his pistol forward at her breast level, but as she came on he turned the muzzle aside and held her off with his bent wrist, shouting commands at her. Anger and hatred made Ana desperate and she beat at the guard's face, striking him repeatedly until he kicked at her legs. She drew off but again rushed at her enemy, but this time the guard seized her arms from behind and told his superior to take the prisoner to the barracks.

The sergeant, embarrassed and fearful of the gathering crowd, nevertheless struck the lad again and led him off. Tears of rage were streaming down Ana's face as she screamed abuse, mingled with the name Juan. When the guard released her she fell to her knees crying, "Juan," still weeping with rage, but when two of the women laid their hands upon her shoulders she suddenly covered her face and cried, "Oh, my son Marcial." They led her into a house and she wept for nearly two hours before her family could persuade her to return home. She wailed and sobbed all night, but in the morning ate a little and afterwards fell asleep in her chair.

Seeing that his mother was now recovering from her grief, Joaquín decided at once to call the family together to hear his decision to go to Asturias. To him the death of Marcial had been the removal of a great burden; a feeling almost of serenity entered him, for an impossible struggle was being relinquished. For years, he realized, it had been Marcial who had kept them tied to that poverty, it would have been impossible for him to do the work in the mines, and the damp climate Ojeda spoke of would have been harmful to him. Even had he proposed going elsewhere it would have been the same; Ana had evidently wished her son to die here, with the support of familiar things and known ways. He saw now that they had all ministered to Marcial's undying pride, for so long as he had been able to do any work at all he had felt that he was not merely being maintained by the family's love. The joy he had shown when Joaquín had consented to the digging of a watercourse had been real, though he had already resolved to do the work in defiance of Joaquín's objection. Perhaps Marcial had known that he had not long to live, he was too intelligent not to have known, and the watercourse had been to him a means of justification.

That evening before supper the family sat down at the kitchen table and Joaquín, by habit taking a notebook from his pocket, told them of his decision. Ursula was the first to speak.

"And what shall I do in Asturias?"

"There are factories, and someday you will marry."

Pascual shook his head, and said, "I shall not go with you, son," but Ana at once answered, "Yes you will; I am going and Ursula is going; you will have to come."

"No, I can't do any other work but this, and I must stay."

"You can do the same work, Father; we will rent a plot of ground and you can have a large garden."

"A large garden," Ana added. "I shall keep house and help you."

"No, the land will be different, they say it rains always in those parts. I shall not understand the ways of the land there."

"There will be water, land with plenty of water."

"Water, Father," Ursula exclaimed, "with water you will be able to grow good crops, think of it." Pascual murmured, "Water," and said no more.

"Very good, tomorrow we'll begin to sell our things. Mother, you will put on one side all that we shall need. When the other things are sold Ursula and I will go to Asturias and find a house; you will follow later."

The girl's face glowed as she heard this, but Pascual rose from the table and stood outside in the yard while Joaquín detailed what would have to be done. After supper the son went into the town upon the first of his errands, and next day a dealer arrived at the house. While Ana and Joaquín were bargaining about the implements Pascual spent his time in building up the gap which the mule had made in the yard wall. Ana quarreled with him over this, calling him a stupid and soulless man. Unexpectedly he replied, "I am."

Ana's comment was a passionate urging of the Asturian

venture, during which they watched her in amazement, never having seen her so excited nor having imagined she could speak in this manner.

Joaquín had no regrets at leaving Los Olivares, but the frequent presence of Justo Robledo was almost insupportable. Again and again he imagined himself with Lucía, dramatizing their marriage, making sentimental pictures of their home in Asturias, with the child in the house. And often these pictures stirred him deeply, yet always he rebelled against acceptance of Mudarra's child. Diego himself was in prison and he had had no other friend; the leave-takings, therefore, were not for him so moving as for others. At the Rincón there was a ceremony of leave-taking and the date of this the organizers had pushed forward, unconsciously wishing to warm themselves with emotion. Nevertheless, going to a toolhouse on Broad Skirt to fetch a few implements of his own, he was suddenly shaken; he was standing within the hut when a thin line of intense red-gold light appeared on the granular surface of the whitewashed wall. In the dusk of the interior the light was so intense as to appear like a strip of burning metal suspended in the air before the wall, yet the irregularities of the plastered wall were copied in the strip and here and there the particles of lime glistened like glass, casting minute blue shadows. He thrust open the door, through a crack of which the western light was streaming, and the deepening suffusion illuminated the flesh of his hands. Outside, the light dyed the olive trunks, and their westward surfaces were gold and purple; the tawny earth burned savagely like ripening maize; scarlet and crimson clods with umber darks littered the hardening surface of the neglected fields, like pimiento fruit. The shadows, softly small at their narrow bases where they sprang off from the trunks, paled as they broadened and the red glow filtered into them; above, a string of small yellow clouds lay over the green-blue sky, and behind the tiger Jabalón a cumulus towered, steeped in all its enormous upheaved mass in blazing chrome. Only the pale gray-green undersides of the olive leaves took no fresh color.

The sun burned its way down through the western sierra as Joaquín hastened home; the silence of the abandoned olivars was frightening. At this hour the bell of Mater Purissima would have knocked and the rap of haft upon haft would have taken the place of the singing, the echoes of the shouts would have drifted up the smoldering cliff like ravens, and men would have been hastening down to the sanctuary to warm themselves with friendship and enmity. The trees stood utterly still upon the bare earth, he had seen them so a thousand times, but now it stirred him with unrecognizable emotion. The trees had been here before man, they had been waiting for this day. . . . The profuse appearance of *varetas* upon the Córdova Whiteleafs was something to be noted with the practical eye; it was impossible that the trees could be left so, no government, no man could be so barbarous. If the trees were abandoned they would put off their own seemly dress and sink back into wildness. The swollen fruit, rich with oil, which man had taught them to bear would shrink into bitter and wooden berries, the thorn and the matted herb would invade and filch all the nourishment and the trees would tinder and die. . . . It could not be so, men would not permit it.

At this time Mudarra's voice would have been heard jeering or singing. The loneliness of the olivars knifed through him afresh as he thought of Mudarra's voice.

The day before his and Ursula's departure Robledo came in early and talked long with the sister, avoiding Joaquín. He was nervous and apparently impatient, for he kept looking at his watch. They could not understand his embarrassment, for he behaved as if he were making up his mind to tell them something, or to leave. Joaquín understood, however, when the postman brought a letter from Lucía. As Caro opened it Justo stood nervously by.

"I'm going to see her," Joaquín said at once, and Robledo lurched forward, his face showing his expectation.

"Yes," Joaquín said firmly and the secretary turned and hurried into the harness shed.

29

Upon the Willows
that Are Therein

OFTEN during the following summer Caro and Lucía set out from the mining town of Sama early upon Saturday afternoon to visit the beach at Gijón or one of the little fishing ports of the Atlantic coast. Neither of them had seen the sea before arriving in Asturias, and in their melancholy first months, repulsed by the alien ways of the Asturian folk, and shrinking from or quarreling with the miners, they sought comfort in the land itself. Pascual's attempt to work a garden had completely failed; it had not even been begun when the father collapsed into a will-less melancholy from which not land nor tools could rouse him. He sat withindoors all the day, finding nothing to say to them, sighing and at times openly lamenting with tears. For a while he found comfort in the friendship of another expatriate Andaluz of his own age, but this soon increased his nostalgia, and the Caros were glad when the old man ceased to visit them. It was, however, not merely longing for abandoned Andalucía which enfeebled Pascual, but the old man's shame at being supported by his son. "But, man alive," Caro said repeatedly, "back in Los Olivares you'd have been content for me to work for you in your old age, wouldn't you?" and Pascual had never replied clearly. The question brought from him a faltering "Yes," or a sigh of perplexity. Gradually it became clear to Joaquín that the custom and usage of their family was something rooted in the land, in the southern land far away. Upon the land Pascual would have been content to be supported, but all the logic and tradition of his life had been destroyed by this uprooting. Nostalgia and shame were destroying him, Caro saw, and he began to search for a remedy. That came in an unexpected way.

It was first of all the sea itself which attracted Caro and Lucía, but rapidly the interest of the port and the fishing quays in particular imposed itself upon the husband. He became friendly with a docking family named Baragaña, the head of which, an unattached Anarchist, loved to protest his love for Andalucía, with which Caro at once perceived he was almost totally unacquainted. Baragaña long ago had joined a company of tunny fishers on the Cádiz coast, and his knowledge of the south was confined to the villages near the tunny traps. He had been well treated by the southerners, and this with the lapse of time he had so exaggerated that the south was now a region of chivalrous and exuberant charity. Caro had been unable to live up to the standard of vivacity Baragaña expected of an Andaluz, but Ursula and Ojeda had delighted the docker. He begged them often to visit his house, much to the annoyance of his wife, who nevertheless did her utmost to make the southern "gypsies" welcome. Caro had often told Baragaña of Pascual's decline, and the docker sympathized with profuse sentimentality. One day he told Caro of a watchman's post which was then vacant in a warehouse in which his son-in-law had a minor interest. Pascual, Ana and Ursula moved to Gijón, and though Pascual's wages were insufficient for the family to live upon, the women soon found employment. Ursula entered the tobacco factory and her mother undertook to hawk vegetables for a very taciturn couple who worked a garden behind the fort upon the headland. Unfortunately this soon came to an end, for Ana, stepping over the barbed wire upon the headland, as was her habit in going up to the market gardener's house, was stopped by a soldier and told she was trespassing on a fortified place. Her Andaluz tongue exasperated the soldier, and putting on his tunic, he informed her she was under arrest. Ana threatened to tear out his eyes, his tongue and his ears if he touched her, whereupon the soldier warned her not to trespass again. He added that the market gardeners were suspected of being counterfeiters, and examining her pay at the end of the week, she indeed found a bad two-peseta piece, an unusual coin to be counterfeited. She did not return to the post after that, and spent more than a month in finding other work.

If often seemed absurd to Caro that he should be making his only contact with men in a city several miles away, and he made several attempts to form friendships. It was the dirt and gloom of his work which dulled his spirit. The work below ground was at first a nightmare to him, the long thundering corridors, the damp drafts, the bruising labor, the ill-lit darkness and the uncouth and, as they seemed to him, wisdomless miners were utterly alien. It was all a fantastic unreality and he longed for the glittering tiger hills and the solemn trees upon the terraced slopes with a desperate nervous longing that made him start violently at any features of the country which resembled Jabalón—an orchard of plum trees or a well, and late in the autumn the red maize hanging from the house walls. He took to wandering about the vast hills of the green-gray Cordillera Cantábrica in the company of Asua, a queer excited Marxist clerk in the mining office. Asua was sincere, Caro knew, though his enthusiasm was spent upon the collection of odds and ends of superstitions, which he called by the dignified name of "folk culture." A doggerel rhyme about the twelve apostles for divining the weather, a garbled tale about the one-eyed Nubeiru, the Egyptian storm-raising spirit, and the measures taken by the parish priests of the cordillero to conjure him, the opinion that grass snakes were displeased if their sexual intercourse was observed, all these things were tremendously important to Asua. Out of this collection of decayed ordure, as Caro described it, Asua hoped to arrive at a portrait of primitive society, when man was a healthy, communal being with a magnificent corpus of mystical wisdom at his command. This portrait was somehow to guide him and the rest of the workers in their revolutionary struggle, but for the present he was content to affect a few local modifications in his speech, ending all his masculine nouns in *u* instead of *o*. Nevertheless, Asua was cheerful company and a knowing walker; with him Caro often covered twenty miles of sierra, the one in pursuit of a rhyme about butter-making the other trying to comfort himself with the great open spaces of the hills. These hills were so different, however: the lush green slopes ran out of valleys streaming with water, where singing birds sat upon the willows; beech and birch and all variations of trees hid the lower slopes, and above, herds of heavy cattle with huge dribbling udders pastured upon the succulent grass. Above these were the green domes for the sheep, and higher there were often huge cliffs and pinnacles of slippery limestone, where the wild goats lived, gray spires worn by the streaming wet winds that forever harped through them. Enormous cumulus clouds forever sailed over the Asturian mountains and often they sank and were broken, drifting for days and weeks about the mid slopes until every leaf and twig dripped water upon the sodden earth. These cloud-roofed hills were echoing halls of the dead to him. Once only he was thrilled by them; from a summit above Sama he saw through a tunnel of the clouds, as if at the end of a huge telescope, a cluster of spired peaks with snow upon them, amethyst and white against the pale rim of the clear sky beyond the clouds.

He railed at himself for searching for the familiar in things and people, yet no railing quickened him to love for the new, till one day, searching for a place in the mine in which to eat his midday meal, he was obscenely invited to sit upon an explosive box by a gang of Asturians. Then he discovered that the mines, the docks and the factories of Asturias were everywhere smoldering with revolt. He joined the mining syndicate affiliated to the C.N.T., the National Confederation of Labor and the Communist group in Sama, and henceforth was rarely at home. Life had once more become real. One thing only was missing. He made the acquaintanceship of many workers, and he was trusted by them, but friendship was missing, friendship of the kind which makes the sweat of a friend's body agreeable to the nostrils.

It was not only Joaquín and Pascual who were spiritless in their first years in Asturias. After the first day or two of confidence following her marriage to Caro, Lucía began to languish. He knew quite well that she was pining for her son but, testing his state of mind, he steeled himself against the temptation to yield to her unspoken need. She brooded and lay awake at night, he knew, because of this, and was sometimes so spiritless that when he embraced her she lay indifferently beneath him. He knew also that he could expect no more from her, but protest at her coldness was wrung from him by some undeniable mechanism of speech. At the second protest Lucía flung her arms around him and frantically urged him to enjoy himself, and then as he burst into expressions of gratitude and love she wrenched herself free and scrambled out of bed. For a moment he was tempted to accept this; he speculated in that instant upon separation, but switching on the light and sitting on the edge of the bed, he said, "Are you afraid of me? Explain yourself, Lucía."

She stared at him with a look of extreme contempt and he bridled at once.

"You have made a mistake, you don't love me?"

"Oh, don't talk to me," she wailed, and turned her side towards him. "Give me my nightdress, Joaquín." He searched for it in the bed and could not find it and she came over and stood beside him and pulled the clothes from the bed. The smell of her flesh filled him with immense craving and he placed his arm round her waist. She stood upright and, trembling, whispered, "Must you, Joaquín?"

"Yes," he said firmly, and, as if drunkenly, she climbed upon the bed and lay still. As he knelt beside her he caressed her forehead and asked, "But don't you love me, then?"

She made no reply, but lifted her arm clumsily and patted him tenderly upon the shoulder. Desire left him at once and he lay down beside her. She slipped her arm beneath his neck and when he shifted about to make his underarm comfortable she shook him and drew him tighter, so that her shoulder hurt the back of his neck. "Don't fidget," she said, as he continued to search for a comfortable position for his arm, "it will go to sleep quick enough." It was a jest she repeated whenever she was affectionate and he was immediately comforted. When they were warmed and peaceful he called her softly lest she should be asleep. She replied at once:

"What is it?"

"I think I could be happy with the baby in the house, now."

"No," she said firmly, but he felt the twitching of her arms. "All right," he answered dully.

Ten minutes passed by, but he knew from the alertness of her body she was thinking much.

"Tell me, are you afraid of having another baby, Lucía?"

She stiffened at once and he seized her and held her tightly as she commenced to struggle. "You're my wife and we're in this bloody mess together," he said.

She said no more, though it was hours before she slept.

Thence onward, Caro thought much about the child and repeatedly expressed his willingness to have it in the house.

"You'll be happier, my dear," he pleaded again and again, but she steadfastly refused.

"You're being damned unfair," he complained one day, "you're expecting me to be more than human. I've said a hundred times you can have the baby back and I mean it. You want me to be happy about it, to make a song and dance about it as well."

"I know you would be unhappy, Joaquín."

"Hell!" he shouted in exasperation. "Don't you see how unfair you're being; how can I feel the same about that kid as I could about my own son?"

"It's you who are unfair, you don't love me as you ought, oh, God, *can't* you see . . . ?"

"See what?" he questioned, his exasperation enduring, and repeated the question, and when she remained silent he said:

"And you are being unfair in another way. You give up the child, you won't have it back, but you still don't love me enough to be a good wife. For Christ's sake do one or the other, have the child, or have me."

The contempt in her face shamed him, though he did not even catch a glimpse of the reason for his shame; there seemed to be another self within him, for his skin began to prickle and perspire at the enormity of an unknown offense.

"You'll never understand, Joaquín; you think so much of yourself, you've got no theory to help you in this." There was both bitterness and a sneer in her words.

"We're that far apart then," he said coldly, and she came across to him in fear.

"No, no, I just married you because I loved you more than my baby."

"My dear, why didn't you say that before?"

"It's so *simple*," she interjected.

"I know I am a fool, but it makes all the difference when you say it. Is that really true, Lucía . . ." He put his arms round her and kissed the hollow of her cheek. "Lobeless ears," he murmured, fingering them, "lobelessness does not become a Spaniard, you're deficient." She jerked her head away as she always did when he jested so, but now her brows were knitted. "Yes, it's true," she whispered, her voice as remote as the expression of her eyes. He allowed her to go from him, seeing that she was unhappy again.

"Perhaps it was because I never had any milk for him," she said at last. He puzzled over her words for several minutes.

"You mean, if you'd loved him more you'd not have married me?"

"Yes, perhaps that's it. God, I'm being unfair, Joaquín, I know."

"I was thinking if you had another baby you might love me more. I'd be the father, you see."

Slowly she looked up at him, shaking with terror.

"What do you mean?" she gasped.

"Mean?" He stared, amazed at her behavior; she was trembling uncontrollably, leaning upon the edge of the table, gazing at the door. "I mean what I say. I think you'd be happier if you had another baby, you'd love me more, a woman . . ."

Lucía suddenly screamed and fell to the floor. For a long time after this she shrank from him whenever he approached her. He never found any formula of comfort for her save, "We're in this bloody mess together, girl," and that often succeeded in pacifying her.

So they lived through that autumn and winter, Lucía gradually drawing away from her husband and he becoming more and more absorbed by the political struggle which, in its revolutionary aspect, became increasingly centered in Asturias. In the month of July of 1934, at the conclusion of yet another attempt to arrest their separation, Caro announced that he would be spending his holiday week in Oviedo, alone.

"You're leaving me here by myself?"

"No, you can go to my parents, they'll be glad to have you."

"Why can't I go with you to Oviedo?"

"I'm going on Party work."

"I wouldn't hinder you, Joaquín."

"No, we should carry on in the same way; we want a rest from one another."

Lucía did not press her request further, but began to lay the table for the evening meal. "You're tired of me," she said suddenly.

"I'm tired *by* you, sometimes. It's your everlasting silence, Lucía, you never speak to me about what is passing in your head, I have to think and guess all the while. Can't you see, woman, that I am doing my best, this is my life, I'm not playing, and you never tell me anything. I have to think it all."

"I know." She came to him with decisive step and sat upon the corner of the table and looked down upon him. "I can't talk, *chico*, I want to talk, but there aren't any words in my head, sometimes I think I haven't any thoughts because I haven't any words . . . thoughts are words, aren't they?"

Caro looked up in surprise at this. "I was reading that in a book myself a little while ago—I don't believe it though. You must try to talk, make a start on a sentence, doesn't matter if you blunder about—talk like you'd do a new job, perhaps you'll say a thing half a dozen ways and none will be right, but I must try to understand from them all."

"No, it's the thought that's too hard and too wicked."

"Too wicked?"

"Yes," she answered sullenly.

"Well, if it finishes things it finishes them. Tell me."

"I think we're like stone, or a piece of wood, Joaquín. When it's broken up, it's broken up and you can't mend it. We're broken up; I am, I know. There's no help for it. There are some things you can do which break us and I have done one of them."

"You mean putting your baby away?"

"Yes. I'm broken. I'm no good. It's not really your fault. I had the baby and I ought to have seen that it was a finish for me, as far as marrying goes, I mean. You were wrong too, you ought to have seen that as well."

"Perhaps so, but I loved you, I do now."

"You didn't do things right, *chico*."

"What do you mean?"

"Do you remember when you told me I'd have to put the baby away. It was when we went to see that giant."

"I remember."

"I said I'd been really alone. You didn't see it was you who made me feel alone. No woman in her senses could ever expect a man to marry her in my circumstances; that was just something cut off, done with, I could have got used to that, I'd have had my baby, you see. Then you kept coming to see me, you let me see you were trying to forgive me and that was worse than being . . . than being . . . I don't know how to say that— it was cruel of you. If you'd even have told me at once, I mean long before you did, that if I got rid of the baby you'd marry me, it would have been better, I'd never have grown to expect him . . . I mean, love him before he came. I had to, Joaquín, it was either you or him and he was certain."

"Yes, I see it, you're right."

"You take on things too big for you. You tried to marry me and let me have the baby; it was too big for you. I don't blame you for not being able to do it, but you ought to have had the sense to see you were only trying to live up to your ideals."

"A man ought to live up to his ideals, oughtn't he, why the hell are you blaming me for that?"

"Yes . . . I suppose so . . . it seemed so clear when I was speaking," Lucía faltered, and, her gaze returning from the pot simmering over the fire, she watched him as he picked at a loose thread in the hem of her skirt. A lock of his hair fell forward and she pushed it back and said, "You ought to have your hair cut, Joaquín, it's getting untidy, and it's dirty at the roots, look." She scratched his scalp with her nail. "Coal dust; you must have it short."

"I know, I meant to, but the shop was so full. I know I was wrong now you say it, Lucía, I ought to have told you about the baby at once."

"Then again, you ought to have loved me properly once you'd married me, but you weren't big enough."

"Good God, I have loved you properly."

"No, you haven't." Turning away from him, she pushed his hand from beneath her dress and adjusted the suspender with which his fingers had been playing.

"You've told me to speak."

"Yes, go on, anything is better than silence."

"You haven't loved me properly—you were playing with my suspender—you haven't had me for weeks and weeks, if you were . . . I don't know—if you were big enough you couldn't do that without wanting me."

His face showed impatience and he closed his lips firmly as if meaning not to speak. "I'm not . . . I mean I've never had enough happiness lately to want you. I've been good to you."

"Yes, but don't you see what I mean, you told me to try saying it all ways even if they were wrong, and now you aren't trying to understand. When you married me you ought to have given me life, you ought to have carried me along, I don't know, it all seems so wicked."

"Wicked?"

"Yes . . . there's something I want to tell you, Joaquín, but I don't know whether it's true always. . . ."

"Tell me . . ." She was trying to speak, he perceived, but indecision went deeper than lack of courage.

"It's wicked?" he said. "Don't worry about that." He saw at once that she was going to speak; it was evident that she was going to speak of something else.

"You ought to have kept on at me—taken me—made me have a baby, kept loving me, made me laugh—made me love you— God, I don't know how to say it."

"I can't want a woman who's not wanting me, not often, anyway; besides, I wanted our marriage to be different, we're equals."

"Yes, I read all that in one of your books, but it's harder than that."

"How do you mean, Lucía?"

"Well, it's right to be equals and to teach me to read and think and all that, you did try. But you're a man, you are better than me, you are the . . . the master. . . ."

"Oh, nonsense, girl; I don't want . . ."

"It's not nonsense, you've got to be master and equal, that's hard. You weren't big enough."

"Now look here, girl, let's have the baby back, I'll make a real effort to love him, I promise."

"To love him . . . you can't love by trying."

"You were saying just now I ought to have tried and how the hell can I like a kid I've not seen?"

"I know, you're trying to argue me out. I told you I can't talk."

"We'll have the baby back."

"No."

"It will be better for us both."

"No, I don't want him back enough to put up with what would happen. I'm not big enough either, I don't love you nor him enough. . . . Oh, Mother of God, I said we were like stone."

"That's because you . . . we've set one love against the other; sometimes two loves neutralize one another, don't you think so?"

Again he was astonished at her conduct; she leaned over the table in the deepest distress and then, wheeling with determined movement, her eyes opened, she gathered in her underlip to begin some word. He waited for her to speak. The will ceased to glow in her eyes and her body lost its tension; she swayed over the table and then bracing herself feebly, she went out of the room.

One day soon after his return to work Caro said to Lucía, "It's this life which is getting me down, the mines, the town, these people, they're real but I don't feel them. They might be something going on behind a shop window."

"Why don't we move then?"

"Move? No." He was afraid of moving, lest he become too mobile, broken off from life and a settled job. She understood this and knew it was the fear of the good peasant. "We can't go back," he added.

"No, but listen. They're going to do some repairs to the Musel breakwater in Gijón; you could get a job there, it would be in the open. There are palms in Gijón."

"Palms! And what after? They look as if they had leprosy."

"You might get work in the docks."

"Might."

"Oh, for God's sake," she screamed.

At the end of a week they were in Gijón and things were easier between them. The growth of revolt also aided them, for while Caro found absorption in the struggle, Lucía herself began to take some part. Not only was the national conflict growing acute but it sounded its bitterest dissonance in Asturias. The attacks upon the Church and the Land Acts, which, although they provided for compensation, dispossessed many of the great landlords, had made desperate the upper and property-owning classes. The Governmental block itself had broken asunder under the strain, and after the fall of Azaña's ministry, government succeeded government and still the storm charge was increased. The election of 1933, which in the Los Olivares province had returned a Catholic Conservative, had enormously strengthened the Right. The landworker had once more returned to his old allegiance, the women had clung to their Church. It was obvious that the old governing classes, now demanding reactionary measures, would soon be in political power. The Republican but divided town vote would soon be borne down by the now united and Conservative countryside. The Fascist and Catholic Action Popular parties descended upon Asturias with intense propaganda. The usual phenomena appeared; prominent workers were beaten up by Fascist gangs, retaliations were made and the various sections of the workers rapidly united. The Workers' Alliance came into existence, Socialist, Syndicalist, Anarchist and dissident Communist joined forces in preparation for the impending crash. Only the official Communist Party withheld its adherence to the Workers' Alliance, though within the Party many, Caro in particular, were in favor of joining. It was necessary to act, to make revolution before the Right became stronger, he claimed, for soon the advances of the Republic would be annulled.

It was while Caro was recounting to Lucía how the speech of the worker Martínez had persuaded the Asturian section of the C.N.T., the revolutionary federation of syndicates, to join the Workers' Alliance, that he caught sight of a column in the Andalucian weekly paper to which he subscribed.

"FIRE DESTROYS GREAT QUANTITY OF CEREALS," it was headed, but it was the final sentences which caused him to spring to his feet. "It is believed that the fires were the work of an incendiary. The police are diligently searching for an Anarchist recently seen in the neighborhood. This man, of a presence likely to influence his hearers, achieved considerable popularity by his performance on the guitar, upon which instrument he appears to be adept."

"Diego!" he exclaimed. "He's out of prison."

"Diego . . . how do you know? Of course he must be, he received only a year's sentence." He paid no attention to Lucía's change of tone.

"Yes, of course," he muttered, reading the column intently.

"It seems that in this town near Ciudad Real, the sheaves had all been stacked upon the threshing floors ready for treading out when the fire started, at the top of a little valley. The threshing floors are all in a line and the wind was blowing down the valley. The whole lot was destroyed, the flames leaped from stack to stack so quickly that all the threshing piles were burning at once, and the sparks streamed down to the next village."

"Would it be Diego? Would he burn corn? It must have been a sight, a fiery wind through the black night."

Caro regarded her with vague surprise. "Yes, if it belonged to two or three big landlords as it says here it did. Oh, here's another paragraph. Listen. 'It is denied by many that the guitarist, while known to be an Anarchist, had any hand in the disastrous fire. The landlord of the inn in which he stayed has stated that his guest was accompanied by a woman and her daughter and that this gave him reason to observe his conduct closely. The innkeeper insists that the guitarist was of exemplary behavior throughout his stay.'"

"That was him right enough. The others would be Conchita and her mother."

"Yes . . . I suppose it would be. He wouldn't be with them if he were going to burn the corn, would he?"

"Probably not; no, certainly not."

"Perhaps he did set fire to it; they say he wanted to blow up the dam at home."

He had felt uneasy as she began to say this, but at the end he laughed, for the first time in many days. Lucía was disconcerted by his laughter and insisted upon an explanation.

"Well, you see, I also tried to blow up the dam, the same night."

"You did? Joaquín." She forgot her estrangement and came over and sat upon his knee, her face glowing. "Tell me, why do you never tell me these things?" Before he had finished her former apathy had returned. Some time after, she said Diego was wrong to want to kill Don Fadrique.

The news about the corn fire was shortly given prominence in the national newspapers because, it was said, the description of the guitarist whose presence had preceded the cereal fire in some ways corresponded with that of a man, also a guitarist, who had been prominent in an agrarian strike a few weeks before. During that strike a Civil Guard had been shot and the man was wanted for the offense. Caro had already begun desultorily to think of how he might get into touch with Diego, when Mudarra appeared in Gijón.

30

Red Corn

IT was a man whom Caro had met in the library of the Workers' Athenaeum who brought the news about Mudarra's arrival to him.

"Where is he?" he asked.

"He said he'd be out on the waste plot beyond the tobacco factory if you wanted to see him."

"On the waste plot? What's the matter?"

"I don't know. I said I could take him to your place but he wouldn't come with me."

"No, he wouldn't." The words were spoken to himself; he was going to ask why he had not given his address, but the agrarian strike might account for his secrecy and he decided to say nothing to his informant.

"What part of the waste plot? It's pretty big."

"I don't know; you go and fall over a heap of cans and he hears you, I suppose. Go if you like, though I should be careful, I thought he looked rather—well—crazy."

When Caro arrived at the waste plot, however, Mudarra was waiting for him on the curb at the street end. He recognized the figure before he drew near.

"Well," Mudarra said. Caro was silent a few moments.

"Well," he replied. The two men faced one another in the semidarkness at the edge of the area lit by a street lamp. He could not see Mudarra's face clearly, but prison had changed him terribly; his cheekbones protruded and his face was sunken and white. The old ease and geniality had gone, and Caro felt the tension of the man's spirit. The sound of Mudarra's greet-

ing continued to echo in his imagination. Why was Diego
here, was he really wanted by the police, had he been im-
plicated in the agrarian strike? Why was he staring so, why
did he not speak? One of them must speak soon.

"Where is Señora Pérez and Concepción?" Caro said.

"Here, they came . . ." Mudarra cut the sentence off sharply
and seem to retreat within himself.

"I am glad to see you, Diego," Caro said at last.

"The hell you are . . . oh, boy." The guitarist stepped forward and thrust out his hand and as quickly as his tone had
changed it changed again. "I am glad, too." He dropped his
hand; Caro had not moved to take it.

"Why didn't you send me your address?"

"Because I didn't want to implicate you."

"In what way?"

"Oh, spies," Mudarra spoke wearily. "I'm being followed."

"Then you were in the strike?"

The guitarist seemed to Caro to hesitate, yet he spoke in
level tones. "What strike? I've been watched ever since I came
out of prison."

"Well, you think that I'm likely to be afraid? . . . though it's
decent of you."

"Oh, very."

"What the hell did you want to see me for if you speak like
that?"

"This howling wilderness," Mudarra murmured, gazing at
the city's lights reflected by the low sky.

"You don't like the place? I don't either. . . ."

"I'd like to see a spot of sun; I've been here three days and
I haven't yet."

"There are palms here," Caro said.

"Yes, they remind me of an ostrich's backside."

"*Real* sun," Caro insisted.

"Yes. Mater Purissima and the shadows of the dulzars, the
olivars in mid June after the second working and the earth as
red as ripe maize."

"Third working."

"Third working, sorry, but red as maize when the sun sets,
Jabalón made of brass and Mater Purissima cut out of snow."

"It's burned now."

"I know. . . ." Mudarra's voice was sad. "Who else could I come to, boy?"

"No one, I suppose, Diego."

Then again the guitarist was silent, but Caro would not leave it so.

"What are you going to do here?"

"Work, if I can. I've got to work, I've spent the bit of money I'd saved."

"It'll be hard to find, and it's different work."

"I've done a few things lately, made hats, shoes, broken stones, made a road, other things, too. It isn't that, I'm being watched."

"Tell me, Diego, why are you being watched?"

"Dangerous subject."

"Christ, there're hundreds of us in Gijón or anywhere in these parts."

"Yes?" Mudarra rubbed the side of his face and sighed.

"I saw a piece in the paper about a strike down Ciudad Real way; a Civil Guard was killed and they said a guitarist was responsible."

"There are a lot of guitarists in the country."

"Now, look here, if you're being watched for that, why not tell me? Why did you come to me if you don't want to say yes or no?"

"I thought if I had friends round me I should . . . shouldn't be so nervy. Go on, laugh, nervy! Oh, Christ, do you hear it!"

"Well, you're right, of course; why do you suppose I'm not to be trusted? Why did you come to Gijón anyway?"

"That's another matter . . . it doesn't concern you."

"No? . . . Well, I think it's time to chuck this conversation; you don't want to speak . . . I thought . . ."

"What did you think?"

Caro wished to say he had hoped they would be reconciled, that he had been twice on the point of embracing the guitarist; it seemed too that Mudarra was thinking the same. He gazed at the man, trying to understand what was passing in his mind; bitterness and distrust were expressed there, and pleading. Then it changed and indifference looked out of Mudarra's eyes. It was the guitarist's place to effect the reconciliation, Caro thought, and resentment, hitherto a tiny spark, grew suddenly into a hot flame.

"That's another matter, it doesn't concern you," he said, and left Mudarra at the edge of the waste plot. Anger burned him. Trust and distrust, affection and indifference, everything was mingled in Mudarra. Well, he could be forgiven that also; prison was no laughing matter. As when he was talking to Lucía, he seemed to be within a few seams of the gold ore of reason which lay below the thinking and feeling. Reason was a little tool that scratched vainly at the covering rocks. Solution of their difficulties lay deeper than reason. He said as much to himself and before greater doubt arrived the chill of failing belief preceded it. Could one make an ideal society, a reasonable society, if such as he and Lucía and Mudarra could not solve a problem which began at such a brute level? The coldness gave way and without awareness he quickened his pace; he was nearly breaking into a run when he reached home, and Lucía was not in; coldness took the place of determination.

When she returned the first thing Caro said to her was:

"Mudarra's here, I've seen him," and after a while she inquired about the strike.

Some days passed by and then, impulsively, she asked Caro if she might still have the baby.

"If you must," he replied. She suddenly paused while putting the bread on the table and said:

"What are we doing?" She was thinking feverishly, he could see, moistening her lips and looking from side to side.

"No, not you," she whispered and closed her eyes. "Joaquín, my husband . . . I cannot do it, I cannot do it, do you hear?"

Her stumble seemed to be deliberate, he caught her as she ran towards him and drew her back to the chair and gazed at her in bewilderment, joy was shining in her face.

"I cannot do it," she said fiercely, and locked her arms so tightly around his neck that he was forced to loosen them.

"What is it you cannot do?"

"My darling, I didn't know I was trying to do it, ah, Mother of God most holy, is it too late, husband? Don't you love me? Love me, husband."

"What is it, what were you trying?" he said, and then he had no need of answers and dashed his mouth against hers, forcing open her lips. She twisted her head aside and gasped, "I'll tell you afterwards." He bore her back to the floor and took her clothing in his hands. "Yes," she gasped again; the breath was hard and dry in her throat, her muscles were vibrating from shoulder to foot; the blood rippled in the veins of her neck. "Hurry . . . tear . . . my husband. . . ."

Afterwards they went at once to bed and when he awakened and struggled to release his underarm she scolded him and said, "Was I good?" For reply he laughed. "What was it you were trying to do?" he added.

"Well, I didn't see it before, I still can't think I could have been so wicked, but it's facts which count, and downstairs, you know, when I was putting the loaf on the table, I suddenly saw the facts as anybody else would see them, as clear as the loaf . . . anyway, does it matter about telling you?"

"Not much, if you don't want to; not now, at least, I'm sleepy."

"But was I good? Mother of God, I'm so happy!"

One of the results of their reconciliation was that when Mudarra next visited Caro the latter promised to aid him to get a job on the breakwater. "It's hellish work," he said.

Mudarra clicked his tongue and then began to grin.

"That'll have its funny side."

"How so?"

"Bad for my guardian angel. There's a police agent who never lets me out of sight. I got a job as a waiter last week; he sat in that café twelve hours a day. There's more than one of them though." Mudarra became serious and peered around him. "It's getting on my bloody nerves, *chico,* it'll be good to work near someone I can trust."

Caro wanted to take the opening, but the guitarist was so tensely strung that he held his peace. Within a fortnight he found a way to keep his promise. There was in the gang a Catholic worker who had made himself objectionable by wearing the badge of Acción Popular, the semi-Fascist Catholic organization led by Gil Robles. Caro and the secretary of the

Socialist trade union picked upon this man and by constant
harassing made him lose his temper repeatedly. The foreman
accepted the gang's account and the man was sacked. Mudarra's stature made the foreman very willing to engage
him. The same day a well-dressed man of authoritative bearing
engaged the engineer in charge of the repairs in conversation.
The next morning a tall narrow-faced individual with a habit
of sucking in his underlip was engaged and put to work with
Mudarra's section. He was useless at the work, he could not
help to lift the blocks nor push the heavy trolleys, nor could he
be trusted to tie a knot or put a load on the stone nippers. At
first the workers baited him, sending him to the foreman for a
No. 2 skyhook, or a bucket of supercharged blast. Then they
tried to work him to breaking point, the well-dressed person
thereupon visited the engineer again, and Roza, the police
agent, was allowed to idle as much as he cared. Many muttered
threats of violence, but though he went in fear, Roza hung on
to his post. When Caro and Mudarra eventually transferred
to Baragaña's gang in the docks Roza went with them. There
were other spies, too. To increase his earnings, for he was
helping Conchita to maintain her mother, Mudarra gave lessons upon the guitar. His pupils were principally southerners,
or criollos from Cuba. One of his most enthusiastic pupils, for
whom he had taken a great liking, was one day seen to leave
Roza's lodging house. Then the F.A.I., with whom the guitarist
was working politically, took up the question of an escort. An
Anarchist docker was moved onto Baragaña's gang on Orient
and Trinity wharfs, but still Roza hung on. A small block of
stone pushed off the wall and intended for his head pulped
two fingers of his left hand. His hand in splints, Roza idled
about on the wall above the gang.

For two days Mudarra was away from work; he had taken
to drink under the strain.

"It's that corn strike," he said to Caro upon his return.

"You were in it, then?"

"Yes, I ought to have told you . . . but things are so hard to
say nowadays."

Caro knew he meant that the trouble about Lucía was still
between them; a half of his will longed to say it was all past,

and a half shrank from facing up to the matter. The tiniest signal would have made him embrace Mudarra, yet he was relieved when the guitarist continued. As he listened he was looking back on that opportunity, nevertheless.

"The strike was organized from Madrid," Mudarra was saying. "I did a lot of the work, most of it, though not much in the field itself."

"Yes, but the guard?"

"No . . . I didn't kill him."

"Why are they after you then?"

"Christ, man," exclaimed Mudarra; Caro nodded. It would matter nothing to the authorities so long as a scapegoat were found, and if the crime could be shackled onto an important Anarchist and strike organizer that would be a fortunate discovery.

"It all turns on my alibi, I guess. I've sworn I was never in Ciudad Real; if they prove I was, I'm for it."

"The other, the corn fire, were you down there, too?"

"Yes, that was just bad luck, that fire. I was going to size up what chances there were of getting the men into the syndicate when that fire broke out. I had nothing to do with it. It was a pure accident."

"Any chance of organizing them?"

"Not a chance; they struck over the harvesting because that's when they have the landlords by the privates. The life's gone out of them, they can't believe anything's to be got by struggle. Thanks to the politicians . . ."

"Do you remember what Robledo said?"

"Yes, he's right in a way, we're going to get it in the neck soon, Joaquín."

"What's the good of talking like that. Make a fight for it!"

"This Alliance is a Communist trick, Joaquín. Make the revolution first and settle the problems as they arise after? That means a new State, the Revolutionary Committee will decide and the party cliques; the workers won't get a look in."

"The other way . . . was Conchita with you?"

"Yes, they were serving as a screen; at least the girl knew she was. But they're all right. The old lady knows how to lie herself to sleep and Conchita could lie the Christ off a crucifix."

"They've been questioned?"

"Have they hell!"

"H'm, better watch that fellow running about after Conchita."

"What fellow, who the hell do you mean?" Mudarra exclaimed, straightening up.

"Don't know his name, better warn her."

At the end of the shift Mudarra borrowed a bicycle and raced off to the shop where the girl was working.

"Who's this hanging about after you?" he demanded, when the girl had come out to the pavement.

"You've no need to be jealous," Conchita quietly replied.

"Jealous be damned, girl, I came to warn you."

"Yes, but I've thought of that."

"You have!"

"He's a spy all right; he showed me some snaps of Ciudad Real last night; there was one he said was of the principal square. I could see it wasn't. He wanted me to say it wasn't, I suppose. I should have told you tonight."

"Well, freeze him off."

"Not yet. If I do that at once he'll guess it's because of those photographs."

"I hadn't thought of that; end of the week then! I can't stand much more of this, it's getting me down."

"Diego, for the Virgin's sake, you *mustn't* let it. You mustn't drink. Can't you see, boy, you'll blurt out something."

"What the hell am I to do? I can't sleep nor eat, and every time a man passes me in the street I want to turn round and watch him. It's hell, girl . . . they'll get me yet."

"For the love of God, Diego, don't say it."

"Why can't you give me a room in your house, Conchita?"

"No . . . there's no bed."

"You've a spare room, I'll buy a mattress and some blankets."

"No, I . . ."

"But I lived with you for years before I went to prison, your mother would like it. . . ."

"No, dear, that was different," the girl faltered and then

continued in a louder voice, "You must have a proper bed, a mattress won't do." Before he could reply she turned and ran into the shop.

The Civil Guard shortly tried new methods with the guitarist. He was subpoenaed as a witness in a case to be tried in Ciudad Real and allowed to go free in that city, agents following him to note whether he showed familiarity with the place. Only the invincible inefficiency of the Spanish police saved him; one of the agents called him by name in the street as he left the court. Then upon his return he was arrested and subjected to endless questionings about arms smuggling. In these days the Workers' Alliance in conjunction with the Socialist Party and the General Union of Workers in Madrid were arming at desperate speed. Trade Union and Socialist lodges were mortgaged, private savings were given and weekly collections taken to provide a workers' army with rifles and bombs. A steamship, the *Turquesa,* was chartered by the Socialist Party and several cargoes of rifles and thousands of rounds of ammunition were landed in Asturias. Being questioned about the smuggling awakened in Mudarra a sickening desire to be in the struggle, to be working for the present attempt at revolution, yet the other motive for his coming to Asturias had been to oppose from within the Syndicates the fusion of workers' organizations into one alliance. That way meant Socialism, or Communism, instead of freedom. The struggle that set up in him brought him to such tension that he was permanently on the point of hysteria. To give him a little more ease a few friends were taken into confidence about the reason for vigilance over Mudarra, Baragaña among them. The Asturian docker as gang leader did his utmost to be rid of Roza, but his discharge was always blocked. Throughout the working day the agent hung on, though he was now aware that his occupation was known to all the workers. His own nerve was beginning to break, but where Roza came from there were many more, they knew.

On Friday private affairs kept Baragaña from work and at about half-past-four in the afternoon he strolled down to the Swiss café in front of the Orient Wharf where he and the others took their evening drinks. The Swiss was one of the most comfortable of the dockside cafés, warm in winter and cool in summer, because of the depth to which it ran back into the block. Baragaña first took a nap on the red-cushioned settle in the back corner, and then fetching the illustrated papers to one of the tables reserved for regular "parishioners," prepared to await the arrival of the gang, who usually called in for a drink before going home. In *Crónica* he read an article on "The Classic Type of Fatal Woman," which was about a Madrid actress or prostitute, it was not clear which, who had built herself a private bar so that she might get drunk at home but in congenial surroundings. Then he read an article about the arrest of a quack doctor at the instigation of the authorized practitioner in a Manchegan village where both lived. The qualified doctor had written a brochure on the curative waters of a local spa, it said. In *Mundo Gráfica* there was also an exciting article about China, where the most grim things seemed to happen, and after that he had just begun to read about the election of a Beauty Queen in Sevilla when the door was thrust open and the noise of a dray swept into the café. He heard the scrape of chairs and a hurried step and looked up. Caro was coming towards him.

A glance at Caro's face told the gang leader what had happened. He leaned over the table and pushed a chair back for Caro and waited; Caro stared at Baragaña with a dazed expression and then lowered his head into his hands.

"He's given himself away?" Baragaña said in a hopeless voice.

Caro nodded. The waiter approached, but seeing the man bowed over the table, halted, shook his head and turned away slowly, then he brought a bottle of brandy, walking quickly on tiptoe.

"Ah, don't take on so, son," Baragaña said. "He'll get off, there's a chance."

Caro did not lift his head, but his body jerked quickly and was still a moment.

"Where is he now? They've got him?"

The Andaluz took the brandy which the docker slid across the table. "Yes," he replied. "But not for that; he cleared off after he'd given in and went up towards Cabrales Street; he was going to the Pérez's, no doubt. I saw him bump into a man smoking a cigar." Caro finished the brandy and stared at Baragaña.

"A man with a cigar?"

"Yes, the fellow said something to him and Diego hit the cigar out of his mouth. They arrested him for it at once."

"Well . . ." began Baragaña after thought, but his companion shuddered and covered his face again; the docker let him sob and took a large brandy himself.

"How'd it happen, son?"

"It was that damned corn; God, it's bad to think a man can be put away for a cargo of corn."

"Corn?"

"Yes, it was this way. We'd got most of the sacks out of her and then we found that nearly all the bottom layer of sacks was split, as you said we should."

"Those bags were bad, yes, they ought not to have been used for grain."

"Well, we just ripped them and got some more sacks from the warehouse and filled them. Roza was shoveling, too. . . ."

"Sod him, I'd like . . ." muttered Baragaña, lifting the brandy bottle.

Caro started violently and whispered, "No, no . . ."

The docker put down the bottle again and said, "Roza was shoveling."

"Roza, too. Diego was shoveling next to me on the other side of the hold, then the sun came out." There was a long pause and then Baragaña said in a reflective voice, "It's been thundery all day."

"The sun . . . God, I knew he was breaking up, you know how he is . . . he was muttering and jumping all the afternoon, and once or twice he cursed me and flung his shovel down. He kept walking off out of the hold, then he took to hanging round Roza; I thought he was going to lay him out. Perhaps he would have done." Caro stared at Baragaña and clenched his fists over the table, his body rigid as metal.

"Take it easy, son," the docker urged tenderly.

"The sun came out and the beam shone on a heap of corn in the center of the hold and Diego laughed suddenly and rushed into it and flung a shovelful up into the air. 'Look, beautiful, golden corn, red corn, little pieces of gold,' he shouted. You know how he is. I don't know whether he had already broken or not, he gets that way sometimes. . . . It got him at his weak point. 'I'll make a song about red corn,' he shouted. He made a song about new bread and olive oil once. Then he flung down his spade and I could see then he was done for. 'Not red enough,' he said, facing up to Roza, he yelled it at him. 'Got to plant all the world with corn, red corn, feed people who are starving—ah, beautiful, beautiful, leagues of red corn, all Europe waving with corn, you've never seen even a mile of corn waving in the wind, have you, you bastard,' he screamed at Roza, plowing through the corn up to his knees. 'I've seen it, miles of it all brown and yellow and bending over . . . miles of it, down Ciudad Real way . . .' We were all watching him, he was acting as if he was drunk, pointing at Roza and staggering about in the corn. Roza flung down his shovel and shouted at him, too, just noises, no words. When Diego said that about Ciudad Real one of the chaps flung down his shovel and said, 'Good Christ. . . .' "

"There, don't take it so hard, Joaquín, there's a chance for him." Baragaña was shaking with excitement; he had screwed up the *Crónica* into a ball.

"He calmed down almost at once and said, 'Adiós,' and left the ship. Roza followed him, grinning, and crying, too; he spewed on the gangway. He was crying all the way along the wharf."

Again Caro began to tremble and he pushed his chair back from the table, his face twitching uncontrollably.

"Here, have another brandy. He may get off at the trial; we can collect for his defense."

"He . . . he won't be tried," Caro gasped.

"They'll have to give him some sort of a trial."

"No . . . no . . . no." Caro's voice sank to a whisper and he stared wildly at the docker. "He won't be tried."

Baragaña returned his stare and then he grasped Caro's

meaning. Leaning over the table, he squeezed his companion's arm and whispered, "All right, son, go to my place and wait, I'll arrange your getaway right now."

Caro rose and hurried away; Baragaña drank hard at the brandy bottle before going out. "God, that was quick work," was the first thing he said.

31

Miracle Play

MENÉNDEZ, the principal figure in the Gijón section of the F.A.I., at once invited Baragaña into his house.

"Here, let me get this clear," he interrupted, "how many getaways have to be arranged, one or two?"

"It's Caro, he's finished off Roza."

"You said he was in prison."

"No, Mudarra's in prison."

"Now, wait a minute, Caro hit a cigar out of somebody's mouth and then what? How does Mudarra get swiped for that? Besides . . . there, start all over again." Baragaña wiped the sweat from his face and swore.

"Now listen carefully," he began.

"Mudarra's in prison then. Well . . . let me see. Listen, if Roza was stopped after Mudarra was swiped there's no need to bother about Mudarra, he's got a sound alibi."

"Jesus, you're clever, Menéndez," Baragaña muttered in astonishment. "I hadn't thought of that." He rubbed his face energetically, screwing up his eyes.

"Now we've got to find out whereabouts Roza was killed and if anybody saw this man Caro, and if so we'll get him out of the town at once. If nobody saw him, that'll be easy, for it's clear he wouldn't have killed Roza if the sod had already been to the police. He must have got him first. You go and collect some dough . . . no, better go home and sleep it off."

"Don't want to sleep, son, give me something to do, and I'll do it."

"Better stay here, I guess, you can lie on that bed. No, wait a minute. If I take you home I can see Caro."

"Brother, I can go home by myself, I'm alri' . . . quite alri'. . . ."

"So I see, but just pretend to be drunk and no one will think it odd for me to be going to your house. Right, you pretend to be drunk, see?"

"Alri' . . . you leave it t'm', I can do it," Baragaña said, patting the Anarchist's shoulder confidentially.

Señora Baragaña angrily assisted Menéndez to get her resisting husband into the bedroom, then she told him that Caro was sitting in an outhouse built against the back wall. He went out at once.

"What's happened, Baragaña's drunk, I couldn't get it straight."

Caro recounted how Mudarra's nerve had broken in the hold of the grain ship and how he had followed Roza, who was still hanging on behind the guitarist. "I think Diego was going to give. himself up; he didn't live in that part of the town, perhaps he was going to the police headquarters. What do you think? God, that's what is on my mind now. If he's confessed . . . I've killed . . . I've killed for nothing." Caro clutched Menéndez's arm. "That's what's on my mind."

"Yes, I understand you, brother, don't let it worry you, keep your head, keep serene, that kind of creature's not a human being. But this about Mudarra, that's a hell of a mess, if he's confessed."

"He was still strung up. The fellow bumped into him but he apologized. Diego wasn't the sort to be offensive after an apology. He must have been screwing himself up all the while; the fellow had a big white face with a baby's mouth, a silly face . . ."

"Well, we've got to chance it; you got Roza before he went to the police?"

"Yes, he'd started towards the police, that's why he looked as if he was following Diego, I think, but when he got near the station he suddenly quickened his pace and walked up another street . . . I followed him . . . I thought he'd see me, I kept so close . . ."

"Yes, go on."

"He went along that road towards the Moreda foundry."

"He was an agent provocateur there during the strike; ah, I believe I understand where he was going."

"He didn't go to the foundry, but cut across that empty yard and went round the corner towards the coal dealer's office. I turned the corner without looking round it, do you see . . . I ran round the corner into him, I had to kill him where he was . . ."

"All right, all right, brother, of course you did. In broad daylight, too. Anyone see you? It's a lonely place, anyone working on those garden plots?"

"I don't know, I didn't have time to see, I bumped into him, he didn't try to stop me, he kept his finger on the bell, he was ringing . . ."

"The first house it would be?" Menéndez took Caro's lapel in his fist. "The first house?"

"Yes, I could hear the bell, it stopped. I could hear it though the foundry was making such a din."

"Thanks be to God," ejaculated Menéndez, "you're in luck. He was going to ease himself . . . if they found him dead outside that house they'd think it was some brawl about one of the girls."

"In broad daylight!" Caro whispered.

"Get it off your mind, boy. Let me think, what shall we do?"

"If Diego's confessed!"

"We must chance that; it doesn't make any difference to this, we've got to clear you. If no one saw you it's O.K. We'd better think up something to stop inquiries though. Here, wait a minute, he was a spy at the foundry, many threatened to do him in; when it was found out, somebody did do him in. No, that won't do. I know! The police'll make inquiries round that quarter first. We've got plenty of men there. Better tell them to plant the yarn that Roza was often seen or heard quarreling around that knocking shop, inside and outside of it. Yes, that's the hammer. All right, you stay here. I am going out to see one of our chaps. . . . Say, brother, what was it, knife or gun?"

"Knife," whispered Caro. Menéndez nodded. "I'll be going," he said.

The lawyer, whom his friends had hired, was able to tell them next morning that Mudarra had been charged with minor assault and language injurious to the uniformed authorities. Señora Pérez, however, brought news at midday that he had not confessed to complicity in the strike, though by the fervor with which he had kissed her she had understood he imagined he was taking his last leave of her. She had shaken her head violently after his kiss but he had not understood. He had been on his way to the Pérez' house first, he had said, and they gathered he had intended to give himself up. It was the smoker's pouting scowl and silly, freshly powdered face which had prevented that, it seemed; it had infuriated him, and the knocking out of the cigar had been preparatory to further assault. He had chiefly talked about the man's puffy stare, she said, despite his belief in the gravity of his position.

They spent a day and a half of suspense and then Mudarra was tried, probably out of deference to the growing unrest. The fines were paid out of the defense collection, and after apologizing to the smoker's representative Mudarra was released. Menéndez took him to his house and there told him the news about Roza. He listened gravely, though his eyes shone brilliantly, and then begged permission to find Caro at once.

"He's not in Gijón, I'm told he starts organizing work for the Alianza Obrera today. I saw his wife this morning. It's as well, for until we're sure about the inquiries he'd better be out of the way."

"What's happening, any news?"

"No more than I told you just now. The police seem satisfied with the tale they've collected. They can't fix it on you and so, well, a dead spy is a spy dead."

"No, I meant about the Alianza."

"The *Turquesa* . . ." Menéndez was suddenly quiet.

"The *Turquesa* what?"

"Nothing, I heard the *Turquesa* was going to fetch another load soon."

"Well, we can't object to arming the workers."

"No." Menéndez was speaking guardedly, Mudarra saw.

"Any news about the Alliance; how many are in it now?"

"I don't know."

"What's the matter, have we been a complete washout?"

"I suppose there's no reason why I shouldn't tell you that I've gone in myself, all the F.A.I.'s in. Everybody's in except the Communist Party. Caro's acting unofficially."

"So that's it. Then the *Turquesa* landed a cargo last night?"

"Yes."

"Joaquín on that job? Distributing? I thought he's seemed tired lately, but he's never told me anything." Mudarra flushed as he spoke.

"No, organizing work in the villages up in the hills, we've got to make the men stay in the places until the time is right. They want to come down here to Oviedo and start an army right away. What are you going to do about it?"

"Better do something, I suppose; anything you can give me to do?"

"Good man, yes, I should think there is, by God. There's three hundred rifles I'm responsible for stuck out in a garage on the Avilés road. It's my first job . . . I only went in yesterday. I've got two milk lorries but I'm short of men. It'll be heavy work, because the Alliance is keeping every possible man at his post. Job by day and this work by night."

"That sounds my style; what about something to eat first? Is there time for me to run around to the Pérez'?"

"Yes; the milk van will pick you up on the road tonight. At the start of the Villar track there's one of those little granaries. You know the sort, built on four pillars with a flight of steps that don't reach the platform, to keep the mice out. Well, you hide in there, you can't mistake it because there'll be two milk churns at the corner, name of Chantada. We'll rattle the cans so's you can be certain; it's the second of the two lorries you get in. I shall be driving. We've got to get the rifles to Trubia, as damn silly a journey as ever was thought of. We shall have to skirt Avilés and Oviedo. Besides, they make guns at Trubia."

"God, this is good, Menéndez," Mudarra said just before leaving. "I'll see you tonight then."

"Oh, by the way," Menéndez called, "we've got to find a man

to go to the Leon province on the other side of the cordillera to sound the agrarian workers. What about you? No, that won't do; if the police as much as hear of you in the country they'll say you were on that Ciudad Real job."

For a moment, when Menéndez mentioned the agrarian workers, Mudarra felt a twinge of doubt; it was only momentary but it sickened him nonetheless, then excitement swept back and he hurried out of the house. A voice in his brain was saying as quietly as the tick of a watch, "Will they rise, will they rise?"

"What's the matter with you these days?" Señora Pérez said when greetings were over. "Didn't you understand why I shook my head?"

"No. Where's the girl, I must be getting thick in the head."

"She's out at a class. Pedro will fetch her; that's the neighbor's little boy."

Conchita returned running and without hesitation threw her arms around Mudarra's neck and took his kisses upon her lips and face and neck.

"Well," burst out Señora Pérez, "why haven't I heard about this, Concha? Concepción, do you hear, why haven't I heard about this?"

"My dear," she panted, struggling to get out of his arms, "how long have you been out?"

"About an hour." The girl blushed and was silent.

"Had to fix up a job for the Alianza," he was quick to say.

"The Alianza? I've been to my class . . . Red Cross class. I've learned how to splint a broken arm; I'm good at it. If you ever get hit let it be your arm. No, I don't like that joke."

While Mudarra ate, the two women made a packet of food for him, a merienda, a Spanish woman's idea of a snack.

"*Madre de Dios,*" he exclaimed, when they placed it on the table, "I'm not quartermaster to the outfit."

"When will you be back?" the girl said at the door.

"I shall be at work tomorrow; now what about a room here, *chica?*"

"No, *chico,*" she replied firmly.

"But aren't things different now?"

"Yes, that's why, you fool," she laughed, and he grabbed at her as she dodged back into the passage.

"Come here, you little devil." He caught her by the skirt and began to wrestle with her. "You'll have to give in, Conchita."

"My darling, don't. They've been different ever since that day in the gate chamber. Listen, Diego, I'd let you have a room here, only . . ."

"Only you remember Lucía." Angrily he released the girl and watched her face.

"No, you know that isn't true . . . did you promise to marry her? Did you? It's you that's remembering her." She said this venomously.

"I never so much as said I loved her; fling that up at me!"

"I'm not flinging anything up."

"You think I'm no good because of what she and I did?"

"If she was willing . . ."

"Of course she was willing, what the hell!"

"Well, you wouldn't be much good if you didn't, then." She spoke sulkily and he burst into laughter at her tone. Conchita tried to restrain a smile and then her laughter rang out also. As he lunged at her she dodged him again, holding her skirt down as she laughed. Señora Pérez came out of the inner room and scolded her for being so noisy. She kissed him decorously and, picking up the package from the floor, he set out for the Villar track. Smilingly she watched him, and then as she returned to the inner room she ceased to smile. She had, while laughing, given mental consent to his occupying one of their three rooms. It would be unwise, she decided, closing her feet and standing firmly upon them.

Two days later Caro and Mudarra met at the Workers' Athenaeum. They shook hands in the committee room doorway, relinquished hands as the door closed towards them and shook again.

"Here, let's go and have a few minutes' talk, boy," Mudarra said as the door swung to against his back. "A drink won't hurt us; I haven't been in bed for two nights."

"Nor I," Caro answered, pushing open the door for a woman visitor.

At the Swiss café they sat awhile, Mudarra speaking of his year in prison and Caro of his own life.

"Things began to go better once she got herself clear about you," Caro said. "I say better; they went like music at once. That was getting me down. Do you know, I began to lose faith in the movement. If we can't settle a little thing like this by reason, I thought, then how the hell can we hope to make a reasonable society?"

Mudarra put his head back and roared with laughter.

"Boy, that's one for those who believe in the present society as well. Man's a savage, unreasonable brute, they say, or an instinctive animal, therefore he cannot make the just and reasonable society; therefore it's reasonable to accept the present, besides the present is such a reasonable order of society. But I don't really bother so much about reason as that. Let's make a society that uses our decent instincts, if we are instinctive animals, instead of our bad ones. They are just as strong, and men would be eternally grieving over the difference between their secret ideals and life as they live it. That's what's wrong with this bloody world. Nobody believes in it, not even the lucky sod who's well treated by it. No, boy, real reason gets down to the instincts too, it's not cold and airy. Besides, in the long run you have done what's reasonable, and good."

It was several weeks later before the two men met again, and then Mudarra received a message from Caro asking him if possible to bring his correspondence and instructions to a village of the hills which he named. There would be a fiesta which would serve as a pretext. Several insurrectionary meetings had been arranged in the group of villages standing upon that headland of the cordillera. Mudarra invited Señora Pérez and her daughter to accompany him.

"No, I don't want to go," she answered. "Concepción may go with you if she wishes."

"Coming, girl?"

"Of course I am."

"Conchita, go upstairs and fetch my workbasket." The girl winked at Mudarra and obeyed.

"Diego, she may go with you, but you'll take care of the girl, you understand?"

"Don't you worry, Mother," he said, kissing her hand.

"All right then, enjoy yourselves at the fiesta. Lucía Caro is going to be there."

"Oh?"

"She's with her husband, they're working together."

"Are they?"

She looked up sharply, thinking she detected jealousy. Then Conchita returned and tried to catch Mudarra's glance. When she succeeded he did not answer her malicious smile.

"What did she say?" the girl said fiercely, when they had left the house.

"Oh, the usual for a mother, you know."

"Nothing more?"

"No."

"You're as solemn as the side of a house."

"Well, isn't that enough to make me?" he said, grinning. "I don't like waiting, and I've got to be on my best behavior now."

"Diego, you're not to say things like that," she said, trying to repress laughter. Neither succeeded, but her laughter was cut short. "Waiting," he had said; what did he mean? Throughout the journey she was perplexed and anguished, wondering whether this man would ever be her husband. Her short answers to his banter dispirited him at last.

When they arrived at the village the tavern rooms were already taken and they were directed to a private house on the outskirts. It was one of the few houses possessing balconies, and these faced south, and from them one would gaze over upsweeping green fields, along the curve of the land, through a belt of leaden cloud that wreathed the loins of the hills, and on upwards to the luminous grays of the final ridges and the billowing peaks of the central cordillera over which small canoe-shaped clouds were drifting.

"God, what a place to sit and play at nights," Mudarra exclaimed, gazing at the balcony, "I wish there was no fiesta tonight; somebody's sure to have a guitar for all it's a heathen country."

"It's cold at nights," Concha said in a shocked tone. "Besides, they won't take us in here."

"Don't sound so damned gloomy," he laughed, and then his laugher gathered fresh impetus. "What are you thinking, *chica?*" he said, cuffing at her head. "You're my sister."

"Then you're a very great sinner, Señor Mudarra." They hushed their laughter as an oxcart approached, its greaseless wheels screaming like pain. When it had passed, the girl began to throw handfuls of water from a runnel bursting from a mossy wall, above which were beehives of hollow trunks. Mudarra caught her by the neck and dashed water in her face, she escaped and raced away along the path. As he sat down to await her humiliated return he heard her scream; he sprang to his feet but a moment later she appeared, walking quickly.

"What's up?" he questioned.

"Nothing, it's an idiot, a man with a big swollen neck, he jabbered at me; he's harmless."

"Let's go and see about bedrooms. Now remember you're my sister and your name's my name. You're the better liar so you must change your name."

"You're the better liar and you must be called Pérez."

"Conchita Pérez, you can leave me standing at lies."

"You can . . . that shows you'll have to be Pérez, you've got the habit of calling me Pérez."

"All right then, I'm Pérez and you're Pérez. What are you thinking about now?"

"Nothing."

"What sort of nothing?"

"Nothing, I tell you."

"Ah?"

"I don't like this sister business, if you want to know."

"Why not, want me to sleep in another house?"

"No."

"Then?"

"No . . . Madre mía, that's not true, Diego, I do want . . . though I'm not going to, but it's you calling me sister, it makes me *feel* a bit like a sister. I don't like it. Sometimes I wish you didn't come from Los Olivares."

"You're a rum kid."

"I'm not." The girl beat her knees with her fists and stood up.

"You are," he said, narrowing his eyes. "You're a tonta, right enough, but you are a most extraordinarily lovely tonta. Olé, *guapa,* blessed be the mother who gave you birth."

Conchita's eyes shone and, tossing her head, she said with gratification and contempt, "Thanks," and as he laughed she repeated, "Thanks, I say, but do you mean it, *chico?*"

"Of course I mean it," and he began to praise her with passionate words in the tradition of Andalucía. "Little gypsy, little piece of fine coral, little morsel of quince, sweeter than a fragment of bread."

"Man!" she exclaimed excitedly, and after a moment added, "Let's be going."

"Going? Listen, I'll ask for a room for you here, I'll sleep on the floor down at the tavern."

"Diego! No, my dear . . . yes, that will be good, it's good of you."

The tenderness of her reply moved him to fresh praise of her, and she listened not to his words, but to his voice.

"Little morning star, my body is broken to pieces by the beauty of your body; oh, Mother of God, since I came here and saw you again I've seen nothing but you; when I play it's your eyes, little lamps of the ashamed sky, that I see in place of frets; in place of strings it's the long lashes of these little glittering pieces of hell, they illumine my nights, my ivory-bodied queen."

After engaging a room in the balconied house they walked arm in arm to the tavern.

"Why are you laughing?" Mudarra asked, feeling her body shaking.

"I was thinking of your great fingers banging on my eyes and pulling my lashes."

"Ah no," he said, frowning, and was silent.

After a while she pressed closer to his side and whispered, "Yes, I am a tonta, boy."

A little before dark, amidst jeers from the onlookers, the

youths of the village began to pile brushwood in the center of the square; presently a few elders solemnly advanced and laid branches of wood on the pile, pretending indifference to the remarks. The young men were careful not to jeer too offensively; domination they would have resented, but they were pleased to receive the older men's help. It was the mature married men, the fathers of two and three children, who took no part; these were full of dignity, as if conscious all the while of fertile loins. Villagers and visitors began to drift into the square till the open space began to grow too small for the youths, who appealed to the mayor, a farmer of forty years, for assistance in keeping the square open. Promptly but with embarrassment he ordered the onlookers to stand back. The words "El Señor Alcalde manda" were heard on all sides. "The mayor orders . . ." A shout was heard from the crooked street that descended the hill, a rocket squirted erratically into the sky and two youths set fire to the pile, cheers rang out and then suddenly ceased.

At the mouth of the crooked street the youths that year performing Los Bardancos were entering. In the middle was the Old Man, a youth dressed in ragged clothes of antique fashion and a long white beard of horse tail, hobbling slowly with the aid of a stick. By his side was Maruca, the Old Woman, dressed in a trailing black skirt, tight bodice and shawl, her head covered with a black kerchief. The youth playing the part of Maruca was the principal wag of the village. Around the couple came the grotesquely dressed escort, insulting the bystanders with coarse epithets. As they approached the bonfire Maruca began to yell at the top of his voice, holding his belly with both hands; by the light of the crackling wood it was seen that his skirt was stuffed out to represent a nine months' pregnancy. Maruca's screams were answered with volleys of advice from the male spectators and screams from the young girls standing by them; the shrill laughter of the mothers of the village greeted every sally.

"Who did it, Maruca? Who did it?" shouted a man near the bonfire.

"He did, he did!" Maruca screamed, pointing at a stout and respectable farmer. Her husband shook his stick at her and tottered about, stroking his beard, calling her a shameless strumpet, swearing that he was the father of the child and praying God it would not be the last. The crowd protested joyfully at Maruca's accusation.

Then the Old Woman began to shriek that she was about to give birth and demanded a doctor at once. A roar of excitement went up and the onlookers nearest the bonfire, whose flames were now leaping high, wilted before a sudden rush of the yelling escort,

"How's this, Señor Doctor?" one of the escort demanded of the bystander whom his companions had seized. "Have a look to see how she's going." Diffidently the captured man stooped and peered at Maruca's belly, while the Old Man tottered about wringing his hands and howling dismally.

"I think it'll be soon," said the doctor at last, and with a shout the escort sprang at him, beating him with their sticks. He broke through their ranks, and raced towards the bonfire, the Bardancos close behind him. With a fierce oath he leaped through the flames into the refuge of space beyond and stood laughing at the escort now turning to seize another doctor. The first man had passed the flames and the feast had properly begun.

It was after thirty or forty had crossed the bonfire that the escort picked on Mudarra.

"Have a look at this, doctor," they said, dragging him before the kicking Maruca.

"Ah, a serious case, señores," shouted Mudarra, waving them back.

"I shall have to make a special examination." The Old Man protested as Mudarra rushed forward and thrust his head under Maruca's skirt.

"Twins, and I think it's wolves," yelled the "doctor," withdrawing his head. "Oh, you careless old lady!"

The crowd roared its approval of the doctor.

"I'll have another look," Mudarra bawled and dived beneath the skirt, the Old Man stomped with rage and beat his hidden shoulders with the stick. While the examination was taking place, the cretin by whom Conchita had been startled blundered out of the crowd and began to mouth and gesticulate, pointing at the heaving skirt. Some of the onlookers encouraged the idiot, but the majority objected to his interference with the visiting and unusually satisfactory doctor and he was pushed back into the crowd.

"Triplets," Mudarra exclaimed, sweeping his arm round at the crowd, "and I'll swear it's bears, oh, you scandalous old lady!"

"Have another look! Viva the doctor!"

"It's quadruplets," Mudarra shouted, emerging the third time, "and my science tells me they are dragons, oh, you daring old lady."

The Old Man danced with rage and belabored the doctor with his stick; suddenly Maruca flung himself to the ground and began to writhe in mock labor.

"An operation!" cried Mudarra. "A pitchfork or a scythe . . . or a spade will do."

Screams of female laughter rang across the square as the guitarist dragged Maruca round towards the bonfire. "More fire, demonios," he yelled, "more fire to chase away the evil spirits; lend me that stick, grandfather." Seizing the Old Man's stick he stood over Maruca and gestured with Caesarean suggestiveness. While others threw brushwood upon the bonfire, two of the escort fell to their knees and thrust their hands beneath the skirt, shouting encouragement. One of them withdrew his hands with a violent exclamation, the skirt heaved up with curious contortions, and the cat which had been hidden beneath it scratched her way out, leaped sideways like a hare as she passed the bonfire and escaped through the crowd.

"A birth, a birth!" the onlookers shouted and, led by the Bardancos, set out in pursuit, hurling sticks and stones at the newly born. The cretin danced round the bonfire waving his arms and a few old men, to humor him, threw more wood upon it.

After the Bardancos, Mudarra and the girl danced together awhile and then Conchita reminded him that Caro and Lucía would be soon arriving from the village above. "Let us go to meet them," she said.

"Right, do you know the way?"

"It's the path by the house where I'm to stay."

They set out and shortly came to a division of ways. A stone shrine stood above the path, its column patchily whitewashed, but the stone flag at its foot broken and displaced.

"Which way now, Diego?" the girl began, drawing near to him.

"I don't know; better ask the saint, I suppose."

"What saint is it?"

"Dunno, yes, there is a saint," he said, clambering up to the shrine. Dimly he could see the staring face of the wooden image, its painted eyes peering through the iron grille with a rapt expression. In the darkness the image was a little being hiding from the mysterious world, Mudarra thought. He winked at its solemnity. The wind made a flurrying noise against the rough stone and he shivered involuntarily; at that moment a wild yell rang out upon the mountainside. It was a cry like no other they had ever heard, in a falsetto voice but hurled out with terrifying urgency. *"Ee hee hu,"* it sounded, a long-drawn *eee* . . . and the last syllables shorter and less emphasized. *"Ee hee hu"* rang again, now a little nearer, echoes as of a monstrous owl were flung down into the hollow from some hidden cliff. The girl was shaking with fear and Mudarra felt his scalp prickling and his hands were moist with sweat. The wind buffeted the shrine behind them and then the cry rang again. *"Ee hee hu."* At the third repetition he steadied himself and put his arms round Conchita and her trembling ceased. The voice upon the mountainside was silent.

In the village a rocket pushed its way up and a glare broke out from inside the circle of rocks. "The bonfire," she said, and put her arm up to his neck.

"Let us sit and wait for them here," he whispered, and she allowed herself to be led to the stones before the shrine.

"Little Moorish queen, my brown one," he murmured and felt for her breast; she lifted her arm a little so that he might caress it and nestled more closely. The bonfire glared more brightly as he did so, and an ash tree across the path stood out against the glow. He laughed quietly.

"Now it's my turn to ask what you are laughing for."

"I was thinking about that old Maruca," he replied. A minute passed and he sat up with a jerk and regathered her in his arms.

"After that I think we ought to get married at once, girl. Shall we?"

"Diego, oh, my darling, yes, if you love me," she said, clutching him.

"Of course I love you, you know—I worship you. My little Moorish queen, my little gypsy. I can't wait, let us marry soon."

"Yes," she whispered fiercely, pressing her brows into his cheek and moving her head from side to side. Her mouth was hot and moist beneath his lips, her breast was rich and soft to his touch and he pressed his palm upon its comfort.

"Dieguito, you don't have to wait, if you don't want to, I didn't know you really loved me."

"Tonta, tonta," he whispered, deliberately placing a finger upon each of her eyes. "You've encircled my heart with a very, very high wall, don't you know that, little hen of a blackamoor?"

"You don't have to wait, my darling," she whispered, clinging to him.

"No, my queen, I know I don't—but I'll wait. It'll only be a little while—or I'll bust," he added. Conchita jerked with laughter.

"I don't want to here either," she said quietly, hiding her face against him. He caressed her head and looking up she said, "What was that awful cry, Diego?"

Mudarra at once put the question to Caro when they came down the path.

"Ah, the '*Ee hee hu'*," Caro said. "It was Chamorro here; that's the war cry of the ancient tribes who lived in these hills. Asua told me about it. They use it still in out-of-the-way parts, to tell people when they are arriving."

"Or to challenge," the man called Chamorro said.

32

Viva La Revolución!

AT midnight, general strike. At daybreak, Civil War.

Even the Radicals had yielded to the overwhelming flood of joyful emotion which the Civil War had liberated. When Caro confronted the leading Radical worker, the man, dry-lipped and half-choking with repressed emotion, had stuttered that they were assaulting a democratic Government. The Prime Minister, Lerroux, was a Republican.

"You can't overthrow a government just because three Catholics have been given portfolios."

"Ca! You'd say the Great War was about the murder of an archduke? Is it democratic to give seats to the enemies of democracy? What did the newspaper A.B.C. say? First support Lerroux, then govern with Lerroux, then supersede Lerroux. This is the second stage. Was there ever democracy under the Catholics?"

"No, but . . ."

"No, but!" Caro scorned. "Isn't that betraying the Republic? They'll twist and turn and intrigue in the Government, they'll split your party about some trumpery business, they'll maneuver you into false positions, they'll jockey you into despair and break your nerve, don't you know what the Church's methods are? Your party was its principal enemy; what the hell are you doing working with the Church now? Against whom? Masters or men? For whom? Masters or men?"

"Yes, but we'll hold them . . ."

"Hold them! Remember Vienna, the Catholics took advantage of the democratic system well enough there. Then they

turned round on the parties that had made it and what
happened? Do you want to be shot down? Hasn't the Catholic
Acción Popular sworn to put down Parliament? Are you going
to make revolution now?"

"Yes, but . . ."

"Yes, but! Say yes, man."

The Radical shouted, "Yes," and dashed out of the building.

In all the working-class quarters of Gijón barricades were
rising. In Oviedo the strikers had at once assaulted the Civil
Guard barracks. From every mining town and village the
miners were streaming down upon the capital, having shut the
Civil Guards in their barracks, or blown them out of them
with dynamite. Confiscated motorcars dashed through the
streets, the letters F.A.I. or C.P. or A.O. painted upon their
bonnets.

Both Mudarra and Caro were sent to Oviedo by the Military Committee, Caro to be attached to the Oviedo committee
for staff work, Mudarra to work with a company in the
streets. They forced their way into Revolutionary Headquarters at Oviedo and waved their slips of paper over the
heads of the officials jammed together in the metal workers'
offices.

"Mudarra! get out to Boquerón de Brañas, there's a miners'
company coming in, you're second in command," shouted the
secretary of the Military Committee, his spectacles close to the
minute book. Searching feverishly among his papers, he threw
over another slip."

"What next?"

The secretary waved his arm in despair and shouted, "What
you like, bring them here, if you can."

Mudarra flung up his hand and went outside. A lorry was
going so far along the highroad and he clambered in and
waited impatiently for it to start and then, passing the suburb
of San Lázaro, he was forced to descend while the lorry was
moving at a terrific pace. Civil Guards opened fire on them
from some cottages facing the crossroads and the driver would
not stop. Skirting a field, he entered a large house to which ran
a telephone wire. With a revolver upon the table before him,

he rang up San Claudio, which the miners' company should have reached by now. There was no answer. "Lines cut," he said to the house owner, a textile merchant. "They've passed San Claudio. I'll take this," and winding the flex round his forearm, he wrenched the apparatus from the wall. "Got a car?" he demanded. The landlord did not answer. "Come on, we'll have a look." At the point of Mudarra's revolver the owner led the way to the garage.

"Right, jump in and drive me towards San Claudio."

Nearing Boquerón they overtook a cyclist riding with desperate haste. He turned out to be a courier bearing the news that a munitions party would be cutting across the slopes of Mount Naranco the following morning to reach them at a certain point on the road. They were to take the ammunition and definitely to attack Oviedo from the north.

"Southern column will do the biggest part of the fighting, I expect," the courier said. "Belarmino Tomás is in command of nearly two thousand."

"Look at this," Mudarra said, holding out his commission.

"You're Mudarra! I left a minute after you did. I must have shifted a bit," boasted the courier. "I'm going back then. Viva la revolución."

"Viva! Be careful of the crossroads, there are guards there."

"Don't I know it! Anybody can have this bicycle; I'm walking."

The company, about two hundred strong, was at San Claudio after all. The local telephone operator was a Catholic and had been caught trying to enter the instrument room; for this reason the communications with Oviedo had been cut. At eight of the evening Mudarra persuaded the miners' own leader to order his men to rest.

"Best move down to San Lázaro in darkness," he said. "We'll move off at three."

Some of the men did not care for this delay and slipped away with their arms and ammunition; when the company was finally got on the road at 2 A.M. several were without cartridges. There was much profanity about the morals of those who had gone ahead.

About four in the morning a ground mist began to blow across the hills and the torch flashes of those sent ahead as vanguard were to be seen only with difficulty. Above, the stars shone dimly. Slowly they mounted over a shoulder of the low Sierra del Naranco, the mist gradually thinning, though now and again a dense cloud would silently move over and the stars grew paler or faded out. It was difficult to prevent the column singing; a good proportion were lads of eighteen to twenty years and the nerves of these were strained to breaking point by the excitement their silent marching on the capital aroused. Now and again they passed a white cottage, and it seemed as if there were mystery about them, their shuttered windows somehow increased the excitement. Near the col a door was flung open and a flood of light shot out onto the steaming mists. The scouts came running towards them.

"They've got a copperful of coffee and a bucket of hot milk. There's wine for those who want it," the vanguard leader announced. A few of the lads were sick soon after they set out once more; others, near to being sick, joked about the waste of coffee.

Beyond the col the road descended in sharp zigzags so that the bushes standing upon the next section of the road were sometimes visible in the gray dawn light. Dense clouds of cold vapor rolled chokingly over the Naranco slopes, chilling them to the bone yet causing them to perspire. Once they heard a shot ring out below and the section of the column halted suddenly, throwing the line into confusion. After a few minutes' halt the head set out again, and were lost in the deepening fog. Five minutes later the leading sections began to sing and Mudarra sent a message forward to forbid it; they obeyed slowly.

Suddenly there was a frightened shout from a youth standing near Mudarra and his shout was taken up by older men. Advancing towards them out of the mist was a company of soldiers. The soldiers caught sight of the column before them in the same instant and a shot cracked dully and the bullet whirred into their ranks. An old man fell sideways. With wild yells the company flung itself against the low bank and struggled clumsily to unsling their rifles.

"Fire!" shouted a youth with no weapon.

"Stop it, stop, stop," Mudarra shouted, "they're our own column." It was true, the head of the column had been approaching them along the next zigzag. That the approaching men were ten or twelve feet below their level was startlingly obvious to him. Cries of "Fire!" rang out on all sides amid the irregular crackling of rifles and shotguns; three or four were already down when Mudarra rushed forward and yelled, "Cease fire."

Almost instantaneously the opposing body realized their error and commenced to dodge from side to side of the road; a few broke away and disappeared in the mist. Three or four random shots were fired from the principal body and then all was silent save for the moans of the wounded. Twelve had been struck, none mortally, but all severely. The miners were too dispirited to count or tend the wounded even, and sat or stood about in groups, weeping and muttering. One of the younger lads suddenly rushed up to Mudarra and charged him with negligence. "It's your fault," he whimpered, "it's your fault."

An old man tried to gather him to his side but he resisted, his wails became louder, others joined him in accusing the guitarist. Mudarra stepped forward and shook the boy.

"What if it is my fault; you're not hurt, are you?"

"It's not your fault, compañero," the old man interjected. "He's an idiot, it's hysteria he's got." The boy began to argue, and as he did so regained his balance and presently shuffled away.

"You're not responsible for this," the old man urged, grounding his rifle; "you're not taking it in that way, compañero?"

"Not likely, brother. I was thinking about the company."

"They're in a bad way; you ought to make them move at once, it's this damned fog."

"I could see they were our fellows right enough. Why couldn't they?"

"No, I mean the fog's got on their nerves."

"Don't they see fog often enough then? There's plenty in these hills. Perhaps they *wanted* to meet an enemy, they've been thinking about it for hours. Perhaps it's my fault, I ought to have let them sing."

"Can't do that, compañero; the Government is bound to have scouts out."

"Yes, but I see it now, a revolutionary army is different from any other."

"You've got to take precautions."

"One moment, I'm thinking." A regular army was a machine, Mudarra saw, in which immediate obedience took the place of emotion and enthusiasm, in which fear had been damped down with hard discipline. Such an army lived in the atmosphere of war as a trade, but a revolutionary army thought of war as a series of triumphs. Its nerve before battle would be less steady though its eventual valor would be much higher, provided they were well led. Good revolutionary leadership must take count of the special character of insurrectionary forces. "Always be doing something or draw 'em right off for rests," Mudarra said to himself. "They'll never do a thing right, so let 'em fight simply."

With immense energy he commenced to exhort the column, the old man and one or two others aiding him. They felled trees and fashioned stretchers and upon these the wounded were sent back to the house where they had drunk coffee. Of the two hundred men only thirty-five or forty would fall in, and some of these began to drift away after a few minutes. Seeing this, Mudarra at once gave the command to advance; another score fell in behind as they moved off.

At the end of a quarter of an hour the mist disappeared and the city lay clearly visible below them; a thin trace of smoke was obliquely rising from the southern side. At once the spirits of the party revived; below was a visible objective, something to be gained. The munition party was nowhere in sight, however, and again the column had to be halted.

"We'll go to a visible place," Mudarra said after a while, "the top of that little peak." They commenced to move across the fields towards the summit of Mount Naranco; when they arrived there they were thirty strong. Three straggling groups were emerging from the mist, going diverse ways about the mountainside. Thirty men out of the two hundred that had left San Claudio that morning, and despair was visible on some of the faces before him.

"Fall in," Mudarra commanded, "and lay your ammunition before you."

They were well supplied, it turned out. Twenty-four possessed rifles with an average of fifty rounds apiece. Three carried revolvers and three shotguns, with twenty cartridges each. Four of the rifle carriers had roughly made bayonets, dangerously sharp.

"All right. We're not going to wait, we're going to do a spot of fighting. What's that large building down there?"

"That's the prison."

"All right, that'll be a strong point; leave it alone for the present. The Government will have occupied that church as well, I guess."

"That's San Pedro."

"San Pedro. Well, I see it's occupied. There'll be soldiers or guards in that house between the church and the prison, too. We'll take the houses first."

At the foot of the hill on which they were crouched were many small fields, bounded by stone walls, a maze of loosely piled slabs.

"The walls will give us cover right down to that pond. We shan't have to climb over them. We'll tear them down."

As they were breaking through their second wall, machine-gun fire rattled fiercely. They could hear the bullets whirring upwards over the field.

"Keep at it," Mudarra shouted, and crawling to the gap, once more began the work of demolition.

"They can't touch us," he said and to prove it he crawled through the finished gap and reached cover. While the company was joining him the enemy halted fire.

"They can't figure where we are," Mudarra said. "The tower isn't high enough to give them a clear view." They were able to advance almost to the houses before they were detected. It was a pole bearing a hunting reservation notice which gave them away; one of the men clutched at its base in passing. The wood proved rotten and the pole swayed away from the wall, was held by a stone and fell sideways and hit a youth on the shoulder. At once a terrific burst of machine-gun fire hammered upon the wall above them.

"Christ, it says 'Private Shooting,'" the lad shouted brandishing the notice board; there was a smothered gust of laughter. When they reached the pond the thudding upon the wall suddenly ceased, though the rattle of the machine guns continued. "What's up?" questioned a file leader, crawling up to the manure heap where Mudarra was crouched. At that moment the boy pointed with the notice board. It slipped from his fingers and he regained it before pointing again. By then they had all seen the miners' party descending the first field they themselves had crossed. The machine guns were trying to drive them back.

"Come here," Mudarra shouted to the boy. He stood up and ran towards the pond and a single bullet came towards them.

"Go back and put that lot wise to our dodge; bring them down here; Christ, there's more of them, look. Tell them we need dynamite."

The stragglers, attracted by the firing, were converging upon the church. At the same time their own present immunity suggested to Mudarra that they might rush the gardens of the houses, which were bounded by a brick wall at the bottom, while the fire was drawn off by the incoming groups.

"Tell them to leave a man behind to warn all the others. Here, take this, compañero." Quickly he scribbled out an instruction to any leader who might show himself among the men now beginning to stream down the Naranco slope. He was to muster a party and repeat their maneuver upon the other side, bringing his force to the left of the church. The boy ran away, stooping low behind the wall.

Five minutes later the first group of miners joined them.

"You've got dynamite?" Mudarra asked of the middle-aged leader.

"What else should we have?" Between the man's belt and his body were more than a dozen sticks of explosive, ready trimmed with fuses. Puffing his cigarette to a bright glow between his lips, the miner gestured with it towards the fuses.

"We want to take the house, but the garden wall is brick. Can you knock a hole through it? You'll have a tough job because you'll be under fire as you cross the field the other side of this wall. We'll give you as much covering fire as we can."

"All right." The miner gave his orders. Four of them would make the rush. They would pitch dynamite from a distance of twenty yards. "Stay away from us if you can," the miner said. "If a bullet hits us in the belt we go up with a big bang. When we've put a hole in the wall, you'll have to rush it. If they miss us, we'll just heave a few sticks at the houses until you get there."

"That's right. Just listen closely until I give you the signal." Briefly, Mudarra explained the plan of attack to his men. They would divide into the two sections. One section would cover the advance of the other.

"It's got to be one straight rush. You must get right up close under the house walls. Fan out now along the wall. Stand up and fire when I yell." Firing broke out on the other side of the church while they were taking position. Suddenly there was a deep boom from the same direction.

"Right . . . let's go," the miner said. "I reckon there's more of us on the other side," and without further comment the four miners lit fresh cigarettes.

"Fire," Mudarra cried at the miner's nod and himself sprang into the gap in the wall and opened fire. Two of the miners went down as the machine-gun fire swathed across the field. The stones on both sides of Mudarra were splintered and he flung himself on his knees, unable to take cover as he watched the dynamite sticks sailing through the air. A moment later the entire length of wall vanished and the two miners were on their feet and racing into the cloud of dust.

"Now!" the guitarist yelled and amidst a furious banging of rifles the assault section ran crouching towards the garden. As they reached it and began to charge through raspberry canes and over strawberry beds, one of the two miners pitched a stick of dynamite through a window of the lower floor.

"Keep back," he shouted as Mudarra's men passed him. "Keep back!" It was too late; short-fused, the dynamite exploded as the first onrushers approached the house. Two of them were struck down by flying bricks. Yet nothing could daunt the men now and they stormed into the house. An attempt to mount the shattered staircase was met with a pistol shot.

"Better surrender," Mudarra called, "I give you two minutes; at the end of that we shall blow up the house."

"Here, wait a minute," said the miner, "it'll take more than that to fix this stuff up properly."

There was a short silence during which the miners hurriedly spliced two lengths of fuse, and then a white handkerchief was flung out. Four Civil Guards descended the stairs, their hands above their heads.

"Give us a few minutes," the senior said to Mudarra. "Two of us are Catholics."

"You're under arrest. If you thought that, what did you surrender for?" the Andaluz replied. "There's a cellar here, get down there."

"Mother of God," muttered the guard and walked quickly to the cellar door. In the upper room they found two machine guns, six rifles and four boxes of ammunition. The capture of the house had cost them four wounded.

From this point onwards the enemies were gradually driven out of San Lázaro; the railway station, the Rescue Home and all the workshops were taken. Reinforcements continually arrived and by dark Mudarra was in command of nearly a thousand men. Only the church and the prison watchtower were left in the hands of the Government. Then, towards morning, an electrifying message was received from Trubia by courier.

"Commander revolutionary forces San Lázaro," it read, "is it safe to bring artillery along your road?"

"By God, what's happened?"

"The Trubia military committee have captured the arsenal; we can send a battery of No. 10's if we can get through here."

"We can bombard the church," exclaimed Mudarra. "Yes, send them along." The message was sent out to all detachments and Mudarra received urgent appeals to permit the storming of the church.

"No," he replied, "with the No. 10's we can blow them out of the tower without losing many men." And then he suddenly remembered that a revolutionary army must be kept attacking; a victory every day, every hour if possible, was the best thing to aim at.

Half an hour later, at the fierce shout of *"Ee hee hu,"* the company rushed upon the church. A searchlight shone suddenly from the tower and the machine guns opened fire and men were falling upon all sides, yet cheer after cheer resounded as the groups drew nearer to the church. Again dynamite was brought to work upon the door, and San Lázaro was captured. An hour later the guns arrived from Trubia and shortly afterwards others from Arellano also, taken under the leadership of a carpenter. One was trained upon the prison tower and by nine of the morning the defenders had surrendered. The company in all lost twenty-eight men, two having been killed and eighteen wounded in the assault upon the church; four had been wounded upon the left flank during the early stages of the battle. There was one piece of tactics of immense importance Mudarra learned that day, that a church is exceedingly vulnerable from the sanctuary end. The roof of the nave masks the tower's fire.

Straightway Mudarra marched the column into Oviedo, which the Southern Army had already entered. Point after point had been taken by Belarmino Tomás' men; after fierce street fighting the Convent of Santo Domingo, the Post Office, the City Hall, San Isidro's Church, the Bank of Spain, the Central Bank and the Herrero Bank. Dynamite had blown open the strong room of the Bank of Spain. It became a popular jest to ask for a stick of dynamite when anything had to be done.

At Revolutionary Headquarters both the Military and Political Committees were in permanent session. When Mudarra reported the capture of San Lázaro, three of the members were sleeping with their heads upon the table, undisturbed by the din of voices and the ceaseless firing from the streets around the Infantry Barracks, while others were working desperately. Caro, who was working as principal organizing officer, entered and with a single "Hola" of recognition forced his way past Mudarra.

"Hola," Mudarra replied, and reached for the order which the military secretary was holding out to him. The secretary's coat was burning, ignited by a dropped cigarette. Asua, now Caro's aide-de-camp, tried to congratulate Mudarra.

"The arms factory, right, the whole company."

Within two hours the arsenal had been captured and thirty-three thousand rifles passed into the hands of the workers, yet the utmost Caro could do to organize cartridge production would probably yield no more than five thousand rounds a day. He motored to Trubia and succeeded in getting three eight-hour shifts going in the artillery works, yet no small-arm ammunition was being produced and many of the shells were without fuses. Trubia was safely held, however, and men released from the gun lathes after eight hours' frantic labor were transported by lorry to Gijón, where the workers were making no headway and fighting only behind barricades. By a blunder of earlier organization there were only fifty rifles in Gijón, but this was the only setback to the rising. Now that the Post Office was in the hands of the Military Committee, lines were repaired and news began to pour in. The Manjoya dynamite factory had fallen to the workers, the metal workers of La Felguera had begun the manufacture of armored cars for street fighting, they would deliver six that evening of October 7th; Avilés, Sama, Infiesto, Pravia reported victory. Delegates arrived from little villages of the hills with requests for further instructions. The second battery of artillery arrived from Trubia and were dragged through the streets by hand to the singing of men drunken with joy.

In Oviedo two points only remained in the hands of the Government, the cathedral and the infantry barracks, with its coveted stores of ammunition. Attack after attack upon the barracks was driven back with severe loss; the cathedral-tower machine-gun fire dominated the center of the city. Neither the light, fuseless No. 10 shells nor the A.G.s could dislodge the enemy, protected by the massive Gothic masonry. Gonzalez Peña, the Committee president, shortly forbade the bombardment of the cathedral, though it was death to present visible target within sight of the Government snipers on the roof. Without the barracks ammunition the Workers' Army could not prevent the approach of larger Government forces.

Yet nothing daunted the street companies; the radio news that the Catalan Left Party had surrendered in Barcelona was disbelieved as mere propaganda.

In Oviedo, faith and confidence. And confidence was increased too by the Revolutionary Committee's reaction to various acts of pillage and private feud. Goaded by their sister, two workers shot the priest of their parish. It was rumored that the sister, whom everyone called La Gloria, had discharged two rounds into the corpse. Several shops were sacked by impassioned men and women. In the early hours of the morning of the ninth an edict appeared. Pillage would be punished with death. All persons possessing arms must report to the Committee and establish their identity. Failure to do this would meet with severe punishment. All food and clothing were confiscated and delegates summoned to regulate their distribution. Members of all parties were ordered to attend to commence the organization of the Red Guard, which was to preserve order in the now quietening city. The restoration of order, however, did something to heighten the nervous tension. Opponents of the revolution and those who by reasons of dissent or cowardice had abstained from taking part once more appeared on the streets. Rumors of revolutionary atrocities at once ran through the city. It was said that in a shop window before the San Francisco park the quartered bodies of several priests were on show—none of those who repeated this visited the shop to verify the rumor; the nuns of Las Adoratrices had been raped and the convent sacked. Yet the Mother Superior, a genial and warmly charitable woman, had opened the building as a refuge for little girls left homeless by the fighting. The convent stood plain for all to see, its worship continued uninterrupted, and the nuns barely knew of the existence of the revolution by other report than that of guns. Mudarra called upon the Mother Superior to request her to be ready to vacate the convent should the Committee need to fortify it against General López Ochoa, now advancing upon Oviedo. Ochoa was held up by the Workers' Army at Grado and the convent was never occupied by the revolutionaries. It was also said that hundreds of children had been killed and that the children of Civil Guards had been blinded.

Mudarra desired to counter these stories with others about the conduct of the Government forces in the villages outside, or about their treatment of the few prisoners confined in the barracks. He lost his temper at the Committee's rejection of his proposal.

"You think they don't do it?" he shouted at them.

Not one of the Committee heard him, even with the physical ear. Nights and days of incessant labor had brought them to that state in which the mind must cling desperately to a proposition to be aware of it. And if any was stronger than his colleagues he learned instinctively to shut out all thought but that of the moment's urgency. After storming at them for several minutes Mudarra called them assassins, counter-revolutionaries, idiots and donkeys. A number of Anarchists among the military direction sided with Mudarra in this dispute.

Yet despite this, everywhere was confidence and faith. The cathedral would be taken by long siege, the barracks with dynamite and shell. That López Ochoa would be decisively defeated if he advanced again was made credible by the news that a company of miners, armed with rifles, shotguns, sticks of explosives, pickaxes and mining tools, had defeated General Bosch at Campomanes. The Spanish worker had risen through the country, Cataluña was red, Viscay was red, Andalucía had risen, Castile had thrown off her sloth. The dreamed and longed-for revolution was approaching its final triumph. Viva España, Long Live Liberty!

As the workers were watching the first Red Guards on parade, airplanes appeared, flying straight towards the heart of the city, but dipping and swerving to attract attention. Cheers rose from the watchers—these were the first workers' planes to shine whitely over the capital of Asturias. As the squadron roared over the roofs packets were flung out. They opened like parachutes and burst into a cloud of fluttering, rocking leaflets; after these came a rain of newspapers. Shouting with joy, laughing in the face of friend and stranger, men and women and children raced to pick up the leaflets, eager to read of the triumph of their comrades throughout the rest of Spain.

The Song of Dynamite

As men read, the poise slipped from their bodies, their hearts raced painfully and the print grew dim. They dared not speak —wives waiting to hear the news read out clutched at their men, children whimpered instinctively. Then after that desolating realization, panic swept them, or rage and vengeful despair.

Spain had not risen. The Government was master of all Spain save Asturias. Dencas had betrayed the revolution in Barcelona and Cataluña had at once collapsed; the second spearhead of insurrection had been treacherously given away. The villages of the steppes and the lost towns of the heart of Spain had never risen at all. The peasant had remained at his plow, the laborer had abided in his apathy. Ah, God, men cried within their hearts, why have they not risen?

The newspapers informed——the leaflets threatened. The Government was now free to throw all its weight against Asturias. Immediate surrender—otherwise obliteration!

Before Headquarters a crowd was clamoring for information for denial of the truth of the leaflets, cursing the Committee for hiding the real state of affairs from them. Many were armed. Red Guards deserted their beats, sentinels crept down from their roof posts with the leaflets clutched in sooted hands, delegates arrived from the barricades.

A long-haired man with disarranged clothing was clinging to a window grille and waving his bandaged right arm over the crowd, shouting repeatedly at them, "They have made martyrs of us. They have made martyrs of us."

Within Headquarters the Military and Political Committees were stricken with dismay when the leaflets were handed across the room. Caro rose from his seat and rocking across the table said, "This must be denied at once, or we must surrender."

Mudarra rose also and laughed wildly. "Ah, you'll deny it now; when I wanted to tell a few pleasant stories you wouldn't consent."

"This may be lies," shouted Caro over the uproar. A Committee man reached up and dragged the leaflet from his hand, and read feverishly.

"But you don't know it's lies, it may be true," Mudarra shouted. Other members rose and cried out against Mudarra or Caro. Some stared at Caro in bewilderment.

"It must be denied if we are to go on fighting."

"Deny it then! Call it a collection of lies—do you know they're lies?"

"Compañeros, order . . ." Gonzalez Peña, the leading Socialist, called, pleading with both men. Anger flared up within Caro and although he knew that his words were absurd he could not contain them. The man in front of him infuriated him, the scorn upon his face, the arrogant gestures, the contempt in his voice, all of this inflamed him and he crooked his arms before his body and shouted at Mudarra:

"Are you going on with the fight?"

"Are you going to deny it?" Mudarra flung back. . . . Who were these organizers, these word-spinners, these politicians! He advanced towards the pale-faced man, blearily regarding him over the litter of the table.

"Compañeros, are you mad?" appealed the chairman again, for this strange conflict had startled the fatigue from them all; none could understand how so much passion could clothe such absurd utterances. Once or twice lately this phenomenon had shown itself, though Caro had always seemed the most resistant of all. In other cases this hysteria had broken out over disputes between Socialist, Anarchist and Communist. The strain of the campaign was indeed disrupting the Committee. The door opened and a woman's face appeared over the shoulder of a delegate. Peña glanced at the woman, then at Caro, and roughly forced his way through the crushing men. "Stand aside please, comrade," he said to the delegate, and the man quickly pushed forward away from the door.

"What is it; you're Caro's wife, aren't you?"

The woman was leaning against the sweating wall of the corridor.

"Yes."

"What is it? Are you wounded, where have you come from?" Peña gabbled, and then, jerking his head, he framed the words with slow care; at the end he relaxed, as from exhausting effort.

"Have you some message?"

"Send my husband out."

The Socialist did not hesitate; as he pushed the door open Mudarra was declaring that they must begin a fresh offensive—the cathedral must be blown up if it cost them all their store of dynamite, whatever Peña might say, or Caro.

"Your wife," Peña shouted into Caro's ear, and after a while the Communist heard and left the room.

In the corridor he lurched towards Lucía and flung out his arms to embrace her; she held him off and pressing back against the wall dragged herself sideways away from him. His eyes stared mechanically at the smear her body left upon the moisture-beaded wall.

"Lucía, tell me what you have to say," he said calmly.

"Gijón," she whispered.

"Yes?" he urged, and Lucía suddenly came forward and, putting her hands on his chest, grappled confusedly with his clothing, closing her eyes tightly.

"We're beaten in Gijón." Then opening her eyes, she drew herself up and screamed, "You must send help."

"Yes, of course, keep control, my dear." Lucía was silent awhile and then she said:

"You must send an army, the best you've got, your best leader—oh, Joaquín, it's terrible, there's a warship in the bay shelling the city . . . the workers' quarter is smashed up . . . it's the cruiser *Liberty*. It's a mile out in the bay. We've no ammunition left, and the Moors . . . Ah, God, the Moors . . . the Moors . . ." Her voice sank to a terrified whisper.

"What do you mean?" he gasped.

"The Tercio, the Foreign Legion from Africa, they've arrived."

"*Moors!* It can't be true . . . they'd never do it," he whispered.

"Joaquín, don't wait, it's true. The Government have brought in the Moors . . . they're terrible . . . they've killed hundreds, with knives . . . women and children, ours and others too, Christians. They're coming here. . . ."

"The Moors," he whispered.

"Send help, Joaquín."

"Yes," he shouted. "Listen, go back and tell the workers we'll send an army at once, and ammunition, we must . . . and the best general, we'll send Mudarra."

"Diego!"

"Yes . . . he's the best we've got for close fighting. That's him in there. It's those leaflets the airplanes are dropping. Hark." The humming of the engines could be heard above the city.

"You can't, Joaquín, you mustn't. . . ." He took her hands quickly and waited for her to speak. "You can't . . . Conchita's dead."

"Concha."

"Dead . . . she was fighting at a barricade in Cimadévilla when the Moors first came, she had a machine gun . . . when all her ammunition was gone she stood up and screamed at them and they rushed at her and shot her . . . the Moors stamped on her and cut off her arms, Baragaña was wounded on a roof and he watched them . . . you mustn't send Diego."

"Yes, we must send him; Tomás is out against Ochoa."

"The Moors, they're joining Ochoa. . . ." Lucía muttered.

"I'm going in," he said, and left her.

"If the leaflets are true there's still a chance," Mudarra was saying. "All Oviedo is with us and all Asturias. We must wipe out the resistance here. The cathedral first, then the barracks."

"The barracks first," Caro interrupted. "We've lost Gijón, we must retake it if we're to go on."

"The cathedral is draining the fight out of our men. It'll be easier than the barracks; it will put heart into the company.

What the hell do all these 'ifs' mean if we're to fight on."

"The ammunition . . ." a delegate began.

"I say the cathedral," Mudarra burst out, losing his temper again, "it will serve us for a stronghold, too. We've got ten tons of dynamite round at the Institute. I'm going to blow a way in by the Cámara Santa. We shall be out of firing sight there. I know you still think we ought to respect the cathedral, Peña. . . ."

"Listen, compañeros." Caro stood and held up his hand. "We've just received bad news from Gijón. The Government has brought in colored troops, the Moors."

For a moment there was complete silence, then a cup rattled in a saucer and instantaneously hubbub broke out. Fierce cries of vituperation and hate greeted the news. Mudarra stood on a chair and held up his arms.

"A civilized Government," he said grimly, his narrowed eyes blazing, "composed of Radicals and Catholic Christians . . . who bring in colored Moslems to put down the Spanish workers. Ah, very well. Do you know what I am going to do first? Something to please Gil Robles and his gang of Jesuits. . . ." He leaned forward and spoke quietly, the wrinkled skin about his mouth white and twitching with bitter hate. "The cathedral of Oviedo is going to be brought to the ground and every church in Asturias if I live and the dynamite lasts. The Church of Christ! The Shrine of Holiness! Well, the Church has chosen to side with the lords of the earth, the bankers and the aristocrats and the little dons . . . I once . . ." He broke off suddenly and leaped from the chair. "Out of my way." The discussion lasted several minutes. Suddenly there was a roar of engines overhead, the broken window panes vibrated. Animal screams burst from the trampling crowd outside and then a lightning-like flash and a grinding boom occurred in the street outside. Shrapnel hurtled through the window and smashed the woodwork and glass to fragments. When the confusion subsided a delegate was heard groaning below the window, and from the street, wailing. A moment later another bomb fell and then the whole house shook as the squadron dived towards the Headquarters, machine guns detonating. Screams again pierced through the din and then the airplanes zoomed upwards and shut off their guns. In the next street two bombs exploded as they raced away. A minute later another squadron arrived and the stamping thunder of bombs again drowned the machine guns. . . .

Silence. Scores of dead lay along the street. Smoke was welling from two houses, the roofs and intermediate floors of which had collapsed. From the neighboring block flames were leaping. The smoke-blinded and choking Committee struggled from the shattered Headquarters, dragging their wounded.

Within an hour and before dissolving, the Revolutionary Committee resolved unanimously to demobilize. Caro, not an elected member, was deputed to carry this order into effect.

Meanwhile Mudarra with a body of thirty men, mostly Socialist Party members from Sama, fought his way through a force of infantry towards the Institute.

"The cathedral," he urged them repeatedly.

"The airplanes will be back any moment."

"No, not while the infantry are on the streets."

Before they reached the Institute, however, an ear-splitting explosion hurled their advance guard to the ground. From some fleeing men they learned that a pair of miners, maddened by despair, had blown up the Institute. The chief store of dynamite had gone with it, the houses around were thrown flat.

"Well, the dump at San Tirso's church will be all right," Mudarra muttered.

"No, give it up, compañero," his lieutenant answered.

"The cathedral . . . God! Are you all cowards . . . you want to give in because of a few bombs?"

He left them and drove a commandeered car to the spot known as Scandal Square, the popular promenade of the city. There he found several hundred Red Guards with weapons piled.

"You're the arsenal garrison?" he inquired of their commander.

"Yes," the man replied. "It's partly in ruins; we've been bombed and stormed out, the infantry's in."

"Fall in." Mudarra climbed upon a bench and addressed the company. "We're going to get the arsenal back," he began.

An hour and a half's furious fighting drove the infantry back to the barracks, a detachment of Ochoa's army, already in possession of San Lázaro, was forced to take refuge in the Convent of the Adoratrices, a lorry full of hand grenades was also captured, and the city workers rallied. Despair had given them courage, and this had been fired by Mudarra's fierce ardor and swift understanding of tactical necessity. Driven by a professional chauffeur, he seemed to be in all places, haranguing exhausted troops in one quarter, clearing out doubtful elements in another, leading a charge to clear the streets of riflemen, or a roof party to bomb out machine-gun posts. Everywhere his appearance was the prelude to frenzied activity.

The news that Ochoa was fighting his way into the town again sent him rushing to Las Adoratrices, intending to drive out the infantrymen and fortify the place. With a hundred men he doubled down the lane approaching the convent; a *ráfaga* of lead greeted them and they leaped to the cover of walls. Two lay motionless and a third squirmed in the dust, his knees shattered. Bullets bored into the soft earth round the wounded man, and then he was shaken violently as by an invisible hand and lay still. He lay still, but bullets continued to thrust at the ground around him. They made no attempt to withdraw, but crouched in cover, staring at the body which was being shattered by bullets; at length the firing ceased, and the spell of fascination was broken.

"The Moors."

"Yes, *los moros*." The vanguard had seen the white turbans at the convent window.

To attempt the storming of the convent with so small a force would have been absurd, and Mudarra therefore drew off and returned to Scandal Square. There he found Caro trying to persuade the revolutionary troops that it was hopeless to continue, they had received news that the Government was sending another army from Santander. It was not true that the dreadnought *Dato* had come over to the revolution. More news had arrived from Spain—in Barcelona, Dencas had kept his armed men in their quarters while he appealed to the unarmed workers to go onto the streets. The Anarchists of Cataluña had not followed their Asturian comrades' example and had refused even to strike. Companys had declared the Catalan Free State and had ordered a banquet to celebrate the declaration. General Batet had calmly proceeded to blow the banqueters out of the City Hall and the Catalan insurrection, barely begun, had ignominiously collapsed.

"Thus we are isolated, we cannot go on. Had the workers risen elsewhere, even had the Catalans only made revolution, it would have been all over by now, as it was here in Asturias."

"You've had your say," interrupted Mudarra. "Now I'll have mine."

"No need," answered a dozen voices, and a volley of cheers acclaimed the military leader.

"You see how they are, Joaquín?"

"Yes, they're the same in other parts of the town." There was great emotion in Caro's voice.

"And you are going to call it off. Hell, man, can't you see that if we can hold out a few days, reconquer the city and get the armies together we can wipe out Ochoa. Then we can invade the Biscay provinces and the workers there will rise."

"I'm not so sure as you are. We were relying on the workers putting the aerodromes out of action and on the railway workers holding up troops."

"Joaquín, listen, you've got to carry on; you must get another committee together; they won't give in; it's useless to ask them; they know the Moors are here, isn't that enough to put life into any man; you can't forgive that, and they know what will happen if they surrender, too."

"Yes . . ."

"*You* know what will happen. The Government won't leave a miner alive in all Asturias if we surrender. They'll turn these barbarians loose in the villages, they'll knife and rape and burn and . . ."

"Yes, yes, but it's despair, Diego."

That the olive worker was frenzied by hatred he could see —what would happen to him if he heard of Concha's death?

"And guts . . . Christ, if that party of yours is any good at all . . ." shouted Mudarra. "Are you going to let those blacks wipe out white workers?"

"All right. I'll answer for it. The Communist Party will form a committee if no others will. . . ."

Mudarra flung his arms around the organizer, who, haunted by the vision of a girl beneath the bare feet of Moors, shrank from his embrace.

"I'll go and get a committee together," he said hurriedly. "But, Diego, don't let this business of the Moors upset your judgment; of course the Government had to call in the Tercio, they weren't sure the army would fight; if the rest of Spain had risen the army *daren't* have fought. It would have been shooting its own flesh and blood. God, it's a tragedy. . . . But keep your head, boy."

"Keep my head! My head's good enough for its job . . . I smashed up Soriano." Mudarra was shaking with rage; it was useless to counsel him, Caro perceived, and, saluting, he moved away. As he left the square he heard Mudarra haranguing his men, telling them of Soriano's tyranny in Los Olivares and of his torture in the Gate Chamber. At the words "the cathedral" a roar of anger swept the square. As Caro searched for the party secretary the hum of airplane motors was heard drawing near and he raced for cover into the church where the dynamite was stored. When he emerged, flames were leaping from all parts of the city. A battle was raging in Uría Street again; from the cheers of triumph it was evident that the workers were winning again. Nevertheless he went about the formation of a directive committee with a heavy heart, because only the Communist Party would undertake it. Even the Party consented only because the mining basin was as yet unentered and undefeated.

Mudarra, having fought his way through Uría Street, led his men to the streets uncovered by the cathedral fire and then placed them in charge of his lieutenant, taking with him a small force to the south side of the cathedral.

"Keep that fire down for me," he ordered, nodding towards the towers. Marksmen spread themselves out and watched carefully for signs of the riflemen hidden among the stonework.

"That's the Cámara Santa entrance," an Oviedo worker said to Mudarra, pointing to a flight of steps.

"Yes, I've read a book written by a priest . . . the Cámara's beyond, that's the antechapel. No good, those steps can be reached by fire. What's that door over there? . . ."

"The sacristy."

"Good. We shall be out of reach there, if we can get through into the cathedral."

"There's a door beyond, they'll have barricaded that."

"All right. Come on then. Get ready, charge."

The sacristy door was blown in with ease, and then the party rushed into the sacristy.

"What's this? Oh, the chapel of San Leucadia!" exclaimed the leader. "I remember reading about it. Right above this is the Cámara Santa!"

"Yes."

"Well, the Cámara Santa's coming down," Mudarra said venomously, leaping towards the pillar of the arch supporting the Cámara.

"We can get in easier this way."

"This will do for me."

"Shut your face," interjected a miner to the man who had opposed Mudarra, pulling dynamite out of his waistband. It was the man who had fought for days by throwing dynamite cartridges, igniting the fuses with his cigarette, walking with complete indifference into the hottest fire.

"One of you as sentry at the door," commanded Mudarra, "and bring over these chests, they'll help to confine the explosion."

The Dynamiter crossed the sacristy for a coal-cutting ax which he had brought and, returning, began to swing it against the base of the support.

"Do you fellows know what's above here?" Mudarra said. "Well, I'll tell you. Of course there's art treasures, oh, yes, things of priceless beauty which you can see once a year if you like to pay for the privilege. There's the Cross of Victories, tenth century, finely enameled, nice brittle substance, enamel! Alfonso the Great cast the metal upon the seashore. Then there's the Cross of the Angel, the book says it was made by two angels disguised as goldsmiths . . . seem to have heard that tale before somehow. . . . That's right, what about cutting the other arch, too, that'll bring the whole floor in. . . . Then there's the Holy Ark with reliefs in gilded silver, that's where the relics are!"

"Here, you splice that again," interrupted the Dynamiter, handing the fuse to Mudarra's lieutenant.

"Looks all right to me."

"It's a bad join, do it again."

"The relics are the finest collection in Spain, they say, though nobody really knows what's in the Ark. My book says Bishop Sandoval tried to open it after prayer and fasting, but when he put the key in the lock he got such a fright that his hair stood up on end and knocked his mitre off."

"The skin of Saint Bartholomew," an Oviedo shop assistant said.

"And two of the thorns from the Crown of Christ."

"Eight thorns," the assistant contradicted. "That's what I've always heard."

"Eight thorns . . . thorns are painful things. Did they dip the Crown in iodine, I wonder? And a bottle of the Virgin's milk, the Lord's winding sheet and the sole of Saint Peter's sandal . . ."

"One of the coins Judas received . . ."

"Ha, that makes them jealous for the other twenty-nine. What else have they got?"

"Some drops of blood sweated by a crucifix profaned by the Jews."

"Well, we're all ready for the fireworks," said the Dynamiter, lighting the fuse and laying it down. "We've got two minutes to get out."

They ran to safety, as they thought, and flung themselves flat to escape the bullets of a detachment of soldiers at the end of the street. While Mudarra's force was vainly battling to clear out the soldiers, the dynamite exploded. The arch of Santa Leucadia's chapel collapsed and eleven centuries came to crumbled stone and billowing dust, settling slowly through the darkness. The loveliness of gold and silver and intricate ivory, the glory of enamels and encrusted stones, the milk of the Virgin Mary and Saint Peter's sandal all alike were buried beneath twenty feet of debris.

The cathedral was never taken. López Ochoa had driven back the defenders upon the outskirts; the soldiers whom Mudarra had engaged were the first of the occupying army. When after ten minutes' rallying and retreating the dynamiting company broke, they ran to a barricade at the end of a side street. The Dynamiter had scrambled halfway up the piled flagstones of the barricade when the shop assistant said, "Where's the commander?"

They looked from one to the other, the Dynamiter relaxed his grip on the stones and slowly slid down the rubble, the shop assistant began to sob quietly. Some let their rifles fall against the wall. "There will never be another like him," the shop assistant said.

"Long live the revolution!" suddenly shouted one of the riflemen.

"The revolution is dead," the Dynamiter answered, and pulled two cartridges of explosive from his waist and examined the fuses. Then he replaced them in his belt, their fuses inclined to the left that they might be easily withdrawn. He patted them gently with a strange smile upon his face and whispered, "Yours'll be the last song in this show, dearies."

"Any of you men got a cigarette," he said, and leaned over the barricade to take the cigarette Mudarra's lieutenant offered. Then, smearing his face with the blood from a wound upon his brow, and hideously masking his identity, he lit the cigarette.

"Well, so long, brothers," the Dynamiter said. "If I find them . . ." and turning he walked slowly towards the street whence the infantry had driven them. They listened. Half a minute passed and then rifle fire resounded.

"They'll have got him first," the lieutenant said; as he finished speaking a deep boom echoed through the narrow street. All the men behind the barricade sighed with relief, thinking of the Dynamiter, and glad for him. The rifle fire ceased and they took off their caps and stood silently. Down in the west the hum of airplane engines began.

When the bullet struck Mudarra in the foot he fell to the ground and, striking his head upon the bolt of a rifle, momentarily lost consciousness. When next he opened his eyes he was in the middle of a group of soldiers who did not recognize him. Nevertheless, judging him to be a revolutionary of importance they forced him to drag himself towards the Pelayo barracks, under guard of two infantrymen. They were met by a posse of Civil Guard, who shouted with triumph on perceiving Mudarra.

"Christ in heaven, do you know who you've got there?" screamed the sergeant of the guard in wild glee. "Hand him over to us, we'll take charge of him." The infantrymen, raw boys, willingly disposed of their prisoner, and the guards carried Mudarra between them to the barracks. Their captain, Pons, sent to Asturias with the express mission of retrieving the money missing from the Bank of Spain, had formerly been recalled from the Philippines because of protests at his brutality. Recognizing the Andaluz, he motioned at once towards the room behind the common hall.

"Well, I give you one chance, where is the money?"

"You'll never know," replied Mudarra.

"Three-motor flight," ordered Pons. The subordinates seized the struggling guitarist and handcuffed him, then, attaching a rope to the connecting chain and passing it over a pulley they hoisted him into the air. A sergeant stepped forward and tore open Mudarra's flyhole and grasping him, commenced to swing him backwards and forwards. This was the torture called the "Trimotor." At the end of a quarter of an hour he was dropped upon the floor and revived with brandy and water.

"Laughter Tube," ordered Pons the moment he regained consciousness.

"We can't do that," the sergeant said. "He's wounded in the foot, sir. He won't be able to run."

"You get another chance," said Pons. "Where is the money? All right, you won't speak, give him a dose of fire, and then a night of the Potro."

After he had been burned they tied a bar of iron to the bend of his knees and lashed his wrists to it and flung him aside. In the morning, Mudarra refused to give any other answer, he declined to say where the remaining dynamite store was or who composed the second Revolutionary Committee.

"Give him Orphean Hell," was the command, this being the name for general torture, because it made all persons sing, however strong. When Mudarra broke lose from his tormentors one of the guards drew his Mauser and shot him through the heart. The same morning he was buried in a common grave.

The Olive Tree

THE days of madness. The second Committee endured ten hours and then Caro confessed that not only the masses but the combatant workers themselves had escaped control. Despairing men were turning to sabotage and among these was a general feeling in favor of setting fire to the whole city. No one sponsored this proposal, it was a ghost of terror, haunting the broken movement—the word "dynamite" was the only word which gave it expression. Caro spent the whole of that day following Ochoa's entry trying to persuade the desperate miners to escape. They would not; everyone spoke the same thought, "Everything is lost, we never had anything to live for but the revolution." . . . "One can only die once." . . . "There is no reason in life—this is as reasonable as anything." Pillage broke out, first by disreputable elements who had remained in hiding throughout the early battles, then by demoralized or starving citizens, then by Red soldiers, now fighting blindly in groups. Searching in Puerte Nueva for the patrols which had been defending that quarter, Caro was told that they had gone into the brothels of the district. Pushing open the door of one of them, he entered. Upon the filthy parquet floor lay a heap of sleeping men, piled one above the other like corpses. Sprawled about the corridors and lying upon the stairs were others. Abandoned arms littered the place and a sack of bombs lay in a corner of the room. The women had fled; the house was silent save for the heavy breathing of battle-spent and drink-stupefied men. Caro found Belarmino Tomás at the

University, which, since an airplane bomb had burst in the chemical laboratory, was now a smoldering mass.

"I've convened a demobilization committee, it's at work in Sama," Tomás said. "I'm trying to stop the fighting here; they talk of blowing up the city."

"All right, I'll get there as soon as I can."

"Good for you. The Anarchists have refused to come on the Committee. We must persuade the miners not to defend the basin . . . that's the only matter I'm bringing up. It'll be difficult."

"Very good."

They both spoke lifelessly, gazing the while at the only thing left intact by the flames, the statue in the center of the quadrangle, of the founder of the University, the Inquisitor Valdés. Tomás at last sighed and said, gazing at the statue:

"Fire was always friendly to him," and walked away.

Then days of terror. Tomás pacted with Ochoa that, against nonresistance to his entry of the mining valleys, there should be no repression. The pact was not kept and the Moors and the regular troops carried fire and slaughter through the defenseless villages, hundreds were slain, dragged out and shot. Torture in prison robbed many of their reason. These were the days when fugitive men, clothed in rags that were less serviceable than nakedness against the bitter nights, longed for rain to hinder the sight of hunting pilots. These were the days when a single revolutionary stumbling across a field was worth a dive and a belt of ammunition, or a couple were worth a bomb. In these days men died by hundreds, hunted, starved and cut down, or shot by the side of the common ditch, or if the firing party had aimed ill and time was short, buried alive.

Lucía arrived in Sama while the third Committee was still functioning, bringing with her the remains of their savings. When the Moors entered and began to kill, they fled into the hills, descending only to buy food at the mining towns, learning to hide in houses whose inhabitants had already been assassinated.

So for six days Joaquín and Lucía moved about the mining villages, being gradually driven towards the main chain by the advancing cordons of troops, now engaged in systematic hunting of the bands of guerrilla fighters who roamed the spurs. Then, seeing that the recently fallen snow upon the topmost crests had partially melted, Lucía proposed they should cross into León.

"We couldn't do it," he replied. "We should be killed by the cold. It will snow again."

"We must do it; we shall be killed if we stay here; it's getting harder to buy food. The peasants are afraid to sell it."

Caro made no reply to this but continued to look out over the valley from the nut clump in which they were resting. She watched him closely and when he sighed she said:

"You are still thinking of the revolution, dear, you don't want to leave this place while any are fighting."

"No, it isn't that," he answered weakly.

"Yes it is; I don't want to leave either, but we must. They are only fighting now because they have lost everything, we have not. . . ."

The color crept into his face, yet he knew that his anger was unjust; at last he said, "We'll try—if it snows we shall be killed."

"It won't snow, my dear." Lucía spoke as she would to a child, with scolding certainty.

While they were still threading through the howling corridor of streaming pastures which lies beyond the Vegarada Pass it began to snow, though the wind at their backs helped them out of danger. Hour after hour they stumbled on, the small flakes streaming past them, till suddenly they heard a bell knock dully.

"There, I said we should get over," Lucía said, pointing through the storm to the darkly visible roofs of a village.

At this village a road commenced and, as they still had food, they did not delay their descent. The following night a road laborer befriended them, selling them all his food, and with quiet courtesy even refrained from questioning them. When they set out in the morning he told them of a path over a spur of the hills which would carry them past the town of La Vecilla, which they would recognize by the railway which there ran parallel to the main chain.

"That path won't take you into the town; there's a limekiln at its start, remember."

"Thank you, brother," Caro said, and shook the man's hand; he stood shaking his head watching them as they turned the corner of the road.

"We shall be safe enough to La Vecilla then," Lucía said. "There'll be a Guards' barracks there."

After La Vecilla a new anxiety afflicted the woman. Her husband, ever since their decision to forsake Asturias, had been growing more strange daily. Even as they had climbed the sodden slopes of the cordillera she had seen how hourly the life drained from him. Now he rarely spoke, but gazed ahead fixedly, an unchanging emptiness in his eyes and his lips pressed together as if sulking. He was at the limit of his powers, Lucía at first reasoned; then it gradually seemed to her that it was not only fatigue which was oppressing her husband. Every impulse had been stripped from him in a merciless denudation of spirit. He had more profoundly wanted to remain behind than she had thought. They were descending to a life that must be an idiot void for him.

She tried to make love to him, and when at last they procured a bed at a village near León she attempted to woo him into desire; nothing she could do brought life to him, however. By day, his body mechanically performed the motions of walking, hour after hour—he seemed never to tire, moreover, and accepted her decision about their route without question, turning this way and that like a beast. He appeared not to notice anything at all, travelers, the landscape, nor even a couple of Civil Guards who were watching a man fishing near a clump of willows.

Then one morning of great beauty, when the wide sky above the opening lands was full of light-reflecting cumuli, they were walking slowly along a lane above a watercourse filled to overflowing with the spill of the cordillera leagues away behind them. Below the watercourses the ground was stepped into terraces covered with a sparse layer of soil, bald and broken slopes rose lazily across the valley. As they turned into a broad gully they saw an old man hastily struggling to repair a gap in the wall of the watercourse. A smooth, twisting spout of water was pouring over the peasant's trunk, enfeebling him and forcing out the stones as fast as he replaced them. Behind the peasant the gushing water was washing a channel through the thin soil of the field.

"Ah," shouted Caro through clenched teeth, and hurriedly searched for a place to cross the watercourse. Lucía called shrilly:

"Here, *chico,* you can jump here," and he leaped across the water and clambered down into the field.

"Both together," he shouted to the peasant, and they jammed their stones side by side in the gap. "Now hold while I lift another."

Lucía ran to a heap of stones at one side of the field and assisted the two men. By and by the stones were able to resist the water pressure without being held together, and Caro and the peasant stood back a moment and regarded the course. The water was escaping in silver ropes through the interstices, soaking their feet. All three were drenched to the skin, but none of them thought of leaving the watercourse in that condition.

"That'll only last awhile," Caro said, and Lucía ran off to fetch several long poles of birch which were lying further back along the path. Dragging them along the path, she stumbled and rolled over on the path and swore mildly. The old man laughed at her and Caro smiled. In trying to push the end of the pole over the course, she let one of them roll into the water and it was swept as far as a bend where it jammed; the younger man retrieved it.

"My wife is right," he said, intently examining the bank. "If we can embed the poles, the water won't press on the weak spot."

"Yes, that's right. I'll cut some thin stakes."

While the peasant was doing this Lucía and her husband fetched more stones from the wall below and piled them at the foot of the course.

"Your wife," the old man said courteously when he returned with the willow branches. "A fine couple, and may I ask how many years of marriage you have?"

Lucía suddenly busied herself with the watercourse, and in

order to avoid the peasant's next question Caro sprang to her side. The old man at once joined them and said:

"Now you get at that end, señora . . . if you'll permit me to order your wife, señor."

Between them they lifted the birch pole into the water; patches of silver skin broke off the bark and swirled downstream. Rapidly Caro hammered in a couple of stakes and the pole held.

"Now it will be easy," he said with satisfaction.

When they had finished, they stood back to take stock of their work and were very pleased with it. "Magnificent," the peasant said, "we're fine engineers," and dipping his hand in the stream to remove the mud, he wiped it on his breeches, and taking off his hat, he held out his hand and said:

"A very good morning to you and to the señora your lady."

"A very good morning, señor," they replied, and after a moment Lucía added, "You have some very good fields here, señor."

"They're not bad," answered the peasant, waving his hat towards the fields up valley, "but now, caballero, let me lead you to my house."

"Perhaps you will have a fire, señor," Caro said, pointing to Lucía's dripping skirt.

"Yes, señor," the old man replied with a dipping inflection of emphasis, "and a bed for you. My house will be your house, señor, if you care to do penance with me."

The fire had been allowed to dwindle when they entered the house, and the peasant upbraided his wife. "And I, señor, who am the *alcalde* of this village, can have no fire kept in my hearth to welcome my guests; cha, cha, cha!"

"You must pardon me, señores," the old woman added, "I did not know my husband was bringing his friends."

They were shown upstairs and left to themselves. While they were undressing Caro said, "Let's go home, to Los Olivares."

"Yes," she replied. "Hurry into bed, my dear, you'll catch cold and they'll be coming to fetch our clothes." Life burned steadily within him again and she rejoiced in her heart, knowing that he would soon recover.

Late that afternoon, when their clothes had been dried, they decided to accept the mayor's invitation to spend the night in the house.

"You are traveling far, señores, if I am not too bold?"

"We are going to Valladolid, señor; we have been to León to see our relatives; this is our honeymoon."

"Ah, may heaven bless you; there's no need to ask whether you have any children." They flushed deeply at the old man's words and the old woman cackled with genial derision, "Ah, see them, the young innocents, they won't be long."

"Are all your children well, señor?" Caro said.

"All that are living are also well, thanks be to God; all well and all but my second son gone from me. He'll be in tonight. He will thank you for helping me with the watercourse."

"There's no reason for thanks," Caro murmured.

They went a little way down the path and presently the view opened. Between two low fan-shaped promontories the violet distances of the great plain were visible. They sat down upon a bar of whitwashed stones at a bend and gazed at the remote horizon. They had been there long without speaking, when a man rode up on a mule; he greeted them and passed on; a guitar was slung across the saddle. Caro looked into space and whispered, "Diego," and suddenly Lucía was in tears. He took her in his arms and tried to comfort her.

"Why do you cry so?" he asked softly, and when she did not reply he added, "Did you still love him?" and she nodded and clung to her husband.

"Ah well, I do also, girl."

Another peasant went by towards the town and then, nerving himself against tears, he spoke long of Mudarra. "There'll be no one like him in Los Olivares, Lucía."

"You will have the revolution to work for, husband."

"Yes, that is true, we shall have to begin again. I have learned much."

"My brother will be glad and you'll have your own children, Joaquín."

"Yes . . ." He stared towards the southern horizon where beyond the immense plains and the snowy heights of central

Spain Los Olivares lay, and then as she turned to him urgently he inclined his head.

"Yes, girl," he murmured, and she whispered, "Yes."

They sat there in the gold of evening while the horsemen rode by and the laborers returned with sad faces to the village above. In his imagination Caro was already going about the solemn olivars beneath the tiger hills of Jabalón, beneath the splendor of a sky that flamed with scarlet and gold. Among the trees of his imagination a voice was singing and he saw himself moving deliberately round the trunk of an olive. It was a lovely *zorzaleño* in the full pride of maturity, its great mother branches holding themselves nobly, the leaves and fruit shining purely in the golden light. The tree put on a richer loveliness as he gazed at it and his heart beat faster and life swelled within him. Then there was a sudden hush as the glow died from the cliffs above Broad Skirt, and once more he heard the shouts of his comrades going down to the great Upper Gate of Los Olivares.

They sat upon the whitened stones until the air suddenly chilled, and Lucía shivered, and then, kissing her upon the crown of her head, he rose and gave her his hand. Silently they returned to the village upon the last slopes of the far-off cordillera. "Tomorrow?" he said before they entered. "Yes," Lucía replied, and they went into the courteous cheer and the light of the hearth.

NOTE

Names of Spanish persons and places often perplex the English reader; those most frequently occurring in this novel are therefore listed here. The story is played first in Los Olivares de Don Fadrique, a small olive-producing town in Andalucía, the most southerly region of Spain, and then in Asturias, a district lying between the Cantabrian mountains and the north Atlantic coast, distant in space and character from Andalucía. The capital of Asturias is Oviedo and its principal port is Gijón. It was in this region that the great revolutionary rising of October, 1934, occurred. The story begins in 1932 and ends in December, 1934.

The Persons of the Story

(Not an exhaustive list. Principal characters are italicized.)

Surname	Christian name (which precedes surname)	
Acorín	Tomás	nicknamed "El Chino" (the Chinaman)
Aguiló	(Dr.)	an Anarchist agitator
Argote	Indalecio	nicknamed "the olivero," mayordomo to Don Fadrique
Asua		a mining clerk (in Asturias)
Baeza		an olive worker
Baragaña		a docker (in Asturias)
Barrera	Pedro (Don)	an olive presser

435

Surname	Christian name (which precedes surname)	
Calasparra		an olive-field charge hand
Cariño		nicknamed "the gypsy." A sereno or night watchman
	Cándida	housekeeper to priests
CARO (family)		
Caro	Pascual	father, a small tenant farmer
Caro	Ana	mother
Caro	Marcial	eldest son, an Anarchist
Caro	*Joaquín*	second son, at first an Anarchist
Caro	Ursula	daughter
Florez		a tenant farmer
García		a Socialist olive worker
González		an olive worker
Gorda, La		the popular name of Señora Molinos, innkeeper's wife
Gordito		nickname ("Little Fatty") of Jesus Caravaca, café proprietor
Guevara	(Don) Full name is Don Fadrique Guevara y Muñaroz, Marquis of Peral, etc., usually called Don Fadrique but sometimes the Marquis and occasionally for dramatic reasons Peral or Señor Guevara or plain Guevara	principal landlord of Los Olivares de Don Fadrique, a grandee of Spain
Guevara	Ubaldo	Don Fadrique's brother, bishop of diocese
Hernández		a Civil Guard. [N.B.—The Civil Guard is the armed police of Spain. It is exclusively concerned with crime and politics, the distinction between which (in Spain) has never been made clear.]
	Inés (Doña)	Don Fadrique's deceased wife

Surname	Christian name (which precedes surname)	
Jiménez		secretary to Rosich
Martínez	Bautista (Father)	nicknamed "the buck mule," rector of San Andrés
Menéndez		an Anarchist (in Asturias)
Menguillo		sacristan at San Andrés
Menudo		an image carrier
Molinos	Vicente (and family)	proprietor of Sevilla Inn
Montaña		captain of Civil Guard
Morcillo		a former olive-field superintendent
Mudarra	Diego	an olive worker, Anarchist and guitarist
Ojeda		olive worker
Ojeda	Catalina	his mother
Ojeda	Escolástica	his sister, an ex-nun
Ortega	Blasco (Don)	nicknamed "——— bell," a lawyer in Los Olivares
Peña	González	Socialist president of first Revolutionary Committee (in Asturias)
PÉREZ (family)		
Pérez	Oliverio	father
Pérez	Paca	mother
Pérez	*Concepción*	daughter (also called Concha or Conchita)
ROBLEDO (family)		
Robledo	Juan	father, a stableman
Robledo	María	mother, nicknamed "half a saint"
Robledo	Justo	son, at first assistant Town Secretary, then Secretary. An unattached Communist
Robledo	Gloria	absent daughter
Robledo	*Lucía*	youngest daughter
Rosich		fiscal, or public prosecutor of the province
Roza		a police spy (in Asturias)
Soriano	Mamerto (Father)	curate of San Andrés
Tomás	Belarmino	commander in chief of revolutionary forces (in Asturias)

Abbreviations

F.A.I.   The initials of the Iberian Anarchist Federation.

C.N.T.   The initials of the National Confederation of Labor, the revolutionary syndicalist organization.

U.G.T.   The General Union of Workers, the Socialist labor organization, until recently reformist. The C.N.T. and U.G.T. are usually in violent disagreement.

A.O.   Initials of the Workers' Alliance, or United Front.

POLITICAL NOTE

THIS is a novel of the Spanish Revolution. It is, however, the human drama and spiritual conflict of that revolution which has moved me. I have therefore tried to keep political matter out of this book save when it becomes a dramatic reality. This brief account may be useful to those unacquainted with Spanish politics.

In April, 1931, the King, Alfonso XIII, was compelled to leave Spain. The first Republican governments were composed of the principal Left and Center parties, Radicals (Center), Radical Socialists and Socialists working in coalition. The relation of the Roman Catholic Church to the State was drastically altered and various land reforms were attempted. At the November, 1933, elections, however, the Right parties regained much of their strength. The Socialists were then deprived of influence and were compelled to leave the Government. Various coalitions took office, the principal of these being those headed by Lerroux, leader of the Radical party. Lerroux eventually invited into his Cabinet Gil Robles, the leader of the C.E.D.A., the Catholic Conservative federation. Steady repeal of the Left reforms was undertaken and when at last three members of the C.E.D.A. became Cabinet ministers, the principal Left parties, under the dominant leadership of the Socialist Party, rebelled. In Cataluña the Esquerra (Left) Party failed to make adequate collaboration. The rising was defeated and since then the country has been governed by Right and Center coalitions, in which the Right has been in steady ascendancy.

THE HOGARTH PRESS

This is a paperback list for today's readers – but it holds to a tradition of adventurous and original publishing set by Leonard and Virginia Woolf when they founded The Hogarth Press in 1917 and started their first paperback series in 1924.

Some of the books are light-hearted, some serious, and include Fiction, Lives and Letters, Travel, Critics, Poetry, History and Hogarth Crime and Gaslight Crime.

A list of our books already published, together with some of our forthcoming titles, follows. If you would like more information about Hogarth Press books, write to us for a catalogue:

40 William IV Street, London WC2N 4DF

Please send a large stamped addressed envelope

HOGARTH FICTION

Walter Allen

All in a Lifetime

New Introduction by Alan Sillitoe

'One of the most magnificent literary portraits achieved by any modern novelist' – *Daily Telegraph*

A classic of working-class fiction, *All in a Lifetime* is a history of a life, but also history as it is lived, in all its strangeness and magical ordinariness. The story of a retired silversmith, born in 1875, this novel is not concerned with world events, but with personal struggles and triumphs in friendship, marriage and political convictions – a moving, powerful testament to a whole way of living in this century.

Richard Aldington
The Colonel's Daughter

New Introduction by Anthony Burgess

Georgie Smithers cycles through the Cotswold villages, hat tugged down against the wind, feeling sure that life must have more to offer than a visit from the vicar or a Girl Guide rally. She longs for a radio, silk stockings – and love. As she stumbles into adult life and the Colonel, her father, dies, Aldington exposes the emptiness beneath the words that ruled her life – Empire, duty, home – the bitter sham of 'this England' that the men in the trenches had died for.

J. F. Powers
Morte D'Urban
New Introduction by Mary Gordon

'This is the book for which his many admirers have long been waiting' – *Evelyn Waugh*

Father Urban Roche is a formidable golfer, raconteur and star of the preaching circuit – no ordinary priest he. Hardly surprising that he harbours less-than-meek ambitions of inheriting the highest of posts, Father Provincial to his Order. Then, banished to a deserted retreat in the wastes of Minnesota, this man for all seasons is forced to confront the realities of life on earth which, through a sequence of events at once uproarious and moving, he triumphantly does. A novel about a priest, a special priest, *Morte D'Urban* is a parable of the straitened role of belief in a secular age. It is also one of the comic masterpieces of our time.

V. S. Pritchett
The Spanish Temper
New Introduction by the Author

'Of all the foreign countries I have known,'
V. S. Pritchett has written, 'Spain is the one that has
made the strongest impression on me.' As a young man,
he spent two years travelling in Spain, and returned
several times before and after the Civil War. Although
the country may have changed on the surface over the
last 30 years, *The Spanish Temper*, first published in 1954
and a classic of travel writing, remains as true as ever.
Weaving together portraits of people, landscape, history
and myth, it is a vivid masterpiece in the tradition of
Borrow, Ford and Gerald Brenan: the perfect introduction to this extraordinary country and its people.